# THE WRECK OF THE MARGHERITA

**a DANNY LANCASTER investigation**

**By BILL TODD**

# The Wreck Of The Margherita

First published in 2012 by DLE Publications - **www.billtodd.co.uk**

ISBN-13: 978-1477495872
ISBN-10: 1477495878

## PRAISE FOR *THE WRECK OF THE MARGHERITA*

- *"Witty, gory, sexy, it's a fantastic read"*
- *"A good dose of gritty realism and strong dialogue"*
- *"Action packed, with some pretty raunchy sex scenes. I fell in love with the main character"*
- *"This book is gripping and exciting, you can't put it down due to the realistic actions from the characters as well as the writer building the tension fantastically!"*
- *"This book grabs you from the first page and plunges you into a dark, sexy and intelligent novel"*
- *"Very well written, a host of vivid characters, pacey and, of course, lots of sex and violence."*
- *"The writing is punchy, the set-up keeps the tension building and the action bubbling."*

The Danny Lancaster crime thriller novels are available as paperbacks and ebooks.
**The Wreck Of The Margherita**
**Death Squad**
The third Danny Lancaster novel will be published in Spring 2013

Find out more about the Danny Lancaster crime thriller series at
**www.billtodd.co.uk**

## FOREWORD

He'd been surprised at the sound his father's skull made when he split it with the axe.

He wasn't sure what he expected, maybe something wet, squashy. There wasn't much mess, at least not until he yanked out the blade. That had taken a bit of pulling and twisting. He'd never seen brains before. They glistened at him through the ugly mouth that had opened up in the bald pink scalp, almost as if they were winking at some conspiracy.

The body made a dull thump as it hit the carpet, like a heavy sleeper rolling out of bed.

And he never saw it coming, not till the last second. He'd outwitted the old bastard, shown who was the cleverer. Total surprise, and the old man's easy certainties had drained away with his own blood.

He had hefted the weapon in his hand, held it up for a better look. The silver curl of the blade stood out against the jet black of the axe head.

A thick teardrop of blood crawled down the curve, slowing as it climbed lumps of jelly in its path, then speeding up until it gathered at the heel of the blade and dripped onto the floor.

Sometimes, when he was on his own, he thought back to that night, replayed it in his mind. And every time he could hear that sound of the axe going in, feel the jolt of the impact run up his arm.

It wouldn't have happened if the old bastard had just listened. But he was like the rest. Why could no one see it? He had skills. He had ambitions. Deserved respect.

He was going to be something, the strongest, the biggest, the most feared. He was going to be a big noise. And if they were all too stupid to realise then they deserved everything they got.

And the best bit was, they never found out it was him. Never found out about the others either. Granted, most coppers, most people, were thick as shit but it just goes to show. He really was cleverer than the rest.

And now, after all this time, it was going to happen, the beginning of something special. Granted, that posh twat could talk for England but his plan sounded good, bloody good.

It made sense, sort of. A mix of politics on one hand and organised crime on the other, fingers in pies above and below the waterline. Takeovers, like big business. Get into the organisation and grab it from inside, take what you wanted, cash, power, and guns too.

Something like that, anyway. The posh twat could talk the hind leg off a donkey but his plan all made sense. Sort of.

He didn't like the guy and, to be frank, didn't understand half of what he said.

But he recognised someone else who wanted power and respect and that was good enough.

And Digby, bloody stupid name, needed skills, skills he could provide. He'd work with him while it suited, until he had what he wanted.

His time was coming.

## CHAPTER 1

**BRIGHTON**

There were only a few of them now, a few hundred left among the millions that had started.

They were tiring after the long journey. Their ranks thinned constantly but the leaders had crossed the cervix, travelled the length of the uterus and were now in the fallopian tube.

The leaders surrounded the egg and began bunting its jelly-like surface as they released enzymes to break down its outer layer. Then a single sperm penetrated and the child was conceived.

At the exact moment it happened the mother was in the tinned goods aisle at the Brighton Marina branch of Asda holding two cans of soup.

She would usually pick the economy version without thinking but the labels told her the more expensive one contained less salt. And the picture on the label, with its curling wisps of steam, made its contents look tastier than the alternative.

She weighed up the tins, as if that might give her a better idea of their flavours, before dropping the economy version into her basket and returning the more expensive soup to the shelf.

Unaware of what was happening inside of her, the woman studied the contents of her basket, wondering how much more shopping she could manage in her backpack and the two reusable bags-for-life she had brought with her.

It was a long journey home that would be made more difficult trying to manoeuvre everything if the bus was crowded. Unsure what to do, she consulted the list she had written on a scrap of paper and weighed up what she still had to get.

\*\*\*

As the new mother considered her options, the husband was stretched out on his sofa two miles away, his hand hovering over the crutch of his tracksuit bottoms.

If he was honest, the film was crap, some butt-ugly fat bird smothered in tattoos on all fours in the back of a transit van getting rogered by some guy with a beard and a beer gut.

The woman was making a lot of noise and tried to look keen but couldn't hide the fact she was bored shitless. Every time she lifted a slack breast in a half-hearted effort to suck her own nipple you could see her cheap implant scars.

Added to that, the picture kept breaking up and he'd had to crank the volume almost up to the max. Sod the neighbours.

He looked at the box the DVD had come in, something about nympho housewives. You'd have more fun cracking one off to the Hollyoaks omnibus.

Still, he shouldn't be ungrateful. The half dozen DVDs had been given to him by one of Eddie's guys, a "thank you". He had to hide them in his old tool box in the utility cupboard. The wife would go mental if she found them.

And, to be fair, he had to do something to pass the day. Repeats of The Sweeney and Minder were okay the first half dozen times, and all the Nazi history stuff was good, but you could only watch so many reruns.

Still, a "thank you" from Eddie was worth a lot, even if the films were crap. Like cash in the bank. Well, the next best thing anyway. It meant Eddie knew who you were. Eddie was grateful for something you'd done. Eddie was a good friend to have. You certainly wouldn't want him as an enemy.

The husband scratched his half-hearted crotch with one hand and hit "eject" on the remote control with the other. The DVD wheezed out of the machine and the picture switched to an old cowboy film, lots of shooting in a canyon, the whine of ricochets off rock. This looked promising. As the husband stretched out and wriggled to get comfortable, the lover was lying on his sofa a mile away.

\*\*\*

When Danny Lancaster woke, Sky News was still on and somewhere an elderly Russian-built airliner had crashed killing more than forty people.

You have a quick kip, forty die, the TV news loop goes on and the world keeps turning. One day it's your turn, random, arbitrary. A tiny ripple, then nothing, and the world goes on turning without you.

The curtains were half drawn but even in the gloom he couldn't stop himself looking at the swathes of yellow brown nicotine that stained the white stippled paper on the ceiling.

The colour and the shape reminded him of smoke rising from burning vehicles. If he looked too long he could hear gunfire and screaming. He looked away but knew he wouldn't be able to stop himself looking back again soon.

He moved his foot and felt something fall. He looked down and saw the half bottle of vodka on the carpet. Didn't matter. It was empty.

Danny sat back low on the sofa, remembering the bayonet going in, the resistance, the blade grating against ribs. He remembered the eyes of the tall talib in the black turban, knowledge exchanged in a look.

Remembered the smell of garlic on his breath. Remembered a flipflop falling from the man's foot as he pitched backwards.

Killing wasn't good or bad, it was the job, stopping them hurting a mate, getting in first. Not good or bad, but intense.

You only survived by working as a unit, one organism, like bacteria or bees, each with a place, all with the same aim, alone together.

Success depends on the completed Rubik's cube, everything planned, everything slotted into place. And when the plan fell apart, usually early on, it was down to order, instinct, training. It was down to the intensity of shared experience, the pooled adrenalin. And it was down to love.

The tall talib's eyes had bulged as he felt the blade, pink spittle at the corner of his mouth.

For Danny there was victory but no hate. Blood chemicals pumping, it was the victory of a world class athlete crossing the line. If the talib had broken the tape it would have been Tyler dead and the Pashtun with the gold medal.

He wasn't Danny's only one. He had seen men drop through the tunnel of his rifle sight. But the talib had been special, the only one close and personal.

It's what you did. What you volunteered for. What you were good at. All the training prepared you for the job they paid you for and that job was war.

It was a world apart. Different country, different culture, different everything. No petty rules, just rules of engagement. No tick-box targets, real flesh-and-bone ones. The only performance-related bonus was staying alive, save someone else the trouble of packing your bags for the journey home.

Danny smiled up at the ceiling. And two feet of sand to stop a bullet, five feet for an RPG. God bless Jimi Heselden.

It was worth having a leg smashed to have been there, cross the line, climb the podium, know as solid fact that you were the best.

His hand fell to his leg. Danny had loved every bloody minute of it.

Since he left he'd had more jobs than he could remember. He enjoyed the physical side of working on a road crew. He liked the slick footwork needed to sell used cars, always look on the positive side, "no" is not an option.

Even his brief experiment with burglary had produced a few memorable adrenalin highs. Danny was always absolutely certain that something would turn up but even his glass-half-full philosophy could take a beating at times.

He missed the feeling of doing something the best way it could be done. And he missed the adrenalin.

Now he was out. He missed Pogo, Si and Dave. He was bored and broke. He was lonely.

Making a fist, Danny hit himself hard in the stomach twice. The six-pack was still firm but he could feel a thin layer of fat creeping across the contoured muscle.

He knew his mind was softening as well, felt the absence of that total certainty and determination that had been hard-wired into his brain not so long ago. He was a blunted knife.

Danny knew he had to get back into his training routine. He needed to cling to his fitness, it was what he knew, what he used to be. The future was enemy territory. And he had to try harder to find some work, seize the initiative.

He was not good at doing nothing. Hard choices had to be made but at that moment he couldn't be bothered to get off the sofa. Too much effort.

Civilian life was hard, so much time frittered away on crap, no focus.

Danny was mystified by TV shows and newspaper articles of people banging on about their problems. People who didn't think they'd had their fair share.

People who didn't think they'd been treated right. Men drinking themselves into an early grave because everything they'd been taught was redundant and all the TV ads made them look like fools.

Women unhappy because they had their careers and their babies and it wasn't the dream they had been promised.

People fretting over the designer logos on their clothes when the most important ones he'd ever worn were his para wings and his blood group.

There's nothing on the birth certificate that promises you anything. You get up and face each day the best way you can. Not being dead at the end of it is a result.

He had seen people living in crap, in mud huts, drinking bad water. Kids cried for lack of food, not lack of PlayStation.

Just keep it simple, expect nothing and give it your best shot. A day without being shot at is a good one. A day without pain is even better.

He hadn't slept properly since he couldn't remember when. Usually it wasn't a problem, head down for a catnap whenever the chance presented.

But for the last week or more he'd only dozed. It was the noises, the sounds of static and shouting. It might be easier if he could hear what the shouting was about but it was urgent and garbled.

Then there was the twitch. The corner of his left eye would suddenly start. It drove him mad. He'd tried pressing down on it with his finger but he could still feel the muscle beneath tapping out some random message he couldn't read.

A gull screeched outside. Danny took a packet of cigarettes from the arm of the sofa and lit one, watching the smoke rise to deepen the stains above him.

He had to get back into running again, maybe lift a few weights. If he didn't, he'd end up as some lardy housebound wreck, shouting the odds, putting the world to rights from an armchair, boring people with war stories.

For some reason, the thought flashed up an image of his grandad. Danny didn't know how old he had been when he'd last seen him but it was a long time ago. The old man had seemed strange and exotic in the small Edmonton tower block flat, like some sort of alien or minor deity.

Old Stan always sat in the same armchair, the one with elbow indentations in the arms that had worn through the fabric.

His forearms were dotted with tattoos. The loose leathery skin made them look as if they were melting.

He spoke in short gasps and his belly quivered when he laughed. The table by his chair was always laid out the same, big old valve radio, that week's Radio Times, Capstan Full Strength and a bottle of Mackeson that Nan always insisted sat on a coaster so it didn't mark the wood.

His breath smelled of tobacco and old age and he kept his dentures in the tray from a large household match box behind the radio.

Sometimes Danny would visit after school. On Nan's baking days the smells made his head swim.

It was a sort of game they'd play where Danny would dip his fingers into the thick cake mixes for a taste. Nan would cuff him round the head and tick him off, then when she had filled her baking trays she would leave him the empty bowls to scrape clean.

On other days he would sit cross-legged on the rug in front of the flame-effect gas fire listening to the old man's stories.

He didn't understand much but somehow he knew it was important to sit still and listen. Grandad's watery eyes would shine with a strange light when he told his war stories. Danny never tired of them, no matter how many times he heard them.

Stan talked of battles and comrades and seemed to be driven by a new energy as he groped around the small shelf beneath his table where his campaign medals were kept in an old biscuit tin painted silver.

Grandad talked a lot about the family, an uncle who had emigrated to Canada and cousins who'd gone to Australia in the 1920s.

Others had spent years at sea, the earliest of them sailing under canvas, times that Grandad spoke of as "wooden ships and iron men".

There were photographs too, yellowy brown images on thick card with cracks across them and chunks missing around the edges.

As Grandad held them out Danny was fascinated by the whirls and folds of his weathered, aged skin.

The pictures were of serious-looking people in tight clothes all buttoned up. Some stood bolt upright in studio portraits that always seemed to include a potted plant. Others showed seaside outings with the family dressed in beachwear that was more substantial than the clothes most people wore to go shopping now.

Grandad reeled off the names and they meant nothing to Danny but sometimes a nose, eyes or a smile would remind him of someone.

Still, he knew it was important. Different lives, different people all linked down the centuries by an invisible steel thread of kinship. He was being watched. There were expectations to be fulfilled.

Danny drew on his cigarette and exhaled hard at the ceiling. The screen of rising smoke made the nicotine stains look as if they were billowing. He pictured the whorls and loops of wrinkles that had covered Grandad's hands. They were the intricate, natural patterns that you saw in the texture of wilderness viewed from a helicopter.

Danny looked at the ceiling again. He was broke, the only money coming in was from that Chinese business. It wasn't really worth the effort but people in need of a detective were not exactly fighting to get through his front door.

He stubbed out the dying cigarette in the saucer on the floor and picked up the vodka. A last trickle burned his throat and he swallowed hard before dropping the bottle back on the carpet.

Danny levered himself up off the sofa with a grunt and padded into the kitchen. The fridge was almost bare, a couple of foil trays and a yellowing lump of old cheese in a fold of plastic. He pared away the mould with a knife and slapped what remained between two slices of dry bread.

He bit into the sandwich and chewed. A bit stale but it filled a hole.

There were still two large cans of lager in the fridge. He took one out, popped the ring pull and wandered back into the living room. It was growing dark as the weak daylight faded but the TV was still on, illuminating the furniture with the flicker of Sky News. Danny dropped onto the sofa and watched as the ticker at the bottom of the screen announced breaking news. He glanced towards the sound of rain lashing at the window.

Gripping his lager, Danny sat forward in the sofa to watch.

\*\*\*

The axe was curved, balanced, perfectly weighted. It was a beauty but it was a tool, a tool for a job. First link in the chain. It would help him towards the guns. Guns were good, precision tools. Just the sight of them would have people shitting themselves. And that was before they whacked bits of metal out at the speed of a jet fighter. No one could argue with that, no matter how hard they thought they were. Guns were sexy. Not like the axe, that was personal, you could see the result, up close, hear the noise, feel the vibration. The axe was a fucking work of art but guns gave you range. A second step. And they would be his. He couldn't wait.

\*\*\*

**MITTE DISTRICT, BERLIN**
Lunch had been excellent, really excellent. For all his faults, Clive was always a wonderful host, always did you proud.

The cream of Bavarian smoked trout was delicious, the Brandenburg beef had been done to perfection and the wines were superb.

Sir Charles prided himself on being something of a trencherman but he had eaten so well that the dessert trolley had beaten him.

And it wasn't just the food. The setting had been quite breathtaking with panoramic views across the city taking in its classical buildings, extensive woodland and the forest of cranes hard at work rebuilding and renewing.

Afterwards, they had stepped outside for a cigar. Beside them stood Norman Foster's glass dome, a hemisphere of shining crystal standing on the thick, dark stones of a building from another age. Inside, beneath its spiral walkway, you could look down into the parliament chamber below.

It really was hard to credit that a building drenched in so much dark history could be transformed into a place that drew millions of visitors to queue for hours in all weathers.

All in all, a thoroughly enjoyable day. Still, there was much to think about. He wasn't sure about Clive, not at all sure. The man was always pleasant but there was something about him. Not sure what, just something.

Still, their discussions had opened doors he hadn't seriously considered before. European politics had always appeared rather sordid, a conspiracy of bureaucrats in support of failed national politicians whose sole interest was seeing themselves commemorated in statues from Cardiff to Sofia.

Sir Charles was confident he had led a full and interesting life, made a contribution, even if he said so himself. The old bones were getting a bit creaky now but that was no reason not to take on a new challenge.

Some of our greatest leaders had combined vision with maturity and a certain wisdom born of experience. If he was called to serve in some capacity it would be wrong not to do so. The liberal, social model had its place but now it was everywhere, affecting every aspect of life. There was no alternative, no counterbalance.

Not that he would represent a right-wing agenda in any nasty sense, if he was asked to step forward. No, his interest lay in respect for national traditions and achievements, judging by what a people had done and who they were, not according to some airy fairy cocktail of rights under an ever-expanding central control fuelled by ridiculously high taxes.

He was ever mindful of what Margaret had said about the contributions of the English speaking nations to the security and prosperity of the world. It was a real tragedy our greatest prime minister since Churchill had been betrayed and driven out by lesser men.

In his mind's eye ideas began to take shape. He had money and contacts and the experience to mould events. Sir Charles considered himself a modest, sensible man but, perhaps, his time had come. Someone had to step up and stop the rot before it was too late, before cherished institutions and a way of life drowned in a sea of consensus politics and red tape. He could be that man.

He had conquered the world of business, politics would be new and challenging territory. Sir Charles considered the idea and smiled.

There was much to think about. He didn't usually like walking but today was a special day. When they parted outside the Bundestag Sir Charles had declined Clive's offer of a lift and set off on foot through the Brandenburg Gate and into Pariser Platz. Despite the biting Russian wind there were still crowds of tourists and a few street performers dressed as clowns or Vopo guards painted silver.

Ahead was the vast and solid shape of his hotel, the Adlon Kempinski. Clive had mentioned that its guests had included Charlie Chaplin, Adolf Hitler and some singer who had swung his small child from the balcony. That alone said a lot about the world we live in now.

He had passed the dull fortress of the American embassy and was approaching the glass fronted building that was once the offices of Albert Speer when a thought occurred to him. What harm could it do, in a spirit of historical inquiry? Decision made, he turned south and cut through to Behrenstrasse.

Filling the view in front of him was a field of huge cubes crisscrossed with paths, undulating across an entire city block.

He paused for a moment, catching the occasional colourful flash of a tourist's anorak within the uniform grey of the memorial as they explored its grid.

Of course it was necessary to commemorate such an event as the Holocaust. If you did not remember the mistakes of the past you were destined to repeat them.

That said, not everyone seemed to support the idea of something so large in the city centre. He had heard the memorial was plagued by graffiti and even a few lunatics who sneaked in to have a barbecue.

That sort of behaviour was clearly grotesque. Such a memorial was absolutely necessary but perhaps it didn't need to occupy quite such valuable real estate.

He pulled his coat tightly around him and set off through the centre of the maze, puffing as the pathway rose. Still, a little afternoon exercise would aid the digestion.

In the south east corner of the block the obelisks thinned out. Wheezing slightly, he reached the pavement and crossed the junction into Gertrud-Kolmar Strasse. A block further on he stopped, collar turned up against the biting wind. He lifted a hand to smooth his hair back down across his scalp. A few people passed by, bent forward against the elements. A small group stood on the corner, looking around.

On his left was an unattractive grey block of apartments with a red roof. Between the building and the road was a half empty car park fronted by patches of grass worn to bare earth in places.

To one side was a sign board fronted with plastic. It looked as though it might contain detail of parking charges or council notices on refuse and recycling collections but he knew it didn't.

He walked up to the board and felt strange at the knowledge of what lay where he trod. He waited until a Dutch family moved on before stepping up to study the diagrams and descriptions of the Fuhrerbunker beneath his feet.

\*\*\*

Axe to guns, guns to money. And money would bring him the stuff he wanted, expensive stuff, and respect as well. Maybe he'd rent a yacht, a big one, all smooth curves, bit like the axe. He could get a really decent tan. Maybe he'd hire a private jet, cruise in deep leather seats miles above all those tossers jammed in their package holiday jets. While they were counting their leftover Euros to pay for a tin of beer he'd be served expensive fizz by some bird with a posh accent in a tight uniform and one of those daft hats.

\*\*\*

**FOUR YEARS AGO**
If this was dying, it wasn't so bad. He didn't know what all the fuss was about. The night sky was fantastic, bloody fantastic.

A rich river of the deepest black carried a cascade of silver that swirled and sparkled and pulsed.

He didn't know much about God, just the usual Sunday school stuff when he was a kid, although somehow he still knew the words to the hymns when he heard them. But if God was real then up there was where he'd be living.

Just the sheer bloody size of it all made you feel small, so alive, so peaceful. He could lie there and watch it for ever if it wasn't for the voices and the hissing in his head.

A shooting star flashed over, a brilliant thread of silver. He was almost sure he could hear it fizzing. A second and a third followed the same gentle arc. Bloody fantastic.

Then a spray of green streaks, luminous against the night, chased by a cluster of red ones, racing after each other at tremendous speed. He felt the ground tremble.

A voice called out, it seemed a long way away. Then he heard a series of rattles and taps, like someone trying to find a beat. Something spattered the ground nearby. The earth was shuddering now. Coloured slashes split the darkness.

The voice called again. Something zipped into the dirt to his left. Then two bulky heads were blocking his view of the sky.

"Jesus, look at the state of him."

"Fucksake, Dave, grab his weapon and let's move." The second head moved close. "Can you hear me, mate? It's Si. Just stay with us, okay, mate?" Si looked back over his shoulder into the blackness. "Pogo! Cover!"

Machinegun fire ripped the night. Si grabbed the wounded man's chest rig and hauled him off the hard earth, began to run at a crouch. "Go! Go!"

After thirty feet they dropped to the ground. An ugly noise swirled around them. The coarse, high-pitched sound grew louder, its frantic, serrated edge slicing through them.

It went on and on until Si stabbed a morphine autojet into the thigh of the screaming man. The darkness crumbled and collapsed on him, swamping the lights and the noise.

\*\*\*

Women weren't a problem, never had been. Some were drawn, like moths, getting their kick off the danger. Others were afraid of him but just as afraid to say no. He did okay but money would make a difference, big time. You could get classy birds, fit birds, not just the usual slags. They'd do anything you wanted, anything, like the stuff in the DVDs. And they'd like it. And they'd smile.

## CHAPTER 2

**THE ENGLISH CHANNEL**

It had been a busy night. The high over the Azores was pushing a low pressure front towards the English Channel.

The severe south-westerly gale began to reach Force Nine with winds of more than 50mph and swells rising up to 30 feet.

Pressed from behind by relentless force, the Atlantic storm resented being squeezed between the English and French coasts.

Driven forward into narrowing seas, billions of tonnes of water formed a tidal stream through the world's busiest shipping lanes, hunting for somewhere to escape, lashing out to show its disapproval.

Water driven forward by the wind pushed long swells up the Channel to the north east.

The flood tide drove on relentlessly until two hours after high water at Dover. Then it turned.

Now the tidal stream was running against winds of up to 70mph, immense forces acting against each other to chop the water into short, steep waves rising to more than 30 feet.

Gerald and Linda Ashton had always enjoyed messing about in boats, exploring the coastlines of Hampshire and Dorset, their estuaries and rivers.

It had been a shock when Gerald lost his job. Insurance had been his life for more than 30 years. The trauma was like losing a limb.

Gerald and Linda were cautious by nature, planning for the future, saving for a rainy day, putting something aside for the kids.

But now the kids were working and earning more than Gerald ever had. Perhaps it was time to take a risk.

With the modest income from their savings and investments plus the rent on their three-bedroom house in Andover they would have just enough money for the dream, to break away from the coast and into the open sea.

It was Gerald's prostate scare that tipped the balance. Life was full of risk but if you were going to do something like this you had to take your chances while you were still fit enough.

So, after much careful thought and research, they had bought Grey Rover, a 28-foot clinker-built centre-plate Bermudan sloop. Admittedly, a wooden hull took a lot of work to maintain but it felt right, more like real sailing.

A summer touring the Med, it really was a dream about to come true. They had spent every available moment honing their boat handling and navigation skills.

But the Bay of Biscay would be too much of an adventure so they had spent many evenings at home with a bottle of wine and maps of the French canal network, working out the most picturesque route from Calais to the western Med, noting beam, draft and height for the waterways.

Gerald and Linda knew from the Met Office forecast that there was a "strong wind" warning with the threat of worse to come but they only planned a brief outing that day to test their new GPS. They would be back in plenty of time.

The Bembridge lifeboat plucked the Ashtons from the debris-strewn deck of Grey Rover after she lost power and wallowed in heaving seas off the Isle of Wight.

They watched as the lifeboat manoeuvred away, unable to tear their eyes from Grey Rover, stern under water and mast dragging alongside the waterlogged hull, as their dream drifted away into walls of driving spray.

To the north east, three drama students competing for the best giant wave photo on their mobile phones were injured when a big one loaded with gravel rushed up the beach and punched through the driving spray to crash over the sea wall onto the prom at Hove Lawns.

Mid-Channel, an RAF air sea rescue helicopter from Wattisham in Suffolk lowered a doctor onto the heaving deck of a ferry from Newhaven bound for Dieppe.

As the doctor jerked like a half-strung puppet above the heaving deck, the wind howled as loudly as Wendy Thornhill, the 22-year-old building society counter clerk who had gone into premature labour.

Sandeep, her green-faced boyfriend, muttered about hot towels and water and wished he'd made the time to attend some of those ante-natal classes as a female member of the ferry's crew tried to keep Wendy calm.

The 52,000 tonne container ship KBS Margherita II was en route from South America to Thames Port with a general cargo including IMDG Class 3 flammable liquids and Class 8 corrosive substances.

The navigator, Petrov, had picked up the storm warning when the ship was still in the eastern Atlantic, just after notifying Thames Port of their arrival within the next 24 hours.

Captain Theo Papadopoulos ordered the crew to secure his ship for bad weather, making sure all equipment was properly stowed, hatches and openings closed and locked down.

The cargo containers were inspected to check they were all solidly stacked.

Satisfied that all the necessary preparations had been made, Captain Papadopoulos reported their progress to the French radar surveillance station at CROSS Corsen, near Brest.

The weather had got worse by the time they reported their position to the radar surveillance station at CROSS Jobourg on the Cherbourg peninsula as the Margherita ploughed through heavy seas heading north east up the French coast, following the Traffic Separation Scheme from Casquets.

The Margherita was just beyond the Greenwich Light Vessel, south of Brighton, when the chief engineer reported the crack.

After a lifetime of resisting the ferocity of the sea, the Margherita was leaking.

The storm force winds and giant waves hammering the ship were driving tons of water through a split in the hull by her stern.

The captain slowed the ship as he waited for his engineers to report, conscious that the Margherita was struggling at reduced speed as she was squeezed between the ebb tide running at her bow and the wind pressing from astern.

When the news came he knew he had no choice. The engine room was flooding fast. If they lost power they would be helpless, wallowing.

Captain Papadopoulos reported the ship's condition to Solent Coastguard which triggered the MANCHEPLAN, the multi-national response to preserve life, property and the environment in a Channel emergency.

His officers gathered on the bridge to assess the situation. Petrov checked their position on the GPS display, said that if they were to run to the nearest safe harbour, the options were Le Havre or Southampton.

The chief engineer, Singh, said the crack was on the starboard side twenty metres from the stern. He couldn't be sure how long it might take but the engine room was filling fast. When it did, they would lose power. They would be helpless.

Someone said an engineer named Agbannaoag had broken his arm in a fall but Captain Papadopoulos was looking out of the bridge window at the swirling murk, weighing his options.

Le Havre would be the obvious choice but if he chose Southampton then the Margherita would take the winds on her port side, using the bulk of the ship to shield the crack.

She would need to slow her speed to reduce the risk of stressing the crack still further but would have to maintain several knots above the tidal rate to reduce the flooding. It would be a delicate balancing act. Captain Papadopoulos radioed Solent Coastguard.

As helicopters, tugs and rescue boats were mobilised, the KBS Margherita II began to turn north west, back towards Southampton, keeping a careful radar watch as she cut across the south-bound shipping lane,

As the Margherita came beam-on to the storm, wind from her left, water from her right, the stacked containers acted like a sail and she began to roll with the punches. The officers on the bridge braced themselves, faces intense in the gloom.

Captain Papadopoulos listened to an update from Solent Coastguard. He had been a seaman for nearly forty years, master of the Margherita for the last twelve.

The ship was his home, the crew his family. If it came to it, evacuating felt like failure but he had a duty to his men. It would be a major challenge in these sea conditions. They would stay aboard until abandoning was unavoidable, then take to the ships lifeboats if rescue craft and helicopters were unable to get close.

As he looked out of the bridge window again, along the huge deck with its towering cargo, a giant cliff face of grey water surged out of the swirling murk and slammed into the ship.

As the surge forced her stern round, a barrage of smaller waves pounded down the ship's side. Then the containers began to move.

The Margherita reeled with the blows, like a tired old boxer, then rolled most of the way back again and stayed there, listing.

As the captain watched he was sure he could hear grinding steel above the howl of the wind, feel the tremors, as a stack of containers tottered and fell away into the seething spray.

Teasing the beads of his komboloi through white fingers, he watched as a second stack, then a third, fell like dominos away into the darkness, scraping and banging the ship's side as they danced on the tide.

Away to the north west, The SAR chopper, bucketing in the wind, was homeward bound and in sight of the Hampshire coast. The crew were quietly pleased with their success in dropping the doctor onto the ferry in testing conditions when they were diverted to overfly the Margherita.

The co-pilot tapped in the GPS coordinates as the pilot, Flight Lieutenant William Wales, banked the helicopter round towards the open sea.

## CHAPTER 3

Money would open the right doors, line the right pockets. And guns would persuade anyone too stupid to get the message. Then it was into the home straight. Politicians were tossers, the lot of them. But people voted for them, believed them. Hard to credit there were so many mugs about. But it worked, like a dream, every time. You put on a nice whistle, smile a lot, kiss a few babies, and you're on the gravy train, on the inside, crooks in suits, making all the rules including the ones you're going to break to line your pockets. Best con trick in the world. Bring it on.

\*\*\*

Lying in his bed, Danny's eyes flickered open again. He sniffed, detected a faint whiff of urine from his mother's room, punching its way through the smell of disinfectant and cigarette smoke in the flat, but his mind was a thousand miles away.

He remembered the night sky, a river of black with its cascade of silver.

The sheer bloody size of it, swooping from horizon to horizon, made you feel small. And peaceful. Shooting stars flashed threads of silver white. Then sprays of green and red, luminous against the darkness, gone in a flash leaving streaks imprinted behind your eyes.

Bloody fantastic.

He remembered the ground trembling and voices.

Static and mumbled voices in his ear.

"Jesus, look at the state of him."

"Can you hear me, mate?"

"Pogo! Cover!"

He remembered being jerked off the dirt.

Bumped across rough ground.

Gunfire.

Men grunting.

"Fucksake, move it. Go! Go!"

That ugly serrated noise that sliced right through him.

Never realised it was him screaming.

Never felt the prick of the morphine autojet stab his thigh.

Last glimpse of the night sky. Bloody fantastic. Then the drug darkness collapsed in on top of him.

Danny rolled over in bed, screwed his eyes tight shut, pulled the duvet tight, blotting out what light there was. He knew he wouldn't sleep.

\*\*\*

Power is the proof you've cracked it. Power gives you respect. You can see it in other people, the way they won't hold your gaze, the way their shoulders dip, all in the body language, fear and surrender. They'd know what you've done, know you for who you are, what you're capable of. You're on a higher level, a different kind of animal. They'd see it all and they'd know it and they wouldn't challenge you because they'd know the consequences. The axe leads to the guns, the money and the women. It was the beginning. The path to power.

He was going to be the biggest, the most feared. He was going to be a very big noise.

\*\*\*

It was something tinny clattering down the street that made Danny give up his efforts to sleep. The wind was moaning through the telephone wires. He rolled out of bed and padded into the kitchen where he started to brew up.

Danny was vaguely aware that the irritating dustbin lid, or whatever it was, had interrupted a hazy half-dream. He didn't normally remember dreams, knew it was a warning sign when he did.

When things piled up his mind started to race, like a speeding train bouncing before it jumped the tracks, he could feel a loosening of control. Not good.

The sudden awakening had left him with faint mental images, something to do with scuba diving across a tropical reef. Crystal clear water and fish sparkling with fantastic colours under brilliant refracted sunlight.

The girl in the blue wetsuit was finning along beside him. Big blue-green eyes seemed to fill the glass plate of her mask.

Her blonde hair pulsed in the water as she pushed forward, arms trailing at her sides. He couldn't be certain but he had a firm impression it was Scarlett Johansson, big lips and a lazy smile.

The thought brought him up with a start. He tried to remember the last time he'd been to bed with a woman. Seemed like a lifetime, certainly far too long. He wished Emma would stop being so bloody moody.

Danny tried to recapture the image of the blonde in the wetsuit but she had gone in the night, washed away by another rerun of that bloody night in Afghan. It didn't happen so often now but it still shook Danny when it did.

The kettle let out its wheezy whistle and Danny poured the boiling water.

His head felt thick from last night's vodka and lager and he used a spoon to stir and squeeze as much as he could from the two teabags in his outsize mug.

Satisfied his brew was as strong as he could get it, Danny flicked the teabags into the pedal bin, splashed in a dash of milk and went into the living room.

The television was still on Sky News. The top story on the crashed Russian airliner had been replaced with one about a container ship damaged in the storm.

Danny vaguely remembered the story breaking last night before he turned in. He looked across at the curtained window, heard the rain lashing, cupping his tea in both hands, trying to imagine what it would be like for those out there, at sea.

The vessel had shed part of her cargo of shipping containers as she ran for Southampton.

The crew had taken to the lifeboats and been picked up by helicopters and lifeboats. Tugs were on their way.

Reports were coming in of containers washed ashore along the south coast. Police in Hampshire and Sussex were calling in reserves to seal off beaches and prevent scenes of looting like those that happened when the MSC Napoli went aground in Branscombe Bay in 2007.

The studio presenter cut to a breathless reporter on a clifftop, trying to make herself heard above the wind and rain. "Despite police efforts, groups of people are already gathering and I can see a line of vans parked behind me on the cliff road.

"On the beach behind where I'm standing a dozen cargo containers have been badly damaged as they washed ashore. Thousands of timber planks are strewn across the shingle. Just fifty yards away I can see groups of men carrying items away from a wrecked container."

Danny looked thoughtfully out of the window. The rain pummelled the glass. He picked up the phone and waited as it rang ten or fifteen times.

"Bob! Morning ... yes, yes, I know what time it is. No, I'm not an insomniac, well, not usually. No, listen, just listen, Bob. Have you heard the news? ... Well stick Sky on. Yes, that's right. The ship, yes, household stuff, tools, there's a bit of everything. It's one big free closing down sale.

"Timber? Yes, they said something about timber. I guess you could use it once it dried out. ... Well, it's worth a try. Fancy giving it a go? Okay, if you bring the van round to mine, I'll give Karol a bell. Yeah, bring a mate if you want, just make sure he can keep his mouth shut. Then we'll see what the early bird catches."

Back in his bedroom he slipped into jeans, shirt, leather jacket and his favourite knock-off Tims. Not ideal for the weather outside but the best he had.

Glad to be busy again, he checked his watch, a Rolex, and grinned at the thought of what the day might bring. He knew something would turn up.

\*\*\*

The man was a giant. Huge biceps stretched the short sleeves of his shirt. The material around the buttonholes pulled into horizontal slits as they strained to contain his chest.

His shoulders swelled like the wings of an old Fifties Chevy and his neck had the squat solidity of a traffic bollard.

Most of the workers sat on their wooden bunk beds in the cramped barracks room.

The few that had been moving about when he came in had frozen in the empty hope that they might not catch his attention. He stood by the door, big fisted hands planted on his hips, a slab of a man in greyish silhouette against the light outside.

As his big head turned from side to side, surveying the room, his spiky gelled hair turned against the backlight like a twisting bed of nails.

He clucked disbelief and disapproval. "What a fucking rabble."

The one they called The Axeman took a step deeper into the room and there was a flurry of nervous, jerky movement as everyone moved to avoid catching is eye.

"I said," he paused to be sure he had their attention. "You lot are a fucking rabble."

Silence.

"What are you?"

His voice booming off the wooden walls prompted a reluctant muttering in a variety of languages. He guessed they were their words for rabble. They wouldn't dare say anything else.

"Louder!"

The volume of the muttering reluctantly increased.

"LOUDER!"

They called out again, voices weary and desperate. The Axeman grinned. "That's better." He took another step forward, to the centre of the room, and looked around, his puffy features made more sinister by eyes set too close together. They glinted in the pale light of the bare eco-bulb hanging above his head.

"Now listen up. It's all very simple. I am the man in charge here. You do what you're told, what you signed up for, and everything will be sweet.

"We've got a job to do here, a special job, important. You've seen the workshop and the range, all you have to do is what you're being paid for. And keep schtum. Just remember I don't take any crap and I don't have a sense of humour. You mess me about and you will regret it, and I mean bigtime."

He looked around. "Do you understand?"

A murmuring came reluctantly out of the gloom.

"Do you UNDERSTAND?"

Whatever it was they had said in their languages they said again, louder.

"Good, now we all know the score. That's what it's all about, eh? The global economy, trading between nations, job mobility. You got a skill, you can take it anywhere. Right?"

They nodded and mumbled.

"Nice one. Now, you've been told already but I'll say it again, just so there's no mistakes. They need to be cleaned, assembled and tested. And I want it done properly. I'll be watching. You start first thing tomorrow so get a good night's kip. You'll need it."

As he took a last look around the gloomy barracks his narrowed eyes stopped on a slim blonde girl who had been unlucky enough to be moving when he entered. She was still standing, stiff and unnatural, where she had been when the door opened.

"What's your name, love?"

She whispered something.

"WHAT?" roared The Axeman. Shadows in the bunks shrank back into the deeper darkness.

"Katya," said the girl, quietly.

"Katya, eh?" said The Axeman, taking a step forward. She stood her ground but couldn't help cringing away from the wall of muscle as it towered over her, blocking out the light.

"So you know your stuff, do you?"

"Please?"

"You know the job, know how everything works?"

"I know."

"Funny job for a girl but I guess we'll find out tomorrow, won't we?"

Katya nodded, shaking.

When a hand the size of a baseball glove closed on her shoulder she couldn't stop the erratic tremors that convulsed through her. She winced as hard fat fingers clamped into her thin muscle.

The Axeman's other hand pinched her chin and pulled her face up to look at him. She screwed her eyes to the side but couldn't hold them there. They were drawn back to look into the puffy face and small, lightless eyes of The Axeman.

"What's a pretty girl like you doing here?"

"I come for my son."

"Your son, eh? Well don't you worry, love. I'll look after you. I'll take very great care of you. Believe it."

The hand released her chin and moved down to cup her breast. His thick lips curled at the edges and a small tongue flashed in and out to lubricate them.

"Stop!"

The Axeman froze, the small eyes widened to their maximum extent in surprise. He released his grip on Katya and turned.

At the far end of the barracks a thin twentysomething with straggly red hair to his shoulders had emerged from the shadows of a bottom bunk.

"Leave her. We come here to work. It is not right you treat her…"

The wet crunch of nose and teeth collapsing punctuated the end of his sentence. The blow threw him backwards. His head cracked hard against the side panel of the upper bunk and he toppled forward, landing in a limp bundle on the floor.

A curl of light traced the edge of the blood pool as it spread across the boards, feeling its way through the grain and knotholes of the ancient planking.

Everyone was surprised at the speed The Axeman had moved. A dark blur crossed the room and he was standing over the skinny man, his boot beating time on the man's ribcage in a series of dull thuds.

"Don't you…"

Thud.

"ever…"

Thud.

"fucking…"

Thud.

"ever…"

Katya tried to grab his arm but he swatted her away. Her frail body skidded off across the floor.

"Ever…"

Thud.

"ever…"

Thud.

The Axeman gave up on the words and concentrated on the kicking to drive home his point. Shadows cringing in the shadows of the bunks winced at the dry crack of a breaking rib.

Then The Axeman stepped back, eyes blinking to clear the sweat that had trickled down from his forehead. A huge hand trawled through his wet hair as he panted.

"Tomorrow," he gasped. "I'll see you rabble tomorrow."

## CHAPTER 4

"How did you talk me into this?" Bob Lovejoy looked deeply unhappy, hair plastered down his face, trousers soaked to the knees. He couldn't resist the compulsion to keep licking the salt from his lips.

They stood in a huddle on the sloping shingle, looking around. Bob had introduced his friend in the van as Skidmarks but they had not had time to talk.

Danny, squinting against the driving rain, surveyed the chaos spread out along the beach. Massive marine containers were gashed and torn in places where the storm had tossed them like kids' building blocks and crumpled them like cigarette packets.

Some had waterlogged and sunk just off the beach. Others had been driven up onto the shingle by the wind and waves.

A gigantic fan of timber planks wheezed, groaned and rumbled like an asthmatic as the restless tide pushed it repeatedly against the gravel beach.

Bob pointed across to a group of police in high-visibility jackets trying to string incident tape against the wind two hundred yards away. "What about them? They're hardly likely to help us load up."

"Don't be such a misery. It's like Christmas down here," said Danny.

Bob surveyed the scene thoughtfully. "Well, that timber would come in handy for that conversion job in Kemp Town. They've got ambitious plans for a conservatory."

Danny looked along the beach to where the police were confronting a group of men. Snatches of angry voices whipped past them on the wind. "Well, let's fill our boots while the boys in blue are busy."

As he looked out to sea, waves of wind-driven spray rushed towards the beach like ranks of smoke-shrouded white horses charging in ranks. The four were sodden in seconds, hair plastered flat, the collars of their jackets whipping their cheeks.

The lashing rain soaked their clothes, opening the way for the knife-edge wind to bite skin. It was hard to see through the drifting spray.

Bob, who had worried that Danny seemed down for so long, smiled when he saw the crazy happy grin that split his friend's face. The first time for a long while, more like the old Danny.

They set off, leaning into the howling wind, their footsteps heavy as their feet sank into the slick shifting shingle, leaning into curtains of spray that masked the ghost army of pounding waves throwing random cargo onto the beach.

Rain lashed stinging skin and made their faces and eyes raw. Bob, socks squelching, thought they weren't properly dressed for the elements but nothing would keep you dry from the relentless scary power of a storm like this.

They trudged through the grinding gravel to the waters edge. Danny and Skidmarks began hauling planks clear of the waves while Bob and Karol stacked them.

The pile was chest high when Danny paused. He looked at the Rolex on his wrist. It was still ticking despite the soaking it had got, a tribute to Chinese engineering. He looked around. "We won't have long before someone turns up for an argument. You guys start getting this to the van. I'll have a scout round, see if there's anything else worth having."

Before anyone could argue, Danny was jogging off along the beach towards three containers jammed against a rock outcrop.

The door of the first one was buckled and hanging from a single hinge. It was filled with what looked like packing cases that began to tumble onto the shingle as the door groaned open. There were no markings to indicate what was in them and Danny didn't have time to find out so he moved on to the next container.

He threw his weight against its handle but it would not budge. He tried three times but the hinge mechanism was bent and the door was jammed shut.

The door of the third container gave at the second attempt. As it creaked open Danny peered in at the jumbled contents, letting his eyes grow accustomed to the gloom.

The container's cargo looked like the leftovers from a car boot sale put through a tumble dryer. He was about to walk away when something caught his eye.

He stepped inside, careful to secure his footing, and began throwing boxes and debris out of his way.

After a couple of minutes he was sweating despite the cold and the damp. He took a step back to study the inside of the container and let out a whoop of delight.

The others were just loading the last of Bob's timber planking into his box van when Skidmarks looked up to see Danny waving.

"Better see what he wants," he told the others and set off across the beach. When he reached the container Danny was inside throwing broken boxes frantically to one side. When he looked up and saw Skidmarks he punched the air. "Result!"

Peering into the gloom, Skidmarks could just make out the fat front tyres and flaring wheel arches of a quad bike sitting in the frame of a broken crate.

"You are joking."

Danny shook his head. "No, I've always wanted one of these. The lifeguards in Brighton use them, neat piece of kit."

"You're barking, mate. How do we get it home?" Danny pointed down to a makeshift ramp he had thrown together out of wooden panels.

Skidmarks scrambled into the container and looked down at the bike.

"I'll put it in neutral," said Danny.

"Hang on," said Skidmarks. He crouched down to look at a crate by his feet. "Label's damaged but it says something about vehicle parts. I've got a garage, might come in hand."

"Chuck it on the bike," said Danny and before Skidmarks could say anything else the quad was rolling gently down the ramp. Skidmarks heaved the crate onto the seat and together they slowed the machine as it crept towards the edge of the container, then pushed to give it the momentum to get clear of the ramp. The bike bounced through the restless water onto the shingle and rolled to a stop.

Skidmarks straightened up and stretched. "You know, Danny, Bob was saying, if you're short I could put some work your way."

Danny grinned. "Thanks but I'm working as a detective now."

Skidmarks looked startled. "A detective?"

Danny shrugged. "Tried everything else, thought I'd give it a go. Beats smiling at people all day in Carphone Warehouse."

"So how's it going?"

"At the moment, it's not but, hey ho, early days. Something'll turn up." He jerked his head towards the police up the beach and braced himself against the quad. "Anyway, we'd better get a move on."

***

## ARAGUA, VENEZUELA, TEN WEEKS AGO

The narrow path was damp and spongy underfoot. Simón walked ahead, holding the thick overhanging foliage aside, but the visitor still had to catch a few branches that snapped back suddenly.

The one he had missed had smacked him across the right cheek and drawn blood. Simón had chuckled and he could hear sniggering from the others behind them. It made the man they called Rookwood angry but he couldn't show it.

Still, he had a lot to be angry about. The journey had been a nightmare. The hotel in Maracay was shit, the food was shit, the weather was stinking hot.

He scratched at his angry skin and turned to see Ernesto walking beside him, grinning. In different circumstances, back home, he'd have punched that stupid smile off his face. But not here.

Ernesto had been waiting for him at the airport and hadn't stopped talking since. Small and wiry, an Adam's apple smeared with stubble, thick black hair poking from the neck of his open shirt and a smile too big for his face, the guy was like a tour guide on acid.

"Welcome to my beautiful country. I am Ernesto, like Ernesto Che Guevara, you know?"

A long drive had taken them to Maracay, the "Garden City", with Ernesto keeping up a running commentary on everything he thought a tourist should know, nodding all the time he spoke so at least someone was agreeing with him.

There had been a lot of military in the city. Ernesto had sung their praises. They'd seen military fighter jets low overhead, big bastards that made your guts tremble. They could do some damage. Ernesto said they were Russian-made Sukhoi SU30s.

With their angled nose and cockpit section perched above big jet intakes and the tall twin tail fins they really looked the business, hunting for prey.

It wasn't so bad when they were on the move, with something to do. Ernesto was at his worst when they were killing time, and they had been killing a lot of it.

"Have you met the queen?" "Why does Margaret Thatcher steal the Malvinas?" "Wayne Rooney is a genius." "Our girls are beautiful. Maybe you have some too. Your Lisbet Hurley is..." For once, Ernesto didn't know the words and paused to carve hourglass shapes in the air with his hands.

According to Ernesto, one of the city's many proud boasts was that it was home to a former Miss Universe, Yoseph Alicia Machado Fajardo.

He'd never heard of the woman but she had to be better looking than the two whores Ernesto had brought up to his room last night. They had been butt ugly but at least they were enthusiastic, and very inventive for kids that young. He'd even given them a bit extra, for the bruises. Maybe he was getting soft.

Thank Christ he'd brought his own condoms. You wouldn't want to take chances with the local rubber. Even the air you breathed in this place stank of disease.

This whole project had been way beyond his expectation. Instead of all this pissing about, why not ship home a few kilos of coke?

He knew the score. A lot of it came through Venezuela from Colombia on its way to West Africa and then Europe. Cash in the bank, that. Money for jam. It was obvious Digby thought he was a wanker but he'd bide his time, see how things worked out, show him who he really was.

He really did have a lot to be angry about but he was much too far out of his comfort zone to risk any trouble with these guys.

His hair was plastered flat to his head and his shirt stick to him like Clingfilm across the back and under his arms where big circles of sweat grew steadily bigger and darker.

The forest was alive with sounds he had never heard. Maybe birds, maybe not. Rookwood slapped his neck at the touch of an insect and nearly missed the backward slash of another branch. Simón grinned but Rookwood bit his tongue.

"Is it much further?"

Simón pulled a face of incomprehension.

"Er ... Mas lejo?"

Simón shook his head and then Ernesto was between them. Talking.

"He says no, no, only ten minutes more."

The small group trudged on through the steaming heat. The others seemed unaffected but Rookwood felt as if he was wrapped in a hot towel, the wet air sucking the breath out of him, clothes clinging to his body.

He slapped his neck again but it was just another trickle of sweat. His eyes stung as mosquito spray rolled down from his forehead on a tide of sweat.

Rookwood settled into a miserable rhythm of stepping and breathing, stepping and breathing until Simón stopped and pointed off the track. "Por ahi."

As he looked, Rookwood could see dappled light thinning the dense shadows around them. Just a few feet ahead they stepped into a long narrow clearing and Rookwood marvelled that the place had been invisible until they were right on top it. God help anyone who got lost in this hellhole.

The visitor glimpsed a man waiting at the far end of the clearing. Simón spoke to the other two in their party. He must have been issuing orders as they nodded and set off at a lazy trot towards the waiting man.

"Smoke?" Rookwood turned to see Simón offering a crumpled cigarette packet. He had tried the local cigarettes. They tasted like shit. He forced a smile. "Gracias."

Ernesto took one too. They stood and smoked in silence as they watched the other three men sling a length of rope across the clearing at head height and attach netting to it at intervals with wire ties.

One tested the rope with his own weight and when they were satisfied they took six melons from their bags and positioned them at even intervals in the netting.

"You know this?" asked Simón. Rookwood turned to see him pull the rifle from the canvas shoulder bag he had been carrying.

The visitor nodded, "Yes."

Simón gave him another of those yellow-toothed grins. He clearly didn't believe him.

"It is modern design of the famous gun. Plastic replaces metal and wood. It can use different sights, for laser or night, and can throw bombs."

Ernesto chipped in again. "It is very good. We make it here, best technology."

Simón stooped to scoop a curved magazine from the bag and Rookwood saw the copper glint of live rounds. Stay cool, stay cool. Simón held the rifle vertically and positioned the magazine beneath the receiver. He hooked the lip at the front end of the magazine into the receiver and snapped it home.

"Like this."

Then he pulled back the cocking handle and released it. It punched home with a satisfying clack. "And like this."

Simón held out the rifle with one hand. Rookwood took it with two and was surprised at how light it was. He hefted it and adjusted the grip of his sweaty hands on the plastic. As he studied the rifle Simón placed a finger against the side of the barrel and gently pointed it down the clearing. Then he gave a loud whistle and the melon men began running towards them to get clear.

When they were safely back behind them, Simón gestured down the clearing. "Go on, try."

Rookwood lifted the rifle to his shoulder but paused as Simón stepped closer, tapping at his feet with a shoe until they were the width of his shoulders apart, pressing the butt firmly into his shoulder. When he was satisfied he waved down the clearing to indicate the melons.

Rookwood slid his finger through the trigger guard and fired. The crack startled him. The recoil forced him to take a step back. The ejected cartridge spun away onto the grass. The melons hung undisturbed in the limp air.

He heard them sniggering behind his back but forced himself to keep looking down the makeshift range.

He rocked to check his footing again, then aimed and fired. Nothing. Rookwood fired a third and fourth time. Nothing.

Someone behind him said something he didn't understand. Rookwood braced again, took careful aim through the V of the sight and squeezed the trigger gently. As the rifle bucked he glimpsed a splash of red and a green chunk flew off a melon. Juice dribbled. He tried to hide a smile as a cheer broke out behind him.

More confident now, he tried again and hit a second melon at the third attempt. When the third one burst the bolt clacked onto an empty chamber. Simón stepped forward and loaded a fresh magazine, offering tips on improving his stance, grip and aim, friendlier now that payday was approaching.

Half way through his third magazine Rookwood smashed the last melon which sparked a bout of cheering and whistling. Simón slapped him on the back. Smiles all round.

He felt better than he had in days. This trip had been a nightmare, he still couldn't wait for it to be over, but the plan was coming together. This might just work.

Simón took the rifle, removed the half empty magazine and put in a fresh one. He handed it back to Rookwood and gestured down the range. The visitor looked and for the first time he saw a black goat tethered at the edge of the trees.

His puzzled expression brought another grin from Simón who waved an arm towards the animal.

"For you. A gift," said Ernesto. Rookwood looked doubtful.

"Si, si, a gift."

He raised the rifle. His arm was aching now and he tried to control a slight tremor. He fired half a dozen aimed single shots. The last one plucked away the animals rear right leg. It toppled over, screaming.

Rookwood looked around at the grinning, nodding group behind him. Simón stepped forward and adjusted a lever on the side of the weapon. His grin grew bigger.

"Automático."

Rookwood turned back to look down the clearing, took aim and squeezed the trigger. Rounds kicked up spouts of dirt and stones as his first burst snaked across the clearing. The cheering behind him grew to roars of approval as his second burst cut the goat in half with a fountain of wet red guts and ribs.

Ernesto jumped up and down, clapping with delight.

\*\*\*

Bob was red-faced and wheezing as he and Karol loaded the last of the planks. He pulled himself upright, blinking away the driving rain, and arched his aching back, massaging his lower spine. Then he looked along the beach. "Oh, for Christ's sake."

Karol looked up and followed Bob's line of sight.

"What the hell is he going to do with that bloody thing?"

They watched as Danny and Skidmarks pushed the quad bike up the incline of shingle. When they reached the van Danny was breathing hard and grinning.

"We've got to be quick about this," he said, wiping sweat and stinging spray from his eyes, "before they lock down this beach and start hanging people for piracy or wrecking or whatever it is."

Something clattered behind Bob and he turned to see Karol unloading a plank. "What's that for?"

The skinny Pole tugged his forelock in a mock salute. "I make a ramp for Captain Jack's bike."

Danny ducked behind the van, tucked his head inside his jacket against the wind and managed to light a cigarette at the fifth attempt. When he emerged he looked back along the beach. Bobbing towards them through the driving curtains of rain was a line of yellow blobs.

"I think we'd better get a wiggle on."

Bob's head emerged from behind the van.

"What's up?"

Danny pointed down the beach.

"I think someone's coming to dispute ownership."

The four of them piled into the van and skidding away across the gravel, chased by the shouts of the approaching police in their high-visibility jackets.

***

**ARAGUA, VENEZUELA, TEN WEEKS AGO**

He'd showered, scrubbing himself all over with the jet on full blast, but it hadn't made any difference. He still stank of the forest - damp, mould and shit. He couldn't get the smell out of his nose.

On their way back to the city, as the sun was setting, the bugs had risen in their million like some vampire army. He liked a day out in the sunshine as much as the next man but this place was mental.

Back in the cool of the hotel aircon, his skin was itching and peppered with nagging red lumps. He had barely had a chance to think through the day's events and neck a couple of scotches from the minibar before Ernesto was pounding on the door.

"The day for you is very good, yes? Very good."

Simón was waiting outside in the corridor, smiling. Rookwood had grabbed his jacket and the holdall and Simón and Ernesto had escorted him to the Merc.

As soon as he stepped outside the hotel he was sweating again. They drove across town through heavy traffic, Simón behind the wheel while Ernesto babbled away beside him in the back. Rookwood didn't listen, just sat looking out of the window and feeling his sweat turn clammy in the Merc's aircon.

He hadn't a clue where he was, just trusting in the plan and this shifty bunch he'd washed up with. He hoped Digby's scheme was solid.

After twenty minutes or so they pulled up at a flash-looking tower block. Ernesto jumped out to open the door and the two men had escorted him through the lobby and into a lift to the top floor.

They walked down a wide corridor until Ernesto stopped outside a door, tapped gently, then threw it open with a dramatic sweep of his arm on the word of command from inside.

"Mr Rookwood, welcome." A chunky hand heavy with gold rings waved him to a chair in front of the desk.

Simón and Ernesto took up station either side of the closed door to the corridor. Rookwood didn't like having people behind him but he'd just have to tough it out. God, he'd be glad to get back home.

"It is a great pleasure to meet you at last, Mr Rookwood. I am Mr Traficante, your host and business associate. I hope my colleagues have taken care of all your needs while you have been here?"

Rookwood nodded.

"You would like a drink?"

Rookwood nodded again.

"I can offer you chicha." He saw the look cross Rookwood's face. "Or some rum, Havana Club."

"I'll go for the rum."

Traficante's head bobbed an inch and Ernesto moved to the illuminated shelves packed with bottles in the corner behind Rookwood.

The chair creaked as Traficante leaned back, revealing three gold teeth as he drew on a thick Cuban cigar. He savoured the taste before blowing out a long plume of blue smoke upward until it boiled across the high ceiling.

The two men sat in silence until the glasses were placed on the desk between them. Traficante lifted his and indicated for Rookwood to do the same.

"A toast, to the success of your enterprise and to our future business."

Rookwood downed the rum in one. It burned but it felt good. Mustn't overdo it.

"Another?"

Rookwood nodded.

As Ernesto busied himself refreshing Rookwood's glass, Traficante leaned forward, placed his cigar carefully in a large onyx ashtray and rested his forearms on the desk, fingers meshed.

"You have the money?"

Rookwood tapped the holdall with his foot. Traficante nodded at the sound of the dull thump. His head moved again and Simón swept the bag up from the floor, took it to a table in the opposite corner and began to count the thick wads of cash.

Traficante raised his glass, opening his arms in a gesture of apology. "I do not mean to be rude but if we are to be partners in business there must be honesty between us. What do you call it in England? Transparency."

Rookwood nodded and took another slug of his rum. The heat in his stomach was spreading outwards now, numbing the bites on his skin. Don't get too comfy.

Rookwood was aware of Traficante studying him through the haze from his cigar. "You seem uncomfortable, Mr Rookwood. Is there something wrong?"

Rookwood shrugged. "Must be something I ate."

Traficante nodded sympathetically. "A pity, but I have heard that the English have a weak stomach when they are abroad. Still, our business will soon be concluded and then you can go home to your … what is it? .. fish and chips?"

Rookwood couldn't figure if this was some sort of wind-up so he settled for another nod.

He stiffened when he saw Traficante's eyes flick inquiringly over his shoulder, towards Simón. Then the big man's face broke into a smile.

"So, my friend, all is correct. Your money is the down payment of your good faith and now we may proceed as planned. You are happy with your purchases?"

Rookwood nodded.

Traficante picked up a sheaf of papers from his desk and tilted his head, squinting, too vain to admit he needed glasses.

"So, you have a business outlet here in Venezuela. I like this. We have done business before, I think. And you will transport the consignment this way, in pieces. It is a clever idea. I wish it every success."

He raised his glass.

Rookwood raised his rum and drained it.

Traficante placed his empty glass down on his blotter, punched the cigar down into the ashtray and linked his fingers again.

"Now, if you are satisfied, Simón and Ernesto will take you to the airport for your flight. I will wish you a pleasant journey."

Traficante levered himself out of his chair and offered a hand. Rookwood felt the hard pressure of heavy gold rings as they shook.

As he turned towards the door, trying to work out the time difference, Rookwood started to calculate how far away he was from a decent fry-up and a proper cup of tea.

\*\*\*

It was a tight squeeze with four of them in the front of the van. Bob had the wipers on double speed to slice through the waves of rain that fell like layers of jelly across the windscreen.

Bob let out a cowboy whoop that made the others wince.

"Steady," said Danny. "You can't line-dance and drive at the same time."

"Bloody marvellous," said Bob.

"What is?" asked Danny, grinning.

"That beach, dashing about like kids in all that rain."

Danny looked over his shoulder at the load rattling and groaning in the back. "And not a bad haul, either."

Bob swung into a bend and all four of them squashed onto the bench seat felt the van slide sideways under the heavy load.

"Careful, old man," said Karol. "You put us in ditch."

"Don't you old man me, you bolshie Polish chippy. Don't forget I'm still paying you, even if there's no work. Conservatories, bloody conservatories. Since the building business went south I've been mooching around the house, bored shitless, getting old, and when I do get any work it's bloody conservatories."

He looked across at Danny and there was a wild light in his eyes. "That was bloody good fun. Best day I've had in ages."

"Glad I persuaded you then?" asked Danny.

"Too right, mate. Charging about back there, legging it from the Bill, better than Viagra."

Worry flickered across Bob's face and he scanned the others in the cab for any reaction.

"Not that I ever use the stuff."

"Viagra," said Karol thoughtfully, "is named for the Sanskrit word vyaaghra which means tiger."

"Trust you to know that," said Bob.

"Very useful for pub quiz," said Karol.

"Where are you going to stash the timber, Bob?" Danny asked.

"I'll use one of my lock-ups, let it dry out a bit."

"Got room for the quad in there?"

"We can squeeze it in, though God knows what you're going to do with it."

The van rocked as a gust of wind punched its flank. Bob hunched over the wheel, concentrating as he gripped the clammy plastic. "Bloody awful weather."

Skidmarks leaned across to Danny and tapped him gently on the shoulder. "I was serious about that job offer, Danny. Give me a call sometime."

Danny shook his head. "Thanks, Skids, but I'm a detective."

Bob, still grinning like a kid, looked across at the others. "Who's for breakfast? I'm starving."

\*\*\*

**HAYWARDS HEATH, ENGLAND, FIVE MONTHS AGO**
"Put Mr Wriggles in the buggy."

Vicky Green had had enough. Her jaw would not stop throbbing but she couldn't get a dentist's appointment until Thursday, not even an emergency one.

She had stood in front of the reception desk, eyes watering with the pain, and been lectured by that dried-up old shrew that she was lucky even to be registered with a dentist. They didn't have the budgets and she would have to wait her turn.

Vicky had read stories in the papers about people pulling their own teeth with pliers. The thought made her stomach turn to water.

She tried to stay healthy, eating proper food and taking exercise. She didn't like taking drugs but the pain left her no choice and she had found herself at the counter in Boots. They had been helpful, sympathetic, but the paracetomol was not even denting the pain. Once they got home she'd see if a stiff vodka would help.

Vicky was tired and her feet hurt. Usually she loved an afternoon's shopping but today wasn't the day. She had spent three hours tramping around The Orchards with Ruby in tow but hadn't found the birthday present she wanted or the new dress she had set her heart on. Money was tight but it would be silly to ignore the sales when they were on. And it had taken her mind off the tooth for a while.

When they stepped outside Vicky saw it had been raining hard, the pavements slick and glistening. A dark, lumpy sky threatened more to come.

"Ruby, I said put Mr Wriggles in the buggy and hold my hand."

As if the toothache wasn't enough, the buggy was close to toppling over with the weight of shopping in bulging carrier bags slung over its handles.

She had overspent again but it was daft to miss the BOGOFs when you could pop the extra in the freezer for later. Looking along the road, Vicky could see that the queue at the bus stop was huge, everyone trying to huddle under the shelter as more rain threatened from the west. There wasn't a cab to be seen.

And on top of it all there was the car. How was she supposed to know what that dashboard light meant? She had enough to cope with, didn't need that smug mechanic explaining the problem to her as if she were a child. Dad had offered to get the car fixed as soon as he'd heard but it still wouldn't be ready until tomorrow.

"Ruby, please put Mr Wriggles in the buggy and hold my hand."

The child didn't budge. She stood on the pavement, eyes lowered, rosebud lips pouting, arms firmly crossed over her chest to advertise her disobedience, pressing Mr Wriggles firmly to her, his frayed ears poking up either side of her neck.

"Ruby, mind the spray. Come away from the road and hold mummy's hand or you'll get all wet. Don't make me ask you again." The toddler's eyes darkened under half-closed lids and she pressed her lips tighter together in sullen defiance.

Vicky winced in silent despair, unable to decide whether to shout or cry. It wasn't as if Gerry was any help. With him on nights for more than a month she'd hardly seen him.

It was like living with a ghost as she tiptoed around the flat during the day to avoid waking him, listening to the buzz of snoring behind the bedroom door. Working nights didn't suit him. He had bags under his eyes and nodded off in his armchair whenever he got comfortable. But they needed the money.

Dad would be happy to help out, he'd offered often enough, but Gerry was stubborn like that. It was his family, his responsibility. The thought of a few little luxuries paid for with dad's cash was very attractive to Vicky but she understood Gerry's point, was quite proud of him, really.

That said, there had hardly been enough cash to cover the shopping and Vicky had maxed her credit cards but she had bought a scratch card at the checkout. It was an impulse, probably wouldn't do any good but it kept hope alive, continued the pretence that there really might be light at the end of the tunnel.

When she got home she would sit Ruby in front of a DVD and give herself a few moments alone to see what secrets might lay behind the little silver panels while she had that vodka.

The stream of rush-hour traffic was throwing up a haze of dirty water from the flooded gutters. As Vicky looked she could see Ruby's coat growing steadily darker.

"Come away from the road, Ruby. You'll get drenched."

The child didn't move, looking solemnly up her at mother, moist bottom lip jutting forward as beads of water zigzagged their way down Mr Wriggles's tatty fur.

"Ruby, I'm not going to tell you again." From the corner of her eye Vicky could see the bus approaching. The crowd that passed for a queue began shuffling out of the shelter into the rain, edging for position.

Vicky looked down at her daughter and gasped in surprise. The little madam had stamped her foot, actually stamped her foot. Vicky tried to speak but her teeth clashed together and she winced as a flash of pain seared around her jaw.

As she screwed her eyes tight shut a tyre sliced through the flooded gutter and a sheet of water broke over her, splashing her face and drenching her coat. She gasped with the shock and tasted something metallic, coppery.

When Vicky opened her eyes Ruby was gone. Unable to understand what she was seeing, Vicky looked down at the spot where she had been standing, confused.

She stared, open mouthed, at the pavement and then at the road, her mind an unbelieving blank. What's happened?

She looked around her but there was no one within ten feet. Vicky looked again at the pavement and the rain-splashed road. What's happening?

The noise of traffic and people suddenly seemed much louder, punching through the roaring that filled her ears.

Somewhere, someone screamed. Vicky looked up to see something fly off the bonnet of a grey car that had just swerved around the bus.

As the vehicle shimmied to regain control the object spun over its roof like a cartwheel and smacked onto the road, flattening itself onto the shining tarmac.

The way it moved, the way it fell, made Vicky think of Mr Wriggles, limp and floppy after numerous trips through the washing machine had pulped his stuffing to clumps of fluff.

The bus's tyres screeched, standing passengers falling like bowling pins as they were thrown forward.

An oncoming van hooted furious as it swerved to avoid the grey car speeding towards it in the wrong lane.

Someone grabbed Vicky's arm. It was funny, she thought, that she couldn't feel the pain in her tooth any more. She looked down and saw something shiny sailing away on top of the rainwater in the gutter. Her scratch card.

Then she saw Mr Wriggles. He was lying in a puddle by the kerb, his dark button eyes staring at her.

As she watched she saw his long frayed ears darken as they soaked up the water. The button eyes caught the orange of the street lights for a moment, then he became a shadow as he sank beneath the oily surface.

Vicky began to scream.

\*\*\*

The vicar paused for effect and took the opportunity to peer down at his notes on the lectern.

The small chapel at Brighton's Woodvale Crematorium was surprisingly full. It was refreshing to have the chance to make the most of an opportunity like this after so many services conducted for a handful of mourners.

He cleared his throat and began the climax of his eulogy. "The number of people who have gathered here today to pay tribute to our sister Ivy is testament to the friends she made and the lives she touched in a long life lived to the full before she was diminished by illness bravely borne." He raised an open hand. "Let us pray."

The congregation shuffled as they dipped their heads. The vicar's voice rose, booming from the ceiling as he intoned the Committal:

"We have but a short time to live.
Like a flower we blossom and then wither,
like a shadow we flee and never stay.
In the midst of life we are in death,
to whom can we turn for help."

Somewhere in the middle of the congregation a suppressed sob exploded and a woman began to cry. The vicar paused, then carried on, lifting his voice to rise above the interruption.

"Deliver us from the bitter pain of eternal death. Lord, you know the secrets of our hearts."

The weeping grew louder. The vicar paused again but it showed no sign of abating. Someone put an arm around the woman, eased her to her feet, helped her shuffle towards the doors of the chapel. He carried on.

"Spare us, most worthy judge eternal,
at our last hour let us not fall from you,
O holy and merciful Saviour. Amen."

The congregation muttered a ragged response. Pleased with a job well done, the vicar gathered up his papers and turned as recorded organ music struck up. An electric motor whined quietly and the curtains closed.

Mourners craned for a last glimpse of the coffin. The chapel doors were opened and the vicar made his way towards the rain-spattered gloom of the car park. Mourners began to file from their pews and follow.

They gathered in little knots outside, clinging to what little shelter the wall of the chapel offered, looking round at the bare flowerbeds, killing time. A lone magpie perched on the back of a commemorative wooden bench, watching.

It was hard to believe they were within a city. The crematorium stood in a wooded valley rich with shrubs, lawns, rockeries and flower beds that would bring a palate of colour to sombre occasions in summer. Now, the spare winter foliage was bowed down by the grey rain that engorged it.

Last to emerge from the chapel were two tall men in long black coats and gloves. They stood to one side and the broader of the two lit a cigarette. The other opened his umbrella and rested it across his shoulder without offering his companion any shelter.

"What the hell was all that about?" asked the smoker.

"I thought it was very moving," said the man with the umbrella.

"Did you know her?"

"No, I picked her out from the notices in the Argus."

"You're bloody mad," said the first.

"Mad? No, Rookwood, not mad. Thoughtful, yes, analytical, yes, but not mad. Don't you understand? This makes the perfect cover. No one at a funeral is going to demand to know who you are. Everyone assumes you're from some distant branch of the family. Besides, if they're not contemplating their own mortality they've got other things on their minds.

"They're thinking about what they might get out of the will or what they can pocket over drinks and sandwiches back at the home of the deceased."

"You know, Digby, if talk was money you'd be minted."

"Camouflage, Rookwood, deception. Now you have recovered from your little South American outing we must meet as infrequently as possible and when we do it must be with the utmost discretion."

"Whatever you say, Digby. That was probably worth another couple of grand."

"I'm serious, Rookwood. If this plan succeeds we will control a highly lucrative business empire and a populist political movement, the two working in tandem. Don't you see, ours is the perfect 21st century business model, vertical integration, each element complementing and supporting the other.

"The business provides the cash cow to fund the political operation which, in turn, shields and protects the source of its funding. And on top of it all it makes us rich men. It's the perfect symbiosis."

"Symwhat?"

Digby rolled his eyes. He found it increasingly hard not to treat Rookwood as the blinking idiot he so clearly was. It was as if the man thought in slow motion, like an old slide projector, pale flashes of smoky light speckled with motes of dust as a thought passed behind his eyes.

But he still needed Rookwood. The man brought certain skills to the plan,

"Never mind," said Digby. "When the time comes we will need a few incidents." He stretched the word to emphasis its importance. "Perhaps a bank robbery or two, maybe the sudden death of a community leader."

He stretched the last two words again to drive home his point, trying not to notice that Rookwood's mouth was sagging open with concentration.

"We create fear and uncertainty, red meat for the tabloids, events that will drive people to our banner. And when that happens people will bind themselves to a strong leader who will make their lives safe and simple."

"I said it before, Digby. If words was cash we could buy the yacht now."

Digby fought down his sudden anger. "Don't let yourself be distracted, Rookwood. This is all for the future. For now, just concentrate on getting that shipment ready by next week. That'll be quite appropriate, don't you think?"

"Why?"

Digby sighed. "Because it's Bonfire Night. You know, Rookwood, you should relax more, recharge the batteries. I have a place in Normandy, a small farmhouse near Bayeux. I go there to relax and think. The local wines are quite passable and the cheeses are excellent. You should try something similar."

"I keep myself in shape."

"I'm sorry?"

"I train, lift weights."

"Well," said Digby. "Each to his own, I suppose. So what was so urgent? Is everything on track?"

He could read the answer from the pained look that flickered across Rookwood's face.

"What's the matter?" demanded Digby.

"The workshop's sorted. The equipment's in, staffing is nearly done and security's in place."

"Yes, but what is the matter?"

Rookwood lit another cigarette. The tip glowed brightly as he pulled hard on the filter, the thumbnail of his other hand worrying away at the paper label on his disposable lighter.

"You're sweating," said Digby.

Rookwood shook his big head with quick, jerky movements. "No, not sweating, keyed up, ready to go. Just don't keep having a pop at me. I don't like it."

"Patience is not one of my many qualities," said Digby. "What is the problem?"

"Have you seen the news?"

"What are you talking about?"

"That ship that came to grief in the Channel. The last consignment was on board."

"You are joking?"

"No, I'm not."

"How the hell…"

"Look, Digby, I can't be held responsible for the weather. Who could know?"

"All right, all right. Let me think."

"It wasn't everything, only 50 items."

"Fifty! That's a tenth of our production run."

"It was a hell of a storm. They're probably at the bottom of the Channel."

"And if they're not? Questions will be asked, the police. You've got to find out, make sure."

"How?" said Rookwood.

"We stay calm and we listen. If the shipment is lost at sea, we order a replacement. But if it should find its way onto terra firma we must retrieve it."

"Terra what?"

"Dry land, dear boy. Just keep your ears open, discreetly of course. Spread the word among the people we can trust and let me know if you hear anything."

"You still think this can work?"

"If we stay calm and stick to the plan."

"I'll get on it right away."

Digby's dark eyes flared. "You do that. I don't care how. Tear this shitty city apart if you have to but find them."

Digby stalked away to shake the vicar's hand.

Rookwood stood and watched him, trying to swallow back a stab of anger. He knew what he was doing.

It was always the same. Why was everyone always having a pop at him? If that bloody Digby started something it would be Rookwood who finished it.

But he'd bide his time, show them all what he could do. Then they'd realise what he was really about. They'd know he had brains as well as muscle. And he'd start getting the respect he deserved.

\*\*\*

Danny could pretty much guess how the meeting would go. He wasn't looking forward to it.

Western Road was busy and when his mobile rang he stepped to the kerb, out of the weaving streams of pedestrians.

He half hoped the meeting might be cancelled but when he pulled out his phone he didn't recognise the number.

Danny looked at the flashing symbol on the screen for a moment, wondering who the caller might be. Somehow he wasn't fired by his usual optimism. He pressed the button.

"Hello? Yes, that's me. A private detective … yes … that's right, very reasonable rates. Yes, did you see it on the website? Oh, the newsagents, okay."

Danny paused to listen as the anxious caller gabbled an explanation of their problem.

"Look … sorry … sorry to interrupt but I can't help you. Yes, I know what it says of the advert but …, yes, I should think it is upsetting for you. A special diet? Yes, that must be a worry. Sorry, the answer's still no.

"If he's on a special diet, have you tried putting some out in the garden, see if it'll tempt him back. Otherwise, try the RSPCA or maybe put up some posters. Yes, yes, I understand that but I still don't do missing cats, sorry."

He slipped the mobile back into his pocket. Okay, so things were grim. He was broke and there was no work coming in. But there were limits.

\*\*\*

"A top-up, Sir Charles?" The old man looked up at his assistant, then down at the cut glass tumbler in his hand.

"A small one, Edmund. Just a small one."

Edmund Salter held the decanter over Sir Charles Wolfram's glass, drizzling the bronze liquid, watching it rise up the sparkling sides until the old man's head gave the faintest of nods.

"Thank you, Edmund. Where was I?"

"Being strong, Sir Charles."

"Ah yes, as I was saying. We need to be strong and seen to be strong. The ordinary working people of this country have no representation.

"I'm not talking about economic migrants and scrounging riffraff. I mean the people who stick at a job, support their family, work through their problems rather than running to counsellors or divorce courts, people who take pride in their independence and self-sufficiency. No one speaks for them."

Salter inclined his head in agreement. Sir Charles waved his glass in circles to emphasise his point.

"The Human Rights Act protects everyone from all the consequences of their actions, Edmund. It's a knee-jerk reaction by Europeans to a century of war and occupation. You can see their reasoning but it's weak, bowing to the bully.

"We British, we are the most welcoming of any European nation. We have given shelter to Jews, Huguenots, a whole mixed bag of refugees down the centuries. But our attitude is different. You are welcome if you come in peace and contribute.

"The Jews lived peaceful and productive lives in London's East End under the guns of the City. Anyone is welcome here if they play the game."

Sir Charles paused to rally his ideas, sipped his whisky and carried on.

"But if you cross the line, if you rob, rape or kill, then you put yourself outside that band of fellowship. If you abuse the welcome and opportunities you have been offered then you, by your own volition, surrender all the rights and privileges granted to you. You put yourself outside the mutual shelter of our society, beyond the pale. Your choice, take the consequences."

"Well put, Sir Charles," said Salter.

Wolfram nodded, sipped his whisky and carried on. "The big parties and opinion-formers are all part of the same conspiracy, London-centric, centre left politicians and media types who know what's best for everyone. Never seen a field of cows or wheat unless it's from the window of a Range Rover or a Volvo as they drive to a Cotswold retreat that costs so much the locals can't afford to live there any more.

"Then they settle down to relax in their rural idyll amid their flavoured coffees and organic veg and moan about cocks crowing and church bells ringing. We have to be strong for the underdog, Edmund, all the tiny links that make up the backbone of this country."

Salter smiled. "We will have that strength, Sir Charles. I'm certain of it. In fact, I have some thoughts of my own on the subject."

Sir Charles nodded vigorously. "I'm sure you do, Edmund. I'm sure you do. That's the sort of spirit we need to nurture, each man thinking for himself, contributing. Perhaps, at some point, we might have a chat about your ideas."

"Very generous of you, Sir Charles."

Salter's thumb stroked the mobile phone in his pocket. He smiled down at the old man in the armchair and tilted the decanter slightly, raising an eyebrow.

Sir Charles looked thoughtfully at his glass.

\*\*\*

"You want fries with that?"

The two children nodded. Cheryl shook her head.

"Well find a table and I'll bring it over."

Danny wished yesterday's celebration after they had stashed the wood and the quad bike had not turned into an all-nighter. His head was thumping, his throat ached and his eyes were sore.

As he carried the tray from the counter to the table he could see that the girl was blinking hard, trying not to stare at him, turning her head to avoid eye contact when he looked at her.

The boy was head down and chin out, surly and determined. Cheryl just looked weary. Danny didn't think he was going to have a nice day despite the assurance of the girl behind the counter.

"There you go," he said, balancing the tray on one hand as he transferred the boxes to the table. "Two happy meals and a cheeseburger. Who's the milk shake?" The girl's arm jerked upward.

"So you're the coke?" The boy's head dipped once.

They settled in their plastic seats and opened their boxes, the children nibbled at their food.

"So," said Danny. "How is everyone?"

Cheryl put down her burger and sighed. Danny thought his sister looked tired. Wisps of hair were escaping from the elastic band that pinned most of it behind her head and there were dark circles under her eyes.

"The kids haven't seen you in months, Danny."

"I've been busy."

"Busy? Doing what?"

"Getting this detective business off the ground."

Cheryl shook her head, breath leaking out of her in a long sigh. "When are you going to grow up, Danny?"

"Don't keep on, Cheryl. I'm doing the best I can."

"But that best doesn't include a proper job."

"It is a proper job. At least it will be when things pick up."

"No, Danny. A proper job is when you turn up when they tell you, do what they tell you, go home when they tell you and pick up a regular pay packet."

Danny went to speak, changed his mind, shook his head.

The boy began to move off his chair. "Can I go outside?"

"No, Wayne," said Cheryl. "Sit still and eat your burger. Your dad's found a bit of time for us in his busy schedule so you'd better make the most of it. God alone knows when you'll see him again."

Danny put down his cheeseburger. "Do we have to do this now?"

Cheryl snorted. "Well when else, Danny? When Kathy died I agreed to look after the kids but that was five years ago. I thought you'd take a bit more interest. Have you any idea how much it costs to dress and feed two growing kids?"

"I've been a bit short."

"Your being short of cash doesn't make it any cheaper to look after these two. Why don't you think about a proper job?"

"I've got a proper job."

"You've always been a dreamer, Danny. Fantastic things are always going to happen tomorrow."

Wayne sat stock still, one buttock on the seat, one off, plucking at the hem of his Arsenal shirt, staring as his burger congealed. Hayley sat with her hands pressed hard into her lap, shoulders quivering as she tried not to cry.

"I'll sort it." Danny picked up his burger and bit out a chunk. "Let's eat."

They chewed in silence, the children picking reluctantly at their food. After a few minutes all four of them gave up, each leaving a crescent of half-eaten burger lying in their cardboard boxes.

"Look, Danny," said Cheryl, "I don't want to keep nagging but you've got to do something. I know things have been tough, what with your leg, then Kathy, now mum, but this isn't going to go away."

"I said I'll sort it."

"How, Danny?"

"I've got a quad bike."

"You've got a quad bike. What the hell for?"

"I found it."

"You found it?"

"Sort of."

"Sort of? You mean you nicked it."

"No, not exactly. Someone lost it."

"Lost it? And I suppose whoever lost it will have the police trying to find it and you'll end up back inside again. What were you thinking of? You wouldn't last five minutes riding round Brighton before you got a pull."

"I'll sell it."

Cheryl shook her head in slow disbelief. "So the best your kids can hope for is a few weeks' food and clothing on the back of a bent bike. Have you had anything like proper work lately?"

Danny poked a segment of gherkin back into his bun. "Sort of."

"What does that mean?"

"Delivering Chinese."

"Delivering Chinese?"

"Takeaways."

"And does it pay?"

"Fiver an hour and a pound for each delivery, two if it's over three miles."

"And using your own petrol?"

Danny nodded.

"But you're not doing that now?"

Danny shook his head.

"Why?" asked Cheryl.

"I'm a detective. It's not what I want to do."

"Danny, for God's sake, what you want to do is look after your kids. I saw a job in the Argus, traffic warden. The pay's not great but it's regular money and there's overtime. At least you could work outdoors."

Danny knew there was nothing he could say but his eyes were dark now. "Look, Cheryl, you've made your point. I'll sort something out, I will."

Wayne was gone before they'd seen him move, up from his seat, weaving through the diners and out of the door onto Western Road. Danny started to rise but Cheryl waved him down. "Let him go. He'll be okay. He's wound up."

Danny dropped back into his seat and rested his chin on his hand as he watched the big red 4 on the back of Wayne's Fabregas t-shirt disappear through the sliding doors into the street.

"Hayley's got something for you."

Danny looked up as Cheryl lifted an Asda carrier bag from beneath the table and handed it to the girl. "Give it to your dad."

Hayley slid from her seat, walked round the table and looked up at her father, holding out the bag with both hands.

Danny opened it and took out a bright blue coffee mug. The word "DAD" was painted around it in large red capital letters surrounded by hearts. Danny turned it over in his hands.

"That's beautiful, baby." The girl broke into a grin but said nothing.

"She painted it all herself, over at some place in Portslade. She did it for Father's Day."

"Father's Day?"

"That's right, Danny. You haven't seen the kids since June."

## CHAPTER 5

She didn't want to do it, didn't really know why they had kept it. Looking at it again was the last thing she needed to do.

If it had been left to her she would have destroyed it but even if she had it would not be forgotten. It had been copied from a USB memory drive to a hard drive and into lawyers' emails. And it had been copied into her brain where there was no delete option.

She could see it with her eyes closed, without having to press play. She didn't know why she was doing it now, why she felt this need to pick at the wound.

It was buried away, in a sub-folder with a meaningless file name in the labyrinth of sub-folders on the laptop that cascaded down from Domestic-Legal-Action-Concluded.

It wasn't at all clear, very grainy and the images jerked, but it was clear enough. She wondered if he ever looked at it, when he was alone, and shuddered at the idea.

She double-clicked the sub-folder named MM. It opened to reveal a long list of files – name, size, type, date modified. Most were Word documents, legal stuff.

Scrolling down, she found it at the bottom, QuickTime Movie MM0001, and pressed play. It held no surprises. She knew every frame, didn't understand why she kept coming back to it, putting herself through this. But she did.

Two circles in the gloom. One black, glossy, the other, grey with a pink circle of glistening skin at its centre.

They move in synch, making circular movements as if they were riding the same wave, back and forth, back and forth. Each move was accompanied by a creaking noise and the image juddered slightly.

She watched the film, forcing herself not to move her head in time with the sway of the image. Then a flash lit the scene. She knew it was coming but it still made her wince.

She watched the film to the end. She had seen it so many times before, remembered every detail, the sweat, the urgency, that smile, the lightning. The grainy images lit by the flashes of the storm outside made it look like some ancient film with Boris Karloff or Bela Lugosi.

She slammed the laptop shut.

It really was a horror film.

***

The cheeseburger perched uneasily on top of too many beers. He couldn't shift the lardy sheen in his mouth. Usually he had the digestion of a wood chipper but today was different.

Danny shifted uncomfortably on his sofa. He wasn't afraid to admit the meeting with the kids had shaken him.

Every time he saw them they reminded him of Kathy. They had her eyes and nose and little gestures that brought her back to life.

Three pints on the way home had failed to take the edge off. So had another half bottle of vodka and the last lager from the fridge.

He had loved her, he was sure of that. It had been good, then it had been bad, then it was over. There was nothing to gain from raking it up. People died, end of. Danny winced at the bedlam of gunfire and shrank lower into the sofa. The faces of the soldiers were engraved with fear. One pulled a cross on a chain from under his shirt and kissed it. Another vomited.

As a ramp splashed down the soldiers, packed in rows, were shredded by bullets. Machinegun fire lashed the water and blood bloomed around sinking bodies.

Muzzle flashes flickered across the slopes behind Dog Green Sector as Tom Hanks tried to gather his men and get off Omaha Beach before they all died.

A bullet punched through someone's helmet. A soldier, one uniformed green leg ending in bloody rags at the knee, clawed across the shingle.

Sometimes, Danny thought, he wouldn't mind meeting a woman, have a laugh, share a few takeaways and the rest.

Emma was good fun, most of the time, good company, good sex. They had first met in a pub when she was at a hen night and the second time by the fish counter at the Hove Tesco.

She had offered to take care of his mum and he paid her when he could. She was the loyal wife when Benny was at home and stayed at Danny's when he was inside. But she was wed to Benny and determined to stay that way. God knows why. Pointless trying to work out women's minds.

No, the idea of a woman, someone fit and fun, without ties, was an attractive thought when he sat in the flat alone, apart from mum wheezing in her hospital bed down the hall, watching late-night films or cop show repeats.

First date, first love-making, little things like the loo-seat-up-or-down tussle. But it could never work. The certain knowledge that it would end, sooner or later, made it not worth the effort.

He remembered the first time with Kathy, on the back seat of the clapped-out Mondeo he'd borrowed from a friend.

Her sweet smile hid an adventurous streak. They'd once had a quickie under the old West Pier in Brighton, before it burned down, on a visit to Danny's parents when dad was alive.

Danny had taught Kathy to swim but gave up on the driving and paid for her lessons, even with money tight. On their first anniversary they celebrated with a bottle of white wine which Danny turned into "Chateau Lancaster Champagne" by gassing it up in a soda siphon. Then the kids, not planned but welcome.

Active duty was as tough on family as it was on the soldiers in the field, probably tougher.

The guys were doing the job they had volunteered for, the job they loved. The wives and kids just waited at home behind brave faces. Going through the alternative domestic routine, the one where the man wasn't there. Making decisions about money and schooling, watching TV news, dreading footsteps on the front path.

All the pressure, none of the fun.

Kathy had been a rock.

Then the cancer. Kathy didn't want to make a fuss, left it late, too late. Danny got special leave, was with her to the end, tried to explain to the kids.

Good sex, friendship and having a laugh sounded great when you were alone in the dark, nursing a cold beer, watching CSI.

But it wasn't worth it because it would end. Fighting in Helmand, getting wounded, was an experience. The other was worse.

Danny took a long pull of the cold lager and stared at the screen. Cheryl was right. He had made a bollocks of it.

Hanks was trying to rally the troops to clear a path out of the killing zone.

Then there was mum. She'd hate it if she knew the state she was in. That was the one good thing about dementia, maybe, the fact that it protected the sufferer from their own decline. That said, it didn't do much for the people left behind. Mum would have hated the indignity, the embarrassment.

A woman who wouldn't use a public loo unless she was desperate reduced to being winched on and off a commode. At least she didn't know, just smiled a lot and stared at blank walls with empty, wide open eyes.

They talked about quality of life. That was a laugh. If she was a bird or a rabbit you'd wring its neck to put it out of its misery, or maybe other people's misery.

The explosion was big. As the dust and rubble came tumbling back to earth Hanks and his men were in among the defenders. Some Germans got shot because the Yank with the tommy gun didn't understand they were trying to surrender, or didn't want to. Tough shit.

Danny drained the last of the lager, crushed the can and dropped it on the carpet. As the Americans poured through the gully he rose unsteadily to his feet and walked through the darkness of the flat.

As he approached his mother's room the acid smell of urine grew stronger. When he pushed open the door it made him swallow hard.

She was lying on her back, head tilted, breath shallow and rasping. On the bedside cabinet was the cluster of pill containers, things to keep her heart pumping, stuff to keep her blood thin and her bowels moving.

At least with the liquid medication he'd just drained from a ring-pull tin in the living room you could enjoy it while you took it. He smiled in the dark.

Her skin was a waxy yellow and Danny remembered the bitter salt tang of it when he kissed her forehead. Afterwards, you couldn't seem to get the taste off your mouth. He didn't kiss her much these days.

It had been different at the start. Some days she was just like she had always been. Later, she sat up and chatted to her father and her favourite uncle. God knows how long those guys had been dead.

It was as if she was being dismantled tiny piece by tiny piece, a slow, living death until it reached the point he couldn't remember her as she had been, only as the wheezing husk in the bed.

Danny picked up a pillow. He gripped each end, stretching and flexing it between his balled fists.

Quality of life? You'd be better off being a teenager blown to bits on a beach doing something useful than rotting away like this.

\*\*\*

"Emma!" The shout was muffled by the door. It wouldn't have mattered. She was too busy staring at the unfolded piece of paper in her hand. For some reason, her eyes just refused to focus.

"Emma! You going to be long?"

She shivered. Suddenly it felt very cold. Her eyes followed the lines of small type on the half-folded page but she still couldn't decipher their meaning. Not that it really mattered, not now.

"Emma! That curry's going right through me. Hurry it up in there, love."

She remembered what Danny had said when his mum fell ill. She was getting on a bit but that evening she'd been on fine form, telling old family stories and laughing until tears ran down her face.

They reckoned she'd had her stroke in bed about midnight and that was it, her life was never going to be the same again.

Emma knew she was having her own midnight stroke moment. She felt shocked. She felt numb and, at the same time, a sense of vertigo, as if she'd fall over if she tried to stand up.

She'd tried with Benny, God knew, she tried. They were married, she was his wife, loyal. It's what she had wanted.

She was 15 when she first met him. The effect of two hours doing her hair and make-up, with the added assistance of her older sister's driving licence, meant she'd had no trouble getting into the club with Karen from school.

Benny had seemed just amazing, a good dresser, plenty of money, always talking, always joking. So much energy, so much fun.

It was much later, after they were married, that Emma was forced to admit what she had known from the start and chosen to ignore. Benny's money came from crime and Benny's inability to keep his mouth shut and his suspiciously overflowing wallet for a man with no known work was why he spent so much time inside.

Yet she knew he was a good person at heart, deep down, and with just a little luck and perseverance Emma was certain she could bring out his good points, change him into the husband and father she knew he could be.

It could be hard at times. There were days when Emma came close to admitting her dreams were just that, dreams, her efforts to grab the life she had always wanted just snatching at smoke.

Danny was something else. Emma felt a stab of shame and embarrassment. Danny was everything she told herself she did not want.

She remembered Bible classes at her parents' church about sin and the sanctity of marriage. Danny wasn't the husband and father type, he'd already proved that once himself. He was a dreamer, but on the up side he did try hard to make his dreams come true. He could be funny and affectionate, protective, even caring but, like smoke, impossible to pin down.

Now new paths were opening up ahead of her, dark unknown paths. She looked down again at the paper in her hand. This wasn't how it was supposed to be.

Emma jerked with surprise as a fist pounded on the door. "Emma! You asleep in there?"

She shivered suddenly and squeezed her eyes tight shut, feeling moisture tickling around her lashes, listening to the drip drip from the leaky old cistern behind her, the porcelain cold against her back.

It wasn't meant to be like this. Emma tore her eyes away from the chipped tiles by the door. She'd been asking Benny to fix them for ages.

Reluctantly, she looked down at the strip in her hand with its two parallel pink lines and then back at the leaflet. What were human chorionic gonadotrophins? She had never felt so alone.

"Emma!"

She stared at the parallel pink lines.

"Emma! For chrissake!"

Her body felt incredibly heavy as she pushed herself up off the toilet seat. Emma pulled up her pants and zipped her jeans before taking a last look at the little strip with its two parallel pink lines. Then she jammed it into the back pocket.

"All right, I'm coming."

***

Danny was always aware of his surroundings. Sometimes it absorbed his full concentration. At other times it ticked away in the back of his mind. But, waking or sleeping, he always had a grip on who or what was around him.

When a habit like that had saved your life more than once it wasn't something you discarded easily.

As he walked towards Brighton Station there was a girl away to his left. She wore a skirt too short for the wet and windy weather and held her head unnaturally high, trying to pretend she couldn't hear the comments from a bunch of lads having a smoke outside the pub on the corner.

Two young guys, hair gelled into spikes, left the station holding hands, eyes bright with the prospect of a night on the town. They didn't see the No7 bus until it hooted them out of its way. The two boys skipped out of its path and set off down Queens Road, laughing.

Danny saw the bus was headed for the marina and that it was named Phoebe Hessel. Many of Brighton's buses were named after people with connections to the city. Danny wondered who Phoebe had been.

M&S was doing a brisk trade with homeward-bound commuters. As he passed, an elderly woman in a heavy coat and wide-brimmed velvet hat burst through the doors and headed off down the hill, clutching a carrier bag with the neck of a wine bottle poking from the top, her walking stick tapping out a determined pace.

At the other end of the station two cab drivers were shouting at each other in a futile effort to free up the cab rank logjam that spilled out into the road. Danny smelled rotten eggs as a catalytic converter warmed up.

A girl with pink hair shaved up one side crossed in front of Danny, arcing away from a tall man with wild white hair and a long coat. The man was jabbering, animated and urgent. With his hair flying, Danny couldn't see if he was wearing a Bluetooth earpiece or talking to the wind.

Brighton was a place of highs and lows, full of luvvies, media types and more than its share of pond life, a centre for theatre, music and all the other arts and the country's injecting drug death capital. Brighton wasn't a city, it was a lifestyle choice.

The guy with the white hair could be a composer, a poet or a lunatic. Danny thought there probably wasn't much to choose between them.

People moved around him at different speeds and angles, posing different levels of threat. Danny's head turned at regular intervals, using his peripheral vision to watch the space behind him through reflections in shopfront glass.

A hunched shape detached itself from the station railings and swayed into Danny's path. The guy's parka was threadbare and filthy. His hair stuck to his head in greasy tongues.

The man looked Danny up and down slowly with wide brown eyes and his cracked lips broke into a private smile. The station lights glittered on a metal spike where a dental cap had once been.

Danny took a pack from his pocket and put two cigarettes in the man's dirty hand. He man looked down at them, then up at Danny but nothing registered in the empty eyes. Danny shrugged and moved on.

"Danny!" He heard his name called above the growl of traffic and looked around.

A woman with neat, short hair zigzagged her way through the crowd towards him. Danny's eyes narrowed when he recognised her. "Detective Pauline."

"It's Detective Sergeant Myers to you, Danny. What are you up to?"

"You know me." He placed his hand over his heart. "Nothing criminal."

Myers tried to fight a smile. "Never give up trying, do you, Danny?

A small woman with short blonde hair eased her way through the press and stood beside Myers who glanced quickly sideways, then back at Danny.

"This is my friend Liza."

"That's Liza with a zed," said the blonde.

"Nice to meet you," said Danny.

"Well," said Myers. "We've got to rush. We're meeting some friends. You and I should have a drink together sometime."

"Maybe," he said.

"Don't be like that, Danny. With your contacts you could be a real asset to an ambitious copper."

"I'm a bit busy," he said.

"It wasn't a suggestion, Danny."

He shrugged. "Well, as I'm in the detecting game now I suppose it wouldn't hurt to help a colleague."

Liza-with-a-zed tugged at Pauline's sleeve. "Don't push it, Danny," said Myers. "I'll be in touch."

Danny watched them disappear into the crowd, then headed for the crossing. The lights turned green and as he started to cross his mood brightened when he saw the warm glow from the windows of the Bellerophon.

\*\*\*

The food was good, it always was. He had made a point of cultivating the head waiter and the chef, sizeable tips, carefully crafted compliments, massaging egos. It always worked.

The pigeon was faultess, the potatoes done to perfection and the chef, Carlo, had excelled himself with the sauce. Light with a subtle yet distinctive taste that complemented the meat without masking its flavour. All things considered, an excellent meal, but the proportions were wrong.

It did not matter how good the food was if it could not be eaten in the proper way, a slice of meat, a section of potato, a certain number of peas and one, possibly two, leaves of mange tout.

Get the proportions wrong and the careful balance he demanded of flavours and textures was impossible. The meal was ruined.

The thought appalled him, aggravating his allergy to failure. Anything short of perfect planning and execution was like a spreading stain. He shivered at the thought, then looked at his plate with weary disgust. There was one pigeon breast remaining but only half a potato and a wholly inadequate scattering of peas.

His hand shot into the air and he snapped his fingers, "Massimo!"

When he looked up the head waiter acknowledge his summons and began moving swiftly towards one of his best clients, swivelling his hips to edge between the packed tables.

He was half way to the table when the special mobile rang. The angry diner scooped the phone from his pocket and waved the waiter away as he answered.

"Digby?"

"Yes," said the diner.

"It's Rookwood."

"Well who else would it be on this phone?"

"I forgot."

"You forgot? "

"Yes, okay, don't make a big deal of it."

"Let's keep this short. Any progress?"

"A stroke of luck. A little bird tells me someone was hawking our property around in a pub in Shoreham, looking for a buyer."

"In a pub! Why didn't the fool just stick them on eBay? Does he realise what he has?"

"Doesn't look like it."

"This could blow right up in our faces. Do you know who the seller is?"

"No, but I know someone who does."

"Well get it sorted out quickly and quietly, no mess, no questions."

"Relax, I know what I'm doing."

"If you say so, and Rookwood?"

"Yes?"

"Don't forget to dispose of your SIM card and use a fresh one next time."

"I'm not an idiot."

The line went dead.

\*\*\*

Emily looked up from her book and scanned the bar of the Bellerophon to check the punters were happy. Marina, the new Romanian barmaid, would be in soon for her evening shift.

She was bright and keen and the customers seemed to like her but Emily thought of the Bellerophon's regulars as hers. She knew the names of most but recognised them by what they drank.

Leaning on the bar looking tired and thoughtful was a young man with spiked gelled hair and flesh tunnels through his ear lobes, toying with the handle of his small wheeled suitcase and staring down into his red wine.

Emily recognised him as an occasional punter but only knew his name was Gavin from the tag on his easyJet cabin crew uniform.

At the table just inside the door was "Mr Stella" and his mate "lager top". Beside the fireplace old Wally was making his Guinness last as he frowned down at his Sudoku puzzle.

Around the other side of the bar, wearing a smart overcoat and with his red leather briefcase against his ankle, was "Mr double Courvoisier with ice." If he was meeting his usual brunette, she would be a medium white wine with a splash of soda. If it was the tarty little blonde, she'd be vodka Red Bull.

At the back of the bar, near the garden entrance, face buried in the Argus, was "Mr Pint of Harvey's In A Jug – could you top that up a bit, please." His drinking pal wasn't in tonight. He'd been Sussex In A Jug as well until the operation, now it was strictly red wine. Emma had spotted the zipper scar when he had the top buttons of his shirt undone last the summer.

Just beyond were Danny's two mates, Sussex for the tubby one, Zywiec for the skinny foreign guy.

Slate, the guv'nor's rangy, silver-grey mongrel, stretched his long legs in the wicker basket by the fire and looked with big brown eyes down his long muzzle at the temporary residents of his empire. Satisfied all was as it should be, Slate looked up at Emily, scratched his blanket into the shape he wanted and settled down again.

Emily shuffled on the bar stool and returned to her paperback. The detective had just received the forensics back on the knife used in both murders and he was in for a surprise.

The street door opened and a gust of damp wind ruffled the gig posters that papered the walls. Emily looked up.

"Danny!"

"Hi, Em, how's life?"

"Quiet, your usual? Pint of Wife Beater?"

Danny nodded. "Very funny, Em. And for the others."

"Sussex and Zywiec."

"Yup."

Danny paid for the drinks and walked them carefully to the back of the bar room. Bob and Karol looked up and smiled when they saw him bearing gifts.

He sat down and took a long pull on his pint. A shadow slid silently up beside him. Danny looked up at a short man in a green anorak clutching a Tesco carrier bag. "You want DVD?"

Danny shook his head and looked back at his friends. "So, how's it going?"

Karol jerked his head towards Bob. "He is depressed."

"Oh," said Danny. "Why's that?"

Bob shook his head dismissively. His chin quivered. "Nothing really."

"Well you don't look full of the joys," said Danny.

"We had a good laugh out on that beach but that was one day. Since the building work dried up it's been, I dunno, weird. Apart from that conservatory job there's no reason to get up in the morning, nothing to do when I do."

Karol rolled his eyes.

"Wanda okay?" asked Danny.

Bob's head came up suddenly. "Why do you ask?"

Danny shook his head. "Just making conversation."

"Wanda's fine," said Bob. "Just fine. At least I think so."

"So what's bothering you, Bob?"

"Drop it, Danny."

"If you say so."

"Just drop it, eh?"

Bob was right. The excitement of their day on the beach hadn't lasted long. Danny put up his hands. "Okay, okay, if I'd known it was going to be like this I'd have stayed in. If I wanted to be miserable I could do it at home and save some cash."

Karol looked keenly at Danny. "You, too, look like a gloomy man. You have problems also?"

Danny watched a thin stream of tiny bubbles jostling their way to the top of his pint, leaving a shallow crater where they erupted onto the white surface. He picked up the glass and took a long pull. "I'm fine, just fine."

Karol persisted. "I don't think so. What happened to 'something turns up' that you always say?"

"I said I'm fine."

Karol swigged from his bottle of Zywiec and wiped the back of his hand across his lips. "You mouth says fine but your eyes are not agreeing."

The sharp crack cut all of the pub's small conversations dead. Bob jumped in his seat, eyes wide and beer foam slopping over the hand that held his glass.

Karol looked over Danny's shoulder and saw every face in the bar turned towards them, pale and startled. Furthest away, Emily had put down her book and was standing on tiptoe, craning to spot the source of the trouble.

Danny slowly opened his hand and the last shards of his broken beer glass tinkled onto the table top. Spilled lager fizzed white on the dark varnish of the table, turning to a frothing pink where the blood dripped.

The light made something sparkle. Danny pulled a splinter of glass from the base of his thumb and dropped it on the table. The silence in the Bellerophon's bar stretched on as Danny looked down at the little mouths that had opened up in the flesh of his palm. They looked as if they were calling. He didn't react when an arm came round his left side and a bar towel began marshalling the broken glass and spillage to the open side of the table, away from the three men, and over the edge into a tin bin.

"Don't worry, Danny. I'll clear it up," said Emily quietly.

"Sorry, Em," said Danny. "I don't know my own strength."

They sat unmoving as she swept the debris into the bin. When she was finished Danny stood up without looking at anyone. "I'm going for a fag."

Even the sheltering walls of the garden failed to hold off the icy wind that spurted in gusts across the bare flower beds and damp wooden benches.

Danny inhaled deeply, tilted his head back and blew a long plume of smoke towards the threatening clouds. Seagulls screeched and wheeled, their white wings washed an eerie orange by the street lights.

Behind him he heard a long sigh of satisfaction through the toilet fanlight as a drinker squared up to the urinal to break the seal after a long evening.

Then the bar door creaked open. Footsteps padded on the mossy paving slabs, a full pint appeared beside him.

"I got you new. Don't break it."

Danny took the glass from Karol. "Thanks. And thanks for the website too. It looks good."

"It is my pleasure. I hope it brings you much investigating business," said Karol. "So, everything is okay then, yes?"

"I don't feel much like chatting tonight."

"Chatting," said Karol, running the word slowly across his tongue. "Interesting word, it comes from First World War, from killing lice in your clothes in trenches. Your soldiers gather together for a chat and they talk as they clean."

"You are a goldmine of useless information."

"Don't be so harsh. I just came for chat."

Danny punched the button on the outdoor heater. The element above them blossomed red and a welcome warmth washed over them. "You're a persistent bastard, aren't you?"

"Polish people are very tenacious. We charge tanks with cavalry. You should find time to read Polish history. You would learn much."

"Karol?"

"Yes?"

"Why do you keep doing that bloody silly accent? You speak English better than I do."

"I tell you before, is for to wind up Bob. He thinks all foreigners speak this way. Sometimes I forget when he's not around. Is good fun."

"You're mad."

"And you are miserable person so what is problem?"

Danny shrugged and pulled down a third of his pint without breathing. "Ah, it's nothing, just little things, Emma's having some sort of moody. The detective thing isn't working, my sister reckons I should be doing more for the kids, get a job."

Karol nodded. "You must ignore people who diminish your ambitions. They are small people. Mark Twain says this."

"Mark who?"

Karol nodded thoughtfully for a moment before he spoke. "You are my friend but sometime you can be a stupid person."

"Go on, cheer me up."

"You are right, my friend, you have much to think about. You go to war, you lose leg, you lose wife, soon you lose mother. These are all bad things."

Karol dragged his fingers through greasy, lank hair. It made no difference. "You have all these things on the inside and you choose not to wear them on the outside. But you are not sick. No tanks crush your harvest and your home. You have roof and money for a little beer and tobacco."

Karol's red rimmed eyes were blazing now. "Life really is lottery. Five fruit and vegetables each day guarantee you nothing. You can eat like pig, drink like fish, smoke like factory and be 90. Problem is you sit too much, think too much, see too much daytime television. So things you want don't happen? Is not disaster, is not fatal disease, is life. You must keep trying because there is no other way."

"You're quite the philosopher."

Karol shook his head. "Me? No."

"Maybe you should be on TV."

"I tell you already. Daytime TV is bad for you."

They fell into a thoughtful silence. Karol spoke first. "How is your hand?"

Danny held it up to catch the light from the toilet window and studied it in the dull glow. "Fine." He drained his pint and looked over at the bar door. "We'd better go back in."

"Why?" asked Karol.

"It's Bob's round."

Danny went first and held the door for Karol. As they passed, Danny said. "Cavalry charging tanks?"

Karol nodded. "I lend you book."

## CHAPTER 6

Scooping the lottery, maybe. Winning the World Cup, certainly. There were lots of things you could wish for to change your life but a good lie-in was a simple pleasure that Danny thought was underrated.

In the army you were always rushing somewhere, even if it was nowhere. But the sheer joy of curling up under your own duvet knowing no alarm clock was ticking away, no one was going to kick your bed and bellow in your ear, that was a real joy.

And sunshine, that was underrated as well. Soft autumn light was pouring in through a gap between storms, throwing extended shadows of the window frame as it tried to explore the room. It you stayed still long enough you could see it move, creeping across the walls, marking the passing of time while you stayed still and snug.

Danny stretched, pushing out his legs, clenched his thigh muscles, his fingers locked together, pressing upward and outward. He could feel the blood and joints moving. Parts of him ached and the feeling was wonderful.

And someone was singing.

As he peeled his ear from the pillow he could hear it, a ballad, something poppy but foot-tapping, muffled by the wall between the kitchen and the bedroom. It stopped when a note went astray. Then there was a little cough and it started again.

Danny watched the sunlight and listened to the singing. His hand wandered under the duvet to his crotch, warm and slightly sweaty. His mind felt fuzzy. He wasn't quite sure where he was or why but it didn't matter. It really didn't. Life didn't get much better than this.

He was squinting through the brightness of the window when a shadow filled the doorway in the corner of his vision.

The girl was short and without make-up. A cascade of glistening chocolate brown hair framed a cute face and large eyes liked oiled black olives shining with possibilities. A dimpled schoolgirl grin showed perfect white teeth.

All that covered her slim figure was one of Danny's t-shirts. It hung long and loose on her petite frame and she filled it in more interesting ways.

Just visible below the hem of the t-shirt, a tattoo encircled her upper thigh, an entwined thorny stem crowned with a red rose. She moved into the room and reached forward, offering a chipped mug topped with wisps of steam.

As Danny pulled himself up on his elbows she smiled again and held out the mug. "Cuppa tea, pet?"

"Cheers."

The girl smiled, cheeks dimpling again. "You're worth it."

Then the bubble burst and Danny woke up. Rain was drumming on the window, making the world outside ripple as it pulsed down the glass.

He rolled over and winced. The palm of his hand stung where the beer glass had shattered.

He moved to push away the duvet then changed his mind and fell back onto the bed. Why get up? He had nothing to do and wandering the flat would just be a waste of electricity and tea bags. Danny looked at his wristwatch.

The flat was silent, the gloomy atmosphere only broken by the rain on the window. Emma would have come and gone quietly, tending to mum without waking him. He couldn't recall the last time she had slipped in beside him and woken him slowly in interesting ways. Whatever it was that was causing this moody he wished she'd get it sorted.

If she wouldn't talk there was nothing he could do to help. But there were other problems he would have to deal with.

Mum's last wish before she lost her marbles was to see out her time in her own home. Danny would honour that but it took money.

And there were the kids, as Cheryl kept reminding him. He didn't need the lectures but she couldn't seem to see how every time he saw Hayley and Wayne he saw Kathy and everything that he kept tightly battened down came bubbling up again.

A little liquid medication now and again helped to keep the lid on but it didn't solve anything. He'd known too many good guys hollowed out by booze.

His problems, his responsibility.

Danny slid out of bed, put on his boxers and went into the bathroom. The cuts to his hand from the broken glass stung and he ran it under the tap to make sure the wounds were clean.

As the water poured, he studied himself in the bathroom mirror. Not a bad looking face, all things considered. The body was looking okay but it needed work. Danny wasn't particularly vain but the damage the months of doom and vodka had caused had unsettled him. Maybe now it could provide the boost he needed to get back on track.

If he was going to make a success of detecting, or anything else, the only tools he had were his body and his mind. He began to brush his teeth as he planned how to get back into shape. The leg still gave him grief but he had mastered the techniques, mastered the pain. No one passing him in the street could tell.

The mind, too, needed exercise and discipline, new things to explore. He needed to spend more time in Jubilee Library.

Computers, that was another thing. He didn't know enough about them but Karol was a genius when it came to that sort of stuff. He'd tap him for a few pointers next time they met. You couldn't know too much stuff, couldn't judge what might come in useful one day.

The mind needed discipline to keep it sharp, keep the dark recesses caged. The darkness could break out at any time, without warning, memories, images, sounds, smells. And they would carry you back, helpless.

Getting emotional didn't get you anywhere. Best to keep the lid screwed tight down and tackle things logically.

The last time, couldn't remember exactly when, he had been walking near the station and came to a dead halt outside a kebab shop. The man behind had ploughed into him and cursed Danny but his attention was elsewhere.

His eyes were locked on three chickens skewered on a metal pole, turning in a rotisserie. The plump, plucked birds were in perfect alignment, like some obscene chorus line. They glistened and sizzled as they turned. Someone inside, a customer at the counter, was admiring them. The fat man in the greasy apron smiled and nodded.

As the crispy bodies turned, all Danny could see were charred babies.

He worked the toothbrush around the ends of his teeth, into the corners, cleaning right up to the gums with a firm up-down motion. When he was satisfied he spat into the wash basin and rinsed his mouth.

His problems, his responsibility.

He turned off the tap, dried his face and hands and went back into the bedroom. His phone was on the bedside table with all the other bits he had pulled from his pocket the night before.

He found the dog-eared business card, squinted at the phone number, then tapped it into his mobile.

"Skidmarks? It's Danny, that job still going?"

***

He was through the pain now, the lack of co-ordination, and pounding along steadily, good rhythm, good breathing, gradually fine-tuning himself back to peak performance.

It felt good, really good. Smooth power and timing eating up the ground under his trainers. A warm breeze rippled his t-shirt and track suit bottoms as he ran.

A line of trees away to his left across the high ground marked the course of the River Ouse. Black Cap and Ashcombe Bottom were way behind him now and he was moving with the lean economic action of a high-performance machine, burning up the yards.

Danny was closing fast on another runner, tall, slim, fiftyish, grey hair, orange headband, head tilted up as he listened to his iPod.

Danny enjoyed music as much as anyone else but he'd never understood the need to run with it, as if you needed help to pass the time, fill the silence. You missed so much, sky, wildlife, scenery. It closed the world in around you when you should be giving yourself all the space you could handle.

Another thing Danny couldn't understand with civvies was that they never looked up, plodding along when they could spot spectacular clouds, fancy buildings and, surprisingly often, someone looking down at you from a high window.

Once he'd been looking up for snipers. Now he just enjoyed horizons.

It had been a while but Danny liked to study the countryside as he ran. Sometimes he saw hills, valleys, footpaths trodden by generations of feet and ancient clusters of rugged trees that had stood as centuries of history passed beneath the wide reach of their gnarled branches. Sometimes a rabbit would streak across a frosted winter field or rustle through new spring undergrowth.

And there were other days when he saw fields of fire, kill zones and dead ground as his eyes read the texture of the terrain and his mind plotted the best way to fire and manoeuvre across its curves and folds, to close with the enemy and kill them.

Sometimes when it was windy he thought he heard the sounds of boots all around him, thundering along in unison.

Danny pounded past the iPod runner but the man didn't seem to notice. The sun was warm after the frenzy of the storm and a gentle breeze kept Danny cool. It was a fantastic day

The path breasted the hill beside the old race course and started down. Below him Danny could see the pretty town of Lewes spread out before him, nestling in a gap in the South Downs where the River Ouse dropped through the chalk cliffs to the sea at Newhaven.

He had always liked the place, even if it was packed with city types and media luvvies in houses with price tags like telephone numbers.

The place made a change from the madness of Brighton. It was the quaint sort of town set in the classic rolling countryside that soldiers were supposed to think of when they fought for king and country.

As he descended the track Danny couldn't help glancing at the dark walls of Lewes Prison up ahead on the right. He was never sure why he came this way so often. The familiar grey bulk sent a cold shiver through him. Perhaps that was why.

He blocked the memory and powered on down the incline. Danny's leg hurt but that was to be expected. A little pain never did any harm.

Despite the recent rain the ground was hard. As he accelerated he misjudged a pile of large pebbles. His left foot landed on them and started to skid. Danny's balance went and he toppled, tucking his arms around his head to roll across his shoulders as he hit the ground.

The breeze block in his backpack punched the breath out of him as he hit the hard grassy ground. He had padded it with a towel and cinched the backpack tight but hadn't planned on landing on it.

He lay for a while, looking up at the cloudless blue sky while he regulated his breathing, feeling beads of sweat tickle their way across his forehead.

"Are you all right?" Danny pulled himself up onto his elbows at the sound of the plumby voice, twisting slightly to avoid a corner of the breeze block digging into his back. A fortysomething yummy mummy with clusters of red hair curling from under her riding hat swung from the saddle of her horse and peered down at him.

Her riding companion, another mum from the school run by the look of her, held her reins as the woman crouched beside Danny, studying his legs.

"I'm fine," said Danny. The woman's eyes ran down his prone body and back to his face. "I've got a first aid certificate. Is there anything I can do? Where does it hurt?"

She spotted the patch of dirt on the material covering his left knee and began to roll up his trouser leg but her hands flew to her face in shock. "Oh my God."

The silver alloy shaft of Danny's lower left leg, rising out of his scuffed trainer, sparkled in the sunlight.

"Just a scratch," he said with a grin. "I probably need a mechanic more than a first-aider."

The woman, still wide-eyed with surprise, looked up at her companion, then back to Danny. "I'm so sorry. I had no idea."

"No reason you should," said Danny, starting to move.

"Let me help you up." The woman took a firm grip on his shoulder and elbow, guiding him to his feet. Danny didn't need the assistance but didn't say no. Rolling down his trouser leg and brushing off patches of chalk dust, Danny smiled at the woman. "Thanks for your help."

She returned his smile, a certain light in her eyes. "A pleasure. Do take care."

The woman remounted her horse and watched as Danny accelerated down the track. Then she turned to her friend and began to speculate.

Danny pounded on, feeling the energy of exercise driving itself into every corner of his body, cleansing tubes, rinsing cobwebs, upgrading electrical connections. It felt good, like coming home.

Time to take himself in hand. Time to stop feeling sorry for himself, sort himself out. He needed to cut back on the booze and start eating properly, pare away the flab creeping across the six-pack.

On the way home he'd pick up some tinned tuna and boil-in-the-bag rice. Knock that up with some kidney beans and a bit of olive oil and yogurt. That should cover a few of the food groups, give him some energy. And he'd lay off the takeaways for a while.

The last stretch downhill into the town was easy. As he lengthened his stride he thought of the soft press of the redhead's breast against his side as she had helped him up.

It was good of her to stop. Not many would. He tried to keep his mind on the warmth of her breast but it kept snapping back to the look on her face when she had rolled up his trouser leg.

***

Her fingers were flying across the keys of the laptop. The rapid clicking was the only sounds in the large lounge, the soft glow of its screen the only light.

"I was thrilled with the pictures. He's shooting up so fast and looks so strong and healthy. And what a lovely smile!!! Do you think he's taking after you or Dan? It's hard to tell at that age."

She was only half aware of a key turning in the lock of the apartment's front door.

"I don't want to be the pushy grandmother but I do so wish I could be part of it all. It's such a special time when they are that young and I do so regret missing it, and missing you too."

Now she could hear the sprung floorboards of the long hallway creaking under heavy footsteps.

"I still hope we might be able to visit sometime soon, I've been looking at flights and brochures, but you know how difficult things are."

The lounge door creaked faintly as it opened.

"Good lord, Margaret, are we having a blackout?"

The light flashed on and Sir Charles Wolfram stood in the doorway, blinking.

"I prefer the dark," she said. "It's restful."

He crossed the room, stood behind her and bent to kiss the top of her head. The smells of whisky and cigars wafted across her face.

"So what have you been up to, dear?"

She closed the laptop lid and switched on a table lamp before she replied. "Just catching up on my email, Charles. Did you want something to eat?"

"No, no, I'm fine. Dined while I was out. I'll just settle for a nightcap, I think."

He eased himself into his armchair and Lady Margaret went to a side table and poured a large whisky.

As she handed him the crystal glass she asked, "Did you have a pleasant evening?"

"Yes, very good, very good. Met some interesting people."

She sat down on the sofa at right angles to his armchair, curling her legs under her. "That's nice, dear. You've been quite busy lately."

She watched his Adam's apple bob as he drank his whisky. When he put it down his lips glistened in the light from the table lamp.

"Yes, I have," he said. "An interesting project's come up. Could keep me occupied for quite a while. Might involve some travelling."

"But what about Perth?"

He twirled his glass, watching the light catch the facets of the crystal as it turned.

"Might need to put that on hold for a bit longer, just until I can get this project of mine off the ground."

"You promised."

"I know, darling, I know. But this could be important. It's not just for my sake, you understand. There are people who think I can make a contribution. How could I say no?"

"But you promised. What about the children? I've be planning for months."

"I know, but we can't all do what we want when we want, can we, darling? Life's not like that, I'm afraid."

He was about to sip from the glass when he realised she had stood up.

"I'm off to bed," she said.

"Already? I've hardly seen you. Oh well, an hour before midnight's worth two after, as they say. Will you be reading?"

"Yes."

"Then I'll use the spare room tonight."

"Yes, dear, you do that."

He winced when the lounge door slammed.

\*\*\*

Danny sipped his pint quietly in a corner. Okay, he was in training but he deserved a treat after today.

The Bellerophon was unusually quiet. Bob, grumpier than usual, had sloped off home to watch something on TV. Karol had stopped for a quick drink and dashed away for some pre-arranged internet gaming session that meant nothing to Danny.

Slate strolled by and looked up. Danny patted his silver-grey flanks and rubbed his ear and the dog walked on.

A gust of cold air chilled the room as the pub door opened. Danny looked across to see Skidmarks come in, a heavy bag-for-life bulging with shopping in each meaty hand. He waved a greeting.

"What will you have?"

Skidmarks put the bags down by the table and looked at his watch. "I can't stay long."

"Just a quickie then?"

"Okay, scotch with a shot of water."

Danny fetched the drinks and studied the new arrival as he approached the table. Skidmarks was a squat, serious looking guy in his forties with a shaven head and wearing a long leather jacket. He looked as if he could handle himself.

"So," said Danny. "You known Bob long?"

"A few years, done each other a few favours."

"Unusual nickname."

"Yes," said Skidmarks without enthusiasm.

They sat in silence for a few moments, then Skidmarks let out a small sigh. "I used to do a bit of driving."

"Professional?"

"In a manner of speaking. No call for it now. It's all computer crime."

Danny nodded slowly. As he moved his foot it tapped one of the bags under the table and they heard the clink of bottles.

"Having a party?"

Skidmarks moved the bags further under his chair. "Been doing a bit of shopping. Anniversary dinner tonight."

Danny nodded. "Been married long?"

"Six months today."

"First flush, eh? I remember that."

"So how long have you been married, Danny?" asked Skidmarks.

"I'm not any more. Make the most of it, mate, nothing lasts for ever. So, about this job you mentioned?"

"It's still there if you want it but I can't guarantee too much. Things are a bit iffy at the moment," said Skidmarks, licking a glaze of whisky from his lips.

Danny shrugged his agreement. "I'm a bit short of cash at the moment so anything would be a help."

"Okay," said Skidmarks. "Just give me a bell and I'll fix you up with a suitable vehicle and a radio."

"What about the documents?"

"Ah," said Skidmarks, "the paperwork might be a bit of a problem but we'll get round it for the time being."

"And if the police stop me?"

"It's simple. Just don't get stopped."

Danny was about to make another point when Skidmarks's mobile rang. He snapped it open.

"Yes, yes, still here. Just having a quick one on the way back, bit of business … No, don't worry, I haven't forgotten. I won't be late. I promise I won't … Yes, I've got the vino and the other stuff. And I've got you something special as well. No, you'll have to wait … Stop worrying … no, I'm not going to turn up late and let it spoil … yes, I'm looking forward to it as well, sounds delicious … No, you go ahead and light the candles. I'm walking out the door now … yes, I promise … yes, I love you too … see you in 20 minutes."

Skidmarks snapped his phone shut. "Look, I'd better be off. Give me a call tomorrow and we'll fix things up."

Danny watched Skidmarks pick up his shopping and walk out of the pub.

***

Bob Lovejoy took his nose trimmer from the bathroom cabinet and looked hard into the shaving mirror. The skin around his eyes was puffy. He pulled at the rumpled bags of flesh with a fingertip and watched them creep slowly back into their original shape.

He stretched his mouth into a humourless grin. The movement sent tiny ripples through his chin. Several of his teeth were crooked. They were a bugger to clean, even with that fiddly string stuff Wanda had bought him. Bob let out a long sigh and stepped back from the mirror. He placed two fingers on each nipple and stirred, watching with a feeling of sinking despair as his moobs jiggled like jelly.

Building work was still thin on the ground and he was spending too much time sitting in front of the television.

It was all rubbish but, with nothing much to do all day, it became strangely seductive. You started to remember the schedules, knew what was coming, and could always fill the boring bits with a sandwich or something from the fridge.

Bob reached down to scratch at the raised vein in the back of his left leg and let out another sigh. Where did all the years go? Why couldn't he stop himself losing his rag over stupid things like late buses and roadworks? He was turning into a grumpy old git.

And Wanda worried him. He was proud and lucky to have her but he was concerned. He didn't know what she saw in him but whatever it was it was heading downwards.

He had read about women's sex drive in a magazine at the dentist's. They got hornier as they got older while guys started downhill before they really knew what to do with it.

Wanda was always a bundle of energy. It was as if the air fizzed around her. She had her line dancing, she was never off that wii fit exercise program and had even thrashed him on the archery game. She was fanatical about her pelvic floor exercises and proud she had no leaking pee troubles like many women of her age.

Bob didn't think they had a problem but you could never be too sure. Maybe there was something she wasn't telling him. The trouble with mooching around at home all day was it gave you too much time to think.

He had thought about getting some of those pills over the internet but drugs from an anonymous source worried him. He felt sure he could get something from his GP if it came to it. Then all he'd need to do was drive to a chemist far enough away.

Bob let out his third sigh, longer than the first two, and jabbed at a cluster of whiskers with his nose hair trimmer.

The vibration made his eyes water and he let out a little hiss when a blade nicked his nostril. Glum and hunched, Bob shrugged himself into his shirt, tucked it into his trousers and tightened his belt, trying not to notice the band of fat that squeezed outward over the straining leather.

Defeated, he plodded downstairs. When he pushed open the living room door he was surprised to see Danny sitting on the carpet surrounded by books. They were arranged in uneven piles with torn strips of paper marking important pages.

"What's all this then?" asked Bob. "I didn't think you were much of a reader."

Danny stretched and felt stiffness and small pains ripple through him from his run. "Bit of research," said Danny. "Trying to learn the job."

"You look a bloody sight more cheerful suddenly," said Bob.

Danny looked up and grinned. "New day, new Danny. I've got a bit of work, just temporary, with Skids, just while I swot up on this detecting business."

Bob picked up a book and snuffled with surprise. "Sherlock Holmes? Are you kidding?"

Danny shrugged, "It might look a bit odd but there's some good stuff in there. In one of them this race horse gets nicked but the guard dog doesn't make a noise."

Bob shrugged, "Maybe it was asleep."

Danny shook his head, "No, that's the clever bit. The dog didn't bark because the thief wasn't a stranger." Danny tugged the book from Bob's hand and flicked through the pages to his marker. "It's what Sherlock calls, 'the curious incident of the dog in the night time'."

"So what about the rest of this stuff then?" Bob waved his arms across the half circle of piled books that surrounded Danny.

"Wanda's a big fan of crime novels. She let me have a look through them and got some more from the charity shop."

"And you really think this is going to do you any good?"

"Well," said Danny. "I've got more time on my hands than I know what to do with at the moment. And anyway, they've all got some useful tips. You'd think it was easy knocking out this stuff but when you really look there's a lot of info in here, clues, little details. You can see some bits coming but others are a real surprise. It's all about being logical and thorough. Like peeling an onion. There's even stuff about working out someone's character."

Danny toppled a pile of books as he plucked one from the bottom, flicking through the pages until he found the paper taper marking the page he wanted.

"Here, it's about smiling. There are two kinds, according to this French guy. Anyone can move their mouth muscles to make a smile but you can't control the muscles under your eyes. The real thing is called a Duchenne smile, when you use both sets.

"If you just turn the corners of your mouth up it's called a Pan-Am smile, named after the stewardesses on an American airline."

Danny waved an arm over the piles of Wanda's crime novels.

"I know it's fiction but the people who write these things really do their research. I mean, it's amazing, there's a copper fighting crime in every town in the country and they're all divorced with drink problems and like music. But there's a lot of complicated stuff as well, real gen about crime scene investigation, forensics, DNA, fingerprints, a lot about stomach contents."

"Bit desperate this, isn't it?" said Bob quietly.

Danny dropped the book and looked up. "Well, I thought about applying to Sussex CID for work experience but I don't think they'd be too keen."

"Okay, mate, okay, I was just saying."

They looked round as Wanda walked in, chin resting on a pile of books held tight in her arms.

Danny looked up at her. "Here comes a Duchenne smile now."

She was not the sort of woman you forgot. Around the fifty mark, the fire in her eyes and the upturn of her wide mouth gave her a sort of permanent post-coital glow that lit up any room she entered.

As he watched her, Danny recalled Bob saying she had done some modelling and bit-part acting in her younger days.

"There you are, Danny. I found a few more in my eBay box."

Wanda bent forward and Danny took the books and piled them on the carpet. She surveyed them with a satisfied smile that crinkled into lines around her eyes.

"That should keep you busy for a while. I hope it does some good."

"Me too," said Danny, glancing up from the blurb on the back of a Rebus paperback. "I need some work. I need some money."

"You could get a proper job," said Bob.

Wanda looked at him. "You are a cheerful sod this morning."

She looked back at Danny. "I was just going to fix Bob a healthy lunch, pasta, smoked mackerel and flageolet beans. Got to keep an eye on his blood pressure. You want some?"

Danny looked up from the book and smiled. "You know me, Wanda, anything with a pulse."

Wanda laughed as she bent forward and ruffled Danny's hair.

Bob was glowering at her back as she headed for the kitchen.

\*\*\*

The arm swept across the vast arc of countryside in front of them. A low pelt of thick dark cloud stretched from horizon to horizon.

Beneath it, the land was dark. Shafts of sunlight punching though the overcast picked out features of the landscape below, a cricket pitch, a pub with wooden benches dotted across its garden, old cottages with roofs of Horsham stone.

"Look at it, Rookwood," said Digby. "Just look at it. You can keep your savannahs, your white sand beaches, your Alps, there is not a sight in the world to beat that, rolling green British countryside."

Rookwood nodded.

"Over there," said Digby, pointing, "is Chanctonbury ring. It's the site of an Iron Age hill fort and a Roman temple. Some say the devil built it, that it was used by witches, that women can increase their fertility by sleeping underneath its trees. Those pale lines you see running up the hillsides are bostals, ancient sheep tracks."

Digby waved his hand over his shoulder.

"Behind us is Devil's Dyke. Legend says it was carved out by the Dark One to let the sea flood the churches of the Weald." He waved his arms again. "This whole area is dripping with history and legend. And that, Rookwood, is what we are going to become, legends, very very rich legends. You know what Chairman Mao said?"

Rookwood shook his head slowly.

"Politics, Rookwood, grows from the barrel of a gun. And we shall have both, the guns and the politics, once you have ironed out our current little difficulty. How is that progressing?"

"There's a man who says he knows the guy who was trying to flog the kit in the pub in Shoreham. I'm checking it out."

"Get it sorted out. Do it quickly. But do be discreet. If we can recover our consignment without attracting attention no one will ever know it was missing. We can proceed as planned."

"I'm not stupid. I know what I'm doing."

They crossed the road to the car park and climbed into the Range Rover. Rookwood, buckling up, turned to Digby. "Do we have to keep it up with these stupid codenames?"

Digby jabbed the tongue of his seat belt into the slot with a loud snap. "I will pretend you didn't say that. I cannot stress enough how important our security is. What we are trying to do is both politically ambitious and highly illegal. We are conspirators. We can take no chances."

Rookwood shrugged, "If you say so."

"I do say so. Just do your job and leave the planning to me."

"You act like I'm some sort of idiot."

"Did I say that?"

"Well, no, but we're supposed to be partners."

Digby ignored the remark, started the engine, revved hard, then slipped the selector into drive.

The Range Rover jumped forward and swung out of the car park and down Dyke Road, Brighton and Hove a distant smudged stain where the sea met the land.

Rookwood glowered through the spattered windscreen, clenching and unclenching his fists, wondering how many people you had to kill to get respect.

"I'll drop you at the bottom of the hill," said Digby. "You can call a cab. We can't be seen together in the city."

He hit the horn and swerved around a figure stumbling across the road. The speeding Range Rover missed the man by inches and swept away.

Digby snorted. "Did you see that grinning yokel, just blundering across the road, didn't even look. Those sorts of people need dealing with."

\*\*\*

The stump was raw, he could feel it with every step, and his lungs felt like they had been pepper sprayed.

Not far now, last few yards. Focus, concentrate, nearly there. Danny crossed the road, never even saw the Range Rover that honked. Each time he ran he pushed himself a little further, extending the distance, increasing his speed, taking more hills.

This morning wasn't anything special but it had felt good and he had just kept going. And here he was.

As he stepped off the road Danny tripped on the low embankment and fell full length, mouth suddenly filled with wet, chalky grass. He'd done it, run up Devil's Dyke, a climb of 750 feet, a run of six miles from the city to the spot where he lay panting. He rolled on his back and laughed wildly up at the dark sky.

\*\*\*

"Hobnobs!"

"What, mum?"

"I forgot to get some Hobnobs."

"They're not good for you," said Barbara Harvey. "You know they get stuck under your plate."

"You forget I went through a war. You didn't get any of this health and safety nonsense when there were bombs coming down every night."

Barbara sighed. "I know that mum but you're teeth were better back then."

Doreen Baines did one of her little pouts, her mouth puckering into a tight anus of tiny wrinkles. Barbara hated it when she pulled that face.

"I might be old but I'm not dead yet. I'm entitled to some pleasure. Anyway, if you dunk them they go soft. Only thing is, you mustn't dunk for too long or the soft bit drops off into your tea."

Barbara felt in her pocket and popped a Feminax from a blister, running her tongue against her teeth to work up enough spit to swallow it dry. She felt lousy and there was a long day ahead.

"It's not much to ask," Doreen continued. "I'll be dead soon enough."

Barbara rolled her eyes and realised the minicab driver was watching her in the rear view mirror. She looked away quickly.

"All right, mum. I've got to pick up the kids this afternoon and collect the car, if it's passed its MoT, but I can get some tomorrow when I do our shopping. Do you think you can hold out for 24 hours?"

" 'Spose so," mumbled the anus sulkily.

Barbara looked up and caught the cabbie's eye again. "It's the second turning on the left."

"Yes, I know," said the driver.

They finished the journey in silence. When the car pulled up outside a neat terrace home in the quiet Portslade side road Barbara jumped out and ran round to help her mother out. That new hip had never really worked out. Her mother hadn't done the exercises properly, no matter how often Barbara had nagged.

Barbara gripped the old woman's arm as Doreen started up the garden path, head down as her misting eyes tried to read the irregular pattern of the uneven paving slabs.

As they reached the front door Barbara looked back and was pleasantly surprised to see the cabbie had unloaded the shopping bags from the boot and was following up the path.

"Oh," said Doreen. "Silly me, I left the door open."

Barbara's head snapped round. "I checked it when we left." It seemed to take her a long time to understand what she was seeing. Her mother's front door stood open six inches. Inside the hallway was dark but what alarmed her most were the thin shards of wood sticking out of the door frame.

"Oh God!"

The cab driver was behind her now, putting the bulging bags down on the step. He looked up, saw her face, then saw the splintered wood.

"Stay here."

Barbara, still gripping Doreen's arm, could feel her mother trembling. Before she could speak the driver had pushed past her into the gloom of the hallway. She patted her pockets for her mobile phone before it dawned on her it was in her handbag on the back seat of the minicab.

She heard a shout and the crash of a door being thrown open, another shout and something smashed, then everything went quiet.

Barbara and Doreen waited on the step but nothing happened. After a very long pause, Barbara leaned forward towards the open front door.

"Hello?"

Nothing.

"Hello? Are you all right?"

Nothing.

She turned to her mother and saw her eyes vacant with an unknown fear. "Stay here," said Barbara. "Don't move."

Doreen tried to mouth something but her lips just moved soundlessly as her thoughts tried to catch up with the speed of events.

Barbara stepped over the threshold and listened. As her eyes adjusted she looked around. Everything seemed normal.

She took three steps into the hall and listened.

Again, nothing.

"Hello?"

The door to the lounge was wide open. She could see the armchair and half of the sofa, a coffee table and bookshelves behind. A standard lamp stood in its proper place, unmoved. Somewhere, Monty was barking.

Barbara tiptoed to the lounge door in her high heels and peered through the gap by the hinges. The door to the patio and garden was wide open. The light outside was dancing in a strange zigzag pattern. It puzzled her until she realised it was catching the jagged edges of shattered glass.

Glancing back to check her mother still in the porch, Barbara stepped into the living room. Everything looked as it should be. She stepped further into the room and saw a shape on the concrete patio. It was rocking rhythmically from side to side.

Two more steps and she had a clear view into the garden. The rocking shape was the minicab driver.

Barbara rushed outside and crouched beside him. "Are you okay? What happened?"

The man's breath hissed through clenched teeth. His fingers were interlocked across his left knee as his body rocked to ease his obvious pain.

"Saw a guy, jeans and a blue jacket, going over the fence."

He hissed again, sucking in more air. "Went after him but tripped over Tiddles there, winded myself on the garden table and cracked my knee on that plant pot."

Barbara looked around. Monty was barking wildly, ears flapping as he charged around the garden in great excitement, determined not to miss any of the fun.

When he saw Barbara, Monty dashed over, jumping up to butt her hand, then he looked at the driver with large wet eyes and began to lick at the man's clenched fingers with a big slobbery tongue.

"Monty! Sit!" snapped Barbara.

The dog looked confused and tried to butt her hand again. Barbara slapped his rump. "I said *SIT!*"

Monty settled on the concrete, a wounded expression on his furry face. His head went down and his long ears flopped across his disappointed eyes as he let out a whine of appeal.

Barbara returned her attention to the driver. "Can you stand?"

The scream startled them both. It wasn't loud but what it lacked in volume it made up for in black despair.

"Billy! Billy! What have they done to you?"

Barbara was on her feet and inside in a flash. The driver levered himself off the paving by gripping the garden table and hobbled inside.

By the fireplace in the living room the old woman was on her knees, her upper body bent forward, arms spread across the carpet, face pressed into a pale grey stain.

"Billy! Billy!"

Barbara looked up at the driver. "That sick bastard."

Confused, the driver looked again at the old woman. It seemed as if the intruder had emptied the Hoover dust bag on the floor. Grey powder trickled across the old woman's wrinkled hands, clogged the spaces between her thin fingers and the loose rings on her wedding hand.

Nearby was a cardboard container decorated with a floral pattern. Beside it someone had thrown down a strange looking green plastic canister.

"Billy! Billy!"

Barbara gripped her mother's shoulders and tried to pull her up but the strength in her withered body surprised her.

The minicab driver saw she was having difficulty. He gently took Doreen's other arm and between them they got the old woman to her feet and steered her into a well-worn armchair.

Doreen looked tiny in the chair, her body sagging, chin on chest, as she sobbed silently, the wobbling of her jowls the only visible sign of her distress.

Barbara disappeared into the kitchen and returned with a dustpan and brush.

"I've got to tidy this up," she said as she set to work.

"What's happened?" asked the cabbie.

"Dad's ashes, some sick bastard has just dumped them on the carpet. Probably thought he could sniff them up his nose or something."

She brushed systematically with short strokes, gathering a little at a time and tipping it carefully back into the green canister.

The driver watched in silence as she worked. Even in the gloom of the lounge he could see a patina of fine grey dust had sunk deep into the pile while larger grains dancing around the surface as she brushed.

Anger and effort made her voice husky. She looked down into the canister and gave a little sob. "There's hardly half of him here."

Barbara attacked the carpet with increasing strength. As her efforts to recover all the ash grew more frantic a blew grey haze rose up out of the pile.

"When I'm done here I'm going to call the police. They've got to find the bastard who did this to my dad."

The driver shrugged. "I don't think the coppers will be much use. I don't think they do burglary these days."

Barbara looked up, her eyes were wet and angry. "You got any better ideas?"

The minicab driver reached into his pocket and handed her a card.

"Detective? Are you having a laugh?"

"Guy who runs the cab firm is a mate. I'm just helping him out. Detecting is my real job. It's kosher, I've got a website and everything."

Barbara looked down at the card again, then up at Danny. "Hold the container for me."

Both heads turned when a distant voice whispered, "Oh, Billy."

## CHAPTER 7

It hurt, it really bloody hurt. His legs and lungs were on fire. It was only now he really realised just how he had let his fitness slide.

Too much booze, too many fags. He hadn't realised how much it had crept up on him, sapped his stamina, fogged his mind.

Wallowing in your problems wasn't going to solve anything. Screw the lid down tight and get on with it. Push the body, clear the mind. That's what he needed.

The answers were obvious. Mum was on her way out. He'd do the best he could for her for as long as she lasted.

And Cheryl had been right about the kids. He had responsibilities.

That left Emma. She was obviously having a moody about something but if she wouldn't say what it was how was he supposed to sort it? Why did women have to leave out these little traps and then let you walk into them to prove they were right? At least with a minefield you knew what to look out for.

He'd set his heart on detecting. It hadn't worked out too well so far but that was no reason to stop, especially as the only other options were probably booking cars parked on yellow lines or frying burgers.

After all, it wouldn't be worth the effort if there wasn't some challenge in it. Life wasn't worth having if you didn't pick through it and try to make the best of it. Someone had said that, Greek guy. Danny remembered reading it one penniless afternoon spent sheltering from the rain in the Jubilee Library.

The slopes of Patcham Down rose ahead of him, the track slick. The going wasn't getting any easier but the pain was part of him now, part of their joint effort, not something to fight.

Making an effort to control his breathing, Danny lengthened his stride. It was only a hill, a bloody steep one, but only a hill. Decide your upper limit, then set the bar a bit higher. We don't do "can't".

He thought of the others, Dave, Si and Pogo, and suddenly he could hear Pogo's voice. "Hill? What fucking hill? It's flat as a witch's tit round here."

And then he was there, over the crest and scrabbling for his footing as the path fell into a steady downward slope.

Just ahead, gleaming under what little light the clouds would permit, was a white marble dome standing on a circle of eight pillars.

The deserted memorial looked oddly out of place on the rain-lashed Downs. A passer-by might have dismissed it as some Victorian folly but Danny had read about it in the library.

It was the chattri memorial to the Indian soldiers who died for their King-Emperor in the trenches of the First World War. The name meant "umbrella" in their language.

Danny tried to recall the book he'd read. Half a million Indian soldiers had served. Around 12,000 wounded were treated in Brighton including at the Royal Pavilion where it was thought the onion-dome architecture would make them feel more at home.

And Danny remembered that fifty-odd Hindu and Sikh soldiers who had died in the town had been cremated and their ashes scattered in the sea. The memorial stood on the site of the burning ghat where the rituals had taken place.

As Danny drew level with the chattri he doubled over, panting, and tasted salt as the rain washed sweat across his lips.

After a few minutes he checked his pulse and was pleased to feel it had dropped almost to normal. No pain, no gain, as they say.

He looked at the memorial. It was a perfect spot, dignified and thoughtful. It was always good to hold the high ground.

Danny shivered as the edge of the wind chilled the sweat on his body. He wondered what those 50-odd Indian soldiers had been like. He had served with Ghurkas. Those guys were living proof that size isn't everything.

Looking down the hill at the memorial and the hills rolling to the sea 500 feet below, he felt pretty certain most people in the city barely visible through the drifting drizzle weren't even aware that this place existed.

They had short memories. Or maybe they didn't want to remember. People were dying in Afghanistan while others were rushing around, worrying about parking, fretting over their café latte with a shot or desperate for the latest iPhone app, whatever one of those was.

When invasion threatened in Hitler's war, Brighton's beach was a no-go area of barbed wire and mines. He'd found that in the library as well.

The city was bombed more than 50 times. One of the worst was in September 1940 when fifty people were killed in Kemp Town. Four kids and two adults died watching the matinee of a film called The Ghost Comes Home at the Odeon in St George's Road.

Everywhere was a battlefield sometime, thought Danny.

He decided he'd better get moving before he stiffened up and he set off down the path at a gentle jog.

\*\*\*

All in all, it had been a good night. He'd had a few drinks, had a laugh and trousered some cash with the prospect of more to come.

As he walked back along the gloomy street towards his Beemer, Mickey D was a happy man. He touched the wad of notes in his shirt pocket. It felt pleasingly thick but he resisted the urge to take it out and count it. That could wait till later.

The two new Romanian girls were proving very popular. He'd set them up in a flat overlooking the estuary and they were doing a roaring trade.

Mickey might have to consider moving them before the neighbours got wise to all the comings and goings and started to complain.

Still, they'd be all right there for a while longer. After all, they should be. That stretch of the Adur estuary under their balcony was a bird sanctuary. That gag always made Mickey laugh.

He wasn't surprised at their success. He'd tried the merchandise himself, just to be sure what his clients were getting, and Ruxandra and Anca were well worth the money, separately or as a double act.

He knew he had to cash in fast while they were still tip top totty, and still scared. The price would plunge once they started to get a bit frayed round the edges.

Mickey listened to the sound of water moving in Shoreham Harbour and smiled.

Then there was the blow. The punters really liked the Moroccan he'd been pushing for a couple of months now. They were puffing away faster than he could get supplies in but that wasn't a problem, it just pushed the price up.

Just went to show that a dodgy economy was good for business. The worse things got, the more people wanted to escape their troubles with a shag or get off their faces with a spliff. Only human nature.

Diversification, that's what they called it, spread the risk and protect the flow of profits. He had the girls, he had the blow and now he had some information.

He had it but it was hard to price. Someone was looking urgently and that ramped up the value but Mickey didn't know how big a price tag to put on it. Wouldn't want to sell yourself short, would you?

If it was a real earner and he played his cards right it might just pay for that trip to Vegas he'd been thinking about. That really would be something. Mickey touched the bulge in his shirt again. He was only fifty yards from the Beemer now but the temptation was just too great. As he lifted the thick wad of bills from his pocket he saw his feet leave the pavement. Something was gripping his arms.

As Mickey looked to left and right he saw a guy each side of him, big guys, shaved heads, mean eyes. The meaty hands dug into the flesh of Mickey's arms. He winced and as he looked down he saw the money, crumpled grubby tens and twenties, falling from his fingers.

"Hey… Hey… that's my money."

He tried to wriggle but the men's grip was solid.

"My money… that's my money."

A breeze took the notes and Mickey saw them tumbling and dancing away down the pavement just before everything went dark and he slammed down onto a hard metal floor.

Mickey tried to get up but a size twelve boot in the centre of his chest pinned him like a butterfly.

Calm down, Mickey, brute strength isn't going to out it here. We need to think. You're a businessman. Do a deal.

He took a breath, opened his eyes and looked up, taking in his surroundings.

The opposite wall of the van was fitted with a tool rack and beside him was something that looked like a work bench. The two bruisers who had lifted him filled most of his vision but there was someone else in the van.

"Get him up," said the third man.

The two men hauled Mickey to his knees. As he came up off the floor he saw the third man was even bigger than the other two.

"What can I do you for, chief?" asked Mickey, trying to give his voice a lightness he didn't feel.

"Cocky sod, aren't you?" said the big man.

"Me? No, just a businessman trying to make a living."

"I'm looking for information, about some missing car parts."

"Well," said Mickey. "You've come to the right man. I was just on my way to see you."

"Oh yes? Where?"

"Well… I… it's just…"

"Clamp his hand," said the big man.

The two others hauled Mickey up, forcing his hand over the work bench and into a vice which they screwed tight around his wrist.

"Hey… hey… there's no need… we can do a deal."

"Too bloody late," said the big man. "When I put the word round I wanted that information straight away, like yesterday."

"I was just … you know … trying to fix a price. It's a rush job, lots of people with their eyes and ears open, so I figured it would be worth something."

"When I want to know something it's an order, not a negotiation."

Mickey flinched as something hard smashed into the bench by his elbow. He tried to pull away but whimpered when he wrenched his arm in the mouth of the vice.

"What this information is worth, you worthless piece of shit, is your fingers."

Mickey saw it now. The man held a hand axe two feet above the bench, two feet above his clamped hand.

As the big man flicked his wrist the axe rotated in his fingers with metronome precision, curved blade downwards, then solid flat butt, blade, butt, blade, butt.

"So what's it worth now, eh?" The quietness of the big man's voice seemed to make it worse for Mickey. His bowels felt suddenly hot.

"I'm just a businessman … you know … trying to make a living."

The big man gripped his hair and jerked his head back. He pressed the axe blade down hard against Mickey's hand and when he lifted it the bit had pressed a white line into the pink flesh.

"I've had enough of you," said the big man. "Bruise it or lose it, your choice."

Mickey's eyes stretched even wider.

"Are you stupid or what, Mickey? Tell me what I want to know now or I'll chop your fucking hand off."

Mickey tried to speak but, somehow, air couldn't get through his throat. He coughed but it came out as more of a gargle. When he found his voice it came gabbling out.

"I was in a pub, down by the harbour. Got chatting to this guy who said someone had been in earlier trying to shift some hooky vehicle parts."

"And…?"

"Someone said maybe they were from farm machinery. No one knew what they were so the guy just left."

"And…?"

"I asked around about the guy."

"And…?"

"No one knew his name."

The axe blade moved down towards Mickey's trapped hand.

"No!.. No !.. No!.. The guy, he runs a minicab business and he's got a garage, repairs and the like."

Mickey couldn't tear his eyes from the axe twirling over his hand.

"And…?"

"He's a poof, runs his business from a little place in Portslade, just off the Old Shoreham Road. Honest, that's all I know, that's everything, please…"

Mickey saw the axe rise, the blade flipping, blade, butt, blade, butt. It was turning too fast. He didn't see which way it was facing when it started down.

There was a snapping noise, like twigs. The pain was excruciating, racing up his arm like igniting petrol. As he threw back his head to scream one of the guys behind him jammed an oily rag into his mouth to strangle the noise. Tears streamed from his eyes as he sobbed for breath, not daring the look down at his hand.

The big man patted his cheek.

"Your lucky night, Mickey. You got the bruising. Next time you jerk me around I will chop your fucking hand off, no lie."

Mickey felt the vice release its grip and he sagged. The pain in his hand was agony. As they threw him from the back of the van he just managed to turn in mid air and take the impact on his shoulder, terrified of his broken fingers punching into the tarmac.

As the van screeched away its tyres whipped up the last of his fallen cash and sent it fluttering off down the road.

\*\*\*

"Thank you for coming."

Danny shook his head. "Not a problem."

He sipped his tea and looked around the living room. The woodwork shone. The new pane in the door to the patio had that sparkle of new glass. Books, ornaments and framed photos were arranged with immaculate, almost obsessive, precision.

Barbara Harvey followed Danny's gaze down to the carpet. "I've tidied up, tried to make everything look normal, but it'll never be the same. Nothing else was touched. Just dad's ashes. It's like the place has been desecrated."

Somewhere in the house, away behind closed doors, he could hear a faint whimpering sound.

"How's your mum?"

Barbara shook her head. Danny noticed her weary eyes were puffy.

"She's not the same. She doesn't say much but ever since it happened she's been quiet, too quiet, brooding. Just keeps on crying. It's like a light has turned off inside. She coped okay when dad died. He was getting on and he'd been in pain for quite a while. It was a release, not just for him, for all of us. It was natural. But this, what happened here, that was sick, perverted."

"What does the doc say about your mum?"

Barbara gave a helpless shrug and looked down at fidgeting fingers in her lap. "Oh, she said mum had had a bit of a shock but there's nothing physically wrong with her. And you were right about the police."

"Was I?"

Barbara nodded sharply. "Yes, a very nice young community policeman took all the details but didn't hold out much hope. They're very busy, apparently. He didn't look as if he was long out of school."

Danny sipped his tea.

"Is it all right?" asked Barbara.

"Fine," said Danny. "So why did you call me?"

"You left your card, the detective one." She picked it up from the table beside her cup and studied the writing for the thousandth time. "You said you might be able to help."

"If there's anything I can do, I will. But I can't promise."

"That's kind of you."

"It's hard to know where to start," said Danny. "Can you think of anyone who might do this, anyone with a grudge?"

Barbara shook her head. "Dad was a lovely man, a real softie. I still can't really believe this has happened."

Danny glanced up at an old photo on the mantelpiece.

"Who's the soldier?"

Barbara looked over her shoulder at the picture and smiled.

"That was dad in the army during the war. He was proud of that picture but he never talked about it much."

She looked back at Danny, twisting her wedding ring, fidgeting,

"Is it expensive, what you do?"

"Depends what's involved," said Danny.

"I've got some money put aside. It's not a lot but I want to do this for mum, and for dad."

"I tell you what," said Danny. "I'll make a few inquiries. If anything comes of it, we can talk money. If I don't get anywhere, well, we'll just forget it."

"Oh no," said Barbara. "I couldn't let you do it for nothing."

"Don't worry," said Danny. "Call it a favour for an old soldier."

"You're very kind. There's just one other thing."

"Yes?"

"Could you take Monty." Barbara saw the startled look on Danny's face. "Look after him for a while, till mum settles down."

"Well, I don't…"

"He's a lovely dog, very sweet-natured. It's just that every time he's in this room he's sniffing around that patch of carpet." Barbara waved a hand to indicate the patch where the ashes had fallen and forced herself to look down at it.

There was nothing to show that anything had ever happened but they could both picture the pool of powder.

"It really upsets her. I have enough trouble getting her to come in here but when Monty starts she can't handle it. It's as if dad had died all over again."

Danny looked at his half-finished, tea, listening to Monty's muffled whining.

"Okay then."

"Oh, thank you so much."

Danny pulled a dog-eared notebook from his pocket and extracted the stub of pencil wedged down its spiral spine.

"I'd better take some details. What about Billy's friends?"

\*\*\*

Dean McKeown's face was creased with concentration into an expression that looked like pain of some kind, perhaps trapped wind.

"It's bloody complicated."

Big Eddie Archer put his Seagulls tea mug down on the kitchen worktop and sighed. "It's not bloody complicated, Dean. It's subtle. It's got layers. If this is going to get me what I want it's got to work in the background, where no one sees it. It's got to be invisible, while every step clicks into place, like a quality lock."

McKeown shook his head. "I still think it's complicated."

"Deano, God knows, I love you like a son. You've been my strong right arm since you were a kid but, honestly, sometimes you give me chest pains."

"I'm just saying it like I see it," said McKeown.

"All right, all right. We'll look at it your way. Yes, it's complicated. But if we do it carefully, set one brick on another, it'll work. Trust me on this."

"Don't I always, Eddie?"

"And I should hope so too, Dean. You all right son? You look a bit peaky."

"I'm fine, Eddie, just fine."

"Right then, about the first step. You up for it?"

"Yeah, you think twenty will be enough?"

"Trust me, son. It'll be enough. I'll leave the details to you. Just let me know when everything is in place."

"Will do, boss."

***

Danny and Skidmarks leaned against the outside wall of the minicab office, blowing cigarette smoke at the sky.

"Thank God it's stopped raining," said Skidmarks. "Mind you, people won't need cabs so much if it's dry."

Danny nodded. "You could go stir crazy stuck in the office all day, especially on that lumpy furniture."

"Especially with nothing to do."

Danny looked across at Skidmarks. "Don't worry. I remember what you said. If the work doesn't pick up I'll be off."

Skidmarks looked at Danny for a moment before speaking. "Maybe not. I've got a bit of news."

"Oh yes?"

Skidmarks nodded. "I've not been entirely straight with you, Danny. I've got an investor, someone prepared to put in a few bob, do a bit of promotion to pull in some punters."

"Must be Christmas come early. Who is it?"

Skidmarks studied Danny, took a long pull on his cigarette and looked back up at the sky. The winds had whipped the cloud away, leaving a patch of blue just above them.

"Eddie Archer."

"Who?" said Danny.

"Eddie Archer."

"What, Big Eddie Archer? The guy who topped Sammy Spoon?"

"That was never proved," said Skidmarks defensively.

Danny shook his head. "This is a bit desperate, isn't it?"

"Danny, mate, I am desperate."

"Even so, it sounds a bit like jumping out of the frying pan."

"Eddie and I go back a long way," said Skidmarks, his voice barely audible.

"Oh yeah? How's that?"

"I used to do some driving for him, way back."

"Driving?"

"Don't ask."

"Fair enough," said Danny. "Anyway, it's your choice."

"Not quite," said Skidmarks, his voice so faint Danny had to turn his head to hear.

"What do you mean?"

"Eddie wants to meet you."

"Meet me, why?"

"Well, I sort of told him you and me were in this together. I thought you could earn out of it as well."

Danny turned and kicked the wall behind him, his boot denting the rusting corrugated metal. "With my track record all I need is to be seen hobnobbing with this neighbourhood's top man for porn, drugs and armed robbery."

"Eddie just wants to meet you."

"And this deal'll keep you in business?"

"That's what the man says."

"I'm not touching anything dodgy, no mystery packages."

"Fair enough, Danny."

Danny sighed. "Sod it, why not?"

Skidmarks closed the distance between them and slapped Danny on the shoulder, relief washing across his face.

"Thanks mate, I owe you one."

A gust of wind set their jackets flapping. Fat raindrops pattered on the crumbling tarmac of the office yard and dappled the water-filled pothole.

Skidmarks looked up at the darkening sky and moved towards the office door. "We'd better get back inside before it starts again."

"Oi," said Danny. "Fag darts."

Skidmarks smiled and stepped away from the building. The two of them stood shoulder to shoulder, toecaps lined up with a boot heel graze in the old tarmac.

"You first," said Danny.

Skidmarks held the glowing butt of his cigarette like a pencil and raised it beside his right cheek, squinting at the ashtray box with its metal grid of small squares screwed to the office wall. He aimed and threw but the cigarette clipped the corner of the grid and spun away.

Danny took quick aim and threw. The butt arced through the air and into the box through one of the squares in the top right quarter of the grid.

"I think we'll call that double 18," said Danny.

"Jammy sod," said Skidmarks.

\*\*\*

The four students looked blank as the scale of their embarrassment began to sink in. The clapping continued, speeded up into something that sounded like sizzling.

The other four students glanced repeatedly at each other along the line, stunned and not quite believing they had come from so far behind to seize the game on the last question.

Gavin had lost them five points for an incorrect answer to a simple starter on Wordsworth and been too unsettled to try again until that last question about the periodic table. It had been a gift.

They looked into the crowd of clapping hands and waving scarves and began to feel the first tingling pleasure of victory. Giles Forrester picked up the video remote control, stopped the recording and deleted it. He looked down at the notepad on the arm of his chair and allowed himself a thin smile, 215 points, beat the lot of them.

He levered himself up out of the chair and moved to the desk. Playtime over, now for some work.

He sat down, looked at the top letter in the tray and sighed. It really was too awful, wasting his talents on rubbish like this. A man with a top notch university education, a brilliantly analytical mind, massaging the egos of morons. It was an insult to his intellect and his skills. The ancestor paradox explained much.

If every person has two parents, four grandparents, eight great-grandparents and so on back in time, why are there more people alive now that at any time in human history?

Part of the answer was inbreeding, cousins marrying and the like. And Forrester had the distinct impression many of his clients were inbreeds looking for some historical justification for their sad little lives, some distant relative with a tenuous claim to fame so they could bask in their dubious reflected glory and feel better about themselves.

He loathed and detested every moment of the work, wouldn't even have considered it if the money wasn't good. But the money could be very good. And it was child's play for someone of his talent.

If he made the right noises, came to the right conclusions, he could virtually write his own cheque. People seemed to lose all reason when it came to their vanity.

Forrester scanned the letter on top of the pile in his tray. The garish headed notepaper, crowned with a positively repulsive cartoon image of a round brown cow with a large lopsided grin bisecting its fat face, announced its author to be Lyndon K Wagstaffe III.

It was one thing for monarchs to be designated by heir regnal number, a clear and unambiguous statement of their lineage and place in the chain of great bloodlines.

It was quite another thing to number the members of a dynasty that founded an all-you-can-eat steakhouse chain across the American south west. Perhaps they thought they might lose track of their relatives. Was it possible, Forrester pondered, that they branded family members with their number as they did their cattle.

Aching with reluctance, Forrester slid a sheet of heavy writing paper from a drawer and placed it on the leather-trimmed blotter in front of him. He took the Mont Blanc fountain pen from the inside pocket of his blazer and began to write.

Dear Mr Wagstaffe,
It is with the greatest delight that I am able to confirm that the family lore you hold so dear, passed down by generations of Wagstaffes, had proven to be correct.
You are, indeed, a descendant of our greatest playwright, William Shakespeare of Stratford-upon-Avon, England.

Forrester rolled his shoulders in an effort to deflect the headache he could feel coming on.

I must stress that the relationship is a distant one but my expertise has proved beyond any doubt that the blood of the great Bard flows in your veins.

I am in the process of preparing a most attractive and detailed family tree to illustrate this fact and will dispatch it to Fort Worth, Texas, by special courier as soon as I am in receipt of the balance of the fee we agreed upon.

May I take this opportunity to congratulate you on the great pride you must be experiencing on this momentous discovery.

Forrester signed his name with a looping flourish and set the letter aside to dry. "Kerching," he said as he picked up the next letter from the tray and scanned quickly through it.

"Declan Callaghan … Boston, Massachusetts … oh God, no. Not Michael Collins again."

He threw the letter back into the tray. That was enough bread and butter work for one evening, better get back to the main business in hand.

Forrester took a sheaf of notes from the desk drawer and leafed through them quickly, refreshing his memory. Then he opened his laptop and began to Google. It didn't take long to find something promising.

He tapped his fountain pen thoughtfully on his lower lip as he speed-read the Wikipedia page.

"The second Anglo-Maratha war, now there's a thought." He began to scribble, adding to his notes, then glanced up at the screen again.

"Wellesley, oh very good, excellent."

The phone rang. Forrester looked at the clock above the fireplace. No one telephoned at this hour. He picked it up.

"Hello?"

"Forrester?"

"Yes."

"It's Eddie Archer. How's it going?"

"It's going very well."

"Don't bullshit me. I'm paying you a fortune. And you're enjoying the fringe benefits too, from what I hear."

Forrester shifted uncomfortably. The caller continued.

"Is the old bastard buying it?"

"Hook, line and sinker."

"Good, keep at him. I want this done as quick as possible."

"A pleasure to be of service."

\*\*\*

"What's that bloody dog doing in the flat?" Danny was elbow-deep in washing up when Emma walked into the kitchen and manoeuvred a thick wad of sodden yellow nappies into a crumpled black binbag by the door.

Danny sniffed the acid air. "I'm looking after him for a client who had a break-in. His name's Monty."

Emma hissed her frustration as she snapped off her rubber gloves and dropped them in the bin on top of the nappies. He saw her hands were mauve and blue-veined, nails bitten, the hands of an older woman, like his mother's.

"Well you be sure to take care of him, Danny, because I've got enough to do clearing up after your mum."

"How is she?" asked Danny.

"She was a bit restless earlier but she's asleep now. The district nurse is due tomorrow."

He stepped away from the sink to let her wash her hands, then attacked something burned onto the bottom of a saucepan with a scouring pad.

"Let's hope they just leave her alone in her own bed."

Emma worked her way through a pile of drug packs, counting a selection of coloured tablets of assorted shapes and sizes into the dosette box.

"They've got a job to do. They have to be sure she'll be safe and cared for."

Danny snorted. "Bunch of bloody box tickers covering their arses."

"That's not really fair, Danny."

He put down the pan and turned to face her. "She's got vascular dementia. The pipework in her brain's rotting. The poor bloody woman just wants to die in her own home."

Emma said nothing. The two of them stood four feet apart listening to the tick, tick, tick of tablets dropping into the plastic box, four compartments for each day, seven days a week.

Danny attacked the pan again. Emma finished counting the tablets and snapped the box shut.

"I need to pop out and get her prescription. Her Warfarin's running low."

Danny held the pan up to the light to check his progress. When he was satisfied he put in on the draining board and picked up a tea towel. As he began to dry he realised Emma was watching him, eating a sandwich.

"You don't like Marmite."

Emma looked at the sandwich as if she hadn't seen it before. "I do sometimes."

"You hate it, you even hate the smell."

She took a large bite and spoke as she chewed. "Well, I'm enjoying this one. Does it matter?"

Danny shook his head. "No, no problem. It's just that you never liked Marmite before."

"Drop it, Danny. Just drop it."

He shrugged. "If you say so."

They stood in silence at opposite ends of the tiny kitchen, the only sound the squeaking of the tea towel on the plate Danny was drying.

"Any more news about work?"

Danny shook his head again.

"Have you thought any more about getting a proper job?"

"I've got some minicabbing, temporary."

The squeak of the cotton tea towel on the dry plate seemed to grow louder.

He knew what was coming. It didn't happen often but when Emma was in one of these moods there was no way out, asking questions that didn't want answers, circling like a shark. Wearing you down, looking for weaknesses, darting in to take a bite, then swerving away to start circling again.

"Couldn't you get something a bit more permanent? There must be something you could do, maybe Bob could help."

Danny banged the plate down on the draining board. "I'm trying my best. Bob's got no work on and I've already taken this crap job driving for Skids, just to tide me over, but there's no way I'm doing that for ever.

"I'm going to make this detecting work, Emma. There is no way I am going to sit in some office shuffling paper or on some building site freezing my balls off.

"Do you know what it's like out there? People with university degrees frying burgers. I'd be right at the back of the queue, over the bloody horizon. Besides, I don't want to be a cog in a machine jumping through hoops for some dickhead."

Emma took another bite of her sandwich and leaned back against the kitchen counter, arms folded. "So what makes you think you're so special then?"

"In the army I was a cog but it was a bloody good machine. There's no way I'll ever match that. The Paras were my family. So was mum but she's on her way out. I'm on my own from here on in. I'm going to make this detecting business work. It's something I want to try. I'm going to put in the hours and make it bloody work. I've got an instinct about it."

"And what's that worth?"

"It's saved my life before."

"And now it's got you dog sitting. How are you planning to solve this one?"

"Not a clue but I couldn't leave the old dear in that state, with no hope."

"It's always about you, isn't it, Danny?"

He said nothing, picked up a dry plate and began rubbing it vigorously with the tea towel.

"So you're on your own, are you? What about me?"

Danny started on another dry plate. He didn't want to look at her.

"You're married, Benny's your family."

"You ever thought of settling down again?" asked Emma after a long, hard pause.

Danny looked up, "With who?"

"How long have we known each other?"

"Quite a while."

"And you still forgot our anniversary last month."

"Anniversary?"

"When we met. At the pub. The hen night."

"I didn't forget."

"Danny, you gave me a Bad Taste Bear and a bunch of flowers the day after. The petrol station sticker was still on the wrapper."

Danny shrugged. "What can I say?"

"You could try."

Danny began to wind the tea towel into a tight knot between balled fists. "Why? This is turning into one of those, 'does my bum look big,' questions. Nothing I say is going to be the right answer."

Emma pressed the back of her hand to her forehead and Danny noticed the wandering blue veins and red skin again. "Danny, I know it's been difficult, with Benny and everything, but have you seen other women?"

"Nothing serious."

Emma slapped the remains of her sandwich down on the worktop. "What do you call serious?"

"I don't know, just nothing serious, that's all."

"So what's serious then?" asked Emma. "A goodnight peck? A back rub. A blow job? Swinging from the light fitting?"

Danny slammed down the last plate and turned to face her. "What's up?"

"Nothing," said Emma. "Nothing's up."

"You sure?"

Emma's eyes flared for a second. "If you say it's something hormonal I'll punch you. Nothing's up."

Danny shrugged. "If you say so."

Emma finished her sandwich, chewing mechanically as she watched Danny polish the last of the dry plates.

"Danny?"

"Yes?"

"Do you love me?"

" 'Course, I'm just not a flowers sort of guy."

Emma licked a spec of Marmite from the corner of her lip and brushed a dusting of breadcrumbs from the worktop.

"It's not just flowers, no, that's not the problem. You're a guy."

Danny looked up, puzzled and wary. "A guy? I thought that was the point, you know, a girl, a guy. It's not my fault if you want to stick with Benny."

"It not sticking, it's not about sticking. He's my husband." Emma manoeuvred around Danny to get to the sink and he noticed she leaned away from him to avoid contact. She started packing away the washing-up in the crockery cupboard, careful not to look at him. Then she turned suddenly, "You still have your funny turns, and the nightmares. What sort of dad would you make? If it happened?"

Danny shrugged. He knew there was a trap here somewhere. He just couldn't see it. "The sort of dad I already am, I guess. Pretty crap."

"You've always got reasons. Something'll always turn up. But when will it turn up? When, eh?

"If you've got something to say, Emma, just say it."

She looked at him, her expression unreadable, then released a long, compressed sigh and reached for her coat hanging on the back of the door. "I need to get to the chemist before it shuts. And I've got to do Benny's tea."

Monty chased Emma up the hall, dancing on his back legs in the hope of walkies. The front door rattled when it slammed. Monty whined his disappointment. Danny filled the kettle and stood looking out of the window as he waited for it to boil.

He saw Emma cross the road with long, angry strides and disappear around the corner. A thin, mean-eyed man in denims was leading a squat ugly dog with a spiked collar along the opposite pavement.

Danny saw him look back over his shoulder to check out Emma as she stormed past him. The kettle began to shriek.

## CHAPTER 8

Giles Forrester stood in the middle of his lounge, eyes screwed tight shut, conducting the first movement of Mozart's clarinet concerto with a large glass of white wine in his hand.

He swayed back and forth, lips curled in a distant smile, as waves of sound ebbed and flowed around him from the six speakers of his Bang and Olufsen sound system.

When the doorbell chimed he ignored it as he waited for the rise of the strings to reach its peak. Forrester had a talent for blotting out the irritating and the irrelevant. He found it helped him enormously in his work, allowing him a laser beam of concentration focussed on what truly mattered.

The music rose around him. He didn't even notice the second chime as his wine glass swayed back and forth, charming that little extra bit of excellence from every section of the orchestra.

When the third chime sounded Forrester let out a little sigh of resignation, put his wine glass down on a coaster on the coffee table, flicked the sound system's remote control to pause and slipped it into his pocket.

His bare feet sank into the deep carpet of the hall as he made his way to the front door. Shooting back the three solid bolts in the same sequence he always did, Forrester pulled the handle and the heavy front door of his flat swung smoothly and silently open.

"Are you deaf?"

Forrester was still smiling. "You look as lovely as ever this evening, my dear."

"I haven't got time to waste."

"Come in." Forrester stepped aside to let the woman enter. He took her coat and hung it in a cupboard, then shot the three bolts home on the front door.

As he followed her down the hallway he admired the way the thin dress she was wearing cupped her bottom, catching her movement as she walked, stretching the material from right shoulder to left buttock, left buttock to right shoulder with each step. The motion was quite hypnotic.

She had good legs, he noted, with well-defined calves. She was above average height and those ridiculous heels accentuated her stature and the way she moved.

It never ceased to amaze Forrester that, despite the fact it was windy and wet outside, women's vanity never failed to drive them out in all weathers in the most unsuitable clothing.

And her hair was different from the last time, long and dark blonde with a tinge of red in it. Interesting.

They entered the lounge in single file. The woman stopped by the coffee table and looked quickly around the room. Her hand slid into the large brown leather bag she was carrying and pulled out a padded manila envelope sealed with wide strips of clear tape.

Forrester wondered why anyone would burden themselves with such an item as the bag, covered, as it was, with a lattice of buckles and straps. It lacked clarity of function, he thought.

She reached out, offering the package to Forrester.

"Here it is."

Forrester took the envelope and weighed it in his hand.

"Is it all there?"

The woman let out a theatrical gasp. "I'm a dancer not an accountant. Check it yourself."

Forrester smiled, revealing a line of expensive even white teeth. "There's no need to be like that. Wine?"

"I'm in a hurry."

"We miss so much in life when we rush. It won't take a moment of your time. It's very good, I must say, a 2006 Domaine Leflaive Puligny-Montrachet."

The woman gave a reluctant shrug. Forrester took the bottle from an ice bucket on the coffee table and poured a second glass. The woman sipped it and gave a little nod of approval. "Hmm, lemony."

"You see," said Forrester. "It pays to set aside a little time for the pleasures of life."

The woman's eyes flicked up over the rim of the wine glass as she sipped. "I said I was in a hurry."

"My dear girl, you know perfectly well your instructions are to make sure I'm happy. It's important that I'm happy. I work so much better that way. And my needs do extend beyond good music and fine wines."

The woman put the glass down hard on the table. Giles winced at the wet ring he could see on the perfectly polished surface.

"I told you, I'm a dancer…"

The smile on Forrester's face hardened. "Let's stop playing games, my dear. I know what you said but you're not a dancer, you are a whore. And for the next fifteen minutes you're my whore so just do as I fucking tell you."

A breath of resignation hissed through her clenched teeth as the woman dropped to her knees.

Forrester unzipped his trousers and was pleased to see he was half hard. The woman moved towards him but he raised a hand. "Ah, ah, don't forget the wine."

The woman flashed angry eyes up at him before taking her glass from the table and filled her mouth with chilled Puligny-Montrachet.

As her lips slid over his erection his head went back and he let out a deep sigh. The wet chill was exquisite. He reached into his pocket, took out the remote and skimmed the stored tracks on his sound system.

The sound of teasing violins blossomed around him, dancing playfully, before the deeper, darker sounds of Ravel's la Valse began to rise. As the woman settled into a fast, regular rhythm Forrester sipped from his wine glass. It was obvious she was trying to get this over with as soon as possible but he wasn't going to allow that.

He cupped his free right hand behind her head and gripped her thick hair. He felt it shift slightly beneath his fingers. A wig, how delightful. A different girl every time.

Forrester tightened his grip, dictating the tempo, beating to Ravel's time. The women gave a little mewl of protest but Forrester ignored it. A drizzle of chilled wine trickled down his balls. Exquisite.

He was very close to Ravel's climax when he let out a series of little grunts. His body shuddered and his hips stuttered back and forth. When he was finished they stayed motionless for a few moments before the woman pulled away.

Forrester waited until his breathing had settled, then sipped his wine. "Thank you, my dear. Now you can get on with whatever it was that was so urgent."

The woman took a tissue from her shoulder bag, spat into it, then began dabbing at the glistening pearl droplets that were starting to run down her chin. Giles chuckled to himself as he watched. "It's quite amazing how something so small as a splash of love custard can affect people's lives. A little puddle like that can control dynasties and even nations."

The woman threw the balled tissue onto the table and Forrester winced at the prospect of another stain.

The dark, angry eyes looked up at him. "What?"

"Never mind, you wouldn't understand. Still, I look forward to seeing you next time, my dear."

The woman rose to her feet, took a mirror from her bag and began to replace her lipstick. "Don't bothering finishing your wine," said Forrester. "I'll show you out."

As he followed the woman along the hall, watching the sway of her body, Forrester considered how to pass the rest of his evening and settled on watching some more of his recordings of Mastermind and University Challenge.

He liked to watch them on the first fast-forward setting so the recording was speeded up but the sound was still audible.

It confirmed many of Giles ideas about himself that, apart from the occasional bravura performance by one or two of the better universities, he still managed to beat the competing teams.

\*\*\*

The Bellerophon was quiet, just the way he liked it. Usually there was too much noise in there, too much noise everywhere. No one these days seemed to value a bit of peace and quiet.

The old man looked up and squinted as the shadow fell across him. "Oh, it's you. What do you want?"

"Just a word."

"I'm busy." The old man picked up his pen, adjusted his glasses and squinted down at his Sudoku book.

"I just want a bit of help," said Danny.

The old man looked up again, squinting. "Do I look like Citizen's Advice?"

"I'll buy you a pint."

Wally's eyes flitted to the last two inches of Guinness in his glass. He'd reckoned on making that last another half hour.

"All right, then. But you'll have to be quick. I'm busy."

Danny crossed to the bar and paid for the pint that Emily had waiting for him. He placed it on the table by Wally's right hand and watched the tip of the old man's tongue flit across his lips. Danny slipped into the seat opposite.

"So what is it you want?"

"I'm trying to find an old soldier. I haven't got an address but I thought you might know where he drank."

"How old?"

"Normandy veteran."

"Ah, proper soldiering, none of this health and safety cobblers."

"As you say, Wally. The guy's name's Joe Walsh."

Wally's eyes narrowed as he drew a yellowed fingernail across his whiskery chin. "Walsh ... Walsh, let me think." His eyes screwed shut, then he opened them and looked at Danny.

"Nope, doesn't ring a bell."

"Come on, Wally. You've got your pint. Try a little harder."

"You tried the Legion?"

"Yes, he's not a member."

Wally drained his glass and drew the new one protectively within the arc of his arm. "There are hundreds of pubs. He could drink anywhere. Or nowhere. Maybe he's signed the pledge."

Danny shook his head. "I'm told he likes a pint."

Wally took a sip of his new Guinness, the tip of his tongue darting like a snake's to clean up the foam on his top lip.

"Search me, son."

"What's your best guess?"

Wally stroked his chin again. "You could try that pub in Hove, by George Street. The beer's cheap and I know a few old sweats used to get together there of an afternoon."

Danny stood up. "Thanks, Wally. Enjoy your pint."

\*\*\*

The flat was on the first floor of a narrow, bow-fronted terraced house in Kemp Town, between St George's Road and the sea. Close enough to the action but off the main drag with its traffic.

Parking in the area, like most of Brighton, was a problem in streets controlled by yellow lines or residents' parking bays but Danny found a space twenty yards up the right hand side. It was quiet as he walked up the front steps, feeling the glowing of his muscles from his last run. He rang the bell. Nothing happened.

He stepped back and looked at the house. The basement and ground floors were in darkness but there was a light on in the upstairs front room and a faint glow visible through the glass panel in the front door.

Danny pressed the bell again, holding it for ten seconds, then he listened. At first he could hear nothing. Then there was an urgent rumble of feet on the stairs.

As he took a step back the door flew open and a women with long red hair and wild eyes stood gasping as she stared at him.

Danny guessed she was in her twenties, tall and slim as far as he could tell from the shapeless dressing gown she was wearing.

"Minicab."

"Thank god you're here. Come in quick!"

She grabbed his arm and towed him, unresisting, into the hallway and up the stairs. "Keep the noise down," she hissed in a theatrical whisper, "The people in the flat downstairs get really arsey if we wake the baby."

The woman led him along the upstairs landing and into the front room.

"Take this," she said, pushing a plastic bottle into his hand. Danny looked down at the label. When he looked up the woman was shrugging the dressing gown off her shoulders, revealing a slender, well-defined body covered only by a thong and push-up bra. As the dressing gown fell onto the carpet the woman leaned forward, spread her hands against the mantelpiece above the gas fire and arched her back.

"Can you finish me off?"

"What?"

"I'm in a tearing hurry. Can you finish me off?"

Danny blinked, unspeaking.

"The bottle," said the woman, indicating the container in Danny's hand with a jab of her hip. "My bloody spray's run out and that's all I've got left. I need you to touch up the small of my back."

Too surprised to speak, Danny poured some of the fake tan into the palm of his hand and smeared it across the woman's back, gently at first, then with growing confidence. As he worked the skin with firm, circular movements he studied the tramp stamp tattoo of a butterfly, its wings spreading upward from the hollow of her back, in an effort to drag his eyes from buttocks separated only by the wisp of thong.

"Make sure it's even, won't you. It looks really cheap if it's streaky."

Danny worked away until the colour was as even as he could judge under the dim glow of a low energy eco-bulb in the shaded ceiling light.

"I think you're done," said Danny, patting the area with a smile of satisfaction. Another first.

"You're a life-saver. Wipe your hands on that towel on the chair. Give me five minutes and I'll be with you. We've got to get a move on or I'll be late."

Danny took the towel and wiped the excess cream from his hands as the woman vanished along the landing into a room somewhere at the back of the two-bedroom flat. He looked around as he waited.

The room was large but crowded with a table and two chairs in the bay window and a sofa to one side facing a flat-screen TV on the wall over the fireplace.

It struck Danny that there was something odd about the room. A shelf of books was immaculately organised, all the spines drawn forward to form a perfect line. Beside the telephone was a pad, its edge parallel to the phone, and beside that a Biro at exactly the same angle. One side of the dining table had a perfect place setting. On the other side was a jumble of tissues, keys, a mobile phone and a half-finished pack of mint gum spilling out of the wrapper.

Something on the mantelpiece above the fireplace caught his eye. Danny crossed the room and studied a small trowel mounted on a wooden plinth. On the front of the base was a plastic panel with an inscription. "With grateful thanks to Claire for making a good job truly great. With the greatest affection, Terry Mallet and the team, The Claudius Dig, August 25, 2007".

Danny was just about to pick it up for a closer look when he heard heels moving fast on the landing. The woman burst breathlessly into the room. This time she was dressed in a sweat top, tracksuit bottoms and a hooded parka. She carried a soft holdall over one shoulder and moved quickly and with confidence on the highest pair of heels Danny had ever seen.

He knew all about the problems of moving around in body armour and helmet, carrying a weapon, ammunition and water but how anyone could walk in those things was a mystery to him.

"I think I'm dry. We'd better get going."

As they left the living room a door banged somewhere in the flat. "Oh," said the redhead, "I didn't know you were still here."

Danny looked across at the flatmate. She was the same height as the redhead but her brown hair was pulled back into a tight knot. He couldn't see her eyes clearly as she wore glasses and moved with her head tilted down."

"No," said the flatmate. "I had some tidying up to do."

"Well," said the redhead. "Gotta dash."

She grabbed the sleeve of Danny's jacket and began towing him down the stairs. He glanced back up at the flatmate but she had disappeared into the shadows at the end of the landing.

Danny led his passenger down the road to the parked Skoda. When he opened the rear door she jumped in and bounced across the seat before arranging her bag beside her.

"God, it's bloody freezing out there." Danny thought she wasn't really dressed for the weather but decided not to say it. "The Pink Flamingo?"

"Fast as you can, love."

He pulled away from the kerb and headed towards the main road, the Skoda's heater slowly wearing away at the chill in the car.

"Lived there long?" asked Danny.

"About a year."

"That your flatmate?"

"She's my sister. You ask a lot of questions."

"Sorry, just passing the time."

"Okay."

"So," said Danny. "You and Claire from Brighton then?"

The girl's head snapped up. Their eyes met in the rear view mirror. "How did you know her name was Claire?"

"I saw it on that thing above the fire while I was waiting for you."

The girl relaxed. "Oh that. Don't ever ask her about it. Don't get me wrong, I love my sister but she could bore for England when it comes to archaeology."

"Archaeology, eh?"

"Yes, she studied it at uni, got a degree, a good one, but there's no future in it. Claire couldn't get a job so now she's working as a supply teacher."

"Shame," said Danny. "She must have been pretty good to get an award."

The redhead laughed. "That thing? She was working on a dig as a volunteer and found something, a coin, that got them all really excited. Turned out the site was much more important than they'd thought. It was big news in archaeology circles … Yawn. The people she was working with clubbed together and bought her that but then the site started to attract big names and big money and she never got a look in. She wouldn't part with that thing for a lottery win but it's like an open wound to her."

"Pity though, said Danny. "It's always a shame when someone's dreams get dumped on."

"You some sort of poet or something?"

"Me? No, just a temporary minicab driver." Splashes of pink neon rippled in the darkness ahead. "Anyway, we're here."

The redhead climbed out, then leaned back in. "Thanks for that." She glanced at her watch. "And almost on time. It's on account. Sign yourself up for a nice tip. What's your name?"

"Danny."

"Nice to meet you, Danny the temporary minicab driver. I'm Minty."

Then she ducked out and slammed the door.

\*\*\*

Sir Charles held the crystal decanter above the half-filled whisky glass and paused to consider before adding another generous splash.

"I must say, Margaret," he said as he settled back in his armchair. "You don't seem very enthusiastic."

Lady Margaret tipped her head to one side as she considered the question. "I'm not sure I am, Charles."

A low growl of disapproval rumbled in Sir Charles's throat. "I really don't understand your attitude, I really don't. This could be a real opportunity to make a difference to this country, to be of service. So few people are prepared to stand up for their beliefs these days. If the call comes, how can I not answer it?"

"Perhaps you have to, Charles, but it's your call, not mine."

"Really, Margaret, so you don't believe in all the things we've talked about."

"Oh, some of it makes sense but a lot makes me uneasy. I don't really think things are quite that black and white."

"Is that meant to be a joke?"

"No, Charles, I was just trying to make a point, the same point I always make. You are obsessed with the idea of saving the country you love in honour of your long line of ancestors who helped to build it. I'm not sure the country you want is the country other people want but I respect your belief. If I have an obsession, it's Australia and the children."

"So you're saying it is all right to put personal desires before duty?"

"Yes, Charles, that is what I'm saying. Sometimes I think it is right."

"Well, I don't know what to say. I had hoped for a little more support, a little more loyalty."

"I think you'll find that works in both directions, Charles."

"At least I have Edmund."

Lady Margaret shook her head. "Edmund Salter is an unhappy young man. He has never accepted he is no longer the business wheeler dealer he was when he was building holiday homes around the Mediterranean in the boom years.

"He has never acknowledged the pain and losses he caused when his little empire collapsed. Your personal assistant is opinionated, ambitious using you to claw his way back up whatever greasy ladder he has in mind."

"Well really, Margaret. I never knew you saw him like that."

"You never asked."

"Edmund Salter is a fine young man, my right-hand man. I will not have you speak of him like that."

The telephone rang. Sir Charles heaved himself from the armchair with a grunt and crossed the room to the small table in the corner. When he answered he listened for a moment, pulled a sour face and mouthed a name to Margaret.

"Mr Archer, wonderful to hear from you."

"Likewise, Sir Charles. I got your email about the DVDs. So it'll be a selection of speeches then?"

"That's right, Archer. A clear and unambiguous statement of policy objectives that will really put across what we stand for."

"Gotta stand up for what we believe in, eh, Sir Charles?"

"Quite so."

"It's just, crunching the numbers, it looks a bit pricey."

"Can you place a monetary value on patriotism, Mr Archer?"

" 'Spose not. Tell you what, I'll ask around, see if I can get a better deal."

"Very well," said Sir Charles. "But you are still prepared to bear the cost?"

"No problem, Sir Charles. You can rely on me. I'll be in touch."

"I look forward to it, Mr Archer."

Sir Charles out put the phone down and looked at his hands as if they needed washing.

\*\*\*

The barman was young but a bad case of acne did not seem to have dented his self-confidence. It was clear from the start that he spent a lot more time gelling his hair into spikes than he did perfecting his customer service skills.

The name tag, pinned just below his "Challenge 21" badge said Dell.

"Not a clue, mate," he said as he handed Danny his change.

"Joe Walsh, old guy, drinks in here regularly."

Dell shook his head and his mouth puckered with doubt. "Look, we get a load of old geezers in here. I've got a lot of work to do and it doesn't include counting pensioners."

"Customers," said Danny.

"What?" said Dell.

"They're not pensioners, they're customers. They're the people who pay your wages."

Dell's eyes widened. He thought for a moment, then leaned forward. "If you're going to cause trouble I can get you barred."

"Who's in charge?"

Dell considered for a moment, then shrugged and called over his shoulder, "Maureen!"

A small plump woman wearing a "Maureen – Duty Manager" tag above her Challenge 21 badge bustled round the corner. She looked at Dell, looked at Danny. Sections of the staff training manual flashed through her mind before she turned to Danny, her face breaking into a wide professional smile. "Is there a problem?"

Danny smiled back. "I'm trying to find an old family friend, Joe Walsh. I'm told he's a regular."

The smile stuck to Maureen's face seem to soften a little. "Joe? Lovely man. Old fashioned manners."

She rose up on tiptoe and scanned the bar, then pointed. "Over there in the booth at the back, with the white hair, reading the racing section."

"Thank you, Maureen" said Danny.

"No trouble, sir."

Danny turned, "And thank you, Dell."

The barman broke away from studying his hair in the mirror behind the bar. "No worries, mate."

Danny was aware of a hissed exchange between the pair as he crossed the room, studying Joe as he went. The man was quite tall but his frailty was visible from the gap between his thin neck and the collars of his shirt and blazer, the space around his wrists within the cuffs. A walking stick was propped against the table.

"Joe Walsh?"

The old man turned stiffly, taking a moment to focus.

"I don't want no DVDs."

"I've come about Billy. Can I buy you a pint?"

\*\*\*

"Digby?"

"Yes."

"I've found it."

"The consignment?"

"Yup, my man couldn't be more helpful after we'd had our little chat."

"Excellent, Rookwood. Do you have it yet?"

"Got to check the place out first, discreet like. Make sure we're not in for any surprises."

"I can't stress the urgency, Rookwood. We need this resolved and quickly."

"Like I said, it's all under control."

"When will you have it?"

"If everything checks out, tomorrow."

"Keep me informed. And change your SIM card again."

Rookwood cut the connection, looking down at the mobile in his hand, squeezing it in his big fist until he heard the plastic casing creak.

\*\*\*

The door was opened by a tall beefy teenager with puffy stupid eyes. iPod leads snaked from his ears and his jaw circled repeatedly as he attacked a wad of gum.

"Yeah?"

"I'm looking for Eddie Archer."

The teen pulled a white lead from one ear.

"What?"

"I said I'm looking for Eddie Archer."

The teenager grimaced at the effort of half turning his head to shout over his shoulder. "*DAD!*"

Danny heard a muffled reply from deep inside the house. "He's in the kitchen," said the teenager before plodding off back up the stairs.

Danny walked down the long broad hallway into a bright modern kitchen packed with top-of-the-range equipment. The place was heated like a sauna. The Rolling Stones's Sympathy For The Devil, blasting out from an iPod speaker dock by the bread bin, was making the windows rattle.

The man standing in front of the gas cooker tore his attention away from a sizzling pan, turned the volume down and looked up.

"Best rock 'n' roll band ever, The Stones. First saw them at Knebworth back in seventy six. You a fan?" His big hands danced along the edge of the marble worktop, tapping out the bongo beat.

Danny nodded.

The guy had been in the papers and on TV but this was the first time Danny had seen Big Eddie Archer in the flesh. It wasn't hard to see how he'd got his reputation. Dressed in a Jack Pyke camo t-shirt stretched across a powerful chest, khaki cargo shorts and brilliant white Adidas trainers, Archer was well over six foot of muscle just starting to show its age.

Cropped grey hair looked like frost against his mahogany scalp. His whole body was burned to a leathery Costas tan. A chunky gold chain nestled in the thick curly hair across his shoulders and neck and he wore a Help For Heroes band on his right wrist, a big gold diver's watch on the left.

Pale blue eyes above a boxer's nose sparkled with a light that could have been humour or madness. On his chin was a razor-neat white goatee.

As Danny studied Archer he saw the man weighing him up in return. Archer broke into a smile of bright white teeth.

"So you're Danny."

Danny nodded. "And you're Eddie Archer."

Archer smiled. "Please allow me to introduce myself. Bacon sandwich?" He indicated the sizzling pan.

"Yeah, why not."

"My speciality, they are. The secret's to get the oil hot and not leave them in too long, otherwise they get dry." He picked up a spatula and chased half a dozen rashers around the pan.

Danny took a step towards the French windows for a look into the garden but stopped when he heard the growling.

"THATCHER!" roared Archer.

Danny half turned to see a bull terrier in the doorway, jaws half open, red eyes locked on.

"Thatcher! Clear off!" The dog's head drooped for a moment. It looked from Archer to Danny and back again, then turned and trotted away into the house.

When Danny caught Archer's eye the man grinned. "What? You think I'm taking the piss?"

Archer waved his spatula at Danny. "That dog knows what it wants and it goes for it. She's single-minded, focussed and courageous. Those are qualities I admire. That's what Maggie had before they shafted her."

"Skids said you wanted to see me."

Archer turned his attention back to the pan, buttering bread as he kept an eye on the bacon.

"Just a social visit, that's all," he said. "I like to get to know my employees, know who I can trust, if you know what I mean."

"I'm not your employee," said Danny. "I work for Skids."

"All right, son, don't take offence. Let's call ourselves colleagues then. I'm always curious about new people."

Archer flipped three rashers onto a buttered slice and pressed the top slice down hard before handing the plate to Danny. As he bent his arm a crown of wrinkles puckered the crest of his big biceps.

"I'm not sure what I'm doing here. I don't want any trouble."

"Trouble?" Archer laughed. "You're worried about being seen hanging around with a gangster? You've been reading the papers too much, son. The media's bollocks. You can't believe a word."

Archer picked up his plate and gestured Danny towards a tall stool. They settled either side of the marble island in the centre of the kitchen.

"Well," said Danny. "I guess you'd know about that."

"You're not wrong there. If I had a pound for every bit of bullshit they've written about me I'd be richer than I am already. What do you think of the sarnie?"

Danny nodded as he chewed, swallowing a little before saying, "Yeah, good. Nice and moist."

"Told you. Very misunderstood animal, your pig. This stuff's good, organic. You are what you eat and these days it's too much salt and chemicals. Just look it up on the internet."

They ate in silence for a while, occasionally catching each other's eye as they formed their impressions. Danny finished first and put down the plate. The house was like a sauna and he was sweating under his jacket but he kept it on. He didn't want to get too comfortable.

Archer put the plates in the sink and switched on the kettle. As he sat down again Danny said, "So what happened to Sammy Spoon then?"

Archer spread his hands on the marble table top. "You're a cheeky bastard, aren't you?"

"Well," said Danny. "You said the media was rubbish. I just wondered what happened."

"You ever meet Sammy?"

"No, just read about it in the papers."

"Well you'll have read about the court case. That bit they got right. There was no body. I was found not guilty. Like I said at the time, I heard Sammy had retired to Florida. You take sugar?"

Danny shook his head and watched Archer brew up in two big Seagulls mugs. The big man blew on his tea before turning pale blue eyes on Danny.

"Bring your mug."

Danny followed Archer across the hall into a vast living room dominated by three white leather sofas grouped under the biggest cut-glass chandelier he had ever seen. On the wall was a flat screen TV that must have been sixty inches.

Archer led the way to a bookcase packed with pictures. He waved his mug at a photo of a large woman in a sundress holding a pink cocktail with an umbrella in it.

"That's my Miriam, been gone six years now, she has. And on top of that lazy lummox upstairs I've got four daughters so I'm an expert on PMT, believe me. That one on the end, that's Vicky, my youngest."

He waved the mug along a lower shelf. "And that's the grandkids, seven so far. Love 'em to bits."

Danny looked at a line of pictures showing kids playing, partying and holidaying, mugging for the camera, sticking their tongues out, pulling faces.

Archer pointed at a portrait of a toddler with her hair in plaits, smiling shyly for the camera. "And that's my little jewel."

Something in Archer's voice made Danny look across at him. Aware he was being studied, Archer turned away.

"Some people think I'm some sort of brain-dead psychopath. In my old line of work you needed a firm hand but I'm a civilised guy. Not opera civilised, ordinary civilised. I watch Dr Who with my grandkids. That redhead's fit. I got a bit teary when Morse died. It's all about loyalty and family values. Trust me, I bleed like anyone else."

Archer waited for Danny to say something but when he didn't he carried on. "We all do stuff when we're kids. I bet you've put the wind up your mum and dad more than once. Okay, so I used to be a criminal. At least we had the decency to admit it, unlike that shower at Westminster with their flipping second homes. Me, now I'm a businessman, a farmer and a philanthropist.

"I invest in local outfits like your mate Skidmarks. I've got some land out near Pyecombe, grow some organics, spuds, carrots, brussels. I love a nice crisp brussel. Keep a few animals as well, goats, some porkers, lovely animals they are, Tamworths, the Ferrari of the pig world. It's a hobby, restful, rhythm of life. Get some dirt under your fingernails. Did you know goats' milk's good for asthmatics? I read that on the internet. Then I do a bit of charity work, golf tournaments, that sort of thing."

"Sounds like you keep busy."

"Don't get me wrong, Danny. I've not gone soft. If I see a red door and I want it painted black it's black by teatime, believe me. I just move with the times. Pillar of society now, me, when I'm not soaking up the sun at our little place in Marbella or surfcasting on Cocoa Beach. I love it there, used to watch the rockets blast off from Cape Canaveral, big buggers, light up the night, they did."

Danny put down his tea mug, careful to use a coaster on the coffee table. "The sandwich was great but I still don't know what I'm doing here."

Archer put his mug down next to Danny's. "You speak your mind, son. I like that. And like I said, I just wanted to put a face to a name. And I might be able to put a bit of work your way."

"I don't need any more trouble," said Danny.

Archer shook his head. "Don't worry, nothing illegal."

They both turned at the sound of footsteps thumping down the stairs. Danny saw the kitchen doorway fill with a big man who obviously worked out. Dark narrow eyes assessed him without giving any reaction.

"Deano!" said Archer. "My go-to guy. Danny, this is Dean McKeown, my fixer, secretary, chauffeur, hatchet man, minder and all round strong right arm. And left arm, for that matter. Deano, Danny's doing a bit of driving for me."

The two men nodded briefly at each other.

Danny heard a scratching sound and looked down to see Thatcher watching them. It struck him that Dean and the dog had the same eyes.

## CHAPTER 9

The door creaked as it opened and the old man stood blinking for a moment before he recognised his visitor.

"Oh, you found it then?"

Danny nodded.

"Well, you'd better come inside."

As he crossed the coconut mat on the front step Danny saw Joe Walsh's place was small and neat with a faint musty smell

"Cuppa tea, son?"

"No thanks," said Danny. "I'm fine."

"Come on in the front room then."

Danny followed Joe into a small room where a worn three-piece suite jostled for space around an old stone fireplace and a small television on its own table.

The old man lowered himself into an armchair with a long sigh. "Make yourself at home."

Danny settled on the sofa opposite. "Thanks, you don't mind the dog?"

"Nah," said Joe, smiling down at Monty as he shook his head. "He's a lovely little fella. And I need all the company I can get at my time of life. Young Barry, my grandson, he visits regular but he's got his own life to lead. Can't fritter it away on an old sod like me."

Monty did a circuit of the room, snuffling his wet nose into corners. When he reached Joe's shoes he licked the toe caps, looked up expectantly, then went on to examine the heels. With a grunt of effort Joe leaned forward in his chair and reached down to scratch the fur behind Monty's ear. The dog looked up with shining eyes.

Danny took the opportunity to look around. The shelf beside the old man's chair was packed with framed photographs. At the centre was a wedding couple. The black and white image was flanked by pictures of smiling children.

The shelf below displayed half a dozen small darts trophies on the left and a collection of books on British birds on the right. The old man watched as Danny took it all in.

"Not much, I know, but I'm comfortable and it's home."

"You live alone?"

"Yes, eight years now since Nora passed but my daughter only lives in Saltdean and her boy, Barry, he comes to see me regularly. He's a lovely lad."

"I was sorry to hear about your mate."

"Ah, Billy, a lovely fella. Must have known him the best part of seventy years."

"And you heard about the burglary?"

"Saw it in the local rag. I was absolutely bloody disgusted. There's no respect these days. Poor old Billy served his country and some druggie yobbo does that to him. Hanging's too good for people like that."

"I know what you mean."

"You been in the army then?"

Danny nodded. "Paras."

"Whereabouts?

"Afghan."

Joe nodded slowly to himself. "So you know what it's all about then."

"Yes."

"Billy and me, we were in Normandy together. That was no picnic either, like the trenches in the first war at times."

"I've heard."

"Scared silly half the time but you soon find out who your mates are."

"I know."

"Would you like to see some pictures?"

"I'd love to, Joe."

The old man reached onto a shelf and Danny was suddenly ten years old again, crossed-legged on the carpet at his grandad's feet, as Joe brought out a dog-eared old album of black and white photographs between thick cardboard covers.

Danny crossed the narrow room and squatted by Joe's armchair as he began to turn the pages. Monty sat up on his back legs, paws begging for another scratch. When no one took any notice he set off around the room again, sniffing.

Joe tapped an arthritic finger on an old brown photo. "That's us in training, hardly old enough to shave but cocky none the less. It was later on we had some sense knocked into us. That one's church parade and that's the old motorbike Billy bought with some money his nan had saved up for him, an Enfield. We had some times tearing about on that thing, I can tell you."

Joe turned another page and looked thoughtfully at the pictures. "These were taken near Caen. That was a dog's breakfast if ever there was one. Supposed to take it on the first day, we were. Took us six weeks and a lot of good blokes."

Joe tapped a photograph of two soldiers standing either side of the entrance to a battered concrete bunker, heads tipped back and cigarettes hanging from the corners of their mouths. "That's me and Billy."

Danny saw the two men grinning at the camera, faces coated in dirt and eyes baggy with exhaustion and fear. He knew those faces.

The old man looked at the album on his lap for a long time, his twig of a finger tapping the translucent foil that protected them. Danny crouched by his side, listening to the whistle of his breathing.

"Can you think of anyone who might want to hurt Billy's memory?"

The old man shook his head.

"It's possible that what happened to his ashes was some sort of accident, just a burglar in a hurry, but it doesn't look like it," said Danny. "Billy's wife's very upset and his daughter's asked me to look into it. I do a bit of investigating."

"He was a lovely fella without an enemy in the world that I knew of. We were like brothers, closer than family sometimes."

Joe snapped the album shut. "Put that back for me, would you?"

Danny slotted the album into its place on the shelf and noticed a box. "You've got a few other mementoes, I see."

As he pulled the box free he was surprised at how heavy it was. The old man blinked when he saw it in Danny's hands. "Just my campaign medals and a few bits of paperwork, that sort of thing."

"Mind if I have a look?"

The old man said nothing so Danny opened the lid. He recognised an old army pay book and some yellowing discharge documents, the fragile paper splitting along its ancient creases.

Beneath them were six medals hanging by their ribbons from a strip decorated with matching colours to ensure the awards were in the right order. Danny held them up to the light to study them, the war medal, defence medal, 39-45 star, France and Germany star, territorial efficiency medal and a Normandy veterans medal. Then he laid them carefully to one side.

Under the medals was a large bronze disc, the metal badly discoloured by age. The disc was decorated with a relief of Britannia and a lion. Inside a rectangular box was engraved in capital letters the name "Cecil Arthur Walsh".

Danny held it up to the weak overhead light as he ran his thumb over the raised images on its surface.

"Death penny," said Joe. "They gave one out for everyone who copped it in the first war. That one's for my uncle, killed at Ypres in 1917." The old man's milky eyes seemed to grow cloudier, their rims redder. "He was blown to bits. They never found anything. 'Known unto God', that's what they put on the memorials."

Danny placed the death penny gently to one side with the medals. In the bottom of the box, half hidden my yellowing papers, was something wrapped in a white cloth. As Danny started to draw it out the old man put a hand on his arm.

"Be careful with that, son."

The package was heavy. Resting it on the palm of his left hand, Danny peeled back the cloth.

"Christ!"

"Bill and I took it off a Jerry officer. Wedged it in some railway tracks and fired it with a lanyard just to make sure our ammo fitted."

Danny lifted out a 9mm Browning pistol and turned it over to examine it. The light from the bay window picked out the eagle and swastika emblems on the grips.

Joe reached out and Danny handed it to him, noticing how his arm dropped as he took the weight. The tips of his fingers went white and the old man's hands quivered as he pulled back the slide.

"Whoa, careful with that," said Danny.

The slide snapped open and Joe tilted the gun to show Danny the chamber was empty. "It's not loaded and I prove it to you before I hand it over. Old habits, son. You never forget. Ammo's in the bottom of the box."

"That's quite a souvenir, Joe."

"That's what I thought back then. It scares the bejesus out of me now. I'm frightened the grandkids will find it but don't know how to get rid of it. Barry's not daft but you know what kids are. And it would drop my daughter right in it if someone finds it when I'm gone."

"You've got years left in you, Joe," said Danny, still looking at the pistol.

"If only, son, if only. Hospital says I haven't got too long, prostate cancer they tell me. It's funny to think you can come through a war in one piece and get killed by some little thing living up your arse."

"Tell you what. If the gun bothers you, I'll take it off your hands."

"Would you? What with you being a soldier too, it would be going to a good home."

Danny weighed the weapon in his hand, feeling the coldness of the black steel. "No problem, Joe."

They both turned at Monty's bark. He had slipped out of the room and was standing at the bottom of the stars, yapping at nothing.

"What's upset him?" said Joe.

"Search me," said Danny, rising from his chair. He clapped his hand. "Come here."

The dog glanced in his direction then looked back up the stairs and barked again. Danny clapped his hands but Monty ignored him.

"Sorry about this," said Danny as he put the pistol back in the cloth and placed it on the table. Then he stepped out into the hall, hooked a finger into Monty's collar and dragged him back into the living room. "I'm looking after him for a friend."

Joe chuckled. "Don't you worry. He's not doing any harm. This place could do with a bit more noise now and again."

As Danny began to drop back into his chair Monty made another dash for the hall but he managed to catch his collar and pull him back.

"Sorry about this, Joe. We'd better leave you to it."

The old man looked up from his chair. "You okay with taking that gun?"

"No problem."

There was a gleam in old Joe's eye.

"You couldn't do me a favour, could you?"

"No problem."

"I do like a drop of brandy now and again, helps me sleep. My daughter won't let me and the district nurse says I can't 'cos off my pills. You couldn't drop me a bottle off, if you're passing?"

Danny patted the pistol lying in its white cloth on the table. "It's the least I can do."

\*\*\*

Danny guessed why the hall light was on in his flat when he opened the front door but he was still wary. It wasn't a habit you could ever break.

He closed the door quietly and called out, "Hello?"

"I'm in the kitchen."

When he walked in Emma was stacking small boxes into a kitchen cupboard. "I was just dropping off your mum's prescriptions on my way home."

"Oh, right," said Danny. "You got time for a cuppa?"

Emma smiled and nodded, "That would be nice." Danny put the kettle on and rinsed two mugs.

As Emma finished stacking the medicines Danny stepped up behind her and slid his hands around her waist. He felt her tense, then relax a little.

They stood for a moment, listening to the kettle wheeze, their bodies hesitantly moulding to each other. He smelled her hair, the scent of some fruity shampoo with a hint of disinfectant.

"About earlier," said Danny.

"Yes?"

"I was thinking … well, what I meant was…"

He felt her suddenly tense, became aware of her looking down.

"What's that?" she asked.

"What's what?"

"On your hands?"

Danny looked down over her shoulder at his splayed fingers and noticed for the first time a dark orange stain etched into the creases of his hands. He looked puzzled. "I don't know."

Emma stepped away from him and turned. Danny turned he saw her eyes blazing. "Well I bloody do."

"What?"

"You bastard!"

"Emma, what is it?"

"Don't play the innocent with me, Danny Lancaster. Do you really think I look that stupid."

"Emma, what are you talking about?"

"Drop dead, Danny, just drop dead."

She scooped her coat off the back of a kitchen chair.

"Emma?"

She grabbed her bag and rushed out of the room.

Startled, he called after her, "What's up, Emma?"

"As if you didn't know. It's fake tan." The front door crashed shut just as Danny's mobile began to ring.

"Danny Lancaster … now? Yes, okay."

The kettle started to boil.

***

Danny left Monty in the Skoda near Hove's big Co-op store and walked across the car park behind a bunch of lively pensioners.

The tall, slim guy with the head of white hair was telling a long story about the entertainment on a Mediterranean cruise they'd had a few years back.

Danny followed them through the swing doors and the lobby and into the bar beyond. It was fairly busy, knots of men sat round circular tables, drinking and studying form.

He looked around the room, studying faces. Nothing clicked so he moved on through to the terrace. He was looking at the odds being offered by the trackside bookies when he heard a shout and turned.

"Danny!"

Big Eddie Archer stood head and shoulders above the crowd, waving a rolled race programme over his head.

When they reached each other Archer clapped him on the shoulder.

"Good of you to come."

Before Danny could reply, Dean McKeown loomed out of the crowds behind his boss.

"You a betting man, Danny?" asked Archer.

"Only when the odds are in my favour."

Archer laughed and clapped him on the shoulder again.

"Nice one, I like it." He opened his programme and held it out to Danny. "What do you fancy in the next race?"

Danny took the booklet and studied the packed text. He used to bet, when he was younger, on the horses. Had a bit of luck but things usually evened out, then went downhill. It was good fun for the odd day out but as a full-time pursuit it was a mug's game. Besides, he didn't have the cash to spare.

Danny ran his eyes down the list of runners. The favourite had good form, winning three of her last four races. The third on the list had a bit of a patchy record but hadn't raced for two weeks. She could be hungry for a win. He tapped the listing with his finger.

"No3, Cloudy Lady."

Archer nodded thoughtfully. "Not bad, I fancy Sarah's Star myself. You having a punt?"

Danny shook his head. "Mug's game. Besides, I'm skint."

Archer pulled a thick fold of notes from inside his jacket and turned to McKeown.

"Here, Deano, a tenner on Sarah's Star and the same on Cloudy Lady." He pushed a sheaf of notes at McKeown. "And get the drinks in as well."

McKeown took the money. His mouth started to move but nothing came out. He looked hard at Danny and turned away.

"He's a lovely fella when you get to know him. He just looks like he bites the heads off babies."

Archer rubbed his hands together. "Bloody parky out here." He glanced up at the sweeping glass frontage of the Skyline Restaurant above them, raised tiers of diners peering out over the track. "Still, you've got to be up close to really enjoy it, see the runners up close, smell the tension."

McKeown returned with the drinks. He handed Danny and Archer a plastic mug of Stella each and placed his own on the ground between them before turning away towards the bookies.

"The Tote's all right when you're dabbling," said Archer. "But you need a real bookie if you're going to take it seriously. They only take bets to win. You've got to take the risk if you want to enjoy the reward, eh?"

Archer waved his pint towards a statue of a racing dog at the front of the terrace.

"Ballyregan Bob," he said. "Racked up his 32$^{nd}$ consecutive win here on December 9, 1986, a world record. Now that's what you call a winner."

Danny nodded, sipped his pint. McKeown returned and handed the betting slips and change to Archer.

The three of them stood in silence as the runners paraded along the path in front of the terrace. On the grass at the far end one dog squatted. Archer laughed. "That one's mine. You wouldn't want to cart that lot around 515 metres. She'll run lighter for that."

They continued to watch as the dogs were led back towards the traps.

"I said I might be able to put a bit of work your way," said Archer.

"And I said I don't need any trouble," said Danny.

Archer shook his head. "Don't fret about it, no dodgy packages. It's nothing illegal. Christ, if I wanted someone to deliver some charlie, and I say 'if', remember I'm out of the business now, you're the last man I'm going to pick."

Danny said nothing. Archer continued. "Skids says you're a good man. It's more … confidential … sensitive, delivering important documents for a project I'm working on, courier work. You okay with that?"

"I need the money."

"You must be a bit curious?"

"So long as it's kosher, no."

Archer turned pale blue eyes on Danny and squeezed his arm. The man's power wasn't just muscle. With a friend like that you could be walking on eggshells but it was better than having him as an enemy.

"Right answer, son."

All three of them turned at the sound of the bell, catching the action just as the hare passed the traps. The six dogs flew along the track, eyes wide and teeth bared, a rippling pack of undulating muscle in a fine spray of pale sand, dolphin-smooth and relishing the challenge.

Sarah's Star, in the blue and white colours, was half a body's length ahead of the pack as they blitzed past the terrace, extended paws hissing on the sand track.

Archer jerked a balled fist. "Come on, my son, come on."

At the bend the pack was still tight. The straight line from the traps had morphed into an ellipse of muscle, rising and falling with lean, economic movement.

As they went into the straight on the far side Sarah's Star had gained a few feet but another dog was clinging to his side, followed closely by Cloudy Lady.

The sounds from the crowd grew louder. It was still tight and too close to call when the six dogs leaned into the last bend and headed for the finish.

As they drew close Archer slapped his forehead with the race programme.

"Fuck me!"

Two seconds later the pack, no more than three dogs' lengths from front to back, crossed the line with Cloudy Lady a head in front.

Archer turned to Danny and there was a light in the big man's eyes he couldn't read. They stood for a moment. Archer and McKeown looking at Danny, then Archer started to laugh.

"I should have known," he said. "There's something about you…"

He held out the betting slip. Danny looked down at it.

"You paid the stake money."

"Yeah, but you cash it in. It was your pick. Look on it as a down payment."

Danny took the slip and raised his pint to Archer.

"Cheers."

\*\*\*

Danny couldn't face going back to the silent flat. He had driven around for a while, thinking. Then he decided he might as well do something useful so he stopped at a Tesco Express before heading towards Woodingdean.

He'd rung the doorbell four times and was about to turn away when he heard the squeak of the Yale turning.

Joe Walsh stood in the doorway, gripping the frame for support.

"Sorry it's so late, Joe."

"No problem, son. I don't sleep much these days."

Danny held out a carrier bag and Joe's face lit up when he saw the stretched plastic outlining the shape of a bottle.

"Come in, come in."

Monty hopped around the old man's ankles with excitement. Danny had the lead on this time and pulled the dog clear before he tripped him.

They followed Joe into his living room and the old man eased himself into his armchair with a sigh of relief.

"You'll join me?" he said, admiring the bottle as he turned it between his bent fingers.

"I'm driving," said Danny.

"Yeah, they don't like that these days, do they?"

Danny and Monty watched as Joe took a tea mug from the table beside him and tipped the dregs into a wastepaper basket. Despite his twisted fingers, he had no trouble breaking the seal of the bottle's cap.

Joe poured a generous measure into the stained tea cup, gulped three mouthfuls, sank back in his chair and let out a long satisfied sigh.

"Thanks, son, I really appreciate that."

"No problem, Joe. Might as well die from brandy as prostate cancer."

Joe rattled a laughed. "You're right there, son."

They both looked up as a floorboard creaked.

"It's just Barry," said Joe. "My daughter's boy. I'm rattling round like a pea in a drum in this place. It's handy for the pubs in town if he's out on the tiles with his mates so he uses the old box room sometimes when he stays over."

Monty dashed for the door, trailing his lead, but Danny stamped on it before he made it.

"Sit!"

The dog waited at Danny's feet, eyes bright, tongue darting. Joe took another slug from his tea cup and sighed again.

Danny was about to speak when Monty made another dash for the door. Danny missed his lead by three inches and the dog was gone. They could hear his paws scampering along the hall and up the stairs.

"He's a lively one, isn't he?" said Joe with a wheezy chuckle.

Danny stood up. "I'd better get him before he craps on your carpets."

He went into the hall and up the stairs, calling the dog's name, following the sound of yapping.

At the top of the stairs he found a toilet and a room with a commode chair beside a bed. Beyond was another door. It was open and he could hear Monty's excited yapping. When he stepped into the doorway he saw a chubby teenager sitting on the bed, folded arms clamping a black shoulder bag to his chest. Monty was dancing around, his barking growing more frantic.

"Who the fuck are you?"

"Friend of Joe's. You Barry?" The boy nodded.

"What's in the bag?"

The boy gripped it tighter, shook his head.

"What is it," said Danny. "Drugs?"

Barry shook his head again. Danny reached out.

"Hand it over."

The boy shook his head.

"Don't mess me about. Hand it over."

The boy pouted his refusal, gripped the bag tighter. Then he looked reluctantly up at Danny, saw the look in his eyes. Danny's fingers flicked a command. Barry handed over the bag.

Danny unclipped the straps and opened it. In the bottom was a jumble of rubbish, crumpled notepaper, sweet wrappers. The only bulky item in there was a Tupperware container.

Danny drew it out and tilted it against the light. A grey powder sighed back and forth inside the plastic tub as he turned it.

"What's this then?"

Barry let out a little strangled sob.

"Grandad said Billy was his best mate."

Danny looked hard at the boy.

"You bloody idiot."

## CHAPTER 10

It was his last job and Danny would be glad when it was over. Despite Archer's assurances, the idea of these courier runs made him uneasy.

It was taking someone a lifetime to answer the door. Danny was about to ring for the third time when he heard the lock start to turn.

"Yes?"

The man in the doorway was tall, dressed in chinos and a striped shirt. A flopped fringe of thick brown hair fell across his face. He pushed it away from his eyes and looked at Danny as if he could smell something.

"Package for Wolfram," said Danny.

"Would that be Sir Charles Wolfram?"

"That's what it says on the packet," said Danny.

"Well," said the man, sweeping away the fringe again. "As the gentleman in question is a knight, it wouldn't be too much to accord him his proper title, would it?"

Danny watched the man for a moment, didn't react.

"I'm Mr Lancaster and I've got a package for Wolfram."

The man in the door shook his head in resignation.

"Oh, very well. Give it to me."

"Personal delivery, for Wolfram," said Danny.

The man gave a theatrical sigh.

"I am Edmund Salter, Sir Charles's personal assistant. I handle all his affairs."

"I'm sure you do," said Danny. "But you're not handling this package."

Salter's weary contempt flashed across into anger.

"Do you know who you're talking to?"

"Edmund Salter, you just said."

"I can speak with your employer."

"Feel free, Edmund. Doesn't change the fact this package is personal delivery, for Wolfram."

Salter held Danny's gaze, then broke away and took a step back into the flat. His voice softened and rose when he spoke, calling down the hallway.

"Sir Charles? Sir Charles?"

A deep, irritated voice from the depths of the apartment. "What is it, Edmund?"

"A package for you, Sir Charles."

"Well take it in, will you."

"Sir Charles," Salter called again. "The delivery man needs to speak with you."

Danny moved into the hallway, forcing Salter to take a step back. As he looked inside he saw a stocky man with thinning hair combed sideways over his head appear in the doorway of the room at the far end.

"You Sir Charles?"

"I am."

"Package for you, sir, personal delivery."

"Give it to my assistant, would you."

Salter snatched the package.

"And give him one of the recordings, Edmund," added Sir Charles.

Salter snatched a CD from the table by the door and thrust it at Danny.

Danny grinned. "What, no tip, Edmund?"

The door slammed.

\*\*\*

Monty was hopping frantically, paws scrabbling at the wooden panels of the front door. Danny could see a metal plate screwed to the frame where repairs had been carried out around the lock.

When the door opened Monty yelped with delight and bolted through Barbara Harvey's legs into the hallway.

She tried to smile. "Mr Lancaster, any news?"

"Mind if I come in?"

Barbara stepped aside and held the door as Danny walked into the hall.

"Go through. Mum's in there. Would you like some tea?"

"No thanks, I'm fine."

She followed him into the living room where Doreen Baines was sitting in an armchair watching an afternoon quiz show on television. On the table beside her stood a cup of tea and a plate of Hobnobs, untouched.

She looked smaller than Danny remembered, shrunken, as if she had been partially deflated. She didn't react.

"How's she been?" he asked.

Barbara shook her head. "Doctor's been. He's given her something but I don't know if it's doing any good. She just sits."

Danny watched Barbara as she looked down at her mother, lost in her thoughts. When she realised Danny was still standing beside her she looked up and forced a smile.

"So, Mr Lancaster, have you any news? Have you found the little bastard that did this?"

Danny drew a bulky Tesco carrier bag from his pocket and held it out for Barbara.

"Sorry about the packaging. Thought I'd better get him back to you as soon as I could."

Barbara took the bag and as she opened it a look of wonder spread over her face.

"How …? How did…?"

"It's all there, all that was taken."

"What about the little ratbag who did it?"

"I was going to ask you about that. Would it be okay with you if I sorted him out, unless you want to press charges. I just thought it might be easier that way, less stress for your mum."

"I just want this over with," said Barbara. "If you can sort him out you go ahead and do it. He deserves everything he gets."

"He's made a start," said Danny, drawing a fold of ten pound notes from his pocket. "That's towards the damage. If it doesn't cover it I'll get some more from him to make up the difference."

"Oh, Mr Lancaster, I … How much do I owe you?"

"Forget it."

"No, please, I couldn't possibly…"

"Okay, call it a tenner for petrol."

They turned at a croaking sound. Doreen Baines had looked away from the television, up at the two of them.

"Is that Billy? Is he home?"

\*\*\*

No matter how Danny shifted, he couldn't get comfortable. It had been a long day and he needed a kip but the minicab office's furniture was a joke.

The old armchair's threadbare upholstery sagged and the springs were shot. It groaned every time he moved.

He recrossed his extended legs and a puff of dust squirted from the cushion on the old stool under his feet. His left leg hurt, even though it wasn't there. A tingling sensation danced around the stump beneath his jeans before it turned into a series of twinges. He flexed his thigh muscles. It helped a bit.

"Those car parts any use?" he asked Skidmarks.

"No, turned out to be some sort of crank shaft, fifty of them. I couldn't work out what they were. The label said vehicle parts but it must have been specialist stuff. I asked around, thought I might flog them, but no one was interested. How are you getting on with your quad bike?"

Danny pulled a face. "Seemed like a good idea at the time. Trouble is, after all the publicity, I'd stick out like a dog's tackle if I start riding it around Brighton. It's stashed in Bob's lock-up till I work out what to do with it."

Danny shifted position again and the armchair gave a slight jolt as something inside gave way.

"Bloody hell, Skids, why don't you get some decent furniture in here?"

Skidmarks put his tea mug down on a table that tilted under the weight. "Believe me, Danny, I would if I could but it's hard enough making the money to keep the lights on and the radio running. The way things are, I'll be lucky to be in business next month unless Mr Archer comes up with the money he promised."

"That bad, eh?"

"Worse, the minicab business can't compete with the big boys like Streamline and Brighton & Hove. It's all automated booking and GPS now. Did you know with these new petrol-electric motors you can get 65mpg from a two-litre engine?"

Danny shook his head.

"That's what you need in this game, cost savings."

"Why not give it a try?" asked Danny.

Skidmarks rubbed his fingertips together. "It costs. And on top of that, the garage is on its last legs. I had a guy in earlier about some servicing work. Dodgy looking character but I can't afford to be choosy."

Danny plucked a red pepper from his doner kebab, then bit off a corner of limp meat and pitta bread, chewing thoughtfully. The meat was cold and clammy. Danny regretted buying it, wished he'd stuck to his training diet. It had seemed a good idea at the time. He tried to get comfortable again but all the armchair did was creak.

"Sounds grim."

"It is mate. And I'm sorry, Danny, but I won't be able to keep you on much longer, the way things are, not unless Archer comes across."

Danny shrugged and sipped his tepid tea thoughtfully. "Shit happens. It's the same all over."

"Things not going well with you then?"

Danny shrugged again. "This detective lark is a tougher nut than I thought. I've just finished one case, body snatching, but it didn't really pay. Still, all you can do is keep on going."

"I suppose so," said Skidmarks with a gloomy grimace. "But it would be nice to see some light at the end of the tunnel. We're supposed to be having a romantic weekend away next month. That's going to cost."

Danny nodded. "I bet, what have you got planned?"

"We thought maybe Amsterdam but it depends on the money."

"Doesn't it always. Does your other half know about the business?"

Skidmarks pulled another face. "Not really. I've tried to explain but Richard just doesn't seem to understand how serious things are."

"Richard?"

Skids looked up sharply. "Yes, what of it?"

"Nothing," said Danny.

"Look, we're gay, okay? It's not all lycra and Judy Garland. You got a problem with that?"

Danny shrugged. "No problem at all."

Skidmarks relaxed back into his seat. "Thing is, Richard's got his own money. Being broke is embarrassing."

"I know the feeling. Emma's been in a funny mood of late. Something's going on but don't ask me what."

"She still with that loser you told me about?"

"Benny? Yes, she's back home with him but comes round to mine every day to see to mum. It's a bit weird sometimes."

They lapsed into a thoughtful silence. Danny lit a cigarette and as the smoke billowed around him he heard the faint sound of shuffling footsteps outside. The noise was replaced by bubbling spasms of violent coughing, then something wet spatted onto the pavement.

Danny watched a hunched shadow move slowly across the frosted window of the minicab office. The shape paused and a spread hand, like an extended starfish, turned pale as it pressed briefly against the glass.

"Punter?" asked Danny.

Skidmarks looked over his shoulder at the shadow. "No such luck. It's Aqualung."

"Who?"

"He used to work here. Knew my old man, helped me set this place up. Then he got into a messy divorce, hit the bottle and it all unravelled from there."

"Sounds grim," said Danny. "What's he doing here?"

"I let him doss round the back of the workshop, bung him a few quid when I can. It's sad."

Danny nodded as he listened to the fading sound of shuffling feet. "It's a comfort to know there's always someone worse off than you are." He looked at the congealed kebab for a moment but decided he'd had enough.

Skidmarks inspected the inside of his mug. "Another brew?"

Danny nodded. As Skidmarks was putting on the kettle he said, "Look, Danny, I appreciate you helping me out, I really do, but it doesn't look like we're going to get any business tonight. If you want to get off home, you go ahead."

Danny stretched in the old chair, listened to the rusted springs groaning. "That's okay, Skids. I've got nowhere to be. Might as well keep you company. Anyway, I'm just starting to get comfy."

\*\*\*

When he thought about it later, Danny was sure it was the sound of skidding tyres that woke him. As he stretched in the old armchair he could see rain wriggling down the frosted glass, lit by the street lamp opposite. His leg ached and his back hurt. Skidmarks was snoring on an old sofa, head back, mouth open.

Danny was halfway out of the armchair when the flash lit the room. A split second later, before he had a chance to realise what was happening, the office was hit by a deafening bang.

The walls creaked and the frosted glass shattered into lethal chunks that scattered across the cluttered office. A mug of cold tea toppled over and ring binders fell from the shelves above Skidmarks's desk. The bare light bulb hanging from a cobwebbed flex in the centre of the ceiling danced a mad jig.

Skidmarks sat bolt upright, rubbing his face in disbelief. "What the f..." As Danny wrenched open the office door a second explosion shook the building. He ducked his head outside, then dived back in.

"The workshop's on fire."

Skidmarks stumbled to where Danny was standing, disorientated and dopey from sleep, pushing his shirt back into his trousers. "What?"

"The workshop, it's on fire."

Skidmarks blinked repeatedly, a look of disbelief on his puffy features. As Danny watched, his eyes widened with shock. "Aqualung's in there."

"Shit," said Danny, ducking his head out of the door again. It was pitch black in the yard, lit only by yellow tongues of fire leaping into the night sky, but he could hear the sound of falling debris clattering off the walls outside. Down the street a car alarm began to wail.

"I'll take a look."

"I'll come with you," said Skidmarks.

"No, call the fire brigade and knock up that house next door. Its flank wall is right up against your workshop."

Before Skidmarks could say any more, Danny was out and running, keeping low, arms wrapped around his head. The cobbles of the yard were slick with falling drizzle. He almost slipped twice before reaching the cover of an outside toilet block.

Its door was hanging by one hinge and water was pouring from the severed pipe behind a shattered wash basin leaning from a broken bracket.

He ducked his head out to take a look. The workshop was on the opposite side of the yard from the minicab office. At the back was an old Ford Escort that Skidmarks had always been meaning to repair. Its fuel tank had burst, sending a sheet of liquid fire across the garage floor and down into the inspection pits.

The front end, with two inspection pits and vehicles hoists, was well ablaze, thick tongues of orange flame curling out of the buckled front shutters and up into the night.

A pile of old car tyres nearby was smoking with the heat and as Danny watched they took fire. Thick black smoke swirled upward, sucking into the rising vortex of heat.

The windows at the far end of the workshop, at the back of the yard by the old fence, were glowing orange and Danny could see it wouldn't take long for the fire to take the whole building.

As he stepped out of cover, a deafening bang split the night. He felt his insides quiver with the shock. A column of flame and debris burst upward, punching through the top of the building, scattering corrugated roofing panels that spun away into the night like gigantic blades. Something smacked into the toilet block and Danny heard more glass breaking. He ducked out from behind the quaking building, pulled his jacket over his head and ran.

At the back of the yard was a single door to the offices at the rear of the workshop. Danny tried the handle. It felt warm to his touch. When he tried it, it wouldn't move.

The yard was lit like day now and the heat ebbed and swirled around him like dragon's breath. He could smell singed hair and realised it was his own.

He tried the door again but it wouldn't budge. Either it was locked or the blast had warped the frame. Danny took a step back, aimed his foot at the lock and kicked as hard as he could. Pain shot up his left leg.

He staggered back, braced his feet against the wet cobbles and kicked again. Nothing. The acrid stench of blazing tyres was burning his throat now.

Coughing hard, Danny took four paces back and looked hard at the handle of the door. He knew the risks of opening a door with fire behind it but he had no choice.

He stepped forward, raised his right leg and kicked as hard as he could. The door snapped open with a crack. Smoke belched out into the yard.

"Hello?" Nothing. "Hello in there?" The only sound that reached Danny was the crackle of destruction. Sucking in three quick breaths, he dropped down onto all fours and crawled into the hazy darkness.

\*\*\*

It sounded like a big one, first they'd had for a while. Nothing that White Watch couldn't handle but it would be good experience for the two new guys.

Echo 02 pulled out onto Old Shoreham Road and swung right. The sprawling cemetery opposite looked like the setting for some old Hammer movie in the darkness as what light there was touching the snaggle of tombstone.

Watch Manager Ken King checked the time. The call to the East Sussex Fire And Rescue Service mobilising centre at Eastbourne had said persons reported.

Experience and training meant Ken King could handle anything, comfortable with any situation. After 16 years with ESFRS he still got that buzz when the alarm sounded at Hove fire station in English Close.

But a shout to a garage fire could get nasty.

King looked across the cab and studied the calm concentration on Kate's face as she steered Echo 02, Hove station's extended rescue pump, accelerating hard, touching 50mph to make the most of a clear, straight stretch of road.

The 11-tonne Volvo tender with its two tonnes of water and battery of tools and equipment took a bend at the end of the straight as if it was on rails, solid and smooth. Kate glanced across at King and smiled.

Whiskey 02, Hove station's water tender, was close behind. Echo 04 from Preston Circus station would join them at the scene. This could be a bad one.

Echo 02 braked hard at a red light, the crew scanning to right and left as they went, then surged across the empty junction. Two hundred yards further on, Kate braked and turned right into Applesham Way.

King checked his watch again. Two minutes ten seconds gone. First response should be on scene in three minutes.

\*\*\*

The office was small. Danny scuttled along the outer wall, using his right hand to maintain contact and the left to search ahead, pausing twice as he doubled up with spasms of violent coughing.

He banged his head on a low shelf, then cut a finger on a screw protruding from the bracket holding it. Something scratched the back of his hand. Through watering, slitted eyes Danny saw a family of mice skittering frantically for the pale oblong of dull light behind him that was the doorway, following the thick belt of smoke being sucked outside.

Finally, his extended hand connected with something soft. He quickly explored the shape ahead of him in the dark, a soft bundle resting on a hard surface.

Reaching underneath he felt the mesh and struts of a z-bed. He pulled at the soft covering and an old blanket flopped onto the floor in front of him.

Then he felt an ankle. Shuffling forward on his knees, Danny located the man's shoulders and pulled him up off the bed. He was only small but he was a limp, dead weight.

The smoke was getting thicker. He could feel the heat rising sharply. The sounds of angry fire battering at the thin wall that separated the office from the workshop was like something alive.

Danny struggled to his feet, wincing as pain shot through his left knee. He hooked his hands under the man's arms and began dragging him towards the door.

He felt a moment of panic when they bumped into a wall, then he felt the flow of air across his face as the smoke sought the escape of the open door and suddenly they were out.

The heat and stench of the yard seemed like bliss after that acrid tomb of the office. As he fought for breath, Danny lost his footing on the wet cobbles and the two men fell in an untidy jumble of limbs.

Danny lay for a moment, his throat closing, fighting to get breath inside him. Then he crawled across to the bundle of smoking rags that was Aqualung and pressed two fingers to the man's grubby neck. No pulse.

Danny shook him and slapped his face a couple of times. Nothing. Levering himself up onto his knees beside the still body, Danny tilted Aqualung's head back. His eyebrows and most of his hair were gone. The man's tongue had flopped to the back of his throat. He wasn't breathing.

Danny pulled his tongue clear of his airway and as he withdrew his hand a denture plate thick with yellow drool flopped onto the man's chest. He placed his hands, one over the other, in the middle of Aqualung's thin chest and began compressions.

"Come on, come on." He watched the face as he rhythmically pounded the chest. The bloodshot eyes were like oysters, embedded in ovals of puffy blue skin.

"Come on, come on."

After 30 chest compression Danny leaned his ear close to the man's mouth. Nothing. He looked down at the thin blue lips, ringed with a circle of scabs like coral.

Somewhere behind him there was a dull thump and a blossoming yellow light made the smoke around then glow before it faded and died. A sudden wind tugged at their clothes as the fire sucked greedily on the air around them.

Danny leaned down and put his mouth over Aqualung's lips. When his kiss of life was sealed against the stubbled skin Danny pinched the man's nose and squeezed a breath into him, paused, then gave him a second. The chest rose and fell slightly, then sank back and stopped moving again.

Danny straightened up, wiped the back of his hand across his mouth and began the chest compressions again. Acid smoke from blazing oil and tyres was eddying around them now, dancing into the updrafts from the heart of the inferno. Danny's eyes burned. Tears ran through the dirt on his face.

"Come on, you old bastard. Come on." He locked his hands over the man's chest and began another burst of 30 compressions. Nothing.

He closed his mouth around Aqualung's lips again and squeezed a breath into him. The chest rose slightly, then fell. Danny pumped in a second breath. The chest rose, then nothing.

As he broke away from the ravaged face he burst into a savage fit of coughing. Danny sucked in a lungful of the poisoned air swirling around him and coughed harder.

***

The streets were narrow, dark and wet. Watch Manager Ken King checked the time again. Nearly there. He looked behind him and saw the rest of the crew, grinning, keyed up, ready to go. One gave him a thumbs-up.

Despite his years of experience King couldn't help running through the permutations in his mind. From the slim details they had from the 999 call it was a commercial garage. That meant petrol, diesel, paint, thinners and cylinders of acetylene welding gas.

It meant thick black smoke made poisonous by burning fuel and plastics creating gases of methane, nitrogen, hydrogen fluoride, sulphur dioxide, carbon monoxide, benzene, acetonnitrile, acetone and nitrogen oxides.

It meant temperatures of 1,000 degrees centigrade.

He knew all the facts and figures, statistics and technical details, the different plans to attack fire, ran them again through his mind. You couldn't prepare too much.

And there were domestic premises close by. This could be a bad one.

Kate threw Echo 02 into a left turn. An oncoming car saw the blue lights sparkling off dark suburban windows and pulled over to the kerb.

King checked the time again. Two minutes 42 seconds. They were two streets away.

As he looked up a boiling plume of orange fire speared up into the night sky above the rooftops ahead of them.

***

Danny, head swimming, teeth grinding in frustration, locked his hands over the man's chest and began more compressions.

"One... two... three... four... five... six... seven... eight... nine."

Aqualung's body jerked like a puppet with each compression. Danny realised desperation was making him press harder and he eased up a little. The sharp crack of heat shattering window panes sounded like rifle shots.

"15… 16… 17… 18… 19…"

Nothing. Somewhere behind him, through the roar of destruction, Danny thought he heard a siren.

"22… 23… 24… 25…"

Aqualung released a little barking cough, then another. As he tried to pull in air he rolled sideways and a slimy paste of half-digested food oozed from his mouth.

Someone, somewhere, was shouting.

Danny cupped the back of Aqualung's head and held it to one side as the old man struggled to clear his throat. A slug of glistening green snot pulsed in and out of his left nostril. When the old man's breathing settled, a little claw-like hand gnarled with arthritis and fuzzy DIY tattoos snapped up and grabbed Danny's t-shirt just as he felt hands on his shoulder.

"Danny!" It was Skidmarks, somewhere behind them. Then an unknown voice.

"Come away, sir. Leave this to us."

Aqualung had surprising strength in his breathless, wasted body. He pulled his face close to Danny. His jaw moved like a landed fish as he tried to speak.

Flecks of thick spit and food spattered Danny's face as the old man tried to form words.

"Danny!"

"Look, mate, get out of the bloody way, let us do our job."

Danny ignored Skidmarks and the firefighters behind him, looked into Aqualung's eyes, the yellowed, bloodshot whites reflecting the leaping flames.

When their eyes locked it seemed to put a last charge of energy through the old man. He wheezed the one word "great," then sank back into the wet cobbles like a deflating balloon.

The grip on Danny's shoulder pulled harder, half turning him. He looked up to see Skidmarks, sweat and smuts creating a bizarre pattern on his shaved head. He was shouting. "Danny, Danny mate, you all right?"

Alien shapes were moving behind him. Before Danny could reply, gloved hands grabbed Skidmarks's shoulder and pulled him upright. "Come on, mate. Come away. It's not safe here."

A second firefighter stepped round them and helped Danny to his feet as two more knelt to tend to Aqualung.

Hunched low against the searing heat from the garage, the group made their way quickly across the cobbled yard, past the minicab office and into the street.

Firefighters working in hose teams of two were attacking the blaze with jets of foam.

Wet tarmac and windows sparkled under the emergency lights of three fire appliances and two ambulances. Further down the road in both directions police vehicles blocked the road.

The firefighters guided Danny and Skidmarks to the nearest paramedic ambulance. One of them slapped Danny on the shoulder as they turned back to tackle the blaze, lumbering dark shapes against the brilliance of the flames that were already beginning to falter under the foam attack.

As Danny slumped down on the back step he saw Aqualung, looking more like a bundle of wet rags than a human being, disappear into the back of the second ambulance.

A paramedic wiped Danny face with a wet cloth and slipped an oxygen mask over his face. He slouched down onto the step of the ambulance and savoured the sweet taste of the gas finding its way through the crap in his lungs.

When he looked up he saw the first of a row of terraced houses beyond the workshop with its front door wide open, the hall light throwing an oblong of light across the small front garden.

A young couple stood on the pavement outside, staring blankly up at the towering flames and column of smoke that rose until it vanished into the darkness.

A little girl was trying to burrow her face into the folds of her mother's dressing gown to block out the flickering brilliance. A small boy, eyes wide with amazement, kept stepping forward for a closer look but failed to break his father's firm hold on his hand.

It was a few moments before Danny realised Skidmarks was gripping his arm. "You okay, mate?"

Danny gave a single, weary nod. "Is that family from next door?"

Skidmarks nodded. "Yes, took a bit of banging to wake them up. What about Aqualung?"

Another single, weary nod.

"Thank God," said Skidmarks.

"At least he'll get a warm bed in hospital but I can't recommend the food." Danny broke into a vicious bout of coughing. A paramedic leaned down to reposition his oxygen mask.

"You want to watch that smoking, mate," said Skidmarks. "It'll kill you."

"Very funny," said Danny, his voice muffled by the mask.

## CHAPTER 11

She closed the door behind her but it didn't make much difference. The old wooden frame was badly warped and the bitter wind whistled through the gaps, bringing a fine spray of cold rain.

Katya moved away into a corner of the deserted shed, feeling her way carefully across the creaking planks of the floor in pitch darkness.

When she felt the comforting vee of the corner against her back she dug a calloused hand into her jeans pocket and pulled out the phone.

She was about to turn it on when she heard the sound and her stomach lurched, acid surging. She froze and listened. Very faint, a rustling. It stopped, then came again. There was something there, moving, in the shed with her.

Katya tried to control her breathing, prayed the sound of her heart pounding could not be heard.

The sound came again and in the thin slice of light that penetrated down the side of the door she saw the dark cat that lived at the farmhouse.

The cat turned to look at her when it heard the hiss of compressed breath escape her lips. They looked at each other, then the cat turned and slipped out through the gap by the door.

Katya's hand was still trembling as she pressed the phone's power button and held it down. When the dark screen flickered to a dull glow her insides clenched with the first flush of joy she had felt in days. Had it been days? How many days? Katya couldn't remember.

The wind howled outside, making the old shed groan and tremble. The phone seemed to take an age to power up and lock on to a signal. She shook it gently, whispering encouragement under her breath, in the vain hope that might speed it up.

After what seemed like a lifetime to Katya, the phone company name appeared on screen. The signal strength indicator moved up and down for a moment before settling on two bars. The battery showed half power. It would have to be enough. She pressed the button for contacts and waited for the phone to bring up the list that contained a single number. Her heart stuttered when she saw the number and its +48 prefix.

She pressed to send a text message and began to tap the keypad, pausing to correct every second word because her hands were shaking.

With the noise of the storm outside, and her concentration focussed on the glowing rectangle of the phone screen, Katya never heard the door open.

The first she knew was when a shaft of harsh light washed over her, searing her night vision and throwing a long twisted shadow up the wall behind her.

"I said no mobiles."

As the pain in her eyes eased Katya could make out the big silhouette behind the light in his fist. The Axeman flicked a bracket on the torch and set it down on the floor, its powerful beam still pointed at her, pinning her to the wall. Motes of dust shone silver in its light. She heard the floorboards moan under his big boots until he blotted out the torch light and she was in darkness again.

"My son," said Katya. "I speak with my son."

She held out the phone, turning it in her hand. When the big man looked down he saw a photograph on the back, a faded and dog-eared image held onto the casing with clear tape. He could see a boy with a quiff of fine blond hair, blue eyes staring seriously into the lens. The man took the phone, studied the picture for a moment, then tossed it over his shoulder.

"I said no mobiles."

Katya tried to dart past him, to reach the spot in the darkness where the phone had clattered onto the planks, but The Axeman gripped her shoulder and slammed her back against the wall.

"Please, sir. I want no trouble. I just want to talk with my little boy."

She tried to push past him again but it was hopeless. He shoved her back against the wall again.

"Please, what do you want?"

"Take off your clothes."

Katya's blue eyes widened, but only slightly. She knew the man, knew what he was capable of. She had seen before what he could do.

"Don't make me ask you again."

Shoulders hunched in defeat, Katya peeled off her t-shirt, scraped her threadbare trainers off against each other and tugged her jeans down her thin thighs.

She paused, shivering in her underwear, hoping that might be enough, but she knew it wouldn't.

"Come on, don't keep me waiting."

A sick feeling gnawing in the pit of her stomach, Katya unclipped her bra and shrugged it off, then slipped her pants to the floor and stepped out of them.

The big man bent down, screwed up her discarded clothes and stuffed them inside the t-shirt. He'd seen all those shows on TV, knew about forensics, traces. Then he threw the untidy bundle over his shoulder. She thought it landed somewhere near her phone.

Katya stood, quivering with a cocktail of cold and fear, her right arm across her breasts, her left hand covering her groin.

The man looked down at her. Her nails were badly bitten and he could see a dark line of dirt beneath them. Why couldn't these people keep themselves clean?

Her skin was pale, almost blue, and stippled with goose bumps. Fear or cold, he wondered. Probably a bit of both. He could see her ribs and her hip bones, too skinny for his taste but you wouldn't kick her out on a cold night.

"Please," said Katya. The Axeman gripped her wrist.

"Please, sir, what do you want?"

He pulled her arm away from her breasts. She tried to resist but he didn't even notice. Katya moved to raise the arm again but he slapped it away.

The man looked at her breasts and gave a half nod. All in all, not too shabby.

"I will do what you want, sir, anything, but please don't hurt me. I have a son."

His huge hand clamped around her neck. The shock turned to pain and she gagged as she tried to suck in some breath, toes scrabbling on the splintered wood as he lifted her slowly upward.

She turned her head to one side and he looked into one wide wild eye as it swivelled in search of salvation.

"Please ..." she bubbled. "What ...?"

"What I want, Katya, is no mobiles."

The sound was quiet, like a twig breaking, as he snapped her neck. She sagged but his iron grip held her upright. He held her for a moment, the tips of her toes grazing the floor, while he tried to remember where the bin bags were stored.

The big man's nose wrinkled when her bowels emptied. He released his hold and took a sharp step back to void getting shit on his boots. Katya's body crumpled limply to the floorboards.

"Bloody foreigners."

\*\*\*

Danny was sitting at the bar of the Bellerophon reading a story in the Argus about the city's rat population when he became aware of someone beside him and looked up.

"Detective Pauline, what have I done now?"

"Nothing, Danny, if you don't count being the mystery fire hero."

Danny shrugged, folding his newspaper. "I didn't do anything."

"You left the scene without giving any ID but I had a word with your mate at the cab office. He said you went into the fire and pulled that old guy out."

"Can I get you a drink?"

"A J2O, I'm on duty."

Danny bought the juice and another lager and set them on the bar. Settling back on his stool he looked at Detective Sergeant Myers and saw her smiling.

"What's funny?"

"Oh, nothing, it just seems strange we keep bumping into each other."

"So what can I do for you?"

"Why did you leave the scene of the fire so quickly? The paramedic said he had you on oxygen, then you were gone."

Danny shrugged. "No reason. I was coughing chunks, just fancied a bit of fresh air."

Myers nodded. "A TV crew turned up soon after, interviewed your mate and the neighbours. I thought you'd have enjoyed the publicity."

Danny looked across the bar room. Slate was dozing in his basket by the fireplace. A man in a green anorak caught Danny's eye and raised a Tesco carrier bag with a hopeful expression, the garish covers of knock-off DVDs poking from the top. Danny shook his head.

"I'm the shy type."

"So you know nothing about the fire?"

"If you've spoken to Skids you'll know. We were in the office, heard a bang and the rest was in the local rag."

"It was a brave thing to do."

Danny took a pull of his pint without reacting.

"Shame he didn't make it," said Myers.

Danny looked up.

"You didn't know?" said Myers. "He died in hospital. His lungs were shot with all that smoke. It doesn't change what you did."

"Didn't do Aqualung much good. He's still dead."

"That's why I came. It looks as if he didn't do himself any favours. He'd had a few drinks and it looks as though he had a cigarette on the go. The fire started with some oily rags and set the place alight. No suspicious circumstances."

"Poor sod."

"Quite, I just thought you ought to know."

"Thanks."

"Don't mention it. And thanks for the drink. I'll leave you in peace."

"That would be nice."

"Oh, we'll be seeing each other again, Danny."

"How so?"

"Trouble seems to follow you so I'll be doing the same. You're a useful contact to have."

"Great."

\*\*\*

"Ladies and gentlemen, welcome and thank you for joining me. You all know me. Some of you are attracted to what I have to say, others are curious, some oppose me.

"That is as it should be. It is part of the great historic democracy that we enjoy in this country and have exported to half the world.

"But let me ask you a question. Do you know who I am? Really know who I am?

"I know. I know who I am because I have made it my business and my passion to know.

"Many of you here tonight will have traced your family tree through public records or on the internet. You will have unearthed many stories, tales of ordinary people making the best they can of their lives. Perhaps you will have found the odd black sheep. We all have them.

"But overall you will have discovered a thread stretching back in time, stories of people who have worked and fought and loved and handed down their genes to make you who you are today in the place you find yourself.

"And it makes you proud, doesn't it? Proud to be part of something bigger and deeply, deeply personal, bonds of blood and tradition that you can pass on to your children and their children.

"I, too, have done this research. My ancestors stood among Harold's housecarls on Senlac Hill. They sweated to pull the 100 pound strain of their longbows at Agincourt, burned their hands on cannon tackle at Trafalgar and stood beside Wellington on the ridge of Mont St Jean in 1815.

"But I haven't come here to tell you about my family's military achievements, proud as I am of them. These same people were merchants, traders, explorers and adventurers, taking our knowledge and our values around the world and bringing home exotic spices, textiles and new knowledge.

"So I do not stand alone in front of you here tonight. Hundreds of achievers stand behind me to warn you of the cancer that is eating away at our country and the desperate fight we face to set things right.

"What was once a free country proud of its traditions is now a sick and crippled thing governed by foreigners for their own interests. And what is worse, there are politicians and others here at home who hate who we are and would stop at nothing, absolutely nothing, to bring us down. Even the mainstream parties offer nothing more than different faces of the same creeping beast of consensus.

"Europe is run by a coven of unelected egos whose only interest is to see their statues put up in every square from Anglesey to the Urals.

"There are others for whom globalisation and profit are a good enough motive to crush the nation state with all its history, tradition and true human values.

"But I am here tonight to tell you that it is not too late, not too late for people of good heart and honest intention to set us back on the right track once again.

"Some call me racist and fascist but that is just cheap bogeyman abuse to strangle proper free debate.

"My family served in the Royal Navy in conditions of disease and privation unimaginable today as they fought the slave trade off West Africa in the 1820s.

"My father fought against Hitler. Many of you today regard our modern wars with mixed emotions but the struggle against Hitler's tyranny was unquestionably a crusade for good.

"So I am neither fascist nor racist. Many mistakes have been made in our long history but we learn from them and we move forward.

"What we achieve, in whatever sphere, can only be achieved by risk. Risk is good, adrenalin builds character. It is the cement of greatness.

"Our health and safety culture is a noose around the neck of individual achievement. If you want to chance breaking a leg chasing a cheese down a hill that is your choice, your decision.

"Children will die on well-planned, well-organised adventure training outings. This is truly tragic for their families but the vast majority that survive will thrive and come away as stronger, better people.

"If you remove every bit of risk and personal initiative you take away the drives and instincts that brought mankind down from the trees to become the prime species of our planet.

"Generations down the millennia have worked and learned and tried to make a better life for their children. All have known blue sky, blue sea, family, pain and loss. It has been a gradual, sometimes arduous, inching forward to where we are today.

"There are those who embrace the hubris of believing that we are the pinnacle of human ambition and achievement.

"But we are part of a journey and it is a journey threatened by small-minded people who are trying to turn back the energy of time, the new Canutes.

"We welcome anyone who wants to join us on this journey, anyone who comes here to our great country to contribute, whatever their colour or creed, but we want Ghurkhas, not shirkers.

"We are not the world's benefit office, driven by some self-flagellating sense of guilt for our past actions. What I do believe in is decency, common sense and natural justice. What I oppose with all my heart is the mindless clipboard, tick box government of the unelected with their juvenile polytechnic politics.

"Earlier I mentioned Hastings. Dusty history to some of you, perhaps, but there are still lessons to be learned.

"The term 'right hand man' is believed to come from the old fighting shieldwall formation.

"The shield, worn on the left side, protects you and the soldier to your left. So your life is in the hands of a trusted individual who is your right hand man.

"And the same is true today, working together as a team, locked together, each responsible for the support and protection of the man beside him.

"Together we can start to halt the creeping rot and change our country into the place that we want it to be, a land of safety, peace and prosperity fulfilling its proper role in the world, a place that our children and grandchildren deserve.

"Thank you."

The man's face, intense and sincere, faded slowly away to be replaced by an image of the Union flag against a blue sky, snapping in a stiff breeze at the top of a white pole.

Then the screen faded to black and the DVD tray whined as it ejected the disc.

Wanda and Bob looked at Danny with startled expressions. Danny shrugged.

"I did a drop off and the guy gave it to me instead of a tip."

Wanda glanced back at the blank screen. "I don't like his eyes," she said, placing the remote control back on the coffee table.

Bob said, "Most of that was rubbish but he does talk some sense. England's a small country. There's only so much room."

Danny shook his head, "Just another bloody politician. I'm off, got to sort something before I go to work."

***

This was insane. If he got caught he was in serious trouble. It had been an impulse. But he had known what he would do as soon as he has seen it in the box.

It was like a talisman from his past, familiar and comforting, a connection to the good times when life was simple. And it could come in handy.

Danny looked at the dismantled parts of the Browning set out neatly on the duvet in his bedroom. He had drawn the curtains even though the room was not directly overlooked. You couldn't be too careful.

The public mood felt that guns were evil but Danny knew that their ultimate safety depended on them, guns in trenches, on ships, at airports.

It was an uncomfortable truth. Like people not wanting to know how the cute cows and sheep living in green fields found their way onto their plate or inside a sesame seed bun.

People felt uneasy at the sight of armed police at check-in. But they'd be a lot happier with an armed copper between them and the nutter with the backpack.

Granted, the odd lunatic ran amok with a weapon but it was weapons that had stopped Napoleon, Hitler and a whole load of lesser lunatics.

Danny had taken old Joe Walsh's wartime souvenir on an impulse but now he'd had time to think. With his track record, being caught with a firearm would mean big, big trouble. He had considered ditching it. Joe had been right about the difficulties of finding a safe place to dispose of it. Dismantling the Browning and scattering the parts off the Palace Pier would do the trick.

So Danny had stripped the weapon. Then he had cleaned it carefully. Now he sat looking at it.

One argument for dumping it was that he could not imagine what he might need it for. But Danny knew that no plan ever survives first contact with the enemy. You can plan all you like but it's always the unexpected that jumps out and bites you.

Guns were just tools for a job, had saved his life more than once.

If he was going to make sure this detecting lark worked he would need all the tools he could get. There was no knowing who he could end up meeting, or upsetting.

He switched off the light. The parts of the Browning were faintly visible now in the dull orange glow of street lights that penetrated the closed curtains.

Looking up at the stains on the dark ceiling, he ran his fingers lightly over the gun parts and suddenly they were coming together, snapping and clicking into place.

It seemed so simple, natural, and he was pleased at the speed. When the Browning was complete he pulled the slide and let it snap forward to cock the weapon.

He knew the decision had been made. He would have to find somewhere safe. Emma would go mad if she found it.

It was a risk, a big one, but the Browning would come in handy sometime, Danny was certain of that. Beyond the curtains was a big black unknown. And the gun was just a tool. The problem solver of last resort.

Danny smiled up into the darkness.

\*\*\*

"You're late." Danny slammed the car door and splashed through the puddles in the pitted tarmac to where Skidmarks was standing by the office door, smoking.

"Yeah, sorry about that. I got held up."

"Well," said Skidmarks, "it's not as if you've missed much. I've only just got back into the office, trying to tidy up a bit. Fire brigade's had the place sealed off to let the gas cylinders cool down, hazard zone they called it."

Danny nodded and lit a cigarette. They stood looking at the ceiling of lumpy grey cloud above them.

"I bumped into a copper I know."

"You seem to do a lot of that."

"They've been looking into the fire," said Danny. At the mention of the garage blaze they both looked towards the gutted wreck of Skidmarks' workshop across the yard. Incident tape fluttered in the wind. A pigeon watched them from one of the twisted roof beams.

"I know," said Skidmarks. "They've been round for a chat, along with the fire investigator."

Danny drew on his cigarette and looked down, rolling the butt thoughtfully between his index finger and thumb. "They reckon your mate nodded off with a cigarette on the go."

Skidmarks nodded once. "That's what they reckon, is it?"

"Yes, it was started with oily rags and cigarettes and they've found no sign of anyone else," said Danny. The harsh smell of charring was still strong. The damp air seemed to wick up the sour stench of burning from the blackened ruins.

"So they've had all their forensic people, all their CSIs, going over my workshop and that's what they've come up with?"

"Yes," said Danny.

"Well, that's bollocks."

"I'm just telling you what she told me, Skids."

"You never met Aqualung?"

"No, just heard him go past the office the night of the fire."

"So you don't know how he got the name?"

"No."

"He loved his baccy, used to be a 60-a-day man, a real fiend for the nicotine. A while back he was diagnosed with emphysema. What do they call it now? COPD, something like that. Anyway, that's how he got the name. His lungs were bubbling like a deep sea diver. It took all his energy just to keep breathing. He'd have given an arm for a ciggie but couldn't hold it down if he tried. There's no way Aqualung sparked up in that office."

"You're sure?"

"Of course I'm bloody sure. He was drunk, not stupid. And I told him to stay out of the workshop because of the inspection pits. If he needed a slash he went round the back. I knew the guy for years but I guess the cops don't give a shit. Gives them a quick excuse to sign an old wino off their books."

Danny drew on his cigarette as he studied the dark wreck of the workshop. "My tame copper said they found fags ends."

Skidmarks shook his head. "No way, not a cat in hell's chance. I never light up in there because it gets too stuffy, no ventilation. And there's no way Aqualung could have if he'd wanted to."

He turned on his heels and hurled the butt of his cigarette at the tin ashtray on the wall. It bounced off the corner and hissed into a puddle.

Danny turned and threw his. Treble 18.

\*\*\*

Sir Charles Wolfram accelerated along Kingsway but he was still fifty yards away when the lights began to change.

The tyres of the Jaguar protested as he braked hard, coming to a halt just over the line, muttering.

It seemed to take an age for the opposing lights to turn green. It was a conspiracy, he thought, a rather juvenile plot by cyclists and tree-huggers to take the joy out of driving, make the open road as big an obstacle course as possible.

Typical leftie control-freakery but it would backfire on the buggers. Their children would grow up cretins from sucking in all the exhaust fumes pumped out by stationary vehicles. A bit like natural selection, when you thought about it.

His thick fingers drummed on the wheel. When he glanced at the traffic island to his right he saw a tall girl with dark hair and long legs, a laptop bag over her shoulder. He smiled. Pretty little filly, nice figure. Reminded him of that girl he'd met in Dorset.

It's not as if he made a habit of that sort of thing. After all, he was a married man, a man with responsibilities and, even if he said so himself, principles.

Still, a little harmless window shopping didn't hurt. And if it went further, well, what was a chap to do? He held no illusions about the plain fact that he was no longer young but he was still alive, still a man.

It had been a rather dreary weekend house party just outside Bridport, organised in the spring by Norman, a Lloyds underwriter of his acquaintance, partly to celebrate the successful sale of the business.

Rain marred the enjoyment of the revellers. Some of the hardier souls went riding while others did a little clay shooting. Most of them hung around the house, talking, drinking and playing cards. The younger ones worked out their frustrations in the swimming pool and gym in one of the larger outbuildings when they weren't disappearing into each other's bedrooms.

The only thing that saved the whole weekend was Norman digging deep into his cellar for some fine clarets and an excellent Napoleon brandy.

By the Sunday evening tensions has begun to surface. Several couples had drifted back to London. Some had driven down to Bournemouth in search of entertainment. One couple bickered loudly over some long-running argument that flared up when the husband had drunk too much on the first night and exhumed some ancient grievance.

The sight of narrowed eyes and accusing fingers provided amusement for some of the guests but grated on the nerves of the marathon poker school that had set up in one corner of the wood panelled lounge.

It had all got rather claustrophobic. He remembered taking his brandy and one of Norman's best Havanas into the conservatory for a bit of peace and quiet.

He had stood in the dark, lightning illuminating the tumbling shapes of the hanging baskets and the lawns outside. He moved to a side door and threw it open, felt a refreshing haze of rain cool his face.

"You like thunderstorms?" The voice in the darkness had startled him. He had turned to see a slender shadow in the gloom.

"Impressive, yes," he said, trying to make out who it was. "Do you?"

"Yes," she said. "They're dangerous."

She moved forward and he could see her now, arched against one of the windows, hands resting on the frame, smoking a cigarette. He remembered drawing on his cigar, the turbulent breeze sucking the smoke out of the door. He heard the girl draw in a deep breath.

"I love the smell of a good cigar."

She tossed her cigarette out of the door, into a puddle. It sizzled and disappeared.

"Have we met?" he said.

"I don't think so," said the girl.

"Are you a friend of Norman's?"

"Yes, he loves orchids, doesn't he?"

"Yes, mad about the things. Have you seen them?"

"No."

"Would you like to?"

He saw her silhouetted head nod.

"It's this way."

They stepped out of the conservatory into a covered walkway that led to a greenhouse at the side of the rear lawn.

The rain was lashing down at an angle and they trotted the short distance. Inside, the greenhouse was hot and humid. Thunder rumbled in the distance.

Rain drummed on the glass roof as the girl made her way through the profusion of potted plants and hanging baskets that filled the room with an array of rich scents, inhaling their perfume.

When she reached the far end she put her handbag down on a wooden bench beside a doorway onto the lawns, lit another cigarette and watched the rain lash the immaculate striped grass.

Lightning flashed again, closer this time. She began to count.

"One-hundred, two-hundred, three-hundred," until her voice was drowned by the crash of thunder.

"It's nearly here."

He was behind her in the doorway now. He pushed it open and dropped his cigar into a puddle. The demon's eye of its glow flickered and closed. The last shafts of moonlight disappeared as ink black clouds rolled over them, carried on a sudden cold gust of wind.

He could smell her perfume, something lemony. It was as if his hand had developed a will of its own. He felt it move slowly around her right side, rest on her hip, stroking gently.

The girl took a step forward into the open doorway. His hand slipped from her hip, leaving him uncertain of her reaction. Water splashed her shoes. She kicked them off. The storm threw a wave of slashing rain against the greenhouse, soaking her long dark hair and making the dress cling more tightly to her body.

A fork of lightning ripped the blackness. She took three paces forward and twirled on the balls of her feet, arms outstretched, face turned upward.

Rain pounded on the roof of the greenhouse and bubbled over the gutters, splashing onto the stone patio and running in rivers down to the lawns. Her hair was heavy with water. He remembered her dress stretched and rippled over her body like a second skin as she moved.

He had stood still in the doorway, watching.

"You're getting wet."

She turned to face him, her dark fringe plastered down to her long eye lashes.

"Yes, I am."

She gripped the hem of her dress and peeled it slowly up her long body and over her head. The sodden material clung to her hips, belly and breasts as if reluctant to be parted from her. She threw the dress over her shoulder and shook her hair wildly.

Her nakedness looked pale in the pulsating white light of the storm. She stood, feet planted apart, hands on hips, studying the hard glint in his eyes.

"You're mad. It's blowing a gale out there. Come back inside."

"You want me to come inside? You come outside."

She held out her hand. He hesitated for a moment, then took it and stepped out into the downpour.

He had grabbed her, kissing her roughly, kneading her wet buttocks. A deafening crash of thunder rolled over them as a flash of lightning lit the rain-washed flagstones with an incandescent white light.

He fumbled with his trousers as his eyes roved from her glistening breasts and down to the shaved strip between her thighs.

Wolfram leaned forward, licking the rain from her breasts and hard, puckered nipples with a rough tongue.

Gently, she pulled his hands away from his trousers and deftly unzipped and unbuttoned him. Then she had dropped to her knees and gripped him hard.

"The storm's arrived," she said, and took him in her mouth.

His mind whirled. I mean, he'd had some adventures in his time, as had any man, but this was extraordinary.

Torrential rain lashed them, pounding their bodies and throwing a fine spray that drifted like smoke across the hard stone of the patio.

Thunder rolled in waves like distant artillery as the storm danced around the enfolding hills. Forks of lightning stabbed at the hilltops like an exhibition fencer.

She looked up into his desperate face. A tongue of hair was plastered down the side of his head. With his eyes narrowed and his mouth twisted he looked to her like one of the stone demons that lined the roofscape of the old house.

He leaned down, tried to grip her shoulders, push her down onto the glistening flagstones, but she resisted him.

"No, let's go inside. I want to smell the orchids."

She had risen to her feet in one lithe movement, took his hand and led him back through the door into the greenhouse.

He remembered she had sat on the bench, then laid back, spreading her legs, her arms reaching back above her head to where she had left her big shoulder bag.

He recalled his excitement, the tension rising inside him, like the lightning all around, a massive charge of electricity that cracked and burned as it searched to earth itself.

Then she had turned over, presented that perfect bottom to him. He had driven deep into her, his strokes short and desperate, face contorted like a maniac in the evil light of the electric storm that raged over them.

There had been that Ukrainian girl, on the business trip to Brussels. She had been very good, very inventive. But the girl in the greenhouse was almost certainly the best sex he had ever had. Pity the little bitch hadn't left it at that.

The crossing traffic had stopped now. The lights were about to change. It seemed to take an age.

As he began to accelerate over the line the young woman with the laptop bag jumped back, eyes startled, mouthing something obscene. Sir Charles hit the horn and powered away, conscious of the erection pressing inside his trousers.

\*\*\*

The place still stank. The walls that were left were black and greasy. The concrete floor was covered with a thick layer of charred debris coated in a varnish of baked ash, oil and rubber.

On one wall the remains of a wooden panel showed the ghostly outlines of tools that had hung there until they had fallen into the fire. Water dripped steadily from the roof through the jagged hole punched in the corrugated panels where a welding gas cylinder had exploded.

"This is a waste of time," said Skidmarks. "What do you hope to find?"

Danny kicked a burned plank out of the way and shrugged. "We'll know it when we see it."

"Danny, the police and the fire people have been all over this. If there was anything to be found they'd have found it."

"Look, Skids, you say it wasn't down to Aqualung. And if it wasn't, there has to be something else. Besides, it's not as if we're rushed off our feet. If we weren't doing this we'd only be watching telly in the office."

"Fair enough, so what do we do?"

"I don't know, just look around. Try and remember it as it was and see if there's anything odd."

"If you say so."

They worked their way around the workshop in a wide circle, taking care where they placed their feet while keeping an upward watch in case anything else fell from the walls or the roof.

Danny turned when he heard a grating noise and saw Skidmarks sidestep a tool box as it skied off the end of a bench that wobbled on its three remaining legs.

"This is bloody dangerous," said Skidmarks.

"Look on the bright side," said Danny. "If business hadn't been so bad you might be compensating a customer for frying his motor on top of everything else."

They continued to move slowly in their circle, Skidmarks using a dipstick to stir the carpet of wet debris in their path.

He flipped a sodden piece of card attached to an untidy coil of wire to reveal the charred remains of Miss October reclining naked over a pile of car tyres.

Danny threw Skidmarks a glance. Skidmarks shrugged.

"It's what the punters expect."

It took them half an hour to circle the inspection pits and reach the front of the workshop where the big sliding doors stood welded open by the flames.

Danny took out his cigarettes and offered one to Skidmarks. "Anything?"

Skidmarks accepted a light and shook his head.

"Nothing odd? Nothing out of place? Think, Skids."

"Danny, the place looks like a bomb's hit it. When that cylinder went off it was worse than a bomb. You can hardly recognise the place."

"Okay, anything missing?"

As soon as he had said it Danny saw Skidmarks pause, the cigarette half way to his lips.

"What is it?"

"Hang on a minute," and he picked his way cautiously across to the far corner where racking for spare parts was hanging drunkenly from the wall after the brackets had given way.

Danny watched him poke about with his dip stick, then walk back slowly to join him at the entrance.

"What is it, Skids?"

He thought for a moment before speaking. "That crate."

"What crate?"

"The one I picked up on the beach when you got the quad bike."

"What about it?"

"It was over in that corner. It's gone."

"Maybe it burned."

"No, it was a solid bit of wood. Even if it had burned the remains would still be there."

"The crate with the crank shafts?"

"That's right. The label said something about vehicle parts."

"But it wasn't vehicle parts?"

"No like any I've ever seen, nothing off an ordinary car. Like I said before, I tried to flog them, asked around if anyone had any use for them but no one I spoke even knew what they were."

When Skidmarks looked across he could see a dark light in Danny's eyes. "What did they look like."

"I can do better than that. Come with me, back to the office."

They crossed the yard just as it began to rain again. Inside the office Skidmarks scrabbled through the cluttered contents of his desk drawer. He pulled out a machined metal rod and held it up.

Danny took it, placed one end in his left palm and turned it with his right hand as he held it up towards the feeble 40watt office light.

"I tried everything," said Skidmarks. "Checked all the manuals, looked on the net, couldn't match it to anything. I was hoping it might be a nice little earner but there must have been fifty in that crate and they were worth nothing but scrap."

"Well someone wanted them," said Danny.

"You reckon?"

"The night of the fire, when I pulled Aqualung out, he tried to say something. It sounded like 'great'."

Amazement washed across Skidmarks's face.

"...but he meant 'crate'."

Danny nodded. "Whoever torched the place, Aqualung must have seen them take the crate before they started the fire."

Skidmarks noticed Danny's intense concentration as he turned the rod between his hands.

"You any idea what it's for, Danny?"

"Yes, Skids, I do."

***

He always liked a good fire. There was something about flames, the light, the way they moved. Beautiful but dangerous. They could suck you into a trance if you weren't careful.

He poked the rod deeper into the furnace, gripping the wooden handle, careful to avoid the metal, turning the crumpled clothes to give them maximum exposure to the fire.

The bin bag had wrinkled to nothing as soon as he had thrown it into the furnace. The bra had already burned away to nothing. The pants were in there somewhere and the t-shirt and jeans were well alight now.

She asked for it, stupid bitch. She'd been warned and he wasn't the sort of guy who repeated himself. Phoning her son, bloody stupid. Did she think this was some sort of holiday camp? Deserved what she got.

Still, it caused a bit of a problem. Left them one short. Maybe the others could work a bit harder, make up time. Or maybe they'd need to get another one in. He'd give it some thought.

The t-shirt and jeans were black and blazing now. No traces, no forensics. He wasn't stupid, knew what he was doing. The Axeman smiled as he stirred.

***

The Skoda pulled away from the kerb. When it reached the end of the road it halted, waiting for a gap in traffic on the main road through Kemp Town.

"So, you local then?"

"No, London. My mum's ill so I'm staying down here."

"Really?" said Minty. "That's sweet. There aren't many people who'd put themselves out for their mum like that."

"No choice, she hasn't got anyone else. There's my sister but she's got her hands full with the kids."

"Danny, isn't it?"

"That's right, and you're Minty. You a local?"

"No, Tunbridge Wells."

"This place is like a magnet," said Danny. "People come and never leave."

"You're right. I love it by the sea, could watch it for ever. I came for university, started dancing to pay for it and never left."

"Dancing pays well, does it?"

"You can make a lot in tips and private dances. Don't think I'm stupid because I dance and I look good. I just liked the work so I dropped out of uni."

"Thought never crossed my mind," said Danny.

"I didn't think it had. You don't look the type. Besides, my life, my choice."

"I'll go with that."

"I just wish my sister would."

"Problem?"

"She's always on at me to make something of myself. She can talk. She got a degree and now she's supply teaching."

"It's a job," said Danny.

"So's dancing. It's a skill, and a talent. People don't realise."

"I believe you."

"Well, Claire doesn't. She's never forgiven mum and dad when they said I had the looks and she had the brains. I know I didn't finish my degree but I was accepted. That has to count for something. And Claire would scrub up really well if she tried. She just can't be bothered."

"Families, eh?"

"Tell me about it. When we were kids, mum and dad sent us both to Saturday drama school, singing lessons, all that. Even got us an agent. They got a bit keen, really, you know, the pushy proud parents. I loved it, did loads of different things. I was a traffic warden in The Bill before it finished. The best one was when I was in Midsomer Murders. I played a barmaid stabbed to death with a pitchfork.

"Claire got a few parts too at the start but she just had to be difficult, go off and do her own thing. Mum and dad were really upset."

"They still in Tunbridge Wells?"

"No, they were killed four years ago, car accident."

"I'm sorry."

"These things happen."

Danny eased the Skoda to the kerb outside the Pink Flamingo. "We're here."

"Thanks, Danny. I like riding with you. You make me feel safe."

"Go and show them your talent."

## CHAPTER 12

The police car cornered hard, its tyres squealing as it started to slide, but the driver knew what he was doing.

The big BMW straightened up with a slight shimmy of her tail and accelerated into the straight, sirens shattering the quiet of the late evening.

Ahead, a line of three cars and a people carrier were indicating left and starting to move to the side of the road.

PC Derek Haines pulled the BMW astride the white centre line and powered past them, grinning, "I always like that bit." As the police car sped past the line of cars they began to pull away slowly from the kerb and continue their journeys.

The BMW's headlights glistened silver on the slick road and the blue lights flashed and sparkled from the darkened windows of the houses on either side.

Haines clicked the wipers to double speed as the drizzle gusted harder, spattering the windscreen.

"Next left, it's just outside Steyning." said PC Sally Drake as she watched the police car's speedometer twitching higher across the dial.

"Hold on," said Haines as he braked hard and turned. The road narrowed as the houses petered out, the headlights the only illumination now.

"There," said Drake, pointing ahead to their right.

A small building was set back among the trees. A car park filled the space up to the road. Standing by the verge was a small woman in a wax jacket and rain hat who was waving a walking stick above her head.

Haines braked hard and the BMW slid to a noisy halt twenty feet short of the woman. Drake jumped out and approached her while Haines radioed their arrival. When he joined Drake and the woman he noticed she had a small white terrier on a lead. She seemed calm.

"You were very quick," said the woman.

Drake looked at Haines. "This is Mrs Betty Holder. She made the call."

The woman nodded a greeting to Haines who turned up his collar against the driving rain. "Lousy night to be out, Mrs Holder."

"I always do it, rain or shine. If Jason doesn't get his exercise he gets overexcited." She indicated the terrier sniffing at his shoes.

"You reported a body, Mrs Holder."

The woman nodded, serious and businesslike. "Yes, over here."

The two officers followed her a short distance along the verge. Then she stopped and pointed down with her walking stick. "There. She looks very young, poor girl."

Haines and Drake stepped onto the grass and peered down into the drainage ditch.

At first it looked like a large doll or maybe a shop window dummy, smooth and pale and almost glowing as it reflected the light from Haines's torch, the brightest object in a dark tangle of wet undergrowth.

"Have you touched anything, Mrs Holder?" asked Haines.

"No, dear, I just saw something white as I was walking past with Jason. When I realised it was a body I called the police straight away and waited for you to arrive. I always carry my mobile phone. My son insists."

"Are you all right, Mrs Holder?" said Haines. "It must have been a shock."

The woman dismissed the idea with a shake of her head, scattering rainwater from the brim of her rain hat.

"I've seen it all before. I used to be a nurse. Still, it's not the sort of thing you expect when you're out walking the dog."

Drake gently cupped the woman's elbow. "Come and sit in the car while we take some details."

Mrs Holder hesitated for a moment, then let out a little sigh. "Yes, perhaps we should get Jason out of the rain before he gets a chill."

Drake walked Mrs Holder to the police car, settled her in the back seat with Jason and radioed control with their latest information.

When she returned to the body Haines was still standing on the verge, looking down into the ditch.

"CID and crime scenes are on their way," said Drake.

Haines nodded. "I supposed we better get this taped off and close the road."

"The old girl was right, she does look young," said Drake. She studied the body. She was lying on her back, naked, head tilted back and her arms at her sides, palms upward as if trying to make some sort of point. The lower part of her body disappeared into six inches of muddy water rippled by rain.

Her eyes were half open and her lips slightly parted. Her skin was blue white and seemed smooth and unblemished in the harsh beam of Haines's torch.

The scene reminded Drake of something she couldn't quite place, an image she had seen before somewhere. She had been good at art at school, had gone on to do a foundation course at Hertford, partly for the challenge and partly to escape from home for the first time.

She'd had some vague idea about a career in art, maybe graphic design. Her parents had been quietly supportive while maintaining a subtle but steady drip drip about the need for a steady job, regular pay and a solid pension.

Drake had resisted but it had been Uncle Eric who had tipped the balance with his tales of 16 years in the Met.

Drake had no regrets. She enjoyed the job, even if Evan had dumped her early on because he couldn't handle her working hours. It would never have lasted anyway.

Hamlet's girlfriend. Drake suddenly remembered an art book from uni, some pre-Raphaelite painting of Hamlet's mad girlfriend drowned in a stream. The victim's expression was distant, almost peaceful. Yet there was something disturbingly submissive about the rain-washed, mud-streaked tableau in the ditch.

The only sign that she wasn't sleeping were the cluster of dark bruises around her neck. Whatever had happened here, at least she was beyond the madness now. Drake shivered.

"You okay?" asked Haines.

Drake shook the rain from her waterproof and nodded.

"This your first first-on-scene?"

Drake nodded again.

"This rain's not going to help much with gathering evidence."

"No," said Drake.

"Rain's a good policeman," said Haines, thoughtfully. "Keeps most of the villains indoors, apart from the drink drivers, of course."

"Well, Derek," said Drake. "I think we're safe to say the poor kid wasn't run over."

They both looked up at the sound of distant sirens.

\*\*\*

Danny hunched down against the biting wind and sucked on the cigarette in his cupped hand. The smoke was whipped away as the phone wires bounced high above his head and discarded food cartons chattered their way along the pavements.

Danny stamped his feet and paced up and down to keep his circulation moving, wishing he'd stayed in the car.

As he looked up the steps of the Pink Flamingo he saw the doorman sheltering from the wind beneath the flashing sign, hands clasped in front of him, licence strapped to his upper arm, watching.

Half a dozen rowdy guys came round the corner and up the stairs. The doorman cast a professional eye over them, gave a short nod and opened the door to let them in. Danny went to draw on his cigarette but the wind had whipped it down to nothing, the tip on the filter glowing like a rivet as the gusts plucked at it.

When he looked up, the doorman was still watching him. Danny returned the look, the two men sizing each other up.

The doorman nodded. "You all right, mate?"

"Fine," said Danny.

"So what you doing hanging around out here in this bloody gale?"

Danny tipped his head towards the door. "Waiting for someone."

"You a driver then?"

Danny nodded. "Temporary, till I get myself fixed up."

The two men studied each other again.

"You ex-army?" asked the doorman.

Danny nodded. "How did you know?"

The doorman shrugged. "Dunno, you just do. Me, I was in Iraq, PWRR."

"Name's Danny, used to be a para."

They stood together in silent communion until the doorman spoke gain. "I'm Rob, by the way, Rob McShane."

"Good to meet you."

"Who you waiting for?"

"Dancer, girl called Minty."

McShane's face cracked into a broad smile. "Ah, Minty, what a cracker. I mean, this place is packed with fit birds, that's what the business is all about, but Minty, she's something special, makes it feel personal, like she really likes you."

"I wouldn't know," said Danny. "I just drive."

"Tell you what," said McShane. "You're freezing your bollocks off out here. Why don't you wait inside?"

"Cheers."

McShane pushed open the door and spoke into his headset radio as Danny walked into the welcoming warmth.

The girl on reception smiled and waved him towards a curtain. He pushed through into a womb of darkness throbbing with music and pulsing with strobes.

As his eyes adjusted he saw a stage backed by a mirrored wall. A flickering spotlight followed a tall blonde, naked except for shiny white thigh boots, her legs clamped tight around a pole, as she slid slowly to the stage floor.

When she sprang to her feet and threw her arms open a crowd at the front started cheering.

Danny made his way to the back of the room and leaned on the bar.

"Drink?"

He turned to see a smiling girl in a low-cut top and shook his head.

"No, I'm fine, thanks."

"It's on the house."

Danny shrugged. "Okay then, an orange juice."

The girl clattered ice into a glass and poured the juice, smiling again as she set it down on the bar at his elbow. Danny looked around the room. The rowdy guys were at the front, near the stage, sparking off each other, getting into the party mood.

Two tables away a group of four men in suits sipped their drinks and talked quietly. On the far side sat a young couple, the man bright eyed, the girl's gaze flicking nervously around the room before it returned to the arm clamped across her shoulder. A handful of lone men sipped their drinks as they stared thoughtfully into the stage lights.

The PA system squawked and the stage went dark. "And now, ladies and gentlemen, please put your hands together and give it up for the sexy, the slinky, the sensational *AMBERRRR!*"

The juice in Danny's glass quivered as the speakers hammered out the first bars of Tom Jones's Leave Your Hat On.

Batteries of lights blasted the stage into wincing brilliance to reveal Minty standing at the back wearing a wide, floppy brimmed fedora hat and a man's white shirt that reached the top of her thighs and emphasised the length of her legs.

As she sashayed forward with an exaggerated swing of her hips the rowdy guys began whooping and clapping. The suits stopped talking and sat back. The solo guys shuffled in their seats and the young man's grip on his girlfriend's shoulder tightened as he pulled her closer.

Minty marched down the stage, grabbed the pole and snapped herself into a u-turn, looking back coyly over her shoulder to reveal one teasing, long-lashed eye and a curl of red hair beneath the brim of the hat.

When she was sure she had everyone's attention she swung round the pole, pulling herself close, then throwing herself back to arm's length like a doll tossed by some fast-paced Latin dancer.

Danny looked around the room and saw heads moving in unison, like a Wimbledon crowd, as the punters followed her moves.

Minty came out of a tight twirl, shirt flaring, and bent double, legs straight, forehead almost to the floor. The hat dropped to the stage. She hooked it with an impossibly high heel and flicked it into the side of the stage, then stood suddenly upright, sending a cascade of red hair sweeping above her head to catch the lights.

She stalked towards the front of the stage, punching her long legs down with exaggerated strides. As she reached the edge one of the rowdy guys reached for her but she ducked away and turned her back, throwing another long-lashed challenge over her shoulder.

She had the room now and she knew it. Even as he watched, Danny became aware that his surroundings were growing dim as his whole attention focussed on the dancing girl.

Minty leaned against the pole and stretched, sweeping the room with a knowing, wet-lipped smile. Slender fingers with impossibly long nails teased the top shirt button open. The rowdy guys cheered.

For a moment she seemed to hesitate, uncertain, before undoing a second button. The cheering grew louder.

Her fingers teased the third button, her face a perfect picture of innocent reluctance eroded by the audience's enthusiasm.

The rowdy guys began to chant, "Three! Three! Three!"

The fingers began to squeeze the button back through its hole but then fumbled to yells of good-natured disappointment. Then it sprang open and a spotlight caught the curve of a breast emerged from her white push-up bra.

The rowdy guys went wild. Even the suits were sitting forward in their chairs, one drumming his fingers on the table.

Minty looked around the room, making eye contact, appealing for advice on her next move in a language that didn't need words.

Still unsure, she turned her back and slipped the shirt down to reveal a smooth coffee shoulder. She flipped it back up and did the same with the other shoulder, wide liquid eyes connecting with a punter here and there who was treated to a slow smile.

Then Minty froze, plucking at the half-open white shirt, shoulders tilted and knees pressed together in a pose of childlike indecision.

The rowdy guys were on their feet. "Off! Off! Off! Off!"

With a speed that surprised the watchers, Minty gripped the hem of the shirt and yanked upwards, the white cotton peeling away from the curves of her body, revealing the lattice of her ribcage. It snagged at the swell of her breasts, then jumped free and she held it scrunched in a fist above her head.

Minty threw the shirt after the hat and high stepped round the stage to wild applause. Danny noticed that the white bra and thong shone in the stage lights and emphasised her lean, athlete's body.

He saw the dark patch of the tramp stamp in the hollow of her back and wondered how much of the tan was real and how much had come out of that bottle. He'd certainly score some brownie points with the rowdy guys if they knew.

Minty danced around the stage, high kicking and grabbing the pole to swing into sudden changes of direction. She swayed and writhed towards the rowdy guys, lashing them with her long hair but always darting back out of reach.

Then she turned her back to the audience, unclipped the bra and threw it after the rest of her stage gear. Cupping her bare breasts she looked back over her shoulder at the audience for more helpful suggestions about what she should do next.

The rowdy guys didn't leave her in any doubt. Minty stalked down the stage, slowly squeezing her cupped nipples, then punched her arms high above her head to expose perfect upturned breasts.

The rowdy guys jumped to their feet and pressed forward against the edge of the stage. A chair fell over. A bouncer at the back took a few steps forward.

Changing gear again, Minty went into a wild high-speed dance of kicks, squats and twirls, showcasing every inch of her body.

As quickly as she had started she stopped, her back to the audience, that look over her shoulder, ribcage rising as she panted theatrically.

The room went quiet, leaving Tom Jones rising to his climax.

Minty's fingers fluttered down the curves of her waist and rested on her hips as they began to pump from side to side with the music.

Slowly, her hands moved round to cup her buttocks and squeeze. A finger hooked into her thong and snapped the elastic.

Cheers.

Her hands moved upward again, as if exploring her curves for the first time, but the fingers were drawn back to snap at the elastic.

Everyone knew the moment had come. It seemed as if the room was holding its breath. Minty stood, tall, curved and slender, with her back to the audience, both thumbs curled under the thong.

She looked over her shoulder, left and right, lashes fluttering, her tongue gliding slowly along wet-look lips.

Then she bent double, legs straight, and whipped the thong to the floor. There was a flash of pink and the audience roared as she turned, totally naked, and twirled the white scrap of material around a finger over her head.

One of the rowdy guys shouted something Danny couldn't make out. Minty looked shy and thoughtful for a moment, then she moved the thong behind her, flipped it between her legs and caught the other end on her other finger.

Her hips began to grind. Back and forth. A pencil thin line of hair pointed the way to her sex as she slid the thong between her legs, head tilted back, face shining.

Minty's head rolled and when her eyes fell on the rowdy guys she looked at them for a moment, then stretched the thong between her thighs and flicked it onto their table. The rowdy guys scrabbled to grab it as she scooped up the fedora from the corner of the stage and perched it on her head at an angle that covered one eye.

She raised her arms high to acknowledge the applause, bowed deep from the waist and vanished. The stage plunged into blackness just as Tom Jones finished.

"You can keep your hat oooooooooon."

Danny found himself breathing in rather sharply and realised he had been holding his breath. When he picked up his orange juice he saw the ice had melted but sipped it anyway.

"You fancy a private dance?"

Minty was beside him, wearing the shirt but it was hard not to notice she was still naked underneath. The brim of the hat hid one eye.

Over her shoulder, Danny saw the rowdy guys surrounding the one with the thong, nudging him and pointing towards the bar. Several of them looked unhappy that Minty had walked straight past them to the tall guy with the orange juice.

Before Danny could say anything a powerful arm with a Help For Heroes wrist band slid around her shoulder.

"Beautiful mover, my little Minty. You enjoy the show, Danny?" said Eddie Archer.

The big man gripped her shoulders and held Minty at arm's length, inspecting her. "Babe! Looking good."

The girl swung her hips, the shirt flaring away from the long legs. She beamed, the glistening smile framing perfect white teeth, and fluttered her eyelids at Archer.

She glanced at Danny, then back at Archer. "You two know each other?"

"Danny's driving for me now." Archer looked across at Danny and smiled. "Well, he's driving for a business associate of mine, isn't that right Danny?"

Danny nodded.

Archer slipped a thick arm around her slender waist. "My little Minty is a very talented dancer. And she keeps an old man company now and again. Don't you, eh? Anyway, you run her home, Danny, and take good care of her. I've got a bit of business to sort while I'm here."

He cupped Minty's buttock through the thin shirt. "And put some clothes on, girl. You'll freeze to death out there."

\*\*\*

"Danny?"

"Hey, Skids, what's up?"

"Look, I might have found something. It's about that crate. Can you drop by the office?"

"On my way."

\*\*\*

"You okay, doll?"

Minty continued trying to get an even coating of low-fat spread on her crispbread. She didn't look up.

"I am not your doll."

"Hey, I'm only trying to be friendly," said Dean McKeown.

She looked up to see McKeown's bulk filling the kitchen door.

"I've got enough friends."

"There's no need to be like that. I'm just making conversation."

"Just leave me alone, Dean."

He grinned, ignoring her comment.

"So how's it going, then?"

She turned to face him. "How's what going? Getting my tits out for a bunch of boozy wankers? Is that what you're interested in?"

"Steady on, girl. It's like I said, I'm just trying to be friendly."

Minty stepped towards the door. McKeown didn't move.

"Excuse me."

McKeown turned side on, leaning against the door frame. Minty scowled, squeezed past him, feeling the wall of muscle press against her.

Out in the hallway she headed for the lounge, then turned. "You know your trouble, Dean. You're trying to play way out of your league."

White teeth snapped down on the crispbread. McKeown's eyes followed Minty's bottom as she sashayed into the other room.

\*\*\*

Skidmarks put two mugs of tea down on the uneven office table and settled in one of the old armchairs.

"So what's all the mystery?" asked Danny.

"Maybe not a mystery, just this." He pulled a tatty piece of yellowed paper from his pocket and handed it across the table. Danny looked at a column of figures adding up to a total scored top and bottom and finished with an exclamation mark. At the bottom of the sheet was the name Toni and a mobile phone number.

"So what's this then?" Danny asked.

"Nothing, it's a quote for a hen night. Turn it over."

Danny flipped the sheet in his hand and held it up to the light. The printed lettering was scratched and faded. He could just make out the words "auto parts" but the rest was too worn away to read. He looked up, puzzled.

Skidmarks smiled. "It's the label off the crate. I'd forgotten it had come off when I unloaded. This girl rang up for a quote to drive her pals around town for a friend's hen night.

"I jotted down the details on the back and forgot about it. Only found the sheet under all that paperwork on my desk when the girl called me back."

Danny held the tattered sheet close to his face, tipping it back and forth to catch the light. "Can't make out the address or the consignment details but there's a picture." He looked closer. "Some guy firing a bow, and a name. It's pretty faint."

"It looked to me like some sort of logo and two words," said Skidmarks. "I got as far as A, R, Q with the first one and the second looks like it ends in 'bean' or something like that."

Danny squinted harder. "Arq … arq … arqu…" he held it up to the light and took a pencil from the desk, noting the letters on a scrap of paper with gaps for unknown letters, like a game of hangman.

Skidmarks watched as Danny scribbled, crossed out and scribbled again. After ten minutes he looked up, smiling.

"I get 'arque' and it ends in an 'o'. I can't make out the letter before last, the paper's worn, but it looks a lot like the second one. That gives us 'arquero'.

Skidmarks picked up his tea. "Does it help?"

"Well," said Danny. "It's a start. And the second word ends in B, E, A, N. The letter before that looks like another 'B'. I'd take a punt on 'Caribbean'."

"Arquero Caribbean?" said Skidmarks, rolling the words around his mouth thoughtfully. "What does it mean?"

"Beats me," said Danny. "But at least it's something. Can I take this with me?"

"If it's going to help you find the bastards who fried Aqualung."

\*\*\*

Big Eddie Archer was lost in thought. Gripping the Seagulls tea mug in his fist, plucking absently at the Help For heroes wrist ban.

He stood in his living room, ignoring Sky Sports News on the giant flat-screen TV, his eyes wandering back and forth over the lines of family photos in their ornate silver frames.

There was a pressure deep inside his chest as he looked into the eyes of the big woman in the sun dress holding the pink cocktail with the umbrella. He remembered that day, the barbie he'd laid on for Miriam's birthday, could hear her laugh above the noise of the partygoers, hear her joking about men and their barbecues.

It had been a blinding afternoon. Hot and sunny, plenty of booze and fat juicy steaks and burgers sizzling on the grill.

Miriam had done them proud with the spread. A whole salmon, cold, loads of dips and that pasta and cream thing he liked. Never could wrap his tongue around that Italian name. He remembered burning his shoulders that day, lobster red they were.

Six years dead. Hard to believe. They weren't just husband and wife, they were mates. She was a rock back in the days when he was doing a bit of business and things got sticky.

And they were lovers, too. He treasured the image of her riding him like a rocking horse, laughing with delight, big breasts bouncing all over like jelly on springs.

A bloody heart attack. There's no justice. It certainly knocked the fight out of Big Eddie Archer. He'd have given up all together if it wasn't for the kids. Instead, he had taken a long look at things and made decisions, easing his way out of the dodgy stuff and into legitimate business, investments, building something solid he could leave for the kids.

Of course, he still had one or two little dodgy ventures, just for the crack, but he was careful, insulated. As far as the outside world was concerned he was Eddie Archer, businessman, entrepreneur and occasional farmer.

He looked along the line of pictures again. That lazy lummox of a son stretched out on his bed upstairs would never amount to much. It was a good thing he had Dean McKeown as his right hand man. But the boy was still his, still blood.

The girls had done better. Melanie had a nice little number going as a nail technician. Vanessa was deputy manager in a travel agents. Money wasn't that wonderful but she got some great deals to exotic places Archer hadn't even heard of. Where the fuck was Langkawi?

Vicky had qualified as a nurse before she'd starting dropping babies and Annie was training to be a vet. Proper qualifications, certificates and everything. It made him proud, his little girls making their way in the world. They must have done something right, him and Miriam.

He looked down at the next shelf. Seven grandchildren, little scraps of Big Eddie Archer that would go on long after he was resting next to Miriam.

He smiled to himself at one of the photos. Jared had spiked hair and a wicked smile, twinkle in his eyes. Next along the line was young Trevor, only seven. There was a bit of tearaway in Trevor but he had a good heart.

Then there was Evie. She was going to be a looker and she knew it. Probably end up the first supermodel in the family. Thank God she hadn't got her looks from him. Archer smiled again.

Then his eyes were drawn to the end of the line of photos and the smile fell away. The toddler with her hair in plaits, prompted by her mum, out of shot, to smile for the camera. Big Eddie Archer's little jewel.

"I'll be off then."

Archer looked at the door. Minty, hand against the frame, red-tipped fingers  gripping the strap of her big designer bag, hip out, skirt revealing long coffee thighs tapering down to slim ankles and killer heels.

It might not be criminal but what they charged for those things was daylight robbery, thought Archer.

"I'll get Dean to drive you."

Minty pouted. "No, it's okay."

"No trouble, babe. He's got to go into town for me anyway."

"No, Eddie, I'll give Danny a ring."

"Minty, Dean's sitting in the office with the car keys. The motor's out the front. Why call a cab?"

"No reason, it's just …"

"What's up, babe?"

"Nothing, I …"

He closed in, gripped her arm. "Has something happened?"

"No …"

"Come on, babe, tell me."

"It's Dean, he gives me the creeps."

Archer laughed. "Deano? Come on, love, it's just his way. He likes to play the hard man."

"He's a freak."

"He's an athlete, babe, trains hard. It takes a lot of dedication to build a body like that."

"And a lot of syringes."

Archer nodded. "Granted, I wish he wouldn't keep pumping himself full of that stuff but he's a big boy. His choice."

"It's the way he looks at me, like I'm naked all the time."

"Well," said Archer, "Fair play, you are a stripper."

"Dancer!"

"Sorry, babe, dancer."

"I know it sounds weird but there's something pervy about him. At the club, when I'm dancing, I know what the punters are thinking. They want to shag me. It's not hard. But it's different with Dean. I can't read him."

Archer slid a big arm around Minty's slim shoulders. "Look, Deano's a good boy. I trust him. But if you want to get a minicab you go ahead and get one. I just want you to be happy."

Minty pecked him on the cheek. "Thanks, Eddie."

"Right," said Archer. "That's sorted. Now you run along and spend some of my money."

Minty smiled and turned for the door.

"Babe?"

She turned back. "Eddie?"

"Those blokes at the club, I'm thinking the same thing, always. You keep your hands off that minicab driver."

"Eddie, as if."

"I mean it, Minty. Like I said before, it's just you and me, unless it's business."

A frowned flitted across Minty's face but it was gone before Archer noticed. She gave him her best smile, teeth white, lips wet.

"I was going to buy myself some new undies. When I get back you can help me try them on if you like."

\*\*\*

Danny wrinkled his nose as he squeezed the J-cloth hard. Grey water drizzled into the bucket. He looked down and saw greasy fragments circulating in the sour-smelling water. There were slivers of orange, probably carrot.

With all of central Brighton to puke over, the girl had to choose the back seat of his minicab. Danny brushed the back of his hand across sore eyes, moistened the cloth again and began to apply some elbow grease to the sheet over the rear bench seat of the Skoda, the cloth in his fist squeaking across the plastic as his elbow punched back and forth.

It had been a crap day, fourteen hours straight. And strange to be back on a radio net again, even one as rubbish as Skidmarks's. It would have been a really, really crap day if it wasn't for the money in the old wash bag under the driving seat. Danny hadn't had time to count it but it felt encouragingly heavy.

He couldn't explain it and neither could Skidmarks. After wasting away hours and days sitting on the lumpy sofa in the minicab office, all hell has broken loose.

Suddenly, everyone wanted to be somewhere else and they had been flooded with work. Skids had been out on the road all day as well and had hesitantly persuaded his reluctant partner Richard to man the phone in the office.

Sod's Law being what it is, the radios had chosen today to play up so Richard had been forced to pass jobs on to Danny and Skids on their mobiles.

Just to make life more interesting, the Skoda was on the blink, the revs falling away as he tried to change up which had involved running in low gears and burning more precious petrol.

The third spanner in the works had been the Skoda's twatnav packing up so Danny had to rely on a map spread out on the front passenger seat to find areas he didn't know. Still, the wash bag felt heavy. A lot of it would be coins but still, it was all money.

He had started around noon with a pick-up from Asda at Hollingbury. It looked as if the woman and her daughter were planning for a siege from the amount of bags he loaded.

When he dropped them home in Withdean there was a job to Brighton station followed by a run to Gatwick Airport, a nice break in pleasant countryside despite the threatening grey cloud. Then there was another supermarket pick-up, this time from Asda at the marina, then another Gatwick trip.

Traffic was heavy and getting thicker. When the main road along the front began to fill up people tried other routes and gridlock began to creep steadily up the hill into the city.

Whenever he was driving along Western Road, St James's Street or any of the others parallel to the front he couldn't help letting his eyes be drawn momentarily down the steep side streets to squint at the light shining from the water or marvel at the ranks of churning green waves. It still struck him as odd, having the sea so close to where you lived, but he liked it.

The traffic was a different matter. More than once Danny had thought that the Skoda was a useful piece of kit for the job but would benefit from a roof-mounted 50calibre machinegun to clear a path, make a red mist of stroppy cyclists, jaywalking pedestrians and wankers in Beemers who thought the whole road was theirs.

Richard didn't sound comfortable manning the office but he caught on fast, arranging for Danny to hold on a garage forecourt near Hookwood until the returning holidaymakers cleared customs so they avoided paying the fees at Gatwick's short stay car park.

It was dark and late afternoon by the time Danny had a chance to catch up with Skidmarks and meet Richard back at the office over a mug of tea and a Scotch egg. Then the phone started ringing again.

His next job had been to collect a couple from Southwick and run them to the Royal Sussex County Hospital in Kemp Town. You didn't need to be a detective to work out it was something serious even though it was outside visiting times.

The woman, small, plump and red-eyed, sat on the back seat sniffling into a scrap of tissue. The man, untidy greying hair, weathered face and eyes locked into a thousand-yard stare, sat beside her, arm around her shoulder, tips of his fingers turning white where they gripped her.

They travelled in silence. Danny nodded his thanks when the man paused to give him a one pound tip before leading his shuffling wife through the cluster of smokers around the hospital entrance.

He wondered what life-changing horrors awaited the couple inside but he didn't ponder for long. Richard was on the mobile again. The woman in the fake fur changed her mind about the address she wanted three times during the journey, then complained at the size of the fare when they finally arrived. No tip.

The guy in the bottle-thick glasses gave street by street directions to his destination along with a detailed explanation of the poor standard of driving and local knowledge among minicab drivers.

Brighton began to come alive with the bright lights of evening as the revellers emerged. Danny had decided early on that he didn't like minicabbing but he needed the money. It was temporary, until the detecting took off.

He was polite, carried bags, made small talk about the weather and road works when required. Some of his fares tipped him, one or two quite generously. He could live with most of the job to earn a few bob but it wasn't what he wanted to do.

And the one thing he really disliked was having people behind him, strangers. As he drove he kept his head down and his headrest up to create the illusion it offered some protection.

When he picked up four girls in Moulsecoomb their battling perfumes filled the car like a sea mist and made his eyes smart. When he dropped them in West Street they offered to pay in kind but he insisted on cash.

They handed over the money and swept off into the night, laughing and arm in arm, with a clatter of stilettos.

Things quietened down as the city partied and he took the chance to leave the Skoda on double-yellows while he grabbed a burger from Buddies on the front. He ate it in the driving seat, listening to the satisfying clink of loose change as he tapped the wash bag under the seat with the heel of his boot.

Then the parties started to die and the streets began to fill, rowdy weaving crowds trying to find home or the next high.

And the work began to pick up again. Danny collected two guys from the Revenge Club in the Old Steine and dropped them at a mews house in Hove.

He made the mistake of taking Kingsway, along the front, and had to brake sharply when a red Vauxhall Corsa cut him up, music blaring from its open windows despite the cold.

Two fingers waved a greeting from the front passenger window as it pulled away.

Half a mile further on Danny saw a policeman in the road waving him down and coasted to a stop.

The four lairy lads in the Corsa weren't so cocky now. One officer was breath testing the driver while two others were digging down the sides of the back seat to see what might have been hidden in a hurry.

The police car that had stopped them was parked at an angle across the road, blue lights sparkling. A queue began to form behind the Skoda.

The officer who had flagged Danny down looked along the line of thickening traffic. Then he looked at Danny who tried to stay still, small and quiet behind the steering wheel.

The last thing he needed was awkward questions about cab licensing and insurance.

The group gathered on the pavement waiting for the red-orange-green lights of the breathalyser to makes its decision. The policeman glanced at them, then at the traffic, then flicked his wrist for Danny to move on.

He manoeuvred the Skoda slowly and carefully around the police car and headed on into Hove.

Danny had just dropped the two guys from the club, and received a generous tip, when Richard came through with the last call of the night.

West Street was a mess. Seagulls, like vultures on a battlefield, fighting over rich pickings of junk food and vomit. Meandering threads of urine trickled from doorways. A dozen police officers grouped around a minibus kept a watchful eye while an ambulance crew treated a girl sitting on the kerb.

Her skirt was round her waist and her head lolled. Two worried friends held her shoulders to stop her toppling over while a female paramedic tried to attract her attention.

"Tracey? Tracey? Can you hear me, Tracey?"

Danny found his fare at the bottom of the road. The guy was grinning and glazed, the girl slumped limply against him, held upright only by his arm clamped round her waist.

It was pretty clear he had been tipping shots down her all night to improve his chances.

Danny knew he should have known better but, hey, they were earning today and he was on a roll.

The Skoda had only gone half a mile towards Whitehawk when the guy began to nod off. His grip on the girl slipped, she sagged sideways, turned her head and emptied the contents of her stomach across Danny's back seat.

"Nearly done?"

Danny looked up as Skidmarks peered through the back door of the Skoda. "Yeah. The whole of Brighton to puke on and she had to pick me. Still, it's been a good day, all in all."

Skidmarks nodded, "You're right there. The place went mad. Still, can't complain. I dropped Richard home a bit earlier. He's in a state of shock but I think he actually enjoyed himself slumming it. At least it's given him a bit of an idea how I make a crust, or try to."

Danny hefted the bucket out of the car and tipped it down the drain. Just as the last dregs were emptying his mobile rang.

"Hello? ...Claire? ...What's wrong? ... You sure? ...have you called the police? ... Okay, I'll be right over."

Danny cut the call and turned to Skidmarks. "I've got to shoot. Okay if I take the Skoda?"

"Sure," said Skidmarks.

"I'll see you tomorrow then."

Skidmarks looked at his watch. "I'll see you later today."

Danny jumped into the Skoda and accelerated out of the yard.

\*\*\*

Richard poured himself another merlot and leaned back with a contented sigh, twirling the stem of the glass between his fingers as he watched the candlelight catch the deep rich red of the wine.

"An interesting guy, your Danny."

"He's not my Danny," said Skidmarks. "He's just a guy who works for me."

"I'm only teasing. Don't be so sensitive. But I can see that now. I was rather dreading it when you talked me into helping out in the office but it's quite opened my eyes. I almost enjoyed myself."

"And thank you for the help, Richard. Much appreciated."

"What are friends for? But I meant it."

"Meant what?"

"About Danny. I think he would be a dangerous man to cross but there's something about him. I sense he has a good heart."

Skidmarks nodded. "I know what you mean. He's a bit old-fashioned like that, a cowboy in a white hat."

"Now you're teasing me," said Richard.

"I'm serious, from what I've heard that streak of decency has got him into trouble more than once."

Richard sipped his merlot thoughtfully, then reached out to put it on the table, water streaming from his chest and shoulders.

"Yes, an interesting guy. Would you pass the soap?"

## CHAPTER 13

The street was quiet and dark, rain streaking past the clouds of orange light that topped the street lamps.

Danny cruised slowly past the flat. There was a light in the first floor window. The two neighbouring properties were in darkness. He cruised around the block before finding a parking space fifty yards beyond the house and climbed out of the Skoda, pulling up his collar against the rain.

Traffic moved on Marine parade and the raised voices of hardcore revellers drifted down from St James's Street but in the quiet side road between them nothing moved, no sound but the hiss of rain on pavements.

Danny started back towards the house, keeping close to the basement railings, eyes switching constantly from one side of the street to the other. When he reached the house next to the one with the light he studied it, peering down into the blackness that pooled in the well of the basement entrance. Nothing.

He walked past the house with the light and studied the next one along. Then Danny turned and watched the houses opposite.

Just a quiet suburban road in the middle of a wet night, no movement, nothing out of place everyone in their beds in preparation for the new day.

Danny padded softly up the steps of the house with the light and tapped on the door, putting his ear to the wet woodwork. Nothing moved. He tapped again, slightly louder, pushing the letterbox open with a finger and leaning closer.

After a pause he heard muffled feet, then whispering voices. An indistinct jumble of footsteps patted down the stair carpet, people moving together. He ducked down to look through the letterbox and saw shapes moving in the glow from the upstairs light that penetrated the stairwell.

"It's Danny," he said, in more of the stage whisper than he had intended.

The shapes moved towards the door but stopped well clear of it, as if some tentacle might slip through and grab them.

"It's Danny. Open the door. It's pissing down out here."

"Danny?" He recognised Claire's voice.

"Prove it. Prove it's you." Minty's voice this time.

"For chrissake, you called me. Open the bloody door."

He took a step back and waited. Bare feet skittered up the stairs. A bolt was drawn, then another. A pale face with a dressing gown clutched tight at the neck was lit by the street light behind him. It was Claire.

"Come in, quickly. Minty's gone back up. We need to keep quiet or we'll wake the people in the flat downstairs."

She opened the door wider and Danny stepped inside, shaking the rain from his jacket. "Come on up," said Claire. He followed her as she padded up the stairs in bare feet. When he reached the first floor landing he looked around.

After the rush to top up Minty's fake tan, this was Danny's first chance to get a good look at what her place was like. If the sisters really were under some sort of threat he would need to check security, doors and windows, entrances and exits.

At the end of the hallway to the rear was a bathroom and small kitchen. Two rooms led off the hallway, one on each side. Through the open door of one he could see an untidy bed, duvet half on the floor.

Danny turned and followed Claire into the room at the front of the house. Minty was sitting forward on the sofa, a tumbler of clear liquid cupped in her hands. Her hair was dishevelled and her face was pale. She looked up and half smiled when she saw him come in.

"What happened?" he asked.

"Have a seat," said Claire. Danny crossed the room and sat down on one of the upright chairs by the table. A wave of fatigue washed over him and he rubbed his eyes.

"Can I get you a drink?" Claire asked.

Danny shook his head. "No, I'm only just awake as it is. It's been a long day. So what's the problem?"

Claire was about to speak when Minty cut in. "Someone was following us."

"Following you?" said Danny.

"Yes," said Minty. "I was so scared."

"Did you see him?"

"Yes ...well, not clearly. Just a shadow really. Claire saw him first. She got a better look."

Danny looked across at Minty's sister. "Well?"

"Someone followed us up the road. I didn't really get a clear look at him. More of an outline really."

"How do you know he was following you?"

"He stopped when we did."

"Did he say anything? Do anything?"

"No, not really. It was over so fast. It was just a feeling, scary," said Claire.

Danny looked across at the sofa. "Minty?"

She sipped from the glass before looking up. "It's like Claire said. I was so scared."

"Any idea who it was?"

Minty shook her head.

"You must have some idea."

"Maybe someone from the club. Sometimes you get weirdos, guys who think it's more than just a dance. They get ideas."

"You danced for anyone like that lately?"

Minty shook her head.

"It could be anyone," said Claire. "This city is full of druggies, mental cases."

"So why call me?"

Minty took a long gulp of her drink and looked up. Her eyes were red and her make-up cried into panda eyes. "We thought you could help."

Danny shrugged. "Why not call the police?"

Minty thought for a moment, then said, "Eddie wouldn't like that."

"So why not call Eddie?"

Minty shook her head. "He'd get angry."

"So what do you want me to do?"

"Protect Minty," said Claire, her eyes suddenly hard.

"Look, I'm a detective, not a bodyguard. And anyway, what makes you think she was the target?"

"Target?" Minty shivered as she said the word.

"I can pay you," said Claire.

"That's not the point."

"Please," said Minty, drawing out the word like a child. "I was so frightened."

Danny rubbed his eyes and blew out a long, thoughtful breath. "I'll do what I can but I'm too tired to think. Best if you lock up tight and get a good night's sleep."

"I'm not staying here, not after that." Minty's voice was harsh with panic.

"You got anywhere else you can stay? Friends?"

Minty looked at Claire. Claire shook her head.

"Okay," said Danny wearily. "I'll try to sort something."

\*\*\*

Heavy rush-hour traffic rumbled along the main road a block away, ill-tempered commuters queuing nose to tail as they crawled their way through the queues of traffic and endless road works to move east out of the capital.

"You really can pick 'em," said Rookwood.

Digby sipped his chenin blanc and paused to assess its flavour as the cool liquid circled his tongue. Satisfied, he swallowed and paused to savour the after-taste.

"And you," he said, "are a peasant to the core."

Rookwood pulled the bottle of beer from between his lips and glowered. "Who are you calling a peasant? I don't have to take that. We're partners."

Digby smiled. "You're right, we are partners. I am the senior partner. You are the junior partner and you'll take whatever I give you."

Rookwood scrambled for a response. When he couldn't find one he just waved his bottle around the old bar to indicate their crumbling surroundings.

"Like I was saying, you can pick 'em. Why come all the way to London? Why this dump?"

Digby looked up from his wine to his companion with a weary expression. "This dump, as you describe it, is the last of the great music halls, 150 years old. It might not look like much to you now but this was the Hollywood blockbuster, the MTV of its day. The story goes that the first can-can in London was performed here at Wilton's music hall in Wapping before they banned it. Great entertainers, household names, trod this stage before the age of radio, television and film. Places like this are an important part of our history. It's what we are about."

"Sounds like bollocks to me."

Digby closed his eyes for a moment. When he opened them Rookwood was swigging his beer again, his small eyes followed a brunette in a short skirt who had just come in from the dark alley outside and shrugged off her coat, shivering. She walked up to the bar.

"This is part of why we are doing what we are doing."

Rookwood shrugged. "That, and the money."

Digby nodded. "Yes, and the money. For too long things have been run by old men while young men with vision and ambition are just used as their bag carriers. That will change when our enterprise succeeds. We will bring modern thinking, modern methods into play to replace a culture of habit and sentimentality. What we are trying to do…"

Digby's voice tailed away as he watched Rookwood, slack mouthed, following the movement of the brunette's buttocks as she walked away from the bar with her coffee and a beer for her boyfriend sitting in the corner.

Digby banged his glass on the table. Rookwood turned back to him with a jolt.

"So how are things going?" asked Digby. "Is everything on schedule?"

Rookwood's head nodded as he gathered his thoughts. "We recovered most of the consignment."

"Most?"

"There was one missing. It doesn't matter."

"I hope you're right."

"And there were no complications?"

Rookwood swigged from his beer bottle and looked across at the girl. The way she was sitting, legs crossed, turned in towards the boyfriend, showing a length of smooth thigh. She was seriously fit, looked like she knew a trick or two. That guy's going to get some tonight, thought Rookwood.

As he watched, she reminded him a bit of Becca, something about the look in her eyes, the smile flickering at the corners of her mouth. Becca had been a fantastic shag, the sort that swallowed.

It had been good back then with Becca, things had settled down, they were a proper family, like it should be, till the bitch had dropped him in it.

Why get the police involved? It was just a domestic, private. He didn't approve of hitting women but she'd asked for it. Then the cops had turned up, found the sword under the bed. It was an antique, for chrissake. It's not as if he'd used it, not that you needed to. Then she'd poisoned the kids against him, even turned the social worker against him, believing everything Becca told her. Silly cow.

He was a good husband, good father, good provider. Why were they all so thick they couldn't see it?

Rookwood looked at the brunette again, running his eyes up and down the bare thigh. Yeah, he'd give her one, then walk away. They were all the bloody same.

"Rookwood!"

His head snapped back to face Digby.

"Did everything go smoothly?"

"More or less."

"Rookwood, this is not a pub quiz. What happened?"

"The stuff was in a garage. I torched it."

"You did what?"

"Torched it, to destroy any evidence, forensics and the like."

"Dear God…" Digby stopped when he saw heads turn and lowered his voice. "But the police will investigate. If they suspect arson…"

Rookwood tapped his index finger to his temple. "It was all planned. They'll think it was just kids mucking about."

Digby stared at the opposite wall until his breathing had settled.

"Do you understand the word discretion?"

Rookwood looked blank.

"Never mind. We just have to hope you're right about the police. At least no one was hurt. So, how are the rest of our plans progressing?"

"We're all staffed up and ready to go. We had a bit of a problem with a couple of them but it's sorted."

"What sort of problem?"

"Nothing, nothing serious. Just discipline stuff. I said it's sorted."

"And you've got the new SIM cards?"

"Yup."

"Remember, security is absolutely vital. We change SIMs after every call and make absolutely sure the factory is tight as a drum. No one goes in or out without our say-so and no one outside can know what's going on there."

"I'm not an idiot. I said it's sorted."

"Very well," Digby raised his glass in a toast, "To the end of old men." Rookwood swigged from his bottle and glanced at the girl with the thighs.

"Now," said Digby. "We've completed this little cultural outing so you will take a taxi to London Bridge for the Brighton train. I will go to Victoria. No one knows us here. No one sees us travel together. Perfect security."

Rookwood chanced another glance across at the brunette in the short skirt. "No such thing," he mumbled.

\*\*\*

They were in the street outside the flat when the man came from nowhere. So did the blow. Claire dropped her night bag and screamed. Danny saw an arcing blur, began to roll away. Minty shrieked. The pole missed Danny's head, glanced along his shoulder, driving him down.

The man came on, looming. Danny, off balance, hit the pavement. As the pole rose above the man's head in a two-handed grip, Danny twisted, kicked, caught the man under his right knee cap. The guy grunted and staggered back.

Claire, fingers gouged into her face, screamed and screamed. Minty jumped on the man, grasping a shoulder. He elbowed her in the ribs. She fell back, tottering on her heels, fell.

It gave Danny seconds. He twisted up onto his feet, wincing as the prosthesis wrenched his knee. The next blow was coming but the force was not yet behind it.

Danny snatched high at the pole, gripped, twisted it from the man's hands, spun, followed the pole's curve, struck the man in the side with his own weapon. He doubled over, snarling through clenched teeth.

The man stepped back. Danny stepped forward, pole in front of him in a double grip. Claire was still screaming. Minty was on her feet now, panting, hair wild, bracing for another charge.

"I've called the police."

All four looked up at a first floor window in the house opposite. Someone in crumpled pyjamas, bed hair sticking up, was leaning out, watching them.

"I said I've called the police. Clear off, go on, clear off."

The attacker turned and ran.

Danny dropped the pole. The clang as it hit the pavement bounced between the houses like a bell.

"Let's take his advice," said Danny.

He spread an arm around each of the sisters, leading them away, aware of the pain in his shoulder, wondering about the damage.

"You okay, Danny?" asked Minty.

"I'll live. How about you?"

She touched her side gently where she had been elbowed. "Bruises, I think. Fake tan'll fix that."

"It was Minty's stalker," said Claire. "That bastard who was following us. Pervert."

"Let's just get a move on, shall we?" said Danny, "and save the post-match analysis for later."

They all turned towards the sound of a distant siren.

\*\*\*

"And I think you'll find this particularly interesting, Sir Charles."

The gangly, tweed-clad shape of Giles Forrester was standing behind Wolfram's chair, bending forward, wound around the old man like a jungle creeper. A bony finger traced a path across the printout on the table in front of them to illustrate his point.

Sir Charles's face puckered to hold his reading glasses on the tip of his nose as he leaned forward.

"Alfred rose to become a colonel in the army of the East Indian Company. He was wounded on September 1803 at the Battle of Assaye."

Sir Charles nodded vigorously.

"As you no doubt know," Forrester continued, "the battle was the decisive engagement of the second Anglo-Maratha war."

Sir Charles nodded again. "Of course, of course."

Forrester paused to smile before he resumed.

"And your ancestor fought under Sir Arthur Wellesley who, as you are no doubt aware, went on to become the Duke of Wellington, victor of Waterloo, 12 years later. Wellesley always said Assaye was his best battle."

Sir Charles nodded vigorously. "Excellent, you've done an excellent job, Giles. This is just what I had been hoping for. The devil's in the details, eh? That's what I always say." He laughed. The glasses wobbled on his nose.

Forrester smiled his gratitude for the compliment and continued. "While Alfred was recovering from his injuries he met Cecilia and they married in Delhi in 1806. Alfred sired Roderick, Reginald and Rodney. Roderick enjoyed considerable business success in tea, spices and textiles in China, opening up quite large new territories to English trade.

"Reginald joined the Royal Navy and rose to the rank of post captain. He was mentioned in dispatches.

"Rodney went into the church and earned quite a reputation for his missionary work in West Africa. He fathered nine children, five of whom survived."

Forrester shuffled the papers on the table and pulled a new sheet to the top. "Rodney's offspring are illustrated on this page which, as you can see, include an archbishop and a deputy foreign secretary as well as an ambassador and a field marshal."

"Very good, very good," said Sir Charles, his fingers playing over the web of fine lines that linked his family tree. This Forrester chap was worth every penny. His researches were just what he had hoped for.

Sir Charles chuckled, his shoulder rocking gently. "It amazes me, with all the effort these men put into building an empire, they found so much time to be fruitful and multiply."

"Indeed, Sir Charles," said Forrester. "They were men of great energy and enterprise." He coughed theatrically. "The ravages of war and pestilence meant only the fittest survived and infant mortality required that they breed prodigiously to ensure the continuation of their name. I have even come across the suggestion that Alfred may have availed himself of some of the local girls but I rather thought you would prefer to exclude that from your family tree."

"Quite right, Giles," said Sir Charles. "Keep that one dark. Mind you," he chuckled again, "Just goes to prove there's always been plenty of lead in the family pencil."

"Quite so, Sir Charles." Forrester stood upright, plucking at his lapel thoughtfully. "With regard to William the Bastard." Sir Charles snorted and looked up at Forrester who smiled an apology.

"With regard to the Conqueror, I am still awaiting some additional research but it looks promising. As we have already established that you can trace your roots back to Harold Godwinson's household, if the new research proves my hypothesis, you will have ancestors among the Norman nobles as well as the Saxon, a sort of early entente cordiale." Forrester let out a little dry laugh. "I hope to have encouraging news for you very soon, Sir Charles."

"Marvellous," said Sir Charles. "Marvellous."

## CHAPTER 14

"BASTARD!"

Danny's gummy eyes snapped wide as the door slammed open against the bookcase behind it with a crash that sent a pile of papers scattering across the floor.

He hauled himself upright and peered around. Emma stood in the bedroom doorway, feet planted apart, eyes blazing. "You've pulled some strokes in your time Danny but this is just … just … fucking unbelievable."

Danny pawed his hair from his face as he tried to focus his eyes and his mind. "What…?"

"And you've still got the nerve to look surprised. You are just … just un-fucking-believable."

"Who are you?" said a voice to Danny's left. He rolled over, looked for as long as it took to recall the previous night, then squeezed his eyes tight shut.

Claire lay next to him. He noticed she had the duvet pulled up to her chest and was wearing the white T-shirt she had on last night. It crossed Danny's mind that at least if she was dressed the truth might just fly.

Beyond her, a mass of hair coiled across the pillow began to move. There was a low awakening moan, then Minty sprang up. The duvet flopped into her lap revealing the superbly perky breasts Danny remembered from the Pink Flamingo.

Emma's balled fists were planted hard on her hips as her ferocious gaze swept back and forth across the bed. "So where did you pick up these two tarts then? I suppose you're going to tell me they're witnesses in one of your high-profile investigating cases?"

"I think there's been a mistake," stammered Claire.

"Who are you calling a tart?" snapped Minty.

Emma was at the bottom of the bed now, waving a fist at the sisters. "Shut up. You're in my bed so just shut the fuck up."

"We can explain," said Claire, her voice quiet as she braced for Emma to attack.

"No you can't, you can't explain. There's nothing to explain. Everything is very bloody obvious."

Danny laid a hand on Claire's clothed shoulder. "Best stop digging, eh?"

He could feel the heat of Emma's anger as her eyes locked on him. "How could... how could ...?" The words choked in her throat.

She turned and stormed away but when she reached the bookshelf she snatched up a big dictionary and threw it. The three in the bed ducked as it slammed into the wall above them and fell behind the headboard. Loose pages fluttered down.

The door crashed shut as Emma made her exit. Danny could hear her footsteps stomp down the hallway. There was a pause, then the front door closed with a bang.

"Who was that?" asked Claire.

"Probably my ex-girlfriend," said Danny.

"Oh my god," said Minty.

"I'm so sorry," said Claire. "It's my fault."

"No," said Danny, weary. "I should have stuck with the sofa."

Claire put a hand on his shoulder. "No, you were exhausted. It wouldn't have been fair after you let us stay. I'll go after her, explain, she's got it all wrong."

"I'm not sure that'll do any good right now," said Danny as he slumped back onto the mattress and pulled the duvet over his head.

\*\*\*

Detective Sergeant Pauline Myers was studying her computer screen intently when the door opened behind her.

She felt a faint movement of air as someone leaned over her shoulder, followed by a distinctive aftershave.

"Not much to go on with this one," she said without looking up.

Detective Inspector Eddie Aziz stood up and straightened his jacket. Myers knew he was very proud of his Boss suits.

"So what do we have so far?"

"The body was found by a Mrs Betty Holder who was walking her dog near her home in Steyning. It had been raining heavily so there's not much in the way of forensics at the scene.

"The victim was naked, no ID and no distinguishing marks or tattoos apart from an appendix scar and signs of childbirth. Looks like the dentistry's eastern European but it will take a while to chase that one up.

"We've got nothing from missing persons. She could be anyone, a holidaymaker, student, illegal, even a smuggled sex worker. I've sent her details to vice but nothing back so far."

"Bit of a dead end then?" said Aziz.

"Not quite," said Myers, scrolling down through the report on her screen.

"So what do we have then?"

"She bit her nails."

"Not exactly a breakthrough, is it?"

"No, but even though they were short there was some sort of oil under them. We're still waiting on the analysis."

"That could take a while. This one's way down the priority list."

"Maybe so," said Myers. "But she's still someone's daughter."

"Fair point. Let me know as soon as we hear anything."

\*\*\*

Danny had just about had enough of a boring day. After Emma's dawn alarm call he had left the sisters in the flat with instructions to stay indoors and started work early.

It was clear early on that yesterday looked like a one-off. Their high hopes of another busy day were going to be disappointed.

The long hours in the cramped minicab office left Danny with the damp and acrid smell of burned workshop in his nose.

Killing time with Skidmarks had been punctuated by a run to Gatwick North Terminal for a couple and their two young kids, a shopping pick-up from Waitrose in Western Road and a couple of runs from Brighton Station for people booking cabs to avoid the queue on the rank. All in all, not much fun and not much money.

He had been about to pack it in when this last job had come up. Danny didn't want to do it but it was another one for Eddie Archer, another pick-up from that snotty family tree git and a drop-off for Wolfram.

Oh well, a job's a job.

The streets were quiet and dark when Danny motored down to Hove. He found the address easily. When he rang the bell the creepy guy opened the door slightly, thrust the package through vertically and slammed it without saying a word.

Charming.

As he walked back down the steps of the apartment block to his car Danny shook the package but nothing moved. He sniffed it but it just smelled of envelope and tape. When he flexed it, the package bent slightly, paper, maybe documents.

As far as he could tell without opening it, the thing wasn't dodgy. Archer had insisted the deliveries were connected to some project he was working on, something kosher. But what was Archer's word really worth? He'd get it delivered as fast as possible and head home.

The address was written on a white label in a flowery script using a fountain pen. Danny remembered his encounter with Wolfram's assistant from his first visit.

He found a rare parking space close by the apartment block and buzzed the number on the entry phone panel.

"Yes?" a woman's voice.

"Package for Wolfram."

The front door lock buzzed. In the entrance hall, Danny ignored the lift and ran up three flights of stairs. The exercise did a little to ease the aches of sitting on Skidmarks's creaky furniture for most of the day.

He found the number and pressed the bell. The door was opened by a tall elegant woman with pale blue eyes and light blonde hair falling to her shoulders.

"Package for Wolfram," said Danny.

The woman opened the door wider and stepped aside. "Come in."

Danny had been expecting a straight drop-off as usual but he did as he was told. He followed the woman down the long gloomy hallway into a large room that served as a lounge at one end and book-lined dining area at the other. There were windows on two sides and a door leading to a small balcony.

The woman took the package, glanced at the label and placed it on a large round wooden table.

"It's for my husband. He's away on business. Do you need a signature?"

Danny shrugged. "They didn't ask for one."

The woman picked up a cut glass tumbler from the table and sipped. "No," she said. "I suppose not. It's only more of Giles's researches. My husband's very keen on his family tree." Danny caught a whiff of gin on her breath. She saw him look at the glass.

"I'm so sorry. How rude of me. Can I offer you a drink?"

"No", said Danny. "That's fine. I'm driving."

"Coffee, then? Or tea?"

Danny almost said no but the thought of putting off the drive back to two anxious sisters in a flat that smelled of pee made him pause.

"Well, a tea would be nice."

"How do you like it?"

"Strong."

"Army tea?"

"Yes, something like that. How did you know?"

"Educated guess. You're Danny, aren't you?"

"Er, yes."

"I'm Margaret. Have a seat and I'll put the kettle on."

The woman went out to the kitchen, leaving a faint tang of expensive perfume in the air. Danny eased himself into a chair by the dining table and looked around.

Spaces on the packed bookshelves were filled with family photos, dozens of them, carefully arranged in matching frames.

Danny didn't know a lot about flower arranging but he could tell the big displays set on small tables must have taken a lot of care and expertise. Over the fireplace was a large painting in an ornate gilded frame. A ragged line of infantry in red tunics faced a dark mass of charging cavalry. Danny guessed at Waterloo.

The woman moved so quietly across the thick carpet that she was beside the table before Danny realised. It was a small thing but he was annoyed at himself. Vigilance was vital.

Lady Margaret put the delicate cup and saucer carefully on a coaster and sat down on the other side of the table. Danny noticed she had freshened up her G&T.

"Nice place," said Danny, looking around.

"Thank you."

"A lot of pictures," said Danny, indicating the bookshelves.

"Oh, those. Most are my husband's illustrious ancestors. The ones at the end are our immediate family."

"You got kids?"

She smiled. "Yes, three. Raymond is a banker, in the City, not the most popular occupation at the moment. Clive is an organic farmer in the Cotswolds, near Chipping Camden. He's an artisan cheese maker with his own brand of sausages."

The pride in her voice was obvious. Danny nodded.

"Our daughter, Mary, lives on a sheep station near Perth with her husband. He's an Australian, a lovely man. They have a beautiful baby boy, my first grandchild."

"You must be very proud."

"I've never seen him. He waves at the camera when we speak to them with Skype but I've never seen him, not in person."

"That's a shame. You don't fancy a trip Down Under then?"

"They send me pictures and film clips. They have a wonderful life there. What's the expression they use, 'No worries'. Perhaps one day I'll visit," said Lady Margaret and she sipped her G&T.

Unsure what to say next, Danny filled the pause by sipping his tea. "Nice brew."

Lady Margaret looked up, distracted for a moment, then smiled. "I'm glad you like it. I wasn't always the decorative wife and hostess, you know. I started life as an army brat. My father served in Malaya. Then, before I married Charles, I worked as a painter."

Danny's cup stopped just short of his mouth. Lady Margaret saw the hesitation in his eyes. They looked at each other in silence for perhaps three or four seconds before she began to laugh. "A portrait painter. You thought I meant…"

Danny nodded and now they were both laughing. The gin jiggled in her glass, ice tinkling against the sides, and she pressed a finger to the corner of her eye as they began to moisten.

"I used watercolours mainly but I did do a little drawing in pencils and charcoal, though I'm sure …" She paused to control herself. "I'm sure if you had a room that needed decorating I could do a perfectly acceptable job."

Lady Margaret looked up at the pictures on the bookshelves, then across at the painting over the fireplace.

"Do you have family?"

"A couple of kids, boy and girl."

"And your wife, what does she do?"

Danny put down his cup. "She's dead."

"Oh, I'm so sorry. I …"

"Don't worry. It happens."

Danny finished his tea and placed the little cup carefully on its delicate saucer. "I'd better make a move. I don't think your husband would be too keen finding a minicab driver supping tea at his dining table."

"Oh, my husband's away. When he's not working on his family tree he's always dashing off somewhere."

"Sounds like a busy man."

Margaret smiled. "He used to be. He ran his family's electronics business after his father died. Charles built it up and got his 'K' for services to industry and exports. He was very successful but globalisation made it hard to compete with the multinationals, economies of scale, that sort of thing, so he had to sell."

Danny nodded.

"He sold at a good time and got a very good price, before all this current unpleasantness, but now he has money and time on his hands. He misses being at the cutting edge, the pressure, decision making, that sort of thing. Sometimes I almost wish he'd buy a motorcycle."

Lady Margaret was looking at him now and Danny could see that she had been stunning in her youth. She had a natural smile and now it was emphasised by a starburst of fine lines at the corners of her mouth and eyes.

Her mouth wrapped itself precisely around her words and her voice had a husky burr to it. There was a calmness and control about her that sparked a long-forgotten memory in Danny of a primary school teacher who had gently helped him master the spelling of his name and address.

When Lady Margaret wanted to know something she didn't mince her words yet she was easy to talk to.

"If you've got time on your hands, perhaps it's you that needs the motorbike."

She laughed again, a clear, honest sound. "I hardly think so. I'm a grandmother now."

"So?"

"Too old, Danny."

"What difference does that make?"

That laugh again. "Oh Danny, you're quite charming."

"First time I've been called that."

"Well it's true, but there's a sadness in you as well."

"Same for everyone."

"No, it's not. Perhaps it's the painter in me, the portrait painter, not the house painter, but you have to see into your subject to truly represent who they are. There's definitely something about you, Danny."

"So I'm a subject now."

Lady Margaret sipped the last of her G&T. Their eyes locked over the rim of her glass. She smiled.

\*\*\*

Rookwood wondered why he put up with it. The guy had no strength in him. He could punch the life out of his smug body any time he wanted to.

But there was something about him, the way he carried himself, the way he spoke. It reminded Rookwood of that teacher at his school, Mr Carter. Sarcastic bastard, could make you feel really small with just a word and a look. You couldn't beat that with all the muscle in the world.

"Why are we here?" he asked, his voice small.

"Don't interrupt me," said Digby.

"It's just, you said we always needed to be discreet. And now you've got us out at the end of the pier."

Rookwood looked around. The Palace Pier was deserted apart from a few hardy souls braced against the bitter wind off the sea. A handful of pensioners sat on the leeward benches, protected by the glass partition that ran up the middle of the pier, tartan rugs over their knees, one man wrestling with the stopper on his thermos flask.

Beyond, the dull and sodden orange shingle of the beach was deserted apart from a few walkers and a lone man with a metal detector.

"True, I hoped we might lose ourselves in a crowd but there wasn't the time to plan carefully enough."

"Plan for what?"

"For your stupidity, Rookwood."

"Steady on."

"Be quiet and listen to me. When we were in Wapping, at Wilton's, you said you had burned the garage to cover your tracks."

"Yeah, so?"

"What you neglected to mention was that you burned a tramp to death at the same time. Even if the police believe the fire was started by children they are going to be taking it a lot more seriously now a life has been lost."

"I didn't know he was there. How could I? I scattered some cigarettes about to make it look like kids had been in there. Besides, according to the papers he was just some dosser. No one's going to get excited about that. Might even work for us. They might think he started it."

Digby squinted into the wind, looking out over the rows of grey waves as they rolled in to slap and hiss on the shingle.

"Perhaps you're right. But we cannot afford any more mistakes. We're taking big risks for high stakes. Get the production speeded up. We need to be finished within the week."

"Will do."

"Now, I will walk back down the pier and leave. You stay here for ten minutes, then go."

Rookwood nodded his big head. "I might stop for fish and chips while I'm here."

"As you wish," said Digby as he turned and walked away.

Rookwood looked at the retreating back.

"Tosser."

***

Danny came awake the way he liked, slowly, warm, surfacing gently. The room was big and flooded with light. He blinked several times but still didn't recognise it. Last time he had slept in a room that size it had been an aircraft hangar, another dream.

"Good morning."

Danny, flat on his back, raised his head and pressed down the folds of the duvet to locate the voice.

Lady Margaret was standing in the doorway, half concealed by the frame. She was completely naked apart from a long necklace.

The puzzle pieces of last night began to shift into their positions in his sleepy mind.

"Hi," said Danny. They watched each other in silence. Somehow he formed the idea that she was nervous standing there like that yet it was something she needed to do.

It was the first time he had seen her in daylight. The curve of her waist and hip were softer, less dramatic, than he was used to.

Her breasts were low and heavy, the nipples drawn into long dark ovals by years of gravity. Stretch marks made a silver cat's cradle of lines across her stomach and faint blue veins wandered across the white skin of her legs.

As he looked closer he noticed notches in the top of her shoulders where bra straps had worn grooves.

At the top of her thighs was a thick bush of blonde hair. Danny had never seen anything like that before.

Suddenly he remembered it tickling his nose in the darkness of the night before, pulling a stray strand from between his teeth when he paused to breathe.

Danny wondered if it should feel weird waking up with someone old enough to be your mum but what the hell. Helen Mirren, Joanna Lumley, they were fit and both looked as if they knew what's what.

It seemed to both of them a very long time before anyone spoke. When they did, they both started together, stuttered into silence and mumbled apologies.

After another pause, Danny asked, "Is that a string of pearls?"

Lady Margaret laughed, the noise sounding younger than her years. "It's a rope of pearls. I think you'll find a string of pearls is a smutty euphemism for a splash of semen."

She saw Danny's eyebrows rise and laughed again. "I told you last night, I wasn't always the decorative wife and hostess. I did have a life once." She looked at him for a moment, then added, "You'd like some tea?"

"Thanks."

Margaret turned to leave and Danny was looking at the swell of her full bottom when she paused and turned back towards him.

"Thank you."

"For what?"

Margaret hesitated, then decided. "For a stupendous fuck."

When he was alone Danny lay back with his hands knitted together behind his head and ran through the sequence of events since he had knocked on Lady Margaret's door with the package last night.

He didn't surprise easily but yesterday evening and the night that followed left him feeling dazed. This wasn't your usual one-night stand. This sort of thing was way outside his experience and yet, lying stretched out under the thick, warm duvet, he felt a peace and comfort he hadn't known in a long time. There was a calmness about her he wasn't used to. He felt safe, which seemed odd.

Margaret returned wearing a pale dressing gown loosely tied and carrying a delicate cup and saucer. A small spoon tinkled against the china as she put it on the bedside table.

She sat on the edge of the mattress and looked at him, apparently unable to tear her eyes away.

"Are you all right?" she asked.

"Me? Fine. Why wouldn't I be?"

Margaret shook her head. "I just wondered. I was afraid you might be ... embarrassed."

"You're an attractive woman."

"Old enough to be your mother."

Danny blinked and said nothing. Margaret avoided his gaze. Then her hand moved slowly to grip the duvet and slide it down to his waist, watching all the way.

"I just wanted to say..." Her voice cracked and she started again. "I don't make a habit of this sort of thing but I wanted to say that I'm grateful. It's been a long time."

"The way I remember it, I've got a fair bit to be grateful for as well," said Danny.

"You're very kind, Danny."

He looked at her full cleavage through the open gown and stretched out his hand to stoke the side of her breast. The skin was warm with the soft furred feel of a much-loved cotton shirt.

Margaret took his hand, squeezed, and pressed it down on the duvet. Then she reached out and Danny studied the lines and raised veins in the back of her hand as she traced the hard ridges of his chest and stomach.

"It's a long time since I've seen this," said Margaret. She thought for a moment, then added, "Charles and I are just friends now, good friends. He's not a bad man, perhaps just a stupid one. He has an idea and it fills his vision to the exclusion of all else. Typical man, I suppose."

He lay back in silence, feeling the pressure in her fingers as she traced the contours. "You never lose the ability to make love," said Margaret quietly, "but you lose the confidence if no one is interested. Sometimes, for a moment, I still think I'm seventeen. Then I remember."

Danny could think of nothing to say so he said nothing. Margaret's hands continued to trace the muscles and scars of his torso.

"You have the body of a young Greek god."

Danny puffed in surprise. "Steady on."

She looked at him and her eyes were wet and serious. "No, last night you were so young, so hard, so serious, so much energy. I miss that so much."

"I …"

Her hand moved to his lips. "No, don't say anything. I don't want to embarrass you, or myself. I know it was just a moment, it will never happen again and I'm happy with that."

"My pleasure," said Danny.

"And mine too."

"I wasn't doing you any favours. We both enjoyed it. You taught me things."

"You're sweet."

Danny looked at her face as he struggled for something more to say and failed. Margaret looked from his chest to his eyes and smiled.

"Your tea will be getting cold."

"Yes."

"I'll make you some scrambled eggs."

"Don't put yourself out on my account."

"You can't possibly go off without breakfast."

***

It had been a night of new experiences. He'd never had scrambled eggs made with cream before.

After a shower and a shave they had said their farewells, Margaret cupping his elbow gently to reach up and peck his cheek. She had seemed thoughtful, serious, her eyes still and deep.

Once back in his car Danny had phoned the flat. Claire answered. She seemed much calmer now, in control, and reported that Minty was more composed.

They had spent yesterday in the flat, Minty watching television and Claire reading what books she could find.

The sisters had ordered a takeaway last night and turned in early. Staying in bed with the door closed until they heard Emma leave after her morning visit to tend to his mother.

They both felt better, rested and calmer. And they both had things to be getting on with so they would be going out soon.

Danny told Claire to take care and call if there was a problem.

\*\*\*

You couldn't call it a smile. His lips retracted to show his teeth to the light but his eyes didn't change.

"Hello again," said Forrester, arm resting against the open door of his apartment. "Come in. You know where to go."

He turned aside on to let her enter. She squeezed past and walked towards the lights of the lounge. With her back to him, Giles didn't see her wince as he slid home each of the three heavy bolts on his front door.

She was standing by the coffee table clutching her big leather bag as he entered. "I do apologise. I forgot to take your coat."

"Don't worry, I'm in a bit of a hurry."

"But I do worry, my dear. You always seem to be in such a hurry but we must maintain standards, mustn't we? Besides, you won't feel the benefit when you go outside again."

She slipped the coat from her shoulders and dropped it over the arm of the sofa. Giles pulled a face at the discordant note the discarded garment made amid his careful décor but this was more than compensated for by what the coat had been concealing.

Her dress was so light it clung to every curve like water, ending quite high above the knee to show a beautifully sculpted length of thigh and those excellent calves emphasised by the height of her heels. And the perfume, something lemony.

"You have my little present?"

The woman rummaged in her bag and brought out a manila envelope sealed with thick overlapping bands of tape.

He took it and weighed it in his hands. "Excellent, I'll check it later but I'm sure everything will be in order. It is a rare privilege to enjoy one's work."

"Well I'm very glad for you but I'd better go. I'm in a rush."

Giles made tutting noises as he placed the envelope on the coffee table. "Haven't you forgotten something?"

The woman shook her head. "No, I don't think so."

"My other little present."

He watched the confusion flicker across her face. Stupid people were a source of constant surprise to Giles. How could they reach an age, any age, and manage to function when the world swirling around them remained a complete mystery, a closed book. Perhaps she was unable to read.

Rather than waste his precious time with more word games he unzipped his trousers. Amusement flickered across his face as he watched her mouth open.

"You want me to..."

"Yes, my dear."

"I can't, I..."

"Don't be tiresome. We've had this conversation before. In the enterprise in which we are all engaged I am a vital component. You are a minor player and one of your roles is to keep me happy in my work."

"I..."

"Just do it!"

"I've got a cold sore."

"What?" Giles squinted irritably at the girl's face but could make out nothing more than a rough patch of skin at the tip of a long red nail that she held to the corner of her lip. His face closed in round clenched teeth.

"This is ridiculous," was the best he could think of to say.

"It's not my fault," said the girl. "I just didn't think you'd want to catch something."

"Catch something!" stammered Giles, one hand covering the limp penis hanging from his open fly.

"Well," said the girl. "It's a sort of herpes, isn't it?"

"This is ridiculous."

Giles rolled his eyes in frustration. He looked at the girl again. Those thighs did look rather sublime. And the calves. He felt himself stiffen.

"I could do you a hand job."

"Get on with it then."

The girl dropped to her knees and moved his hand away from his groin. He gasped as she gripped him and started work. Clearly, this was a new area of expertise he was unaware she possessed.

As she got into her rhythm he planted his hands on his hips and tipped his head back, pushing his pelvis forward.

"That's good ... that's very good."

She began to pump harder with longer strokes and he felt his scrotum tighten.

"That's good ... just don't get any love custard on the carpet."

## CHAPTER 15

Danny looked at the phone box again, then swept the street around him. Not many people about. He swept the rooflines and the corners of the buildings. No cameras.

He hadn't had many to choose from. The rise of the mobile made phone boxes an endangered species. And those that survived were used as toilets or for drugs deals as often as they were for phone calls.

The first he had tried had too many people wandering by and in the second the handset had been ripped out. But Danny had persisted. This was not the sort of phone call where you wanted to leave a trail.

He stood a little longer, watching and waiting, before he was satisfied. Then he slipped into the box. It smelled of piss and dark stains marked the concrete floor. Someone had used a thick ink marker high on the wall to reveal Chas's sister's enthusiasm for anal sex.

He dialled. The phone began to ring. Danny waited, rocking on the balls of his feet, reading the exotic range of services advertised on the cards Blu-Tacked to the wall, a blonde in a straw boater and mini-kilt, a masked woman whom specialised in punishment, a pre-op transsexual with full wardrobe.

The phone clicked. A voice, quiet but with a clipped edge of authority. Lancaster, yes, Daniel, yes, 2006, that's right. The conversation was short and deliberately vague. It didn't answer all his questions but it set him on the right track.

If the man he was looking for was around he would be at Chelsea Harbour or St Katharine's Dock. Danny flipped a coin, St Katharine's.

\*\*\*

Karol's finger drummed on his bottom lip, his thoughtful face lit by the glow of his laptop. As Danny watched he knew the skinny Pole liked nothing more than a pub with wifi and a puzzle.

"You're good at this," he said.

"Not good," said Karol without looking up. "I am excellent. I study computer science at Jagiellonian University, Krakow."

"So why are you working for Bob as a chippie?"

"To make money, to save. And without me he would have no dog to beat."

Something on the laptop screen caught Karol's eye. He leaned forward, squinting.

"You make joke, yes?"

"No," said Danny. "What's funny?"

"This company, this Arquero Caribbean, is import-export business in Venezuela, Caracas."

"So?"

"Arquero is Spanish word for Bowman. Arquero Caribbean is owned by Bowman Enterprises, it has offices in London and Rotterdam for shipping cargo."

"And?"

"They make trade with containers all over the world, all kinds of merchandise. But now it is closed. The company does not do business."

Karol saw the disappointment in Danny's face.

"So it's a dead end then?"

Karol shook his head.

"Maybe not. Do you know who is boss of Bowman Enterprises?"

"Karol, stop playing quiz show host and tell me."

"Archer, your friend Eddie Archer. Archer is Bowman. Is joke, yes?"

Danny looked down at the floor, his features suddenly dark. "Well if it is, it's not bloody funny."

***

Giles Forrester peeled back his foreskin and worked the soap round the bell of his penis with a thumb. It still tingled.

Personal hygiene was a vital and regular part of his day. He dreaded germs or dirt of any kind, spent a small fortune on antiseptic wipes and soaps and moisturisers to avoid his hands drying out from the frequent washes.

Pushing his crotch further over the sink, he ran his penis under the cold tap and started again with the soap.

She was good, that girl. Stupid, obviously, but very talented in matters carnal. His enthusiasm had got the better of him, which almost never happened. As he had felt his orgasm rising he had pushed himself into her infected mouth and pumped his life juices down her throat. It had been a risk, reckless, but so, so sweet.

And it avoided any nasty spillage. God alone knew what a nightmare it would be getting semen stains out of a deep pile carpet, even if it was Scotchgarded.

He rinsed thoroughly, then started again with the soap. Attention to detail, so important.

When Forrester was satisfied that all traces of the woman and her diseases had been removed he dried himself on a hand towel and walked back to the lounge.

Odd, he thought as he padded silently along the carpeted hallway in his slippers. He didn't remember leaving his laptop on. He was sure he had turned it off before the girl arrived.

When he stood in the doorway he could see the lid was up, the screen glowing. The girl was sitting at his desk.

"What on earth do you think you are doing?"

Something was winking. A small red light pulsed beside the laptop. It took him a moment to understand. Then he realised, it was one of those memory stick things.

That girl, that stupid, diseased girl, was stealing his researches. Outraged, Forrester started across the room towards her.

\*\*\*

Danny could never get his head around London, a vast, sprawling mishmash of a place. For a lad brought up in North London, south of the river was a foreign country.

True, there was plenty to see and do but he still couldn't work out why tourists braved the fumes and the prices.

His train had queued outside London Bridge Station for fifteen minutes before it found a platform. The place was busy with commuters desperate to get out of the city at the end of their working day but those arriving were a trickle.

He had wanted to be early but now he had time to kill. Danny crossed Tooley Street and walked through Hays Galleria to the riverside walkway. He checked the Rolex, bought himself a pint and sat by the river, watching the cruise boats and ferries churn the restless brown water.

They looked tiny as they passed the fearsome bulk of HMS Belfast, veteran of the Arctic convoys, Normandy beaches and Korea, her hedgehog of six-inch heavy gun barrels aiming high to the north west.

Danny remembered reading somewhere that from where she sat her shells would hit a motorway service station on the M1. That would be something to see.

He drained his pint and set off towards the Testicle, the egg-shaped office block that housed London's government.

On the other bank of the river the squat brown fortifications of the Tower of London were dwarfed by the weird and wonderful picket of skyscrapers in the City.

Mishmash London still amazed Danny as he passed the Testicle and climbed the steps onto Tower Bridge. Down river the banks were lined with blocks of yuppie flats built in the boom years.

Behind the thin waterside strips of lifestyle development were the old districts of the East End where English was a second language.

Danny hoped the ridiculous piles of cashed pumped into the 2012 Olympics would deliver the promised improvements to the area because it certainly needed it.

He paused in the middle of the bridge, one foot on the north ramp, one on the south, and looked down at the dark strip of water below, feeling the vibration of passing traffic.

On the north side he cut through into St Katharine's Way, in the ugly shadow of the Tower Hotel. Ahead was the towering greenhouse of the Thomas More office complex in Wapping. He began to study his surroundings.

It was a pleasant evening, cool and still. Hands deep in his jacket pockets, Danny set off at a brisk pace, keeping to the shadows and steering clear of the few people he saw.

The City folk would be tucked up in their minimalist warehouse apartments sinking a bottle of something fashionable and wondering if they'd have a job in the morning.

As Danny rounded a corner he became conscious of shapes moving at the edge of his vision. He turned quickly to assess the two men heading towards him, one tall and thin, his companion shorter and thick set. Each carried a small shoulder bag.

The Browning hung heavily in his waistband. Danny began patting his jacket pockets as if searching for something, hand inching towards the weapon.

As they cut across his path to intercept him, Danny's hand was on the butt of the Browning. They were too close.

As the shorter of the two pulled something from his pocket Danny pulled the pistol free of his waistband and held it behind his back.

The short man pushed something towards him. "Please? Liverpool Street Station?"

There was a pause as he studied them and they shuffled uneasily, uncomfortable at having strayed off the main tourist track.

Danny let out a long, silent sigh, pushed the pistol down against the small of his back and took the offered street map.

He pointed out their destination and when they seemed alarmed at the distance he directed them straight up to the main road and suggested they get a cab.

The two young tourists thanked him in heavily-accented English and began to jog up the road, backpacks bouncing.

Danny watched them go, annoyed at his hair-trigger reaction. He suddenly thought of Emma and pictured her watching television with Benny, putting cups in the sink, maybe, switching off the lights, then going to bed.

He shook the images away. Things weren't going to get any better till this business was sorted. He needed to concentrate.

Danny moved forward into the exclusive darkness of St Katharine's Dock. Even at night the dock was an impressive site, an executive oasis risen from crumbling wharves.

A fascinating mixture of boats rode gently at their sheltered berths. Old canal and river boats weathered with age and salt shared their haven with cabin cruisers and the sort of fuck-off high-tech yachts that would-be lottery winners dream about.

Sharply aware of CCTV all around, Danny turned up his collar and dug his hands in his pockets, keeping his head down. He might look overdressed but there would be no record of his face.

He made himself stroll casually, a passer-by taking in the sights, going somewhere in no particular hurry, slow enough to recce the place without looking to watching eyes as if he was loitering.

Danny walked down the cobbled path and circled the kidney-shaped double basin. He soon found what he was looking for and smiled to himself.

She looked big to Danny, even in the dark, a sleek, raked yacht, the breeze tapping strands of rigging against her soaring mast. Pegasus, very appropriate.

The last of the drinkers were finishing up at the Dickens Inn pub, smokers grouped on its wooden balconies among the hanging baskets of flowers.

Danny took his time, smoked a cigarette. When he saw a concealed position that offered a good view over the dock basin he ground out the cigarette on the cobbles and slipped into the darkness of the covered walkway that ran along Commodity Quay.

A trickle of people passed along it but their footsteps rang out loudly on the stone, giving him plenty of time to assume the air of the curious tourist or to melt away into the shadows.

High up in one of the luxury penthouse apartments Danny could see a figure silhouetted on the balcony, looking out over the dock and the brooding eddies of the broad River Thames beyond.

The light from the room behind flickered through the wine glass in the watcher's hand. Someone had told Danny that Cher had an apartment up there somewhere. He wondered if it was true.

It was a long wait but that didn't bother Danny. He was well practised at waiting. As time wore on the drinkers and diners drifted away from the dock.

Danny scrutinising every shadowy shape that passed. Then he saw him. The man was tall, dressed in a dark jacket and chinos. He walked slowly, leather-soled shoes clicking on the stone as he talked quietly with his companion.

He whispered something and the woman laughed, a rich sexy sound that echoed in the stillness of the dock.

They strolled arm in arm along one of the walkways, then dipped from Danny's sight as they went down a flight of steps to one of the pontoons. Danny slipped from the shadows and followed. He could hear their footsteps on the wooden decking and kept his distance.

Then the low rustle of conversation stopped moving. He looked down into the dock and saw two shadows standing by the gangway to the boat. The man led the way as they boarded and disappeared below. A light came on.

Danny looked around carefully and listened. Water whispered against the stone quay and slapped gently against rocking hulls. There were voices some way off and a car in the distance.

Trying to look casual to the casual observer, Danny strolled along the walkway to the spot where the couple had gone down onto the pontoon. The top of the steps were blocked by a gate held by a lock with a keypad.

There was no way Danny could defeat it so he looked quickly to right and left, then stepped over the chain fence beside the gate and dropped onto the wooden decking of the pontoon.

It was a short distance to the boat. Danny walked carefully, putting his feet down gently on the planking to minimise the noise.

He reached the gangplank and tested it carefully before easing his weight down onto it. A sliding door down into the interior stood open, dim light creeping round the edges of the curtain that screened the entrance.

Danny heard a clink of a glass and then the woman's laugh again. He hadn't banked on anyone else being there. It had thrown his plan.

The salon of the yacht fell silent. Danny wasn't sure what to do next. He moved forward slowly onto the deck, sliding his feet softly to avoid making a noise or tripping on anything. He eased his way the few feet towards the door and paused. Then he heard the woman moan.

Shit!

Danny considered his options. He could come back another time but he couldn't be sure she wouldn't be there then. And time was a luxury he couldn't afford. He leaned down towards the stripe of light at the edge of the curtain and peered in.

The salon was large, very neat and immaculately fitted out with cream sofas and pale wood panelling. The couple were in the centre, about ten feet away.

The woman had her back to him. All Danny could see was the top of the man's head as he bent to kiss her neck and his hands as they kneaded her buttocks through the sheen of a silk slip. Her legs were long and slender, the colour of toffee. Danny's eyes wanted to linger admiringly on them. He could hear the woman's breathing and the faint mewling noises she made as she nuzzled the man's chest. "Oh, Will."

Danny turned around to look out across the yacht basin and tried to work out what to do. "Hello, Danny." The voice was soft and amused. The stripe of light by the door had widened slightly. Danny turned towards it, hands in his pockets.

"It is you, Danny, isn't it?"

"Hello, Mr Tyler."

The voice still had that soft edge of amusement. "We ought to recognise each other in the dark. We've had to do it often enough."

Danny nodded and looked down at the squat snub of a pistol sticking through the gap between the door frame and the curtain.

"Is that a Sig, sir?"

"You know perfectly well it is."

"Nice pistol," said Danny. "Very reliable." The nose of the weapon came up slightly. When he spoke the humour had gone out of Tyler's voice.

"Take your hands out of your pockets, slowly." Danny did as he was told. "Are you armed?" Danny nodded. The muzzle of the Sig jerked down towards the deck. "Carefully, Danny, carefully."

Danny drew the Browning slowly from his belt, pinching the butt of the weapon between finger and thumb. He crouched slowly, never taking his eyes off Tyler, and laid it on the deck before taking a step back. Tyler seemed to relax.

"You heard me coming?"

"Nothing so basic, Danny." Tyler indicated the top of the doorway and in the faint light from the edge of the curtain Danny could just make out a pencil-thin webcam.

Tyler swooped to snatch up the Browning. "Oh, and there's a pressure pad on the gangplank. You can't be too careful, Danny. Get sloppy and you never know who you'll find waltzing into your living room with a pistol in the middle of the night. Come in."

He held the curtain open and gestured with the Sig for Danny to enter, stepping clear to maintain the distance between them. They ducked through the door and into the saloon.

Tyler waved Danny towards a bench seat and took the one opposite. Beyond one of the forward cabins Danny could hear the girl moving around.

"She's a beauty, isn't she?" said Tyler.

Danny looked from the skylights above his head to the cabin door. Tyler laughed.

"I meant the boat, Danny, although you're right about Sammy as well."

Danny looked around him. The place smelled of leather, polish and money.

"How did you find me?"

"Mutual friends," said Danny.

"Ah, I see," said Tyler. "Look, Danny, it's nice for old comrades to keep in touch and all that but you didn't come here in the middle of the night to discuss the finer points of automatic pistols. Are you looking for work? There's good money to be made, security, close protection. You'd be perfect."

"Not work, a favour."

"There's no profit in favours."

"All I need is a bit of information, some intelligence."

"Intelligence is something you were never short of, Danny. You were always the serious one, always the thinker. The deep ones are the dangerous ones.

"As for information, it's a commodity like anything else. Some people trade in metals or orange juice. I trade in information and the hardware required to exploit that information. I don't do favours, Danny."

"I understand that, Mr Tyler. Normally I wouldn't ask but there's no other way."

Tyler made a noise somewhere between a laugh and a sigh. "You ought to be in business yourself, Danny."

"I am, Mr Tyler, I am."

The forward cabin door creaked open and Sammy emerged wearing a black silk dressing gown, her hair loose. She sat beside Tyler on the opposite bench and lit a cigarette, a section of sinuous, tanned thigh visible where the dressing gown fell open.

Danny had to make a conscious effort to drag his eyes away from her legs. It was made harder by the look that flickered across her face as she studied him, her attention focussed at his feet and moving slowly up his body to study the scars on his face. Tyler looked from one to the other. "Sammy, be a darling and fix us some drinks."

"Certainly, Will." She rose with a whisper of silk and looked inquiringly at Danny.

"Beer if you've got it," he said. He tried not to watch as Sammy swayed the length of the salon to the galley. She returned with a tin of Heineken and passed a crystal tumbler with a large measure of scotch to Tyler.

"Could you give us a minute, darling? It's business. I won't be long."

Sammy pouted at Tyler, glanced again at Danny and disappeared into the forward cabin.

"Nice girl," said Danny.

"If you're asking if she's a great fuck the answer is yes but I think she's a bit out of your league."

"Nice boat," said Danny.

Tyler laughed. "Yes, an Oyster 46. We took her round the Med last summer. She's got a Volvo diesel with plenty of poke but under sail she flies. Not exactly in the Abramovich league, I'll grant you, but it's a start. Pegasus was a nice touch, don't you think? And she keeps me mobile. You need to be mobile in this business."

Danny nodded. He lit a cigarette and offered one to Tyler who shook his head. "Given up," he said.

Tyler gestured towards the curtained entrance and the chequerboard lights of the skyscrapers in the City of London beyond.

"This place was a trading centre before the Romans came and it's been a dock for a thousand years, part of a network that made London the trading capital of the world. Fabulous wealth has passed across these quays, ivory, sugar, marble, wines, rubber, carpets, spices, perfumes, even precious shells and feathers.

"Generations of merchants, whores and sailors have plied their trade here. And over there," he waved his tumbler towards the City, "is more money than you could dream of, power bigger than governments.

"Did you know, Danny, that on September 7, 1940, the Luftwaffe made their first big daylight raid on London and this place was smack in the middle."

"No."

"The warehouses were set ablaze and it spread to barges loaded with copra. Burning fat and wax floated on the water of the dock. The place was an inferno for days. The dock never really recovered."

"And?"

"My point is, Danny, where you have money you have danger. And there's a lot of work there for guys like us if you know the right people. Dave, Si and Pogo too, if they're interested."

"They're still in."

"Are they? I didn't know. So you're on your own? It can be lonely on the outside."

The two men sipped their drinks in silence, each staring at the opposite wall, both drifting back to another time, another life.

Danny could picture the stunning, savage countryside, the dust and the incredible heat that sucked the breath out of you. Different world.

The locals were as hard as nails but with no TV and no pub to keep them entertained they had bacha bazi, "boy play".

The sort of thing that could get you the death penalty in Afghan, or Rule 45 back home in prison to save a nonce from getting the shit kicked out of him, was a normal recreational activity for many of them. But when girls were a strict no-no outside of marriage you had to find somewhere to put it.

Allegiances to family and clan were everything but loyalties could shift like sand. If your worst enemy asked for your hospitality you fed, watered and entertained him and couldn't lay a finger. But once he was outside…

Danny remembered a labyrinth of canals, irrigation ditches, mud brick compounds punctured with murder holes, fields of poppy and corn, the riverside dense with greenery, elephant grass shooting up from patches of sand and pebbles on its banks.

Another world.

He remembered thick greenery, the Talib, the bayonet.

Danny glanced across at Tyler who looked up and blinked, returning to the boat's saloon from the same place he had just been.

When he spoke, Tyler's voice was quiet and almost hesitant. "Ironic when you think the empire's long gone but we're still fighting the same enemies in the same far off lands of which we know little."

Danny couldn't think of a reply so he said nothing.

"You know," said Tyler, "I used to have nightmares about that day. It's funny when you think about it. We've both been in worse scrapes. The guy just came out of nowhere. I remember it so clearly, I looked down at the map, looked up and there he was and I knew I'd had it."

"But you hadn't," said Danny.

"No, thanks to you. I'd never seen anyone killed with a bayonet before."

"Me neither."

"All the training, all the planning, and something like that turns on a second of dumb luck."

Danny sipped his beer. "I guess he's sitting on a cloud somewhere with his 72 virgins thinking the same thing."

Tyler let out a brittle laugh. "You're probably right, Danny."

"I never knew it bothered you. Seems a funny line of work for you to go into if it did."

Tyler took a mouthful of his scotch and washed it around his tongue as he thought. "It's like riding a horse, Danny. The only thing to do when you fall off is to get back on again. And look at the advantages, a Morgan Plus 8, this boat, the beach house in Florida."

He nodded his head towards the cabin. "And, of course, there's Sammy." Tyler looked at his watch. "Speaking of which, I have a hot woman waiting for me in there so, just this once, I'll do what I can to help. What's the favour?"

"Guns."

"Buying or selling?"

"Hunting, I need to know who might be importing weapons, parts for Kalashnikovs, for assembly in this country."

"Why would someone do that?"

"Search me. Maybe they think it's easier to bring in the bits, hope they get mistaken for engine parts or something like that."

Tyler shook his head. "This is out of your league, Danny."

"I didn't volunteer for this. It sort of got dumped on me. A friend's involved and I'm helping him out."

Tyler drained his scotch, stood up, looked out at the light of the City. "I did hear something."

"What sort of something?"

"A contact told me someone was looking for people in this country with experience of Russian weapons."

"And why might that be, do you think?"

Tyler rubbed a thoughtful finger across his lips. "It would make sense, if what you say is true."

"And are these people still looking?"

"I can find out."

"Thanks a lot, Will. I appreciate it." He slipped the Browning into his waistband and moved towards the door. "Have a pleasant evening, sir."

Tyler grinned, white teeth shining in the gloom. "Depend on it, Danny."

\*\*\*

He was woken by the warbling of his mobile phone. Danny rubbed his eyes. He had got back late from London and watched TV into the early hours, unable to settle.

He needed time to think. He had promised to help Skidmarks but still had no clear idea how. Tyler and his network of contacts were his only lead. This detecting lark was a lot harder than it looked on TV.

He needed some space. Step back and assess the situation. Take his mind off it. He was too close to the wood to see the trees.

The phone was still ringing. He picked up the phone from the nightstand but didn't recognise the number.

"Hello?... Oh, hi... What's up?... Are you all right?... I will if I can... Okay, okay, tell me when you see me..." He glanced at the time on his watch. "Yeah, that's fine. I'll see you there." The call rang off.

Interesting, but no point in guessing. He'd find out when they met.

## CHAPTER 16

Danny shook his head in disbelief. Whenever you were dumb enough to think you'd got a handle on the world it smacked you around the head from a direction you hadn't expected.

You looked for patterns, logic, a sense of things fitting together and what do you get? Turdus.

He looked at the book again, pressing it down on the table as he ran his finger along the text.

There was an illustration and beside it the description, garden songbird on the threatened Red List, known for repeating song phrases, eats snails by breaking them against stones, lives around bushes and trees.

The song thrush was an attractive little bird. Nothing special to look at, not in your goldfinch league. But the sound that it made was magical, hard to see how tunes like that could come out of something so small and simple.

The book said they were rare, endangered. He thought he might have heard one, caught a glimpse, when he was walking through St Ann's Wells Gardens a while ago, but he was new to this twitching business and couldn't be sure.

And some muppet had named it turdus, turdus philomelos.

What the hell had that got to do with birds and singing? Just went to prove there was no justice.

After being woken by the phone call, Danny had gone for a run before returning to the flat for tea and a shower. With nothing to do until he heard from Tyler he had decided to take it easy before his meeting.

Danny liked Jubilee Library. From the outside it was a black cube of glass but inside it was light and airy with a floating deck above the main floor that stood on a row of tall columns.

When he had time he would relax in the comfy chairs overlooking the square and browse for a while or just sit and think. He liked the peace and quiet in the womb of the library. Sometimes he just people-watched through the dark glass or just stared into space, thinking, apart from the city, which was pretty much his usual position.

Danny didn't like waiting, it didn't feel like a good use of his time. He didn't like it but he was good at it. Soldiering was ninety five per cent hanging around.

Danny liked to pluck books from the shelves at random, pick up a few facts on something he knew nothing about.

But today he had hunted down the bird book because he wanted to find out about starlings. It had just fallen open at Turdus philomelos.

He found the page for starlings, Sturnus vulgaris. Short tail, pointed head, triangular wings, glossy with a sheen of purples and greens, gregarious, starlings spend a lot of the year in flocks, another one on the Red List.

Danny scanned the page again. It said large numbers arrived to spend the winter but didn't say much about their gatherings, the murmurations. That's what interested him. Maybe he'd get Karol to look it up on the net for him.

He put the book down and looked around. You could spend a lifetime and still not touch on all the interesting stuff packed into this place.

But he was pretty sure that nowhere on the long, packed shelves was a book that would tell him what was up with Emma.

A librarian glared at him when his phone trilled. Danny shrugged an apology and went outside into the square to take the call.

Tyler was brief, a rendezvous and a time. Danny tapped the phone thoughtfully against his chin.

\*\*\*

The sun had dropped below the clouds now, low to the south west. It threw a path of shimmering gold across the water and in among the charred ribcage of the burned West Pier, making the wedding cake facades of the tall Georgian houses along the front glow with a honey light.

Seagulls bickered at the water's edge. A big Alsatian danced on its back legs, waiting for the stick to be thrown, man and dog in hazy silhouette against the dazzle of the waves behind them.

Danny had hoped the starlings would be there. They gathered in their thousands at day's end, forming a single ghostly cloud that swirled and pulsed, growing lighter and darker as the birds circled in perfect unison, like millions of iron filings dancing to the commands of a single magnet.

It was still early for them. The dusk gathering was called a murmuration. He'd read that in the library too. But there was no sign of them today and he felt strangely disappointed.

The café by the peace statue on the border between Brighton and Hove was still open and Danny suddenly fancied a tea.

He joined the queue and ordered but when he patted his pocket it was empty and he remembered he had used the last of his change buying a paper.

Danny saw the look on the face of the young guy in the Pride t-shirt behind the counter.

"I'll pay for that, young man."

Danny turned to see an elderly woman swathed in a thick woollen coat. She had a large handbag hung over her shoulder and a worn wooden walking stick hooked over one wrist. Bright red lips framed a smile half hidden by the big floppy brim of a large velvet hat.

"That's okay," said Danny. "I'll skip it."

"Nonsense," said the woman, pushing past him to the counter. "Make that two teas and..." She turned back to Danny. "Would you like a slice of cake as well?"

"No, I'm fine, thanks."

The woman carefully counted out the correct change and Danny picked up the two mugs.

"Will you join me?" she asked.

"Okay," said Danny, uncertain. Being a Londoner, he had never quite got used to the Brighton habit of talking to strangers.

The woman picked what Danny guessed was her favourite table close to the protection of the snapping yellow wind break and settled herself carefully in a white plastic chair. She tucked her large handbag by her feet where she could keep an eye on it and looked out to sea, sighing with satisfactory at the panorama of shining water. Her husky voice had the whistling exhalation of a former smoker

Danny blew on his tea and took a sip. It was hot.

"Thanks for that," he said.

"Nonsense," said the woman. "You look as if you need it."

He took another sip.

"You look tired," said the woman. "Are you sleeping well?"

Danny looked up, startled. "Yeah, fine."

"A good night's sleep is so important, gives you a chance to process the events of the day before and sets you up for the new one."

Danny held the mug half way to his mouth, looking at the smile under the floppy brim of the velvet hat.

"But look at me, an old bird rattling on like this. You must think I'm mad. In fact, I'm Sara."

"Nice to meet you, Sara. I'm Danny."

"You needn't worry. I'm not some sort of nutcase. Talking to people keeps me young. And it's just nice to meet new people. It's what Brighton is all about, don't you think?"

Danny nodded.

"I like to get out every day. Use it or lose it, my doctor says. It's too easy to get stuck indoors now I'm alone. I like to keep busy, get involved in things. Are you familiar with Rapunzel's plant?"

Danny shook his head. Sara ploughed on.

"The spiked rampion, *Phyteuma spicatum*, a member of the bellflower family. It's endangered, you know. I'm part of a group helping to preserve it, although there's nothing much we can do now in winter. It's native to East Sussex but now only grows in eight known sites."

"Really?"

"According to the Grimm fairytale it's the plant Rapunzel stole that got her banged up in the tower."

"Oh?"

Sara laughed. "There I go again, blathering on. Relax and enjoy your tea, young man. You look as if you have a lot on your mind."

"Does it show?"

"Just a little. I was an actress once, many years ago. I study faces. It's a professional habit."

"Would I have seen you in anything?"

Sara laughed again, leaning forwards against the bulk of her large coat to pat his knee. "I doubt it, Danny, I very much doubt it. Z Cars?"

Danny looked blank.

"No, I thought not," said Sara. "I was working in provincial theatre before you were born."

Danny could hear it now, the rich, deep voice and the way she formed words. He could imagine how Sara would push that voice across a big room and her whole audience would hear every word.

He sipped his tea and lit a cigarette. Sara leaned forward, tilted her head back and hoovered at the blue strands of smoke before the breeze took them.

"Sorry, used to be a forty-a-day girl. Gave up ages ago but I do still love the smell."

Danny nodded. They sat in silence for a while. Then Sara leaned forward again.

"I don't mean to pry, Danny, but the only solution to a problem is to hit it head on. Unlike elderly actresses, they don't improve with age, they only get worse."

"Speed and aggression?"

"You're a soldier?" asked Sara.

"Used to be. How did you know?"

"Daddy was in India. So you've left the forces?"

Danny lifted his leg and slapped his knee. "Left a bit behind."

"Really? That must have been dreadful for you. Of course, I couldn't support Blair's wars but I have the highest regard for the work you boys and girls do. I just hope they're giving you the support you need. It must be so difficult adjusting after all the dreadful things you've seen and done."

"It's just a job," said Danny.

"Dulce et decorum est. I think that's just your stiff upper lip talking. You must need expert help to adjust back into normal life."

"It was normal life."

Sara looked startled. "Well, I suppose you would see it like that. Do you have a therapist?"

Danny nodded.

"I do a lot of work with local charities for people with difficulties. Perhaps I know her."

"I doubt it."

"What's her name?"

"Stella."

Sara looked sideways, eyes creased almost shut as she thought.

"No, no, doesn't ring a bell. Stella, you say. What's her last name?"

"Artois."

There was a pause. Then Sara flipped up the brim of her hat, bright eyes aiming straight at him.

"You're teasing me."

"Sorry, couldn't resist."

Her laugh was rich and deep. She slapped his knee. "You're a bad boy, Danny, teasing an old lady like that. Still, you'll have to excuse me." She gulped down the last dregs of her tea and thumped the mug down on the plastic table. "They'll be cutting the prices on the date-expired stuff at Waitrose about now. And remember what I told you, get a good night's sleep and hit those problems head on."

Danny nodded again. "Perhaps you're right."

Sara laughed again. "Of course I am, my boy. I am your muse of fire." She gripped her handbag and hauled herself to her feet, fine tuning her balance with the walking stick.

"It was a pleasure to meet you, warlike Danny."

"And you, too, Sara. If we bump into each other again the teas are on me."

She laughed. "I'm sure we will but don't leave it too long. I'm 78 you know. And don't forget, speed and aggression."

She turned and walked away, waving an arm in farewell. Danny smiled as he watched her go.

Then he drained his tea and looked towards the pier. In different circumstances he wouldn't have taken kindly to being given a pep talk by a game old bird of 78 but this was Brighton. Different rules.

Maybe Sara had a point. She was the first person he'd spoken to in ages who didn't have a problem he had to solve. Perhaps she was right, get some kip, then go for it.

He checked the time on his Rolex. Forty five minutes to his appointment. Then he turned and looked across at the old pier.

No starlings today. But it had been worth the outing.

\*\*\*

Danny sat at the bar, nursing a pint of Stella and watching the door of the Bellerophon. He checked his watch.

"Expecting company?" asked Emily as she bent to open the dishwasher.

"A client, hopefully."

As he turned he saw Emily pop a Pritstick back on a shelf.

"What's that for?"

Emily shook her head with disapproval. "Someone's been snorting off the top of the cistern in the ladies again. They'll get a surprise the next time they try."

They both glanced across as the bar door opened. Slate looked up from his basket. The woman stopped on the mat and looked around. Her face was without make-up, pale and drawn, her hair scraped back into a bun, her shape concealed by a baggy overcoat.

Danny jumped up from his stool. "Can I get you a drink?"

Claire Marshall nodded, a small jerky movement. "Yes please, a pinot grigio if they have it."

"That's a wine?"

Claire gave another jerky nod and Emily ducked down to take a bottle from the chill cabinet.

The bar was quiet and they moved to the furthest table and sat down.

"You guys settled back in your flat?" Danny asked.

Claire nodded briefly. "Minty was still worried but you convinced her, I think. You scared away that guy with the pipe."

"Well, if there's any more trouble, you've got my number."

"Have you sorted things out with your girlfriend?"

Danny shrugged. "Haven't had a chance. Been busy. So how can I help?"

"It's Minty, she disappeared."

"Disappeared?"

Claire's head jerked again.

"We've been sitting here chitchatting and now you tell me Minty's disappeared? What happened?"

"I don't know. I didn't want to panic. After we left your place we went back to ours for some fresh clothes. Minty called the club the night before and said she was sick but didn't want to miss two days. It's just that she didn't come home last night. That's not unusual. Sometimes she stays with ... friends. But she's never out of contact for long and now her mobile's not answering."

Danny looked at his watch. "So, she's only been gone, what? 15, 18 hours. She's a big girl, Claire, perhaps she met someone."

Claire shook her head. "No, I understand what you're saying but it's not like that. We're more than family, we're sisters."

"Have you tried the club?"

"It's not open until later this evening."

"Maybe you should wait until then and check."

Claire shook her head. "I know you're the detective. You must know all about this sort of thing. But I've got a feeling, a dreadful feeling. It just can't wait."

Danny tapped an index finger on his lower lip as he thought it through.

"If it's money," said Claire. "I can pay you." She dug in the pocket of her overcoat and pulled out an envelope. Danny looked at it on the table.

"There's two hundred pounds and I can get more, whatever you need."

"Why me, why not go to the police?"

"I want to keep it quiet. I couldn't face all the questions and publicity."

"What about Eddie Archer. He'd help."

"I don't trust that man. Minty likes you, she said so, and you've helped us before, with the stalker. I thought maybe he had something to do with it. That's why I came to you."

Danny slid the envelope towards him, felt its weight as he lifted it.

Claire squeezed her hands together. The fingers went white. It looked as if she was praying.

"Please, Danny. We're sisters, as close as two people can be, closer than anything. Even in these few hours, not knowing, it's like losing a part of myself. Can you imagine what that's like?"

Danny looked into her red eyes. "I think so, yes."

\*\*\*

Brighton is a travelling city, thought Danny. Everyone was going somewhere, aisles blocked, bags stacked, everywhere humming to the sound of wheeled luggage.

People arriving, leaving, visiting, people in a rush, white iPod leads in their ears, cardboard coffee cups in their hands.

Danny didn't understand the cult of coffee with its shots and daft ingredients. Coffee was something you had strong and simple for a hangover or a morning kick-start. After that, good, strong tea powered you through the day. And what was the point of decaff?

He had been thinking about Minty, running things round in his head. Claire's story had been pretty vague.

There were a thousand reasons why a girl like Minty might want time alone. Danny tried to convince himself of the idea, guilty that he had not started looking straight away.

He had tried her mobile but it still wasn't answering. He had called the club but they hadn't seen Minty and seemed pretty angry she hadn't turned up.

Danny knew he should be doing more but he had an appointment he just had to keep.

The previous train had been cancelled and the one he caught was only four coaches. It was packed. People jostled for seats, employing all the usual commuter tricks like spreading out and putting bags on seats to put off all but the most determined from squeezing in.

He had found a seat next to a tall man in a sharp suit and open-necked shirt who was scrolling through some sort of report on his iPad. Opposite were two girls, language students, Danny guessed. One a brunette, the taller one a bottle blonde. He couldn't identify the language but placed it somewhere in Eastern Europe.

Just as the departure whistle blew a large woman levered herself through the doors, wheezing as she leaned her weight on a walking stick, bluish lips quivering with the effort. Standing travellers shuffled reluctantly to make space for her. The people with seats avoided her eye as she peered around, cheeks puffing.

Danny looked up and down the carriage, then rose from his seat and waved at her with the copy of The Sun he'd bought at the station.

The woman smiled with snaggled teeth and shuffled down the aisle. Compressed air burst from her lips as she dropped into the seat, nodding her gratitude till she had got her breath back. "Thanks, son. There aren't many gentlemen left."

The man with the iPad looked across and glowered. The bottle blonde flashed Danny a smile.

He spent the journey leaning against a glass partition, reading his paper. A Premier League footballer said it was the pressure of the game that had driven him into the arms of three prostitutes in a motel room.

Now he wanted to make amends to his wife who was the only real love in his life.

Danny looked at the picture that went with the story, a sweat streaked man nursing the ball towards the penalty box, a guy on 150k a week with a testosterone level higher than his IQ who would jump on anything with a pulse, not so much a news item, more a confirmation of what bears do in woods.

Two pages on, an MP pledged to spend what little free time he had working with the homeless following his arrest in a public toilet near Paddington Station.

A wannabe pop star was being treated by a top psychiatrist for nervous collapse after being ejected from a TV talent show.

Danny looked up from his paper and smiled as the train burst from a tree-clad cutting and soared over the Ouse Valley on the Balcombe Viaduct just north of Haywards Heath.

He always liked that bit of the journey, always looked out for it. Thirty seven arches and 11 million bricks, he remembered reading that in Jubilee Library.

Emerging from a groove in the earth the train was suddenly a hundred feet above the valley. It felt like you were flying, terrain-hugging in a chopper.

As they came back to earth Danny went back to his paper. The usual crowds of travellers shuffled on with their luggage at Gatwick Airport. The passengers thinned out at East Croydon and he found a seat.

\*\*\*

Danny took his time. It didn't pay to rush this sort of thing. He waited until the crowds had cleared before he followed them down the broad platform and on to the escalators.

He ran his ticket through the automatic barrier to leave the station, wincing at the cost of rail travel, and walked out into the shopping mall.

The food market was doing a brisk trade. Danny set off along the shopping arcade, walking slowly, zigzagging from side to side, using the big plate glass windows as mirrors to watch what was happening behind him. It was looking good.

He made his way to the upper concourse and stood for a moment watching the shiny yellow-nosed snake of a Eurostar train gliding away from its platform, heading for Paris or Brussels. That was the way to travel, thought Danny. Maybe one day.

The upper level of St Pancras International was quieter. Small groups of travellers hurried about, checking their watches. A cluster of train spotters huddled around their tallest member, looking at something on the preview screen of his digital camera.

In the champagne bar two guys in sharp suits were talking loudly, competing for the attention of their glossy female companions.

Danny looked up. He was the first to admit he knew sweet FA about architecture but this place was definitely something special. The powder blue lattice of the station roof curled over him like a giant wave.

He walked on a bit, pausing to study a bronze statue of a jolly fat bloke clutching his hat to his head and wondering who the guy was.

A bit further on was another statue. It must have been thirty feet high. This time it was a couple locked together, bidding a tense and tearful farewell. He knew what that felt like.

Danny took another long, lazy look around, a guy in no hurry, someone with nowhere to go. Satisfied, he walked around the end of the Eurostar platforms, stopping to look at some complicated carvings of station life around the bottom of the tall statue, and entered the pub in the corner.

There were a few punters scattered around the Betjeman Arms but it was pretty quiet. He walked to the far end and ordered a pint of lager, biting his tongue when he heard the price. Leaning back against the bar he took a sip and looked around.

Four guys in business suits were comparing Blackberries. At a table further on two elegant women were sipping white wines, their slender legs disappearing amid a cluster of shopping bags bearing designer names beneath their table.

At a table on the other side of the room was a man looking hard at the screen of his iPad. He looked perfectly at home in his surroundings, just another businessman making use of the station's free wifi.

As Danny watched, the man looked up and saw him, picked up his coffee and walked out. Danny took another sip of his pint, then followed. It wasn't hard to see that the body beneath the cashmere crombie had not been honed behind a City desk.

Outside on the pub terrace the cathedral quiet of the upper concourse gave way to the fume-draped traffic hell of Euston Road.

The rain had held off for a couple of hours but it was still cold enough on the terrace to deter all but the most hardy of smokers. Tyler was the only person there, sitting at a table sipping his coffee, reading the Daily Telegraph on his iPad.

He looked up as Danny emerged from the pub and waved to the next seat. Danny put his pint on the table and sat down. "Coffee?" he queried, indicating the man's half-empty cup.

"I've got an important meeting next door in a few minutes." Tyler waved up towards the exotic Victorian towers and spires of the St Pancras Renaissance Hotel.

Danny sipped his pint. "Chilly out here," he said, rucking up his jacket around his neck against the wind.

"We've seen worse. Remember Norway? This is nothing. Anyway, as I said, I'm on a schedule so, small talk over."

"You found something."

Tyler nodded. "You know Lincolnshire at all?"

Danny shook his head.

"Very flat, big on agriculture, cabbage, caulis, that sort of thing," said Tyler.

"And?"

"They hire a lot of foreign workers, mainly Eastern Europeans, to do the work the English are too lazy to take. A man has been asking questions there. Who's done military service? Who knows Kalashnikovs? Who wants to earn more than a few pounds an hour?"

"So who is this guy?"

"He's not important, a one-man band. Runs export business in Vilnius and a job agency for harvest workers. He's small time, like you."

Danny lit a cigarette. The wind whipped the smoke away. "So who's he working for?"

"That is the puzzle. He speaks regularly by mobile with a man in Brighton. Whatever they're looking for, I think they've found it."

"And the man in Brighton?"

"Bit of a puzzle. This Brighton contact works for an import company. I checked the name. Once, ten years ago, the company did big business, connections all over the world. Now it does no business. It's dormant."

"So an inactive company is using a middle man to recruit people who know Russian-made small arms."

Tyler nodded. "That's about the size of it."

"I need contact info for the recruiter."

"Danny, I am a businessman. Time is money."

"But you'll do it."

Tyler shrugged.

"As soon as I have the recruiter's information I will let you know. The name of this dead company is…"

"Bowman Enterprises," said Danny.

\*\*\*

Danny had caught a train to Brighton before the rush hour kicked off and there was space to settle quietly and think.

He called Claire to be told there was still no sign of Minty. He had tried Minty's mobile again. No reply. He rang the Pink Flamingo but it wasn't open yet and there was no answer.

Danny looked out of the window at the blur of countryside, wondering what to do next. Perhaps taking Claire's cash had been a mistake but he had taken it and that put him under an obligation to earn it.

The problem was, how? Claire didn't want Archer or the police involved. All Danny had were two phone numbers, Minty and the club, and other problems to solve. All he could do was give it a bit longer and see if anything happened.

He wasn't comfortable with the idea but without a way forward he didn't see any other choice.

Fingers crossed Minty was tucked away somewhere quiet partying with an admirer of her dancing skills.

As the train pulled out of Balcombe station his phone rang. It was Tyler. Danny dug a stub of pencil from his jacket pocket and noted down the information on the back of his cigarette packet.

The call lasted 25 seconds. When Tyler rang off Danny sat back in his seat and looked out at green countryside blurring past the window.

Tyler had come back to him fast, which was both a relief and a surprise. He had the information he needed. Now it was time to do something with it.

Danny didn't notice when the train dashed across the viaduct.

## CHAPTER 17

As the train approached Brighton he called Bob and Karol, a pleasant ache of anticipation in the pit of his stomach at the prospect of things moving forwards, action at last. As an afterthought, he tried Minty's mobile and the club again. No reply.

And he was hungry, hadn't eaten all day. It was dark when the train pulled in to the long curved platform at Brighton Station and he jogged through the barriers and set off into town to get food for the troops. An army marches on its stomach.

Danny had spotted the shadow before it moved from the dark doorway of the shop.

When he emerged Danny saw the guy was about his height, jeans hanging in folds, a dark hoodie covering his head and upper body, only a spotty chin peppered with pale whiskers visible in the orange of the street lamps.

The light also caught the blade, about five inches, double edged.

"Gimme your cash and your phone."

Danny drew his hands from the pockets of his jacket, let them fall to his sides.

"Why?"

" 'Cos I fuckin' said so."

Danny eased his feet slightly further apart, bracing.

"That's not an answer."

The man looked as if he was trying to spit but couldn't summon the fluids. Danny could hear snot bubbling in the guy's nose. His free hand disappeared into the hood, wiping.

The knife hand was shaking now. Nervous could go either way, thought Danny. The guy might run or he might panic and do something stupid.

"Give me your cash and your phone. I need them."

"Me too," said Danny.

The guy was breathing hard now, too quickly to extract the oxygen he needed. He rocked on the balls of his feet, the knife sawing circles through the cold air in front of him.

"I'll stick you in the guts." A ghostly white plume of breath curled from under his hood as he spoke.

"You ever seen them?" said Danny.

"Seen what?"

"Guts."

The guy's trainers grated on the ground as he shuffled. The blade continued to circle.

"Horrible things," said Danny. "Like rolls of big wet purple sausages, miles of them."

The breath plume was punching out of the guy now, like an old steam engine labouring.

"Once they're out it's a bastard trying to shovel them back in, hurts like hell. There's a lot of screaming."

The man's feet were moving now, restless, almost dancing, rolling back and forth. The light striking the blade in his shaking hand was flashing Morse messages.

"You're fuckin' mental." And he was gone, shabby trainers rasping on the pavement as he ran. Danny slipped his hands back into his pockets and walked on to collect his takeaway.

\*\*\*

They sat in a circle, hunched, gripping mugs of tea, thoughtful, a cloud of cigarette smoke hovering over them.

The remains of their Chinese was congealing on plates stacked on a tray to one side by Wanda when she had cleared the table. Tendrils of noodle hung over the edge of a foil tray.

Danny turned the rod from Skidmarks's office between his fingers. "Whoever these people are, this is what they killed Aqualung for."

"And what is it again?" asked Wanda.

"It's part of the bolt mechanism from a Kalashnikov, cocks it, fires it and loads the next round. And they have a crate of them. It makes sense. Components would look far less obvious than the finished article in transit. Now the stuff's here they're looking for people to put them together. We don't know why but it's got to be bad. We need to sort them out before something kicks off."

"So that's it? That's your plan?" said Wanda.

Danny nodded. "Yes."

"You want to send Karol off to a secret factory run by men with guns. He gives you all the details, then you tip off the police?"

"Something like that, yes."

Wanda, Bob and Karol looked at Danny, then at each other.

"Not much of a plan is it?" said Wanda.

"Trust me, it'll work."

"Why not just tell the police now?" she asked.

Danny shook his head. "Skidmarks's mate got killed. I said I'd find out why. Besides, the bill already have it down as an accident and we don't know anything really, no solid proof. We don't know the where and we don't know the why. And on top of all that, the less contact I have with the boys in blue the better, and the girls."

They looked at him. Danny turned to Karol.

"You happy?"

The thin Pole leaned forward to look at the map. His face showed no reaction.

"Happy? No. It is as I say, Poles can be crazy people. It is cavalry against tanks. But I will go."

Danny turned to the others. "You see. He can phone us, pop out for a dental appointment, even leave a message in a tree stump. It'll work."

"I said I will go," said Karol.

"Sounds desperate to me," said Wanda.

\*\*\*

Archer led the way into his vast living room and gestured towards one of the big white leather sofas.

"Take a seat, Danny. I appreciate you coming."

Danny sat down. "I'm guessing this isn't about a cabbing job. Like I said at the start, I'm up for a bit of courier work if you need it but nothing dodgy. I don't need the aggro."

"No, it's neither. Just shut up and listen. Minty's missing."

Danny nodded.

"You don't look surprised."

"No," said Danny. "Her sister told me."

"Right, well, are you any good as a detective?"

"I think so."

"Well I want you to find my Minty."

"I've already got a client."

"What?"

"Her sister hired me."

"That mousey little school teacher? No, I'm talking about a proper investigation, not sticking a few posters up on lampposts. If you want a grand a day, son, you got it."

"Sounds tempting but ..."

"Don't try giving me any of that professional ethics bullshit. I want her found."

They looked at each other. "Okay," said Archer. "I don't care if you tell the sister everything, whatever. Just find my Minty."

"Okay."

Archer seemed to relax a bit, shoulders dropping as the tension eased. "That's my boy. Sorry I shouted. It's got me a bit wound up."

Danny said nothing.

"You probably think it's a bit odd. You wouldn't be the only one. I'm old enough to be her dad, her grandad, probably. But she's a sweet kid, good fun. Keeps an old man young. And she's company, if you know what I mean. I haven't had a lot of that since Miriam was taken."

His voice tailed away. Archer glanced up at Danny, afraid he'd said too much, revealed too much.

"I'll give it my best shot, Eddie. Have you got a set of keys to Minty's flat? I'd like to recce the place, see if that turns up anything, without her sister hovering over me."

"I should have," said Archer. "Dancing's a nice little earner but it doesn't pay Kemp Town rents so I bought the lease. The keys are in my desk. Come on through."

\*\*\*

Passengers trickled out of the entrance to Haywards Heath station as the train above them on the raised track pulled away towards Brighton.

A man carrying a laptop bag waved at a Peugeot saloon that pulled into the forecourt and stopped. He jumped in, kissed the driver and the car sped away into the traffic. The passengers scattered in different directions. Some headed for the bus stops and others joined the short queue at the taxi rank.

A middle aged woman puffing under the weight of her shopping bags set them down in the station entrance and massaged her red-striped hands as she looked from the bus stops to the taxi rank. Decision made, she heaved her bags off the ground and joined the taxi queue, her last treat of the day before preparing dinner.

When everyone was heading home, Karol stood alone, a small rucksack over rounded shoulders, looking up and down the road. He had been standing still, looking casually around, for a little over ten minutes when a black people carrier with tinted windows pulled onto the forecourt.

"We're on," said Danny.

Bob started the engine of his white van. They both watched as a figure slid open the side door of the people carrier and beckoned to Karol. He stepped inside.

"We ready?" said Danny.

Bob glanced down at the van's instruments. "We've got a full tank of petrol."

Danny patted his pocket. "I've got half a packet of cigarettes. Right, let's do it." He picked up Bob's binoculars from the bench seat between them and pressed them to his eyes.

"Hard to make out what they're doing through that smoked glass. There's a lot of movement. Christ! It looks like they're hooding him."

"Bloody hell," said Bob.

"Too right," said Danny. "I hadn't planned on that. This looks heavier than we thought."

The people carrier began to move, turning from the forecourt.

"Right, Bob," said Danny. "Remember what I said. Keep them in sight but don't get too close. We don't want to be spotted."

Bob put the van into gear and eased into the flow of traffic. The people carrier was six vehicles ahead of them.

"He's indicating," said Danny.

They followed at a discreet distance as the people carrier made its way out of Haywards Heath. As the houses on the fringe of the town started to thin Danny spread an Ordnance Survey map on his lap and began to study the options.

"How's it going?" he asked Bob without looking up.

"Slow and steady so far. They're seven ahead, behind a Land Rover."

"Keep tucked over to the left. Use the vehicle in front for cover. We've got to get this right. If we lose them we lose contact with Karol. Relax, smile, we're just a couple of guys going about our normal business."

"You still think this is going to work, Danny?"

"Has to."

Danny ran his finger along the roads radiating ahead of them, trying to anticipate their destination. It was too early.

"He's indicating right, taking the third exit at the roundabout," said Bob.

"Stay with him."

They both watched as the people carrier entered the roundabout, heeling over as it turned tightly. Bob's white van was just approaching the roundabout when the people carrier went past the third turning and back on into the road they were on.

"He's doubled back," said Bob. As he swung the van onto the roundabout they both fought the urge to look across as the people carrier passing them, going in the opposite direction.

"Don't look across," said Danny. "Don't make eye contact."

"I don't like this," said Bob.

"Stick with it," said Danny. "We've got to know where they take Karol."

Bob drove fast round the roundabout and back onto the Haywards Heath road.

"What if they spot us?" he asked.

"Relax," said Danny. "It's a white van, almost invisible."

They drove in silence for a few minutes, both sets of eyes glued to the black people carrier.

"He's indicating left," said Bob. "There's a petrol station coming up."

"Slow down."

Bob braked gently in the stream of traffic and the vehicle behind hooted.

"Ignore him," said Danny.

The horn sounded again.

"I can't keep slowing down," said Bob.

"Ignore him, just hang on."

A hundred and fifty yards ahead they saw the people carrier turn onto the forecourt of the petrol station.

"Do we go in after him?" asked Bob.

"Hang on," said Danny.

The van was crawling now, the driver behind was leaning on his horn. They watched the people carrier coast between the rows of petrol pumps.

"Well?" said Bob.

Danny chewed his lip. Decision time. As they watched, the people carrier moved slowly through the line of pumps, turned back towards the road and shot quickly into a gap.

"Sneaky bastard," said Bob as he accelerated.

The vehicle behind, a silver Beemer, pulled out to overtake them. Danny saw a pale finger jerked in their direction as it roared past.

They drove on, both beginning to relax a little when the people carrier started to manoeuvre again.

"He's going left at the lights."

Danny looked down at the map. "They take their security pretty seriously. That can't be good news."

They could both see the people carrier eight vehicles ahead of them now, moving steadily in a string of traffic.

"Don't get too close to the one in front," said Danny. "Give yourself room to pull out if we need to."

"How do you know all this stuff?"

"It was in a book Wanda got me."

Bob pulled a face. "How far can it be?"

Danny shrugged. "They're heading south east. Just stick with it."

There were two small boys in the back seat of the Renault hatchback in front of them. Through the sunroof Danny could just make out the mother at the wheel, head half turned as she argued with her children.

The boy on the right threw something to the floor in a temper. Danny could see the mother mouthing threats. The second boy, the younger one, stared out of the rear window, bored, and began pulling faces at Danny and Bob.

As they came out of a gentle bend, the woman's brake lights came on. Bob slowed down.

"What's she playing at?"

Then they saw the bus pulling out from its layby.

"Hell," said Bob. "What do I do?"

"Nip round her, quick."

Bob dropped a gear, pulled out and accelerated. An oncoming van flashed in anger. Bob pulled in between the Renault and the bus.

Danny caught a glimpse in his door mirror of the woman in the Renault as she gave her boys her opinion of rude van drivers.

"I can't see them," said Bob.

"Go round the bus."

"I can't see ahead."

"Try."

Bob pulled over the white line but served back in behind the bus when he saw the articulated lorry. As it thundered past they glanced at each other.

"We can't lose Karol," said Danny.

Bob eased out again but a string of cars were coming in the opposite direction, each one making a zooming noise as it sped past.

"Come on, Bob."

"I'm trying, I'm trying but it won't help Karol if we're in a head-on."

He eased out again from behind the bus.

"There's a gap."

"Go for it."

"It's too small."

"Go for it."

The van heeled over hard as Bob pulled out sharply, dropped a gear and floored the accelerator. The old van's ageing engine protested at the effort, the gear box screamed. The plastic dashboard vibrated. Danny looked up into the faces of startled passengers. The bus seemed to take forever to slip behind them.

Then they were ahead and Bob swerved into a short gap between the bus and the vehicle in front, the horn of an oncoming coach bellowing as it tore past them in a blur of bright paintwork.

"Nice one, Bob. I see them," said Danny.

Bob, heart pounding, said nothing. Danny went back to his map.

They followed the people carrier for another ten minutes, southbound along the A275, Danny tracing the route.

"If they don't do something soon we'll be in Lewes."

"They're indicating left."

"Okay, keep back, stay with them."

They watched the people carrier turn and followed it onto a quiet country road, a single Ford Focus between them and their target.

"We'd better hang back as far as we can," said Danny. "Our cover's wearing a bit thin out here."

Bob, hunched over the wheel, concentrating, just nodded. Danny looked down at the map. "There's not a lot around here. They must be close."

The Focus turned off and now the people carrier was two hundred yards ahead of them on a country lane with nothing between the two vehicles but empty road.

"He's turning left," said Bob.

"Okay," said Danny. "Get ready to follow him." He looked at the map again and glanced up to see the people carrier disappear behind some trees. Bob slowed for the turn.

"No," said Danny. "Keep going."

"What?"

"Just keep going."

Reluctantly, Bob changed back up and drove on. They both looked down the lane on the left but there was no sign of the people carrier.

"Pull in under those trees," said Danny.

As the van rolled to a stop Bob turned in his seat. "What was that about?"

Danny indicated the map.

"That lane just loops around and rejoins this road about three quarters of a mile further on. According to the map there are only a few buildings along there. It has to be one of them."

"So what happens now?"

"We wait up ahead where the road rejoins for a bit. If they don't come out, we go home and wait to hear from Karol. Besides, I've got a few things to sort out."

"And what if that lane's just another diversion to throw us off?"

"Trust me, Bob. I've got a feeling."

"Well I hope you're right, for Karol's sake."

\*\*\*

Claire Marshall stepped out of her front door and looked carefully up and down the street. It was daylight and there were people about but with everything that had happened it made sense to take precautions.

She pulled the door closed, pressed to check it had engaged, then used a second key to close the deadlock.

Satisfied the front door was secure, Claire took another look up and down the street, then set off towards the seafront.

She had always prided herself on her power of observation, her attention to detail. It was an essential skill for a good archaeologist.

Claire didn't spot the man behind the van.

CHAPTER 18

When Claire Marshall had turned the corner of the street Danny slipped from behind the parked Transit van and walked swiftly up the front steps.

Eddie Archer's keys in his hand. He looked around as Claire had done, let himself in and closed the door quietly behind him.

He remembered the layout from his earlier visits. There was no sound from the ground floor flat but he tiptoed past anyway. No need to wake the baby.

Danny padded quietly up the stairs and opened the door to the upper flat, another Yale, another deadlock.

When it clicked open he listened and slipped inside. The only noise was a clock ticking somewhere.

He knew burglars often slip on the door catch to delay anyone returning. Instead, Danny turned the key in the deadlock from the inside.

He sniffed. Faint smells, cleaning fluid, a whiff of cigarettes and the slightest tang of a perfume, lemony.

Danny went into the front room. He stood in the centre and turned slowly through a full circle. Small sofa and two armchairs. TV with a DVD player on the shelf beneath. Bookshelf with an old encyclopaedia, two modelling directories, local street finder, three Dan Brown paperbacks and two Bridget Jones.

Glass-topped coffee table, copies of Hello, Current World Archaeology, Grazia, The Guardian, a weekly soaps magazine and TV listings. To one side there was an unwashed coffee cup and some make-up cleansing pads.

On the mantelpiece was the ticking clock and Claire's archaeology award that Minty had told him about.

Danny didn't know what he was looking for, hoped he would spot it when he saw it. Nothing chimed.

He took a quick look in the kitchen at the end of the hallway. It was small and basic, clean and neat. Danny guessed that would be down to Claire more than Minty.

He opened a few cupboards at random. Slimming soups, rice, pasta. In the fridge he found non-fat milk, fruit yogurts and a half-eaten meal in a foil tray.

To Danny's eyes, the bathroom looked like a pharmacy closing-down sale, soaps, creams, gels, sprays mouthwash and two sizes of tampon.

It wasn't hard to identify Minty's room. As soon as Danny opened the door he saw the Brad Pitt poster on the wall, the sweaty, bare-chested warrior with the thousand-yard stare.

Danny remembered it from that film about some ancient Greek love triangle, good battle scenes.

He stepped inside. The lemon scent was stronger here, as if a trail had been laid for him.

The bed was big, pillows scrunched, the z-shape of her body impressed into the mattress and highlighted by the parallel ridgeline of crumpled duvet that trailed off onto the floor.

The make-up table was covered with bottles and jars and had a mirror with lights around it. Wardrobes packed with clothes ran along two walls, dresses, tops like handkerchiefs, denims with ragged slashes across the thighs.

At the bottom of the wardrobes were racks packed with high heeled shoes except for the one on the left which held Minty's collection of thigh boots, four PVC, two leather. Ridiculous heels.

Danny opened a drawer. It was packed with underwear, bras, thongs, delicate tendrils of lace, mostly white, black or pink.

Something caught his eye. He reached into a corner of the bottom drawer and pulled out a spray can of mace.

Beside it was a knife. Danny pressed the switch and a thin, viscous blade flicked out. At some time, Minty had been worried about her security.

He dug into the drawer again and drew out a vibrator, turned it over in his hand, marvelling at the size and wondering what the knobbly attachments did.

Danny turned to see Brad watching him, the thousand-yard stare. Then he spotted the cork board.

It was big and packed with photos and scraps of paper held with map pins. Minty with a group of girls holding empty shot glasses, sticking their tongues out at the camera. Minty in a long Victorian dress, tiny waist, big hat. Minty on stage, wrapped round a pole, long legs encased to mid-thigh in white PVC.

Minty on the set of EastEnders, posing with some of the cast. Minty in a carefully staged head-and-shoulders picture, serene and distant, in black and white like the old studio portraits.

Minty feigning shock as she woke to discover her female flatmate in bed with her in one of those newspaper problem picture stories. Minty with her arms flung dramatically around Big Eddie Archer.

Dotted between the pictures were scraps of paper, agents' business cards, a dental appointment and a modelling card. Danny pulled out the pin and examined the card. On the front of the A5 sheet was a moody portrait shot of Minty, eyes smoking at the camera, framed by long dark hair.

On the reverse was a picture of her in a short skirt and boots, hands on hips, and beneath that her vital statistics – Height: 5' 9". Weight: 8st 8lb. Bust: 36b. Waist: 24". Hips: 33". Shoe size: 6. Eyes: Blue. Hair: Black. Nationality: British. At the bottom of the page was contact information for her agent, Bowman Talent.

Danny nodded in approval, but still nothing chimed. He pinned the card back on the board and looked around again, trying to see anything he might have missed.

In the far corner, screened by the open door of a wardrobe hidden by clothes on hangers, was a small desk. Danny moved the door and saw a laptop. It was plugged in and the screen was up.

He pressed the power key and was surprised when it came to life. Danny wasn't good with computers but he had picked up a few tips from Karol.

He sat down and studied the screen. Minty had Facebook as her desktop. Danny scrolled through her friends, all 486 of them. Pictures of people mugging for the camera, people in clubs, on beaches. No one he recognised.

Careful not to damage or disturb anything, Danny moved the mouse to explore her documents folder. There were a few letters and a file labelled "Diary". Danny opened it but it was a short account of everyday activities that had obviously bored Minty quickly as it only ran for three weeks.

He tried the My Pictures file. There were hundreds of pictures including a number of photoshoots, Minty in a flowing ballgown, Minty playing tennis in a short, pleated skirt, Minty and a blonde girl sharing a foamy bath.

Some images were taken on film sets, Minty as a policewoman, as a Victorian flower girl, behind the beer pumps of a pub bar. Danny scrolled through the thumbnails, opening the occasional image to full size, thinking to himself this wasn't such hard work.

At the bottom of the folder was a file named QuickTime Movie MM0001. He clicked it and the movie player opened with a fuzzy black screen.

As Danny leaned closer he could make out two circles in the gloom. One black, glossy, the other, grey with a pink circle of glistening skin at its centre.

They move in sync together, making circular movements. There was a creaking noise and the picture juddered.

Then there was a flash and a rumble that seemed like thunder. Danny wasn't sure and moved the volume slider to increase the sound.

The movement in the foreground stopped. The woman pulled forward, disengaging with a little sigh and Danny realised what he was looking at.

She was lying on a flat surface, or bench maybe, and the camera was behind her, looking at the top of her head.

She sat forward, swinging her legs down from the bench, exposing her long slender back to the camera.

There were some muttered words, too indistinct to make out, and the squelch of a kiss followed by a light laugh.

Then the woman stretched out on the bench, flexed and arched her back. The camera picked out the outline of her breasts and a red, sweaty face beyond.

The woman turned to face the camera, placed her hands wide on the bench in front of her and bent forward. She arched her back and from the movement of the camera you could tell she was wiggling her bottom.

The man said something but her body blocked the camera's microphone. Then there was the sound of a slap followed quickly by another. The woman squealed.

Her mouth formed a perfect theatrical "Oh" of surprise as she was penetrated from behind. Then her pert breasts began to rock towards the camera, back and forth, back and forth. The bench creaked. The camera rocked with the rhythm.

As the pace increased the woman's nipples traced dark ellipses in the faint light. Then a heavy hand with thick fingers and a single gold ring clawed its way up her body from behind and gripped a breast, squeezing.

Lightning lit the scene again and the woman let out a long, rising moan. The man was talking urgently now but the woman's rocking body blocked the sound from the microphone. He spoke again but thunder drowned the sound.

Another flash of lightning, closer together now. The man was shouting. The woman lifted a hand from the bench and plunged it down between her thighs, reaching for something.

As she did so, her breasts were bouncing towards the camera before being jerked back by the pull of the big hands on her hips.

The woman stared straight into the camera now, black hair cascading across her pale shoulders, eyes wide with excitement. Wet red lips parted to reveal brilliant white teeth lit by lightning into a smile of triumph.

As the man behind began to bellow, the woman let out a long, lingering howl.

Then it stopped. The man took a step back, looking dazed. The woman bobbed down, picked up a small black dress and wriggled into it, flicking the thin black straps over her bare shoulders.

The man said something. It sounded impatient.

The woman reached towards the camera. "I'll just get my bag." The picture went haywire. Danny sat back in the chair and looked at the black screen, wondering what it meant.

Could just be a home movie, making your own entertainment on a wet Saturday night. The guy in the background was pretty big, could have been Eddie Archer but the picture was too indistinct to tell. Danny wondered about making a copy of the film but he didn't know how.

As he considered his next move he pulled open the drawer of the desk. Paperclips, a leaky Biro, pink heart-shaped Post-It notes and a thick paper packet half-filled with Minty's model cards. He pulled one out and slipped it into his pocket.

He took a last look around the room and stepped out into the hall. It had felt strange digging through Minty's personal things, personal life, but that came with the job.

He looked at the door opposite for a moment, the last room, then pushed it open.

***

The light seared his eyes as the hood was wrenched off his head. It seemed as if he had been waiting for hours, had lost track of time. The man blinked against the bright light and looked around.

Two guards stood behind him, one at each shoulder. The one on the right held his small backpack. In front of him a cliff of muscle grinned down at him.

"Don't your mothers feed you bastards where you come from?" The Axeman shook his head in disbelief as he looked up and down the scrawny figure standing round-shouldered in front of him.

The man said nothing. The Axeman reached forward and gripped his bicep, squeezing hard. "Look at you, muscle like a sparrow's kneecap. It's a miracle you can stand up on your own."

As The Axeman's grip loosened the man twisted his arm free and rubbed it with his other hand.

"You sure you know the job?" asked The Axeman.

The man nodded.

"I asked you a question. Do you know what you're doing?"

"Yes," said the man.

"Don't give me attitude. Don't give me attitude. I run this place. I'm the boss, you know, the big chief or whatever you call them where you come from. I shout 'shite' you jump on the shovel. Savvy?"

The man nodded.

"And don't you forget it because I'm not a man you want to upset. Now listen to me and listen good. Security, we take it very seriously here," said the wall of muscle, grinning.

"Welcome to the only farm in Britain that grows Kalashnikovs. Your fellow workers call me The Axeman behind my back but as far as you are concerned I am God. You keep your nose clean and we'll get on fine but you break the rules, and we have a lot of them, you, my friend, will wish you had never been born."

The Axeman glanced at the man holding the backpack and nodded. The man put the bag on a table, unfastened the straps and tipped out the contents. He poked through the jumble of socks, t-shirt and underpants then squeezed the side pouches. His hand closed around something solid and pulled out a small zip bag.

He emptied the contents onto the table, toothbrush, paste, bar of soap. The man picked out a small packet and held it up. The Axeman roared with laughter.

"Condoms! You think you're going to get lucky in here? You people, you make me laugh."

The guard with the backpack indicated for the new arrival to repack it. The Axeman watched him work.

"You're a replacement so you'd better catch on quick. You start work tomorrow."

The man nodded.

"Now these two nice gentlemen will show you where you sleep."

The thin man shouldered the bag. The Axeman held out an open hand the size of a shovel.

"And I'll have your mobile phone."

The man dug his hand into the pocket of his jeans.

The Axeman grinned gain. "Like I said, we take security very seriously."

\*\*\*

Claire's bedroom was neat and sparse, everything in its place, a complete contrast to Minty's. The bed was small, duvet and pillows carefully arranged, smoothed, all creaseless parallel lines.

The only wardrobe contained a small selection of clothes. It held all the personality of an operating theatre, thought Danny. Nothing caught his eye.

He tried a drawer. Underwear, pretty but sensible. Tucked in the corner, a small pocket vibrator. He glanced at a cluster of certificates on the wall, caught the word archaeology.

Beside them were some framed pictures. Claire in a muddy trench, smiling, floppy hat, dirt on one cheek. Claire sitting on a bench in a tent with half a dozen others. Claire standing in front of a crumbling ancient wall of small red bricks.

If Danny was missing anything he couldn't begin to image what it might be.

There was a small desk in the corner. The centre drawer held a small, neat laptop. He powered it up but it wanted a password. He tried all the options he could think of but it wouldn't let him in.

The drawers to either side of the desk were packed with paperwork, all arranged in clear plastic folders with coloured tabs separating the sheets into different sections.

He wondered about the laptop, was about to look at the papers, when he heard the scratch.

Instantly he was out of Claire's room and down the corridor. Behind him, the deadlock yielded to the key. As the Yale started to grate Danny swerved into Minty's room. No space in the cupboards. He looked under the bed, jammed with crap but he could make room if he needed to. The front door opened and closed. Footsteps walked past into the kitchen. Cupboards opened. The footsteps returned.

Danny heard Claire enter her bedroom. He crouched by the door, listening, ready to dive into the debris of Minty's life under her bed if it sounded like Claire might come into her sister's room.

Claire was inside her own room for just over two hours and ten minutes before Danny heard her move again. Footsteps went along the hall. He could hear the sound of the television. Whatever Claire was watching lasted 90 minutes.

The flat went quiet for a while, then more footsteps as she went into the bathroom. Danny heard the sound of peeing, then the hiss of the shower.

He gave it sixty seconds, then eased open Minty's bedroom door and passed along the hall. The bathroom door was half open. Danny could see the curve of a pale hip swaying beneath the water through the translucent plastic shower curtain.

He looked at his watch. Skidmarks had booked him a job for the evening but there was still time. Danny moved silently to the front door and let himself out.

\*\*\*

"This is outrageous, bloody outrageous."

Sir Charles Wolfram's face was purple with rage. Edmund Salter could smell the tang on his breath, knew his blood pressure would be through the roof. He looked like an over-ripe fruit about to burst.

"I am a serious politician," said Sir Charles. "I came here to debate the issues." Salter winced as spit flecked his face.

"I did not come here to be abused by that pack of animals. Call themselves journalists? Bunch of smug pinko hacks. They wouldn't know the truth if it bit them."

Salter looked at the beads of sweat breaking out on Sir Charles's forehead, smelled the whisky. He laid a restraining hand on the old man's shoulder but Sir Charles brushed him away.

"If ever I needed proof that this country is long overdue for a damned good shake up it's that rabble in there, only interested in themselves and their naïve polytechnic politics."

Salter could see Sir Charles was shaking. "I know you're upset but please do try to calm down. It will only make it worse if they see you like this."

He put his hand on the old man's shoulder again, tried to guide him along the corridor from the meeting hall, but Sir Charles brushed it away. "No respect for age and experience. No respect for traditions. Fair play? Hah!"

Sir Charles's shoulder drooped. Salter took his arm and began to lead him towards the exit. "Time to go, I think, Sir Charles. We need to draw a line under this evening, formulate a response, perhaps turn it to our advantage."

Sir Charles huffed. "Where's my driver, Edmund?"

"He's right outside, Sir Charles."

\*\*\*

Danny, hands deep in pockets, stamped his feet against the cold. He stood under the canopy of the meeting hall, leaning in against the wall to escape the worst of the icy rain that slashed in rippling sheets through the orange glow of the street lamps.

He glanced at his watch, then fished a packet of cigarettes from his pocket and opened the neck of his jacket to shelter the flame of his lighter. Behind him a handful of vehicles gleamed in the wet of the car park, a few hunched figures on the pavement beyond. Danny hoped this wouldn't take all night. It was a favour for Skidmarks, a special job. But it had been a long day and he'd had enough.

"Danny!"

He peered into the patchy darkness of the street. Two figures bent against the wind, struggling to stop their umbrella turning inside out. A bus went by, hissing as its tyres bit through the water on the road.

"Danny!"

Then he saw her, dressed in a soaked and clinging hoodie top, her hair plastered to her head. Water flicked up from the heels of her trainers as she ran.

"Danny!"

She ran across the car park, clutching at the neck of the hoodie top as if that would make any difference. Then she slammed into him, arms gripping him, head pressed against his chest, sodden rats' tails of her blonde hair sticking to his chin.

He prised her head away from his body and looked down into her pale face. Her lips moved but no words formed.

"Emma? What's the matter? What's happened?"

"Oh Danny, Skidmarks told me where you were. I had to talk to you. I'm sorry."

"Look, I'm working. What's the problem?"

"I need to talk to you, explain."

"Explain what?"

The double doors behind them burst open.

"Where's my driver?" Sir Charles staggered as he stepped out into the rain, his white hair dancing above his head.

"Here," said Danny, raising an arm. He looked down at Emma. "I've got to go."

Salter was right behind Sir Charles. He walked straight to Danny, gripping his arm. "You're late."

"Sorry about that."

"Never mind. I brought Sir Charles here in the Jaguar but I have to go on to a meeting in London. You're here to run him home, quickly. Clear?"

Danny nodded, taking the minicab keys from his pocket.

"But Danny, we need to talk."

He looked down into Emma's tortured eyes.

"Driver!" yelled Sir Charles, blinking as the rain spattered his face.

Salter was waving Danny forward when another figure appeared in the doorway behind them. "Sir Charles! Sir Charles! Could you just clarify your immigration policy? Do you still stand by what you said about medical examinations and intelligence testing?"

Salter turned round, arms wide to block the man. "Sir Charles has nothing further to add this evening. He will be making a full statement tomorrow."

Danny looked down at Emma, still clutching him, her arms round his waist. He reached back and began to pry her locked fingers apart. At first she resisted, then her grip slackened. Danny took a ten pound note from his pocket and pressed it into her hand.

"Look, I've got to sort this. Get a cab back to mine. I'll be there as soon as I can. We can talk then."

Danny could hear shouting from the doorway and the sounds of a scuffle.

"But Danny…" Emma's face was twisted in misery. He pushed her gently away.

"Go on," said Danny. "I'll get there as soon as I can."

Emma took a step back and stared at him, cold rain extinguishing the falling tears, then she turned and ran away into the night.

Danny spun round and walked into the doorway. Three journalists were watching the confrontation as Salter and the man who had challenged Sir Charles faced off, faces eighteen inches apart.

"You can't stop us. My readers have a right to know what that old racist is proposing."

"I have told you already there will be a statement in the morning," said Salter. The journalist took a step forward. Salter squared his shoulders. Eyes locked, neither saw Danny step up and take the journalist's wrist. The man gave a grunt and looked to his side.

"Who the fuck are you? One of his fascist bodyguard?"

"No," said Danny, smiling. "I'm one of the silent majority and I'm going to break your wrist if you don't back off."

It wasn't the pain that convinced him, it was the look in Danny's eyes. The man took a step back and Danny released his grip. The man stuffed his notebook in his jacket pocket and began to massage his wrist.

"Blood Nazis, you're all bloody Nazis." Danny just looked at him as the man backed away into the safety of the three who had been watching.

Salter turned. "Bit drastic, that, but thanks anyway. After Sir Charles's performance tonight things couldn't get much bloody worse."

The journalists huddled in the doorway, heads tilted together, muttering and glancing across at them. One spoke into his Blackberry, reading from his notepad.

As he watched them, Danny saw a large figure elbow his way through the group who started to protest until they saw the size of the man. He ignored them, slipped through the doors and into the shadows, striding briskly off across the car park.

Danny nudged Salter with an elbow. "What's he doing here?"

"Who?" said Salter, looking around.

"Eddie Archer."

Salter hesitated. "He's … Mr Archer is a local entrepreneur. He is a valued supporter of Sir Charles's work."

Danny shook his head and Salter looked around. "Where is Sir Charles?"

They stepped out into the rain lashed car park but nothing moved. Salter looked around the parking bays and gasped. "Oh Christ, he's taken the Jag."

Then they heard the crash.

## CHAPTER 19

Salter was fit but Danny left him standing. Legs pounding, arms chopping, he powered across the car park and into the street.

He saw it straight away, a shapeless bundle by the kerb a hundred yards ahead. Someone bending over it.

As Danny skidded to a halt a haggard, dripping face looked up from the body on the tarmac. "He came out of nowhere, going like the clappers, some bloody boy racer. He must have been doing seventy."

The man peeled off his coat but Danny laid a hand on his shoulder. "Don't move her. She might have spinal injuries."

"You a medic?" asked the man, hopefully.

"I know a bit."

Danny knelt down and peeled the limp and crumpled clothing from the victim's face.

Emma's eyes were closed and her face was deathly white, made paler by the blood that trickled from her nose and mouth.

"Emma? Can you hear me, Emma?"

He gripped her wrist and felt a faint pulse. Her breath was low and gasping. Gently, he gripped her chin and opened her mouth to check she hadn't swallowed her tongue.

He dug his mobile from his coat pocket and dialled 999. "Yes, ambulance, hit and run. The victim's got a faint pulse and shallow breathing but she's unconscious and not responding. Yes, fast as you can." He gave the location and dropped the phone back in his pocket.

"Anything I can do?" the man asked.

Danny looked up and down the road. "Just stand over there and wave if you see any traffic. Make sure they see us."

"Right you are." Happy to be useful away from the casualty, the man hauled himself to his feet with a grunt and began waving at an approaching minibus to take a wide berth.

Danny checked her pulse and breathing again. "Emma? Emma?" He listened to the night but there was nothing but the hiss of rain. "Come on, come on." He looked down again. "Hang on in there, Emma. You'll be okay."

"How is she?" asked the man, waving a bus into the opposite lane. Danny shook his head. "I don't know."

A BMW slowed to take a look. Danny waved it away. Emma's face seemed to grow paler beneath the orange glow of the street lamp beside them. Wet hair curled across her forehead like question marks and he smoothed them away.

"Come on."

Danny looked up when he heard footsteps.

"How is she?" asked Salter.

"Unconscious, I think it's pretty bad."

"Do you know what happened?"

"Yes," said Danny. "And so do you."

Salter tried to look puzzled. "What do you mean?"

"It was that cunt boss of yours."

They both looked towards the sound of sirens.

\*\*\*

The newcomer was different. His surroundings didn't seem to distress him as it did the others. He had not provoked The Axeman but he had not cowered either.

The man seemed to know things the others didn't. He seemed to have some inner strength and Olexei found that comforting.

Olexei tried to settle in his bunk but every position hurt. He knew a rib was broken, others probably cracked. He winced at the memory of The Axeman's boot. He shifted again and grunted as pain flashed around his ribs like shorting electricity.

The newcomer looked up at the sound and gave a nod of greeting. Olexei nodded back. The small barracks was gloomy, the light dim, half an hour to lights out.

Most were already asleep. At the far end Arkadi was snoring, long rasping exhalations punctuated by wet snuffling. In the bunk above, Stepan read an old copy of the Argus, the paper tilted towards the glow from the single bulb.

The newcomer slid from his bunk, padded silently across the floor and slipped in beside Olexei. He looked down at Olexei's t-shirt and raised an eyebrow. Olexei nodded and the man lifted the t-shirt to reveal purple bruises across his whole body.

"Three ribs, I think," said Olexei.

"They will mend," said the newcomer. "But it will hurt."

"We can sit for the work. It will not be so bad but it is not what we expected."

"What did you expect?"

"We knew the work could not be legal but they treat us like dirt, like animals. We are locked in here when we are not working. We cannot go out or make contact with family. We are prisoners."

"And what happens when the work is finished?"

Olexei shrugged. "Who knows? I try not to think, just hope we can get our money and go."

The newcomer nodded. "What about the others. Do you know them?"

Olexei shook his head. "No, we are all strangers. And they do not like us to talk."

"You have no friends?"

"No," Olexei thought for a moment. "Maybe one."

The newcomer put his hand in his pocket and pulled out a scrap of something. Olexei leaned forward to see what it was and gave a little gasp when he recognised it.

"I found it between the planks behind my bunk. You know this child?"

Olexei took the picture and studied it. "No, but I know his name is Peter. He is seven years and wants to play the piano."

"How did the picture get here?"

"It belonged to his mother. She had the bunk before you."

"Did she leave?"

"No one leaves, not until the work is done."

"Then what happened?"

"I don't know. She came here to make money for her son to go to school. Her husband is dead in an accident at home. She missed her boy very much. Sometimes I could hear her crying in the night, pushing her face into the pillow so no one would hear. But I heard. She was gentle, beautiful and she did this for her son. I think she was my friend."

"But she didn't leave? Escape?"

"No, Katya went outside the barracks one night, late, after they put the lights out. She did not come back. Now her son is alone in Rumia. It was her home, in the north of Poland. Do you know it?"

The newcomer nodded, memories of drinking Luksusova with friends at his favourite bar, the smell of his grandmother's bigos made from a recipe handed down through her family.

His father Janusz using his carpentry skills since he lost his job at the Stocznia shipyard in Gdynia. His mother Krystyna cleaning. The pay was pitiful but what choice was there with so many out of work.

His brother Daniel chasing around with his friends, getting into trouble. The newcomer hoped his brother was exercising Bax regularly. He had to be the world's ugliest mongrel but he missed him.

The newcomer knew his sister, Goska, would be scribbling away in her notepads, fingers locked in her long blonde hair as she wrote another of her books about local history.

"I know Rumia," he said.

"Perhaps you know Katya," said Olexei.

The newcomer shook his head.

"She went out at night and did not come back?"

Olexei nodded.

"The Axeman?" said the newcomer.

Olexei's shrug confirmed it. They both looked down at the creased and faded picture of the boy who wanted to be a pianist.

"Katya," said the newcomer, quietly to himself, then tucked the picture between the boards behind Olexei's bunk.

"You are Olexei?"

"Yes."

"A pleasure to meet you. I am Karol."

\*\*\*

He drank bitter machine coffee from a plastic cup, sitting on a plastic chair under the sickly lights, lost in his thoughts.

He had tried not to think, blot it all out by reading the posters on the walls, warnings not to smoke, warnings of what would happen if you threatened the staff.

It wasn't working. He could still hear screaming tyres, see blood floating on the fallen rain.

A mumble of conversation drew him slowly back into his surroundings. He looked up to see a nurse at the far end of the waiting room talking to a fat, round-shouldered guy wearing an anorak, stained jeans and worn trainers. The man shuffled towards him and stopped a few feet away.

"Nurse says you're the man who brought her in."

Danny nodded. "I was minicabbing in the area. Heard the crash."

"Nurse says you gave her first aid, might have saved her life."

Danny shrugged.

"Name's Benny Driscoll. Emma's my wife."

Danny nodded. "Pleased to meet you."

"I just wanted to say thanks, you know, for what you did. It's nice to know there are still a few good Samaritans about."

"It was nothing."

"Well it is to me," said Benny. "I don't know what I'd do without my Emma." His body wobbled under the impact of a sob. "I mean, you're sitting at home watching telly and the phone goes and your whole life turns inside out. If she ... if she dies ... I don't know ..."

The bank of plastic seats heaved as Benny collapsed into the chair next to Danny. Tears squeezed between the fat fingers pressed across his eyes. "I'm sorry ... I'm sorry ..."

"That's okay," said Danny, unsure what to do. "Look, I'll get you a coffee."

Benny snuffled a yes and added, "Sugar, please."

Danny waited as the machine clunked and whirred, watching Benny's hunched bulk jiggling as he sobbed. He walked back, handed him the cup and sat down again.

"It makes you think," said Benny, wincing as the hot liquid scorched his lip.

"About what?" asked Danny.

"You know, life and stuff. You don't know what you've got until you look like losing it. I mean, it hasn't been easy. I haven't always been the best husband. I've been away a few times, if you know what I mean, haven't always been the best provider.

"She's a lovely girl, great cook too. I don't deserve her, not really. I've been a bad boy at times and I know it. Sometimes I wonder why she puts up with me."

Benny slurped his coffee and looked down at the floor for a moment, then carried on.

"You know, Danny, once I even got to thinking she might be shagging someone else. I felt bad about that, thinking it. Don't get me wrong, she's a cracking girl, but, no, not my little Emma. She wouldn't."

He finished his coffee and put the cup on the floor, peering down at his hands, turning them over, studying the other sides. "She'll get through this, won't she?"

Danny just looked into Benny's dull eyes. He had nothing to say. The man began to shake, quivering as if something alien was bubbling up from his chest, shoving its way up his throat. He let out a wail and collapsed against Danny's shoulder, body wracked with spasms.

Reluctantly, Danny stretched an arm around Benny and patted his shoulder.

"Hang on in there, pal. You need to be strong for her."

Benny's blotchy red face turned up towards Danny but he didn't pull away. An elastic slug trail of snot hung from one nostril.

"I'd be lost without my Emma. If she ... if she gets through this, I'll make it up to her. We'll start again. I'll be a proper husband. We'll be a proper family. If she ..."

They both turned as the swing doors opened. A tall man with scruffy brown hair and dressed in green scrubs was talking to the nurse. She pointed towards them and he walked briskly down the waiting room, a clipboard under his arm.

"Mr Driscoll?"

Benny raised a finger, straightened in the chair, then hauled himself to his feet. Danny stood beside him as the doctor threw an inquiring look.

"It's okay," said Benny. "He's a pal. So ... is she ...?"

"There's a concussion and she's lost a lot of blood. We won't know for sure if there's any permanent damage until we get the results of the x-rays and scans. But she's strong and the signs are good. I'm hopeful."

Benny clapped his hands. "That's good, good."

The doctor tilted his head to put a brake on the celebrations. "I'm afraid I do have one piece of bad news."

Danny and Benny froze.

"Yes?" said Benny.

"She's lost the baby."

\*\*\*

They stood by their bunks, some of them upright, some hunched, some shaking. The Axeman's boots cracked on the old wooden floor as he stamped up and down the cramped barracks room.

"If I've told you once I've told you a thousand times. And I'm not in the business of repeating myself. Is that crystal?"

No response.

"Is that CLEAR!"

A mutter ran round the room.

"Again!"

They agreed with him, louder this time. He walked around again, pausing to stare into eyes. Some tried to meet his gaze, most flinched away.

He stopped in front of Karol and their eyes locked.

"I don't like you."

They stared at each other.

"I don't like you. What did I say?"

Karol looked hard into The Axeman's red-rimmed eyes. "I don't like you," he repeated.

The punch took him by surprise, knocking his back against the bunk. He lost his footing and stumbled to the floor but gripped the planking and hauled himself upright. The Axeman moved on.

"If anyone, ANYONE, is hiding a mobile phone they had better tell me now. If they do, I might just break a leg. You can work sitting down. If you don't tell me NOW, things will get a lot worse."

He looked around, head snapping from face to face. He stepped forward and paused in front of Olexei.

"You bunch of Pakis better be taking me seriously."

"My name is Olexei. I am from Ukraine."

"Same difference," said The Axeman. He looked sharply across at Karol, then round the room.

"Last chance. Anyone?"

There was the smallest of movements at the end of the barracks. The Axeman's thick neck whipped round.

"You, what's your name?"

"Arkadi," said the fat man. His voice was barely a whisper.

"Speak up!"

"Arkadi."

"What are you looking at?"

"Nothing. Nothing, sir."

"You were looking."

"No, sir, no."

The Axeman crossed the room in three strides, pushed Arkadi aside, grabbed the thin mattress from his bed and threw it on the floor. He bent his bulk, thick fingers scratching and scrabbling as they probed around the slats and crevices of the bunk.

He straightened up, snorting. "Go on, where is it?"

"Nothing, sir, nothing," His hands were reaching out in front of him, palms upward, pleading. The Axeman stepped towards him but stopped suddenly, looking down. He was standing on the mattress, his right boot rocking on something hard.

"In the mattress, eh?"

"Please," whispered Arkadi. "It is for my mother. She is ill. She worries."

The Axeman grinned. "In the mattress, is it? You know, if brains were dynamite you couldn't blow your hat off."

The smile dropped from his face and the first punch took Arkadi full in the mouth. He flew backwards, falling, skidding across the floor.

He crawled away, found a corner, his face turned to The Axeman, watching for the next attack while his hands scrabbled behind him, as if the planks might magically part.

The Axeman stamped down hard on the lump in the mattress. He stamped down again and again. Something cracked. He kept stamping. His breathing grew ragged. Spit flew from his lips.

The Axeman was away in a world of his own, stamping and stamping. Everyone was startled when he stopped. It was so sudden. A taut silence gripped the room, broken only by The Axeman's ragged breathing.

He looked across at Arkadi on the floor, his head tilted, eyes slits. "You miserable little piece of shit." He drew out the words, left space between them, to drive home his point.

The Axeman took a step forward. Arkadi whined, quaking, trying to roll himself into a tight, tiny ball, praying he might fall through a crack in the floorboards.

"Mother."

The Axeman took another step. Everyone braced themselves for the beating to come. The Axeman took his third step. As he did he reached down and opened the flap of the axe holster on his belt.

There was a hiss of breath around the room and Arkadi whimpered as everyone leaned away, trying to make themselves small.

The Axeman drew out the weapon slowly, hefting it, spinning the haft in his hand so the head rotated.

Arkadi's nails scrabbled at the wooden wall behind him in a hysterical attempt to claw his way out. He tore his eyes away from The Axeman and tried gouging his fingertips into the narrow gaps between the planking. A fingernail snapped. His skin tore and began to bleed but nothing moved.

The Axeman took another step and stood over him now. The last whisps of will seem to drain from Arkadi.

The Axeman spun the haft in his hand again.

"So, blade or butt?"

Arkadi sat, back against the wall, eyes so wide they looked as if they would burst from his head, a faint keening noise rising from his throat.

The crack of the axe head's flat butt smacking into Arkadi's temple echoed off the walls of the small room. The terrified watchers twitched as if an electric shock had passed through them.

Arkadi let out a little sigh and sagged sideways. The Axeman changed hands and repeated the blow from the opposite direction. The dying man's eyes rolled up into his head.

The Axeman kicked him but the only response was air wheezing from his throat.

"Come on, you piece of shit, make an effort, do something."

The breath continued to wheeze.

The Axeman turned, bright eyes sweeping across the others in the room. "This is boring."

With a speed that startled them he spun the axe in his hand, swivelled on his heel and brought the weapon down in a fast, high arc. They all heard the thud as it buried itself deep across the top of Arkadi's head, the haft throwing an angled shadow across his face like some sort of obscene sundial.

It seemed like a long time before anything happened. When they heard The Axeman's breathing start to ease everyone began to rise slowly, like a time-lapse film of plants waking to the sun.

They couldn't help turning, drawn to look into the corner of the barracks room.

Arkadi's body was slumped back against the wall at a slight angle, a halo of blood spattered against the woodwork behind him, darkening as it soaked into the old, dry timber. The blank whites of Arkadi's eyes pointed unmoving at the room.

Nobody moved. The Axeman looked down at the body. Then he looked down at the axe and seemed to see it for the first time.

He looked at the body, then the axe, body, then axe. Slowly, he tilted his big face to the ceiling. "Oh, fuck."

His teeth were grinding, a harsh sound like nails on blackboard. Then he started to laugh.

Karol, watching, could feel his eye closing up from The Axeman's blow and knew he really didn't like him.

\*\*\*

The doorbell rang, on and on. It stopped for a second then rang again, on and on and on.

"I'm coming."

She hurried into the hallway, dipping briefly to slip the elastic at the back of her right slipper over her heel.

The bell whined on. What could be that urgent at this time of night? The ringing stopped, then started again. "I'm coming, I'm coming."

She pulled back the bolt and fumbled with the catch on the lock. When the door swung open she took a step back, startled by the tall figure silhouetted against the dim lights in the hallway.

"What's happened?"

Lady Margaret gasped as he stepped into the light of the flat. Danny's clothing was crumpled and soaking but it wasn't that. It wasn't even the blood stains spattered on his jacket and up his arms, on his neck and in his hair. What really stabbed a chill through her were the black, empty holes where those sparkling eyes should have been.

"Danny? What ever's the matter?"

He took another step.

She opened her arms. He fell against her, arms circling her waist, punching the air out of her with a ferocious grip.

She felt his silent sobs shaking her body, his face pressed hard into her neck, hot tears burning her skin. She cupped her hand over the back of his head and pulled him closer.

***

It had been easy, maybe too easy. The buildings sat in a natural dip in the hillside and were well screened from the outside by bushes and trees.

A single unsurfaced track wandered to the farm, its last 400 yards following a line of trees in clear sight of the buildings and anyone watching.

The men who ran and guarded the place lived in the main farm building. Beside it was what had once been a multiple garage and was now converted into the barrack block.

Behind that was a large barn, a third of its space occupied by the workshop. Its heavy wooden door was secured with a large old padlock. After several attempts, Karol had managed to pick it. He took a quick look round and moved on, closing the padlock behind him.

The entire compound was fenced by razor wire carefully meshed with the surrounding bushes to make it invisible to anything but the closest inspection.

They had CCTV but it was limited to avoid anything being seen from outside the compound. The cameras were hidden under the eaves of the buildings. Karol had studied them carefully and worked out that if he kept close to the walls he would be below their arc of view.

The cameras were operated from somewhere inside the farmhouse building but from what he could see of them they were not infra-red which was good.

The pathways around the perimeter used by the guard patrols offered plenty of cover if anyone approached the wire.

That just left the little shed. Karol watched it for a while. Nothing moved, apart from the silent shadow of a cat near the farmhouse

He had waited a long time after they had dragged Arkadi away and thrown a bucket of water at the blood-stained wall where he had fallen.

Karol wondered where they would take him, whether he would be with Katya from Rumia. Whatever happened, there was nothing he could do, not yet.

The guards toured the farm regularly through the night but, watching and listening, Karol had found there were fewer of them in the early hours and they patrolled less often, drawn back too easily to the warmth of the farmhouse fires.

He looked at the shed again. Apart from the night movements of the surrounding woodland, everything was quiet. He crept closer and pressed his ear to the planking. Still nothing.

It was the only building he hadn't checked. It made sense to do it now, so he had a complete picture for later.

Then the wind whipped the sound of boots on gravel to him and he shrank back into the shadows.

The guard, black padded parka and woolly hat pulled down tight, walked within twenty feet of Karol, rubbing his gloved hands, too numbed by cold to look at anything but the inviting lights of the farmhouse.

Karol, freezing in t-shirt and jeans, watched him go by. The cold was painful but he ignored it. He had things to do.

When the man was gone, Karol slipped silently along the front of the shed and pushed open the door. He stopped just inside, holding it slightly open to allow the farmhouse lights to penetrate the darkness.

In the gloom he could make out sacks stacked in a corner, an untidy pile of crates, straw scattered across the floor. The room had a smell of toilets.

The faint illumination picked out something pale, half buried in the straw. He bent down and pulled up a piece of material. When he dusted off the clinging straw he saw it was a pair of white pants.

Karol dropped them on the floor and flicked straw back over them with the toe of his trainer. As he turned for the door his foot connected with something which skittered off into the dark.

Dropping on all fours, he searched with his hands until they connected with a small box. He held it up to the dim light. A battery.

He searched a little further and found a larger box, rectangular. As he lifted it to the light from the door he saw a picture of a boy secured to the back of the mobile phone with clear tape.

"Hello, Peter," said Karol quietly.

\*\*\*

Nursing his third tumbler of whisky as he sat at the breakfast bar, shoulders slumped and loose, face a foot from the marble top, Lady Margaret thought Danny looked smaller than usual, even younger.

When he looked up his eyes were unfocussed, distant. She moved across the kitchen, took a length of kitchen towel, dampened it under the tap and bent down to dab at Danny's eyebrow.

"Missed a bit," she said, gently stroking away the last smears of Emma's blood.

"I'm sorry," said Danny.

"You have nothing to be sorry for."

"Earlier, the way I acted."

"You're a man, Danny, a real one. There aren't many like you any more but you're still not Superman. You've had a shock. Just let it out."

"I ... I ..." Danny sighed, gave up and gripped the cut glass whisky tumbler.

"Finish that one if you want it, then you've had enough," said Lady Margaret. "I'll make some tea." Danny nodded.

As she busied herself around the kitchen Danny struggled to regain control of the night's images as they wriggled in and out of his consciousness like a desperate eel. The sound of screaming tyres. A heavy, wet thud. Sodden hair plastered to Emma's bloody forehead. Benny's moon-faced disbelief. A baby dying in darkness.

He didn't feel sick. He wasn't in any pain. He just felt nothing, empty, as if he had been hollowed out, everything inside him scooped away and dumped by some giant blunt spoon.

He jumped when she put the tea cup and saucer down beside him. She brushed a limp lock of hair away from his eyes. "I think you're in shock, Danny. Drink this when it's cooled down. I've put plenty of sugar in it."

She sat down and watched him, catching glimpses of the eels writhing behind his eyes.

"It was him, wasn't it? Charles?"

Danny nodded.

"He was here earlier, drunk as usual, and agitated as well. Something about a journalist. Just dashed in and dashed out again. He's often drunk. I know the signs. It doesn't take much to set him off these days but tonight I knew there was something different. Do you want me to call the police?"

Danny shook his head.

"Let me guess, you're going to deal with this yourself."

Danny dragged his head up and looked at her. She saw his face was blank. The eyes were dark and still. The eels no longer moved.

"You're right," she said. "I know I shouldn't say this, it's disloyal of me, but Charles would get himself a good barrister, might even escape a ban. He's very good with lawyers. They're saved him more than once. Besides, they would never send him to prison. He's very thorough. 'The devil's in the detail,' that's what he's always telling me."

Danny tested the tea, found it had cooled and took a sip.

"He's not a bad man," said Lady Margaret. "Just a weak one. Once he had ambitions, dreams. Their passing has made him bitter."

He rose, walked to the kitchen units and took something from a cupboard. She placed a key on the marble breakfast bar beside Danny's cup and saucer.

"He has a garage behind the flats."

\*\*\*

There was no rush. He had all night. Better to get it right than do it quickly. Any mistake, even a small one, and there would be no second chance.

Karol lay on his side, back to the barracks wall, hands folded under his head, eyes closed, listening to the breathing all around him.

Some of it was a rhythmic hissing. At the far end of the barracks, Stepan made a sound like sawing as he snored.

Slowly, Karol opened his eyes. The pattern of sounds around him remained unchanged. He clawed the blanket from his body and bundled it behind him.

Planks creaked as someone turned over, snuffled and settled again.

Karol still wore his trainers. He swivelled silently in his bunk and placed his feet on the floor, applying his weight slowly to hear if the floorboards would creak.

A sleeper three bunks away, deep in a dream, drew in a deep breath and whispered, "Anna, Anna."

Karol levered himself to his feet and padded to the door. As his hand closed around the handle he heard a pop, pop, pop, pop away to his right. Stepan farting.

Karol opened the door four inches and listened. The compound was silent. The outline of a guard passed against bushes on the far side.

It was good there were no dogs. He would not be able to move at night if they had dogs. It was a big weakness in their security but Karol knew they wanted the farm to go unnoticed in the countryside. People around would have heard the dogs, noticed the change in routine. The dogs were a lucky break for Karol.

When the shadow of the guard passed behind the farmhouse Karol slipped out of the barracks door like smoke and made his way to the unused shed, pressed tight against the walls to keep below the arc of the CCTV cameras.

When he was satisfied the building was empty he went inside. Katya's mobile phone was where he had left it.

He pressed the power button and waited, shielding the light of the screen with his hand.

When the mobile had locked on to its service provider Karol smiled. One bar of battery power and two bars of signal. Enough.

He couldn't know how much credit there was on the phone but he thought of Katya and her need to speak to Peter, hear his voice as she sat, trembling, in the darkness, and knew there would be enough for what he needed.

Karol tapped in a mobile phone number and saved it into the memory. Then he opened a blank text message and began to type.

## CHAPTER 20

The old Jaguar under the dust sheet was some sort of classic, worth a few bob, probably.

It was parked neatly, perfectly straight, and hadn't been used for quite a while. The front near-side tyre had gone soft and the even silvering of dust was undisturbed. Beyond it was a dark blue Mini One.

The nearest car was different. A modern Jag, obviously quite new from the gleam of the paintwork and the blackness of its tyres. It had been left at an acute angle to the wall, one window half down and the driver's door pushed to.

It had almost hit the rear wall as it had come to a halt. Danny squeezed between the wall and the front of the new Jag. The bonnet was faintly warm.

As he looked around something caught his eye, trapped in the claws of broken glass that jutted from the smashed near-side headlamp. He reached down carefully and pulled out a matted sprig of blonde hair.

\*\*\*

It was dark and something was buzzing. Danny opened his eyes but remained perfectly still. The cotton pillow pressed against his head felt crisp and fresh. He didn't recognise it.

As his night vision adjusted he felt a gnawing in his stomach. Something was wrong. He tensed at the sound of movement and watched the shadows of feet flicker through the strip of light at the bottom of the door.

His head hurt. He couldn't recall where he was or why. Then suddenly he did and his stomach turned over with a sick vertigo lurch.

He remembered Sir Charles, drunk and angry, Emma sobbing in the driving rain, tyres screaming, Benny at the hospital, Margaret mopping blood from his face, putting him to bed in her spare room.

Danny's throat closed as he tried to control his breathing and calm the wild drum roll of his heart.

Beyond the darkness was a buzz of traffic. But the buzz that had woken him was close by.

He levered himself up from the mattress and saw an oblong of pale light on the night table. He picked up his mobile. A text from a number he didn't recognise. He opened it and read the message. It made no sense at first.

"Payne's farm ... barn ... barracks ... guards."

Then he realised. Danny carefully reread the message, then tapped out a brief reply and sent it.

He lay back on the mattress, staring up at the ceiling in the dark. The pain of yesterday and the fuzzy remains of last night's whisky fell away. A cold determination spread slowly through his body and mind, like ice rising up a pane of glass.

He had people to see, things to plan. It was time to take the initiative. Danny wondered what else the day would bring.

\*\*\*

"You talk to me like that again and I'll break your fucking legs. Show some fucking respect."

"Respect? Maybe when we met, but not now. Not after I find out you've been backing that drunken old fool."

"You don't storm into my house and talk to me like that. No one does. I won't warn you again."

They stood, shoulders squared, snorting like bulls. A deep rumbling growl from Thatcher in the corner as he hunkered low, baring his teeth.

"Where's Wolfram?"

"What am I, his mum? How the hell should I know?"

"You're one of his barmy backers."

Archer jabbed a thick index finger under Danny's nose. "Don't push it."

The dog's growl wound up into a snarl, flashing yellow fangs set in gluey wet gums.

"Back! Thatcher, Back!"

"Where's Wolfram?"

"You won't be told, son, will you?"

"Don't 'son' me."

"Look, you'd be better off spending your time trying to find Minty. How far have you got with that?"

"Don't change the subject. Just tell me where that bastard is."

"And why do you want to know?"

"You think this is funny?"

"No, son, far from it. Believe me, I can understand why you're upset and I can see why you want to take it out on Wolfram."

"It's a bit more than 'upset', Eddie. There's a girl, she's lying all smashed up in A&E after that drunken bastard ran her down, killed her baby. I want him."

"And what are you going to do when you find him? Rough him up a bit, smack his head on a concrete floor a few times. That right, Danny?"

"I'm going to kill him."

Danny saw something change in Archer's eyes. The tension went out of his shoulders, then he threw his had back and barked a cold laugh at the ceiling.

"Join the queue."

"What?"

"I'm first in line."

"But you're his mate. You've been backing his barmy politics campaign?"

"I had my reasons. That accident, it's not the first time he's done this, Danny."

"He's got form?"

"And some."

"One of yours?"

"My little jewel, my Ruby. She was only two, been out shopping with her mum, Vicky. Car just swiped her off the kerb, squashed her to a pulp. It destroyed Vicky. I bought the best shrinks there are but it took six months before she was even talking again. Even now we have to keep an eye on her, make sure she takes her meds."

"And it was Wolfram?"

Archer nodded.

"Why didn't you tell the police?"

"And see that fat fake grinning from behind a team of smug lawyers? No."

"You've got other ways."

"Top him, you mean? Too easy. My one blessing with little Ruby was it was quick. Doctors said she wouldn't have felt a thing. I have to believe that. But death's too good for Wolfam. I've got other plans."

"Such as?"

"I'm going to destroy his family, see how he likes it. I'm going to smash his precious reputation, smash his career, ruin him so he never has the chance to crawl back up again.

"I want him humiliated, disgraced. I want to trash what he loves, kick him in the ego, make him nothing, just like he did to my little Ruby. Once he's been through all that, and he knows who and he knows why, then the bastard can die."

Danny sat back in his chair. "How long have you been planning this?"

"Since the day of little Ruby's funeral. I don't care how long it takes, how much it costs. I even used Minty. I feel bad about that but I want Wolfram ground into the dust like the piece of dog shit he is."

"I didn't realise."

"I don't give a lot away, son, not unless I want to."

"Doesn't get round the fact I want him too."

"You're a persistent young bastard, aren't you?"

"Yes."

"You know, Danny, I like you. You're one of those people who says what they mean and does what they say. That's rare. It's a gift, or maybe a curse."

"Don't change the subject."

"Fair enough. Just making a point. Maybe we can co-operate."

***

Sir Charles's lips opened and closed like a stranded fish, pumping soundlessly as he tried to form words and force them out.

"We spoke of protection." The mouth pumped silently again as his mind tried to grasp what he was seeing. "Those who oppose us can be violent and desperate people."

The others stood quietly and watched him wincing his way slowly through the painful process of comprehension, mouth deforming as if he tasted something rotten. The wrinkles around his eyes creased and recreased in an ever-changing pattern of anguish.

"We must be able to defend ourselves if we are to be free to spread our message, fulfil our mission. But this! THIS!"

He held up the Kalashnikov in his hands, offering it to the others for comment. No one spoke. His knuckles were white, fingers flat and pale.

"This is madness. I never approved it. By resorting to this we make ourselves as bad as our enemies. We make ourselves criminals. It flies in the face of everything we are trying to do."

The others watched him in silence, no reaction on their faces. "Have none of you understood? We support order and the rule of law. This ... this ..."

He threw the weapon down and stepped away, as if it might sting him.

"I have to go home. I have to think. This is wrong, very wrong."

Sir Charles turned and walked towards the door of the barn. The others watched, letting him get half way there before they followed.

The last man out slammed the doors behind him. When silence had returned to the barn a shadow glided from behind a wall of straw bales. He listened, watching a rat scuttle through the straw.

When he was satisfied he padded silently across the wooden floor and carefully picked up the Kalashnikov using a rag to cover his hands. He slid the weapon into a hessian sack and slipped back into the darkness.

\*\*\*

What would it have looked like? Emma was a petite little thing but Danny was more than six foot. And Benny, well he was Benny.

Calling it "it" kept it at a distance, "he" or "she" brought it uncomfortably close. Boy or girl, dark or fair, Danny tried to push thoughts of a cocktail of characteristics from his mind.

It was like that kids' game where you stuck plastic features on a potato. But the thoughts kept creeping back, promoted by memories of his own kids, the milky smell, bright eyes, toothy smiles, sticky-up hair.

Pointless anyway. The baby, whatever it might have been, was dead. Probably the best thing anyway.

Danny shrugged himself deeper into his jacket and quickened his pace along the prom. The taste of salt spray on his lips reminded him of that day on the beach among the wrecked containers. How long ago had that been? Seemed like ages.

He felt better for the fresh air but very tired, drunk with fatigue. When he had rung the hospital they said Emma was "comfortable." What the hell did that mean? You've been run over by a drunk driver. You've lost your baby and you're "comfortable". Danny wondered how they'd describe a really bad day.

Fragments of unrelated problems whirled in his mind, crashing into each other and bouncing off like bits flying off a car wreck.

Brown eyes or blue? Maybe green?

He didn't want to be alone but couldn't face company so he had caught the No7 bus out to the marina and walked back along the front, following the line of the Volks Railway which was closed for the winter.

A light aircraft burbled by, following the coast towards Shoreham Airport. He watched it go, puzzling how it was that it managed to stay up there. Danny had never understood how flight was possible, the invisible forces at work. Something else to look up at Jubilee Library, when he had time, when he had sorted everything out.

Just before he reached the Palace Pier he stopped by a black anchor on a plinth, marking the spot where the cargo ship Athena B had run aground thirty odd years ago. The Margherita wasn't the first ship to come to grief in the turbulence of the English Channel and she wouldn't be the last.

He walked on. It was bitterly cold but the wind had dropped and the cloud was beginning to break up a little.

The mercury sea stretched to a grey horizon. At the end of the pier he could see the feint skeins of fishing lines.

There was a lot going on and Danny needed to think it all through carefully. A lot had happened. He winced at the memory of the night at Lady Margaret's. Not the sex, that had been a real education. It was the crying that bothered him, sobbing like a baby on her shoulder.

The memory made him uncomfortable but, even as he tried to blank it, he knew the reasons why. Sometimes the lid came off, no matter how hard you tried to keep it screwed down tight.

The night it came open there was no way he could let it happen in front of the others. He didn't do that. But if it had to happen he somehow knew Margaret would understand. And she had. He pushed the memory away with the plastic facial features and the potato and stepped aside to clear the path for two runners, monitors strapped to their arms, faces dark with concentration as they pounded by.

It was all starting to crowd in on him. Events were moving fast and he had to move with them. The kid was dead. Emma was in hospital. Nothing he could do about that. He would have Wolfram, that was certain. The guy deserved it, for Emma, the baby and for Archer's granddaughter.

Archer might think he had first claim but not if Danny got to him first.

Danny walked past the black ribs of the old West Pier. Beyond that, a small freighter chugged westward towards Shoreham Harbour.

He barely noticed as he walked, head down, thinking. Then there were the guns. Some bunch of nutters in a remote farmhouse planning who knows what. Their actions had killed Aqualung and he had promised to help Skidmarks.

He had to deal with Payne's Farm and get Karol away safely. The little Pole was tough, resourceful, but in among the opposition he was vulnerable. And he was Danny's responsibility.

That left Minty. He'd only met her a few times but she seemed lively and energetic, as happy with her life as anyone could expect to be. Not the type to vanish. Added to that, her room had enough stuff to open a fashion shop and nothing was obviously missing. Minty wouldn't travel without clothes for every occasion.

If he was right up to that point it meant something had happened to her. But what? She was close to Big Eddie Archer so anyone touching her touched him. They would have to be crazy but that didn't mean it wasn't possible.

And the sister was an odd one. They looked and acted so differently you wouldn't know they were related if you weren't told. Still, despite their differences Claire had hired Danny to find Minty so there must be some sisterly feeling there somewhere.

This detecting lark was a bit like soldiering, ninety five per cent hanging about and the rest of it frantic. Now was the time for frantic.

Danny had a lot to sort out but it wasn't like the army, no planning group, no flow of intelligence. You had to do it all on your own. And time was not on his side.

He stopped at the café by the peace statue and rummaged in his pocket for some change. When the couple in front moved away he stepped to the counter.

The guy in the Pride t-shirt looked at him and smiled. "What can I get you?"

"Mug of tea, please," said Danny.

"Make that two, young man." said a voice behind him. Danny turned.

"Sara."

\*\*\*

All in all, it had been a bloody good evening, thought Kenny Connor as he stuffed his semi-limp penis back into his jeans.

There had been a good turnout, especially considering the weather. Took a lot more than a bit of rain to put that bunch off an evening's fun. And that Brenda was a game girl. Her husband really was a lucky bugger.

It had been quiet when Kenny had arrived but things had picked up after an hour or so. At its peak there must have been getting on for a dozen vehicles scattered around the car park so there was plenty of entertainment for everyone.

Kenny always parked the van away to one side, under the trees. That way it gave him a chance to watch the comings and goings, as he liked to call them, and get an idea of how the evening was shaping up. They were a good-natured crowd and you got to recognise quite a few regulars after a while, just a nod of greeting, nothing more. And you had to be a bit sensitive. Different people were into different things. It was only human nature.

Some let you watch, some let you join in. There was always a ripple of excitement when a vehicle's interior light flashed the signal and the watchers started to emerge from the shadows.

Sometimes you stood by the car and followed the action, like a porn film with live actors. Sometimes they'd wind the window down and let you have a feel. Then there were the ones who bent over the bonnet and let anyone have a go.

Different people had different needs, were comfortable with different levels. It was all just good fun, really, all consenting adults, a real community.

But as far as Kenny was concerned there was no denying that Brenda was the star turn. The things that woman could do he'd only ever seen in magazines. It was a wonder her husband ever let her out of the house, let alone to gatherings like these. That said, he seemed to enjoy it as much as she did. Lucky bugger.

Brenda was a star and this evening she'd excelled herself. Kenny and three others had been standing by the car, right by the front passenger door. They had the seat back and Brenda and her old man were going at it hammer and tongs.

She had her eyes shut and the most amazing look on her face. Then, just as hubby got into his short strokes she opened her eyes, looked straight at him and smiled. Bright blue eyes with those long lashes. Straight into his eyes.

That had never happened before. It had been such a shock, such a kick, that he'd shot his bolt straight away, all over their wing mirror.

What a night.

Things had quietened down now. And there was no way you were going to top an experience like that. Time to head home. The thought of going back to the tiny bedsit with the dodgy old TV took the edge off Kenny's pleasure.

Why couldn't he have been married to Brenda instead of that grasping cow who'd taken everything?

Kenny tried to blot out the thought of his ex. Maybe he'd treat himself to a bucket of wings and a few tinnies on the way home. As he walked towards his van he ran his fingers through the change in his pocket. Just about enough.

He had reached the van and unlocked the driver's door when he decided he needed a pee and went round the back between the rear doors and the woods.

Kenny was in full flow, whistling quietly to himself and rocking up on the balls on his feet, when he looked down into the ditch that surrounded the car park.

He was so shocked he had wet his trainers before he realised. Some heartless bastard had run over a dog and just dumped it. He could see matted black hair spread up the far side of the ditch's bank.

Sometimes it was hard to credit what some people were capable of. Kenny finished and zipped up before taking a careful step forward. With all the rain they'd had recently the bank was slick with flattened grass and mud.

It must have been a big dog as far as he could tell from the area of fur that he could see. Must have been a posh one, too, from the look of the black gloss on the parts not matted by mud and water.

He looked back across the car park. Most of the others had gone. The only illumination was a pale orange street lamp by the entrance which wasn't throwing much light his way.

Kenny decided he needed to check if the poor thing was still alive. He wouldn't be able to sleep if he thought he'd left it there in pain. Testing the bank with a urine-soaked trainer, he took a tentative step forward. It was hard to make out the shape.

Kenny pulled his disposable lighter from his parka pocket and flicked it three times before it lit.

Later he wished he hadn't.

There was something beside the black hair at the bottom of the bank, a pale patch with some sort of pattern.

He squinted in the weak light, turning his head to make out what it was, following the lines.

When the penny dropped. It was obvious. He was looking at a butterfly.

\*\*\*

Danny's finger traced the gentle curve of the contour line as it curled round the foot of the low hill. When it reached the crossroads he tapped it twice with his finger.

"There, that looks promising." He glanced up at the dull glow of Google Maps on Wanda's laptop, careful not to touch the surface of the screen. Sticky finger marks on computers annoyed him.

Bob and Wanda watched as Danny sat back and thought for a moment, his gaze moving from the laptop to the 1 to 25,000 scale Ordnance Survey Explorer map of Brighton and Hove spread out on the coffee table.

The county town of Lewes was a historic picture postcard place with property prices to match. It straddled the river Ouse, filling a gap in the high ground of the South Downs as they ran parallel to the coast like a large protective wall.

The town boasted its own brewery, castle and prison, all the essentials of life.

The terrain on the map to east and west was packed with the tight swirls of contour lines showing steep hillsides that hemmed in the river, railway, the A26 running north east and the A275 heading north.

Towards London there was rolling open country dotted with woods. Danny's finger traced a route north of the town and tapped twice when he found what he was looking for. He looked up to make sure Bob and Wanda were paying attention, then picked up the rod from Skidmarks's office.

"Here's Payne's Farm." He said, using the rod as a pointer.

"The junction here is about three quarters of a mile away and from the Google satellite picture it looks like a quiet road with good cover."

Wanda flapped a hand. "Don't make a mess with that thing."

Danny looked at the rod, turning it between his fingers. "Don't worry. It's clean, never used."

"Well do you have to keep waving it around?"

Danny placed the rod carefully on the coffee table and rested his finger on the map to indicate a wooded area just south of the farm. Wanda watched his good leg bouncing with anticipation. The random movement annoyed her but she said nothing.

"We can leave the van there and take the quad bike on to the farm using this line of trees for cover. It's a shallow valley that climbs up towards the buildings which sit in a slight dip so the terrain and the trees should mask any noise. I might need to borrow your fancy phone, Bob."

"Why?"

"It's got GPS, just in case I get lost. I can't risk reading the map in the dark."

"I've never worked out how to use it. I'll dig the manual out for you."

"Or you could just tell the police," said Wanda.

Danny looked up. "You know I can't do that. Karol's in there and I can't drop him in it. I got him in there, I've got to get him out before anything kicks off."

"Well I don't know anything about soldiering," said Wanda. "But it sounds like a tall order for one man on a quad bike."

Danny smiled. "You might not be a soldier, Wanda, but you've spotted the flaw in my plan. Still, it's the only plan I've got. Surprise is the best weapon, that and a 9mil Browning."

"You've got a gun?" she asked, her voice suddenly harsh.

He patted his jacket pocket.

"I don't want that in my house."

Danny was about to reply when Bob cut in. "I'll go."

"What?" said Wanda.

"I said I'll go. You said yourself it was too much for Danny on his own so I'll go with him."

Wanda wasn't often lost for words but her mouth opened and closed three times before her thoughts came together. "Don't be daft. You've never done anything like this before. And anyway, what about your blood pressure?"

Bob shot to his feet, his face dark. "I'm not that bloody old, and I'm not a bloody invalid."

Danny felt the heat of Wanda's glare and took his queue to chip in. "She's right, Bob. It's good of you to offer but it could turn nasty."

Bob's eyes flared. "Don't you start. You both seem to think I'm some sort of cripple. And you're the one who's always banging on about mates helping each other, brotherhood under fire or whatever it is. Anyway, it's my van and you're not going anywhere without it. Besides, you'll need a hand getting the quad in and out."

"What about your back?" asked Wanda.

"For God's sake, woman."

Wanda and Danny sat still in their seats, looking up at the anger and frustration that ebbed and flowed across Bob's face.

"There's nothing to discuss. Karol's in the shit. Danny's going to get him out. And I'm going with him."

The creaking silence that followed seemed to stretch on for ages. Danny picked up his tea mug and downed the last cold mouthful.

"Well," he said, dabbing a dribble off his chin. "If you put it like that."

"It'll be all right, won't it, Danny?" said Bob, forcing a smile in an effort to hide the tremor in his voice.

"It's all about what your mind and body is prepared for, Bob. Skewer your hand with a kitchen knife and it's panic and a dash to casualty. Donate a pint of blood and it's a nice brew and a biscuit. Expectation, that's the key."

Bob nodded. Danny looked across at Wanda and saw her eyes were glistening. "I'm not nagging, Bob, honestly," she said. "It's just I'm scared."

Bob still towered over them but his shoulders seemed to droop just a little. He took two steps towards Wanda's chair and slapped his hand down on her shoulder. "To be honest, love, so am I. But it's got to be done."

"Well if you're going, I'm going."

Bob cupped his hand under Wanda's chin and shook his head. Danny sat in silence, watching them speak without talking and remembering times past when he had enjoyed that same special intimacy. He didn't know how long it took before a tiny relaxation in their posture signalled that some sort of agreement had been reached. Danny leaned forward and pulled the map across the table.

"Okay, let's synchronise watches."

A look of panic flashed across Bob's face. "What? Already?"

Danny looked up, grinning. "I was joking. Just jump."

Bob looked confused. "Do what?"

"Jump."

Bob glanced across at the watching Wanda, then did an uncertain hop, landing with a flat-footed thump on the carpet to the sound of clattering metal. Danny put his hands out. "Keys."

Bob dug in his pocket and handed over a large bunch of keys.

"Change," said Danny. Bob pulled a fat handful of loose coins from his pockets.

"Try again." This time Bob landed with another thump but no other noise.

"Let me see your watch."

Bob pulled up his sleeve and offered his wrist. Danny inspected a large gold wristwatch dotted with knobs and dials.

"Okay, push it as far up your arm as it'll go and keep your sleeve pulled well down. You can sit down now."

"What was all that about?"

"When we get out to the farm it'll be night but we don't want any stray light sparkling off your watch and we can't have you clanking around the countryside like a suit of armour. Now you're dark and silent."

Bob grinning as he considered the image of himself dark and silent. Wanda watched him with a pinched, brooding expression darkening her face.

"Wanda?" said Danny. She turned her head to look at him. "It'll be no fun sitting around at home, waiting. I might have a job for you if you want it."

Bob and Wanda glanced at each other. Danny indicated the OS map on the table. "Anyway, let's just go over this again. I've got a few things to sort out but we go tonight."

Wanda saw the look of raw excitement in Danny's eyes and shivered as a chill ran through her. "I'll put the kettle on again."

## CHAPTER 21

Big Eddie Archer stood in front of his bookshelves, eyes roving back and forth across his family pictures, Miriam, their boy and four girls, the grandkids.

He stood still, shoulders slightly rounded, but there was an aura about him, something like an electrical surge searching to break free.

"How?" he said.

"Stabbed, so I heard," said Danny.

"And you're sure about this?"

"Copper I know told me."

"What did he say?"

"It's a she, and not a lot. Found in a car park near Lancing. They're got her down as unidentified at the moment. I couldn't ask too much or I might have looked interested."

"Car park near Lancing? That's a dogging site."

"So she said."

"Bastard."

Archer turned away from the bookshelves and looked straight at Danny. His eyes were burning with a strange light. "I lost my Miriam, then little Ruby, now this. I tell you something, Danny. I've done some stuff in the past but I don't deserve to be punished like this. Not like this."

They looked at each other in silence for a moment. Then Archer pulled himself upright and clapped Danny on the shoulder.

"You did well, son. And thanks for coming to tell me. It's better coming from, you know, a friend."

"You hired me to do a job. I'm just sorry it didn't turn out better. She was a lovely girl."

"Job's not over, Danny," said Archer.

"How so?"

"I want you to find the bastard who did this to my Minty."

"It's a murder investigation now, Eddie. They won't like me treading on their toes."

"Sod their toes. I don't care if you have to cut their bloody legs off. I want that bastard found."

"Okay, Eddie, I'll do what I can."

"Unidentified, you say?"

"Yes."

"Her parents are dead. I'll take care of her. I owe her that."

"You any idea who it might be?" asked Danny.

Archer shook his head slowly. "No, not offhand, but I'll think it over. Everyone knew Minty was with me so whoever did this to her is either stupid or mad."

He looked back at the pictures.

"There was one guy, Giles Forrester, some family tree expert. I had him doing a job for me, part of the plan to set up Wolfram. He's bent, and a greedy bastard. Happy to do dodgy work but wary of getting too illegal. He'd heard of Wolfram, knew it was big, wanted more. I was happy to pay but not silly money so I had Minty deliver his pay packets and provided a little performance bonus as an incentive every so often to keep him keen."

"You got his address?"

"I've got his card on my desk."

Archer led the way towards the door. As he reached it he turned.

"Whoever it was, Danny, I want him."

\*\*\*

It would have been better to take notes but nothing could be written down. He could carry nothing that might be found.

It didn't bother him. He knew he could move quickly and silently. He knew he could remember every detail and repeat it when necessary.

Some people liked to work with weights to harden their body. Danny ran to keep himself in shape. Karol's pleasure was to exercise his mind.

He had sat, curled up in the shadow of the barn, and watched for nearly an hour, still and invisible in the dark, noting details.

One of the guards must have a weak bladder, or perhaps it was the cold. He had a favourite tree he used to urinate.

Another was a heavy smoker. They patrolled in rubber-soled boots but Karol often smelled a whiff of cigarette smoke before he came into view.

On other occasions he had heard a guard even further away when he paused to spit, announcing his arrival with a harsh bubbling sound as he hawked to clear his throat.

Karol sat, watched and listened, and made careful mental notes of routes, timings and any little habits and mannerisms. It was hard to be sure how many men were guarding the compound. Some patrolled while others were in the farmhouse. Karol could not be certain but it seemed like there were more of them now.

Fifteen minutes ago the bladder guard had passed. The steam from hot urine in the cold night air had been clearly visible rising from the bark of his favourite tree.

Five minutes ago the hawker had passed by. The faint light from the farmhouse had caught the silver streak of phlegm as it arced across the farmyard.

Anything might be useful. You could never know when some tiny piece of insignificant information became important once it was linked with another.

When the others had gathered to meet the big man in the barn Karol had not known who he was. But by the way they spoke and the way the others, including The Axeman, had reacted, it was clear he was important to the operation at the farm.

And he had been surprised, angry. Disagreement was a fissure that might be prized open with little pieces of information. The rifle the man had handled was still in its Hessian sack, buried in a corner of the barn where no one would find it.

Karol knew he had a five-minute window before the next patrol. Time to slip back into the barracks. He started to rise, legs stiff, but froze at the crouch when a door opened. Silently he lowered himself back onto the ground and waited.

It had been impossible to mistake the bulk illuminated by the light from the open door, The Axeman.

Karol watched him close the door, walk down the farmhouse steps and pause to light a cigarette in his cupped hand. Then he moved away across the yard.

Something about the way he moved, the way he kept looking around, seemed odd to Karol. The Axeman's usual swagger was gone. He seemed nervous.

The big man walked to the far side of the yard, close to the padlocked double gates, and drew himself into the shadows. He looked around again, then plunged a gloved hand into the pocket of his parka. There was a pause, then a faint glow. Karol leaned forward to watch and listen.

"Digby? It's Rookwood. Yes, I know that. How's it going?"

The Axeman listened to the reply.

"Well, he seemed seriously pissed off when he saw the gear in the barn. What if he says something? ... You sure? ... implicated? You think so? ... So you're saying Wolfram'll keep his mouth shut? ... If you say so... yeah, yeah, of course I will. I always do. Okay."

The Axeman ended the call. Karol watched as he scrabbled at the mobile phone, trying to detach the battery and remove the SIM card with gloved hands. When he finally succeeded he weighed it in his palm for a moment, then threw it towards the perimeter fence.

As he turned The Axeman lashed out with his foot and cursed. The boot failed to connect and the fleeting silhouette of a cat vanished into the bushes.

Karol waited as The Axeman walked back to the farmhouse. Then he slipped through the shadows to the spot by the main gate where the SIM card had fallen after bouncing from one of the thick wooden uprights. He slid it carefully into his pocket and melted away into the shadows, everything filed away in his trained memory.

In the wooden shed he retrieved Katya's mobile from its hiding place. When he switched it on he saw the battery had one bar of power left.

Karol sat in the dark, weighing up whether he could risk sending a message about the increased security or save what little power was left in the mobile.

He switched off the phone and sat in the dark, tapping it thoughtfully against his lower lip.

\*\*\*

As plans went it was crap. A five-year-old would see through it straight away and laugh.

It was a seriously crap plan. He'd given it a lot of thought, weighed the options, but this was the only idea he'd come up with. And as it was the only plan he had it must have something going for it.

Danny held the parcel and stood in the street by the entrance to the front door. Couldn't stay too long or people would notice.

It took ten minutes before he saw someone, a woman with two bulging shopping bags. He waited for her to turn up the path to the entrance of the flats, gave it a few second, then started after her.

She put the bags down and rummaged for her keys in her handbag. As she put it into the lock one of the bags tipped over and two oranges rolled off and bounced down the step. He heard the woman swear under her breath.

"Don't worry, I'll get them."

Her head swivelled round, eyes alert. They locked on to Danny and stayed there as he scooped up the escaping oranges.

"There you go." He held them out. The woman took them and placed them back in her bag. He held up the parcel.

"Delivery for number 12."

"Bit late, isn't it?"

"Well, when we say 24-hour delivery, we mean it. Can I help you with those?"

Before the woman could reply Danny put the parcel under his arm, picked up the bags and headed through the door to the lift. He pulled the door open and held it with his foot before following her in.

"Which floor?"

"Fifth."

He pressed the buttons. They travelled up in smiling silence until the lift sighed to a halt on the second floor.

"This is me," said Danny.

"Thanks for the help."

"No problem."

He stepped out and walked along the thickly carpeted corridor. It was still a seriously crap plan. 'Oh, I brought the wrong parcel. Sorry to bother you' was pretty bloody lame. Still, if it got him inside for a quick look round all well and good.

If it didn't he would talk his way out of it somehow. Amazing how trusting some people could be if you looked right and smiled a lot. Maybe that's how politicians got away with it.

He slowed as he approached the door, rehearsing what he was going to say. It was only as he reached for the buzzer that he saw the door was open a crack.

Something fizzled across the back of his neck and down his spine. There was a light on through the gap. Thirty seconds and no movement, no sound.

He pushed the door with the corner of the parcel. It swung silently open. Still nothing but the faintest tang of perfume in the air. He stepped inside.

"Hello?"

Nothing. He tapped the door shut behind him with his foot.

"Anyone home?"

Still nothing. He walked towards the light at the far end of the hallway, pausing by each door on the way to look and listen.

When he reached the lounge door he stopped again, then moved slowly forward.

There was a lot of blood. Giles Forrester lay on his back, arms thrown up, mouth open and eyes rolled halfway back into his head like an extra in some cheap zombie film.

The whole of the front of his shirt was sodden with blood and it had spread out either side of him on the carpet like dull red wings.

You'll never get those strains out thought Danny as he took a step forward, careful not to tread in anything. He leaned forward for a closer look.

Stabbed, by the look of it. You could see the slit in his shirt, several of them. The lower parts of his body were purple where the blood had pool inside him, dragged down by gravity once his heart stopped.

He felt a moment of panic, the thought that he was standing there, stone still, shedding stray hair, skin cells, rare seeds and dirt with traces of something unusual that would bring forensics to his front door.

You've been watching too much CSI, he thought, grateful he still had his gloves on.

He walked carefully in a wide circle around the body, avoiding the blood, but there wasn't much to see. A chair was on its back. A fountain pen lay on the floor. An empty glass of wine lay on the carpet, its contents spread into a fan shape as it sat on the thick pile. What was it they called it? Spray pattern?

Danny didn't think there was much to learn, couldn't linger. He was about to turn for the door when he noticed the man's laptop was open on the desk.

If Karol was with him he'd have been able to rinse it of everything useful but that wasn't an option now.

He was about to go when something sparkling caught his eye. It was at the side of the computer. Danny moved closer and bent to look. A piece of freshly torn metal shone silver in a slot at the side of the machine. Danny struggled to remember what they were called, JCBs, something like that. He'd seen Karol use them.

But you didn't need to be a computer nerd to see what had happened. One of those memory stick things had been fitted into the laptop and something must have come down on it with some force to snap off the plug while it was in the machine.

He crouched to look under the desk. The memory end of the broken stick was lying in the corner by the skirting board.

Danny scooped it up and put it in his pocket before circling around the blood-winged body and back out of the front door, pulling it closed behind him.

\*\*\*

Bob and Wanda stood, uneasy and self-conscious, in his lock-up, unsure what they should say or do next.

Behind them, steel racking stretched to the roof. Most of the shelving was empty apart from a few boxes of Italian tiles and some copper piping. The timber from the beach was stacked on the far side, a dark stain of damp spreading out beneath it. Parked close in front was the quad bike.

"Right," said Danny. "Let's get it loaded."

They each took the best grip they could and eased the bike up the plank ramp into the back of Bob's white van. Danny took the greatest weight and it moved easily. Once inside, Danny lashed it to the side and jumped down, dusting his hands together.

"Okay, let's have a look at you."

Bob and Wanda straightened as if they were on parade. Wanda wore ordinary street clothes in the darkest colour her wardrobe would allow.

Bob was dressed in black cord trousers, grey jumper and a dark green parka.

"Got your gloves?" asked Danny. Bob patted his pocket in confirmation. He did a little hop and nothing tinkled when he landed.

"Good man," said Danny as he put his hand in his own pocket. He drew out a tin of boot polish, looked at it and returned it to the pocket. Then he took out the Browning, checked the safety and hid it away again in the fold of his jacket.

"Right, won't get much chance for chitchat once we leave here so is everyone clear on what we're doing?"

Bob and Wanda nodded.

"Any last questions?"

"Do you have to take the gun?" asked Wanda.

"Yes," said Danny. He looked from one to the other. "Anything else?"

They shook their head.

"Right, mount up."

***

The streets were quiet. Danny was pleased. The odd whoosh and sparkle of fireworks glittered in the winter sky.

The route was straightforward and Wanda had studied the map carefully. She wasn't going to stand for any jokes about women and navigation.

"On the left, just round this next bend," said Danny.

"I know," Wanda replied without taking her eyes off the road.

She coasted off to the side and rolled the van onto a patch of ground under the long branches of an old oak tree. When she killed the engine the sudden silence seemed to jump at them.

None of them spoke as they set the plank ramp in place and rolled the quad bike out and into cover behind the van.

Danny climbed into the back of the van and lit a cigarette in his cupped hands. As he looked up he saw the others watching him.

"Last gasper before we go over the top," he said with a grin.

Wanda shivered.

Danny could see their unease, tension stretching their determination. He took a last, deep pull on his cigarette and ground it out on the bed of the van.

"Right, let's get moving."

He jumped down, took the boot polish from his pocket and daubed it across his face in thick finger streaks.

"Is that really necessary?" asked Wanda.

"Yes," said Danny. He held out the tin to Bob but Wanda took it, dug her manicured fingers into the thick black paste and set to work, breaking up the curves and lines of Bob's pale face with short, dabbing strokes.

Danny looked at his watch. "Time to go."

Wanda carried on blacking Bob's face. Big white circles round his eyes made him look startled. She seemed reluctant to finish the job, biting her lip as she worked. Then, some silent decision made, she dabbed a spot of the cream on the tip of his nose.

"There, done. Now you go off and get this over with."

Danny saw the worried look on Bob's face.

"If you need to, now's the time."

Bob nodded and disappeared behind the van. Danny and Wanda stood looking at each other as they listened to the trickle of Bob peeing against a tyre.

"You don't need to say it, Wanda. I'll look after him."

She nodded just as Bob came round the back of the van, zipping himself up. Wanda dabbed at some clumps of boot polish on his face until she was satisfied with the effect.

"You hurt yourself, I'll kill you." She said and kissed him on the cheek.

The roar of the quad bike's engine startled them. Danny mounted up and twitched the throttle. Bob climbed on behind and gripped him tightly round the waist. The quad circled out from behind the van and stopped by the roadside, then it started to move off.

Wanda saw Bob break his grip on Danny for a fleeting wave. She watched the quad out of sight, then listened until the wasp buzz of its engine faded away behind the sound of branches moving above her.

She touched the back of her hand to her mouth. It came away marked with a boot polish lip print. She stood in the country night, looking down at it.

\*\*\*

Detective Inspector Eddie Aziz plucked a speck of dust from his dark tie and flicked it towards the waste paper basket.

"This is turning into a busy week. Anything more on our mystery blonde in the ditch?"

Detective Sergeant Pauline Myers shook her head. "Still waiting on test results but the bruises on her neck show she died from manual strangulation. No signs of sexual assault. From the dental work it looks like she's probably Eastern European but we'll need more to go on before we can extend our inquiries."

"Big place, Eastern Europe," said Aziz. Myers nodded.

Aziz continued. "I guess they'll keep the murder team pretty small until we get more to go on, especially with this latest one in the car park. What's the score there?"

Myers looked at the computer screen in front of her. "Still early days, brunette, five nine, early twenties. Very toned, so the pathologist says. Could be an athlete. Only distinguishing mark is a butterfly tattoo in the small of her back."

"A tramp stamp," said Aziz.

"Doesn't mean anything," said Myers.

"No, I suppose not. Everyone has them these days." He grinned. "Maybe even you."

"Well, you'll never find out," said Myers.

Aziz pulled a face. "Any ID?"

"Nothing, clothes were fashion brands, expensive. We've no reports of missing persons. It was reported by an anonymous call from a phone box a mile away. The man sounded scared."

"Suspect?"

"Obviously, but the place where the body was found is a popular dogging spot. I don't think we're going to have witnesses queuing around the block with this one."

"Dogging? In this cold?"

"It seems to be an all-weather hobby for the real enthusiasts," said Myers.

"So," said Aziz. "We've got next to nothing."

"Not quite," said Myers.

"Oh?"

"She was killed by a single stab wound to the chest, pierced the heart. Death must have been instant. Again, no sign of sexual assault. There was no weapon at the scene and not much blood so she was probably killed elsewhere. Whoever did it didn't make much effort to hide the body. It was tipped into the bushes at the edge of the car park.

"There were no defensive wounds so she was surprised or might have known her attacker. The odd thing is the blade, thin but wide. They haven't managed to identify it yet."

\*\*\*

Never before in his life had Bob realised just how dark darkness could be. It was a disturbing revelation to a born-and-bred city boy that you could put your hand six inches from your face and only know it was there by the kiss of your breath.

His eyes were playing tricks. The faintest glimmer of light burning fuzzy patterns that smeared his vision as he turned his head.

And the noises. Things creaked and rustled. Shadows crept up on you. It was like being goaded by some invisible mutant army, the nameless unknown, the stuff of kids' nightmares.

Bob pressed two fingers to his wrist and started to check his pulse but lost count when something rustled through the trees above him. He felt acid in his stomach and his joints ached from humping the quad and from the cold that constantly probed the weak spots of his jacket.

Bob knew if he could go home now he would but it was too late. He tried to take his mind off everything by keeping as still as he could, looking and listening as he had been told, trying to read the language of night. It didn't work but as least it kept him busy.

And he still jolted with fright when a black shape slithered into the ditch beside him.

"Bollocks," said Danny. He eased himself down and turned to face Bob.

"You scared the life out of me," Bob gasped.

"It's what I used to do for a living, Bob."

"Well you must have been bloody good at it."

"I was."

"So what's up?"

"The message said four guards. I count seven, maybe eight."

"What do we do?"

"No choice, we crack on. At least there aren't any dogs."

Danny looked at Bob. Even in the occasional faint starlight that peeped through gaps in the cloud he looked pale and frightened beneath the web of boot polish streaks that criss-crossed his face.

"You okay, mate?"

"'Course I am. Why did you say that?"

"Just checking. You sure you want to go on with this?"

"Too late to turn back now, Danny."

"Right, let's do it. Stay behind me, stay close."

Danny rolled onto his front, crawled to the lip of the ditch, looking and listening. As he prepared to move he felt a hand on his leg.

"Bob?"

"Danny."

"What's up now?"

"It's ... I ... What's going on with you and Wanda?"

Danny slid back down into the ditch.

"What?"

"Seems to me you've been pretty close of late. She fusses over you, pats your hair. I'm not getting any younger and you, well, you've got a bit of a reputation."

Danny went to speak but stopped, not sure whether to laugh or lose his temper. They sat in silence for a while.

"You really pick your moments, Bob."

"I'm serious, Danny, if she left ..."

"And that's why you were so keen to come? Impress her with what a hard man you are?"

"Not exactly, well ..."

"Bob, you muppet, Wanda's a beautiful lady, one of a kind, but she's more woman than I could handle. Besides, I've got enough on my plate. She's just a friend, Bob, a good friend. And for some reason she thinks the sun shines out of your wrinkly old arse. Don't ask me how women's minds work, Bob, but she does."

"Really?"

"Trust me, Bob."

"Thanks, Danny mate."

"Don't mention it. Now can we get on with this?"

Bob nodded.

"You sure you still want to go?"

"Too late to back out now."

## CHAPTER 22

Danny rolled onto his front again and began to crawl forward slowly through the undergrowth, conscious of the Browning in his pocket pressing against his hip.

The darkness eddied around them, the sounds of the breeze, the rustle of birds, insects and small animals, resting, hunting or just watching.

An alien environment for Bob was home to Danny who wrapped the philosophy of night around him like a cape.

As he eased himself gently up the incline Bob followed, grunting each time he dug an elbow into the ground and hauled himself forward.

Danny looked back over his shoulder. "Can you keep the noise down? You're keeping people in Crawley awake."

A whisper. "Sorry."

They reached the hedge line and moved right fifteen feet to the spot Danny had seen earlier. There was a good-sized gap between the ground at the bottom of the hedge between two trunks.

The strands of razor wire stood out clearly against the farmhouse lights beyond.

Danny slipped the wire cutters from his pocket and snipped the top strand at one edge of the gap, bending it back and snagging it against the hedge trunk.

He waited, still and listening, then cut again and bent back the second strand. He had severed half the strands across the gap when he heard the whisper of rubber-soled shoes on frost. Bob heard it to. They melted silently onto the ground.

Blackened cheek pressed to the earth, Danny saw his gloved hand resting two feet from his face. The same distance beyond that, a black boot crunched on the ground and stopped.

It turned slightly one way, then the other, as the body above it moved to look around.

There was a rasping sound. Danny held his breath and hoped Bob was doing the same. The boots rocked slightly as the guard shifted his weight.

Then something trickled across Danny's shoulder, the liquid rustling off his waterproof jacket.

Then something was pattered on his woolly hat. Droplets sprayed his face. He knew what was happening long before the steam rising from the icy ground brought the acid smell of urine to his nose.

The sluggish stream meandered across his shoulders and over his woolly hat. It seemed to take for ever. At last, it faltered to a trickle and then into drips. Danny heard a sigh of satisfaction and the rasp of a zip being pulled up. The sound of boots faded away.

Neither of them moved for long minutes of deafening silence. When Danny was sure the area was clear he crawled back slowly down the incline until he was level with Bob.

His friend's face was deathly white between the dark streaks of boot polish.

"Jesus, Danny," he hissed. "How did he miss us?"

"Secret of camouflage," said Danny. "Stay perfectly still."

"You okay?"

"Don't worry, I've been pissed on by experts. I don't know what that guy's been eating but he should drink more water with it."

After half a minute of looking and listening, Danny clawed his way silently back up the slope and began cutting again.

He was bending back the last strand when they heard more footsteps. Both watched, pressed hard to the ground and holding their breath, as legs crossed the farmhouse lights beyond the gap.

Bob lay, eyes slitted, remembering Danny's lecture on camouflage, regular shapes being easily spotted, eyes attracted to the tiniest movement.

Bob held his breath, heard the blood thumping in his ears, wondered what his blood pressure was doing. The legs passed by.

When Danny was satisfied, he gave Bob a thumbs-up and crawled into the gap.

***

Eliška Mlynár did not understand the English. Her homeland was famous for its beer and wine but no one drank like the English.

Since she had been here she'd practised the language and was confident she could make herself understood in most situations, although newspaper headlines and slang still confused her.

She missed Košice and the mountains, missed skiing and country walks, but Brighton had its compensations. There were the concerts and the theatre and she enjoyed the clubs but not some of the mad-eyed people who took drugs in them.

It was an exciting place and she had met and made friends with people from all over the world. She had 76 friends on Facebook and they were real friends, not the ones people accepted just to make themselves look popular.

The people in England had more money than she had imagined was possible yet they had no idea how to live their lives.

Many would rather take money from the government than work hard. The idea grated against everything she had been told as a child, everything her parents had taught her.

When she had first arrived Eliška had worked as a nanny for six months. The Johnsons had been good people, kind. She had had a nice room and they had given her an iPhone as a welcome present. But it couldn't last.

They had fretted constantly about their children, Tristan and Penelope, yet they gave them no guidance, no boundaries. To Eliška, it seemed that Mrs Johnson lived in fear of her children's disapproval, would buy anything they wanted to secure their love.

That was no way to raise a child. Adults needed to guide them in the world or how would they know what their responsibilities were?

Mrs Johnson was always very pleasant, smiling, but Eliška could feel the tension rising when she tried to exercise some control over Tristan and Penelope.

They said it was something to do with their domestic budget, cutbacks, the recession. But Eliška knew the real reason when they let her go.

They had been very pleasant, smiling sadly, even gave her a new iPod, but Eliška new the reason.

Still, life goes up and it goes down and you go on. Other nannies she met had had similar experiences so Eliška decided to try another path.

She had always helped her mother clean back home in Košice so she thought she would give that a try. A small advert in the Argus brought an encouraging response and word-of-mouth soon built her client base.

She was proud of her reputation. If you did a job you did it properly, not like the English. She cleaned, she polished, she vacuumed, she dusted. Eliška went into corners and crevices untouched for decades.

One client had said that you could eat your meals off Eliška's floors. It seemed a bizarre suggestion but Eliška took it as a compliment. She walked briskly up the last flight of stairs. Why join a gym when you could just avoid using lifts? She pressed the doorbell and listened. There was no sound from inside the flat so she rang again.

Eliška tried to take a Christian view but this client made her uneasy. He smiled a lot but it was a movement of the face, not the heart.

She could feel him watching her as she worked, one hand in his pocket. He was very fastidious and complimented her on the work when he was there but she never felt able to relax when he was around.

It was good that he liked not to be disturbed, good that he usually liked her to clean at unusual hours when he was out at a concert or visiting a gallery. Eliška preferred to work alone, without the strange eyes following her.

She rang again. No response. Eliška slipped the key from her bag and opened the door.

"Mr Forrester?"

When there was no reply she walked down the hallway.

"Mr Forrester?"

It was as Eliška walked into the living room that she saw the body.

\*\*\*

They sat with their backs pressed to the wooden wall. Danny studied the yard in front of the farmhouse.

They had been clever, just enough light for the guards to patrol by, nothing bright enough to attract local attention. But no security, however expensive or cunning, was perfect. The lack of dogs and infra-red cameras was a weakness.

Danny watched the yard for ten minutes, following the guards as they paced out their routine patrols, turning his face from the light when they came close.

When he looked across at Bob he saw him still sitting with his head tilted back against the wall. He was wheezing, the line of his chest rising and falling heavily, laboured. Plumes of breath curled upward.

"You okay?" whispered Danny.

"Never felt better," said Bob, gaspy gaps between the words. He took a ventilator from his pocket and inhaled, containing the sound in cupped hands. Danny was pleased to see Bob was starting to get the hang of this stealth lark but no amount of enthusiasm would overcome his lack of fitness. Danny knew he could encourage him a bit further, but not far.

"Are we going to be okay?" asked Bob. "There's a lot of them."

"We'll be fine. Remember the Spartans."

"What about them?"

"Three hundred Greeks against a million Persians. I read about them in the library."

"And did they win?"

"No, they were slaughtered to a man but they made a big dent in the opposition."

"And that's supposed to cheer me up?"

"Stop worrying. Wanda will love you whether you go back with your shield or on it."

"What's that supposed to mean?" said Bob between breaths.

"Forget it," said Danny. "Right, I'm going to need to zip about a bit. What we need is a rendezvous point we can hold. You up for that?"

"Whatever you say."

"Right, see that big building over there, the barn, that's where we're headed. Keep close, stay low and stay very, very quiet."

Bob nodded and, levering with his hands on his thighs, hauled himself to his feet with a grunt.

\*\*\*

They waited until the guard has passed and turned the corner before the final dash to the door.

Danny waited for Bob to catch up, then slipped the bolt cutters from his pack and watched it slice the padlock chain with a single bite. He caught the chain just as it started to rattle through its retaining eyes.

Danny eased the big door open, relieved it glided silently on newly oiled hinges. He gestured for Bob to go inside, pulled the door almost closed, then reached outside to loop the severed chain back into position. Hopefully, it would fool a casual inspection.

Inside the barn was pitch black. Danny slipped a hooded Maglite from his pocket and swept the vast space. Close to them were two long, solid wooden benches with tools grouped at a dozen work stations.

Beyond the benches, crates were stacked neatly in rows. At the far end of the barn, where the torch beam faded, Danny could make out piles of hay bales stacked high in two long rows with more stacked at the far end.

He recognised a crude firing range, the bales stacked to soak up the sound and stray rounds. Clever, he thought. The bales were too tightly packed to burn but there was a lot of stray straw scattered about, certainly enough to cause a problem if they didn't damp it down before firing.

They moved deeper into the barn, Bob sticking close behind Danny in the pool of light the torch threw at their feet. Danny listened until he was sure the barn was empty, the only sound was Bob wheezing at his shoulder.

Danny padded towards the crates. Each stack had different markings. The crate on top of each pile had the lid on but was unfastened. He pulled the lid off the first one and lifted something out, held it up and shone the torch.

"What's that?" asked Bob.

"Russian RGO hand grenade," said Danny. He looked down into the crate again. "RGN grenades, too." He reached in and pulled out a rectangular packet, turning it over to examine it.

"PETN," said Danny.

"What's that?" Bob asked.

"Plastic explosive, very powerful stuff, hard to detect. It's Al Qaeda's favourite."

"Bloody hell," said Bob.

Danny opened the next crate and took out a pistol. He popped out the magazine and opened the slide to check it was unloaded.

"Czech CZ75 9mm semi-automatic."

"Bloody hell," said Bob.

They shuffled in the gloom to the third crate. Danny pulled off the lid and Bob could see the whiteness of his teeth as he smiled.

"And here we have the special guest at the party."

He pulled out an assault rifle.

"Jesus," said Bob.

"AK103, modern version of a classic. Plastic furniture, laser, night and telescopic sight options and you can fit a grenade launcher."

Danny probed further into the darkness with a torch and found a smaller crate. He took something out and showed Bob.

"Magazines, loaded."

"There's tons of it," said Bob. "Danny, this is serious stuff."

"You're not wrong there, Bob. Now listen, I've got to go and find Karol. The longer we hang around the greater the risk. You stay here and hold our rendezvous point."

"You're not trying to dump me, Danny? Fob me off?"

"Don't be daft. It's an important job."

"And how do I hold this rendezvous?"

Danny held out the Kalashnikov. Bob's eyes were wide with a curdling mixture of fear and excitement. "I've never done anything like this outside of a fairground when I was a kid," he said.

"Win anything?"

Bob shook his head. "Just a goldfish. It died two weeks later. My mum flushed it down the loo."

"Okay," said Danny. "Now concentrate. It's easy."

Bob's eyes followed the gleam of live rounds as Danny hooked the banana magazine against the lip of the receiver and snapped it home. "Like this," snapped back the cocking handle, "like this," and clicked on the safety catch, "like this."

Danny handed the rifle to Bob who braced to take the weight and looked suddenly surprised.

"It's light."

"A kid could use it, they often do. Okay, pay attention. Don't fire unless you absolutely have to. If you do, remember the key is speed and aggression."

"Speed and aggression," Bob mumbled.

"Right," said Danny. "You have a full mag and the safety is on." He leaned forward and flicked a lever. "That's single shot." He clicked again. "That's full auto."

He tapped the front and rear of the weapon. "Foresight, backsight, line those two up with your target. Makes a hell of a noise and tries to pull upwards so make sure you hold her down tight or she'll climb up off your aiming point."

Bob nodded dumbly, gripping the AK tightly, fearful of moving his hands in case he touched anything.

"You sure you still want to do this, Bob?"

The older man gave a single tight nod.

"Then what?" he asked.

"Right, when you need to, click off the safety, select the fire option and squeeze the trigger."

"How will I know when?"

"Don't worry, Bob, you'll know."

"What happens then?"

"You spray and pray."

***

Slowly and carefully, Danny made his way along the buildings, pausing to check the speed and timings of the guards' patrols.

He had left a nervous Bob crouched in a corner of the barn nursing the Kalashnikov. As he had slipped out Danny had rearranged the chain to make the door looked locked.

When he reached the spot where he and Bob had been sitting earlier he made himself small against the wall and waited.

He heard the sound first, then picked up the movement soon after. The figure slid along the wall of the building opposite and dropped down beside Danny.

"I came earlier but you weren't here. You are late and you smell bad."

"Nice to see you, too, Karol."

***

Danny glanced over his shoulder, through the slit of the barn door, and scanned the compound. He turned back to face the others.

"You're bloody mad."

"I insist."

"Karol, we came to get you out before the police turn up and all hell breaks loose."

"I insist."

"Look, there are more guards than we planned for and we don't have the transport. This isn't the Great Escape."

Karol's red eyes stayed fixed on Danny. "I still insist."

"Bob?" asked Danny.

"He's got a point. This place is nasty. Doesn't seem right to leave the others here to fend for themselves. There's no way the people who run this place are going to let them walk away."

Karol nodded firmly. "You would not leave one of your people on a battlefield. You were not left when you lost your leg. These people are my people."

Danny thought for a moment. "Fair point. Okay, if you're both up for it, we leave no one behind."

"Have you got a plan?" asked Bob.

Danny shook his head. "Short of vaulting the wire on a motorbike, no. But give me a minute."

\*\*\*

Aziz walked into the lounge and scanned the room, shaking his head. The apartment's lounge looked cold and empty, most of the contents videoed, photographed and then bagged and removed by the scenes of crimes team.

The body was on its way to the mortuary but you could see where it had been found by the pattern of blood on the carpet. It looked like a giant pair of angel's wings, he thought.

Detective Inspector Eddie Aziz shook his head. "Where's Pauline?"

"Off tonight," said Detective Sergeant Bill Oldfield.

Aziz pulled a disapproving face. "They're not going to be happy."

"Who aren't?" said Oldfield, looking up from the blood stain.

"Upstairs. First we had the mystery blonde, then the one with the tramp stamp, now this. The SIO is going to get his ear bent over budgets again. Upstairs aren't going to like this."

"I don't suppose the victim was too happy about it either."

"No," said Aziz, "I suppose not. Giles Saint John Forrester."

"It's pronounced 'Sinjun'."

" 'Sinjun'? Well if that's the way it's pronounced, why doesn't he spell it that way?"

Oldfield shrugged. "Sounds posh, probably worked well in his line of business, massaging rich egos."

"What do you mean?"

"From the look of the correspondence in his desk he was researching family trees for rich clients. He seems to have been telling them what they wanted to hear, for a fee."

"What?" said Aziz. "So great great grandad shagged the chamber maid and someone killed him to preserve the family honour?"

Oldfield shrugged again. "I can think of flimsier motives, especially if there's money or an inheritance involved."

Aziz considered the idea for a moment. "So what do we know so far?"

"Looks as if he walked in and surprised someone but there are no signs of forced entry, just a chair knocked over and the blood. SOC said there was some damage to his laptop but they want to take a closer look.

"In addition to the blood there's wine on the carpet and another fluid that might be semen. It's possible Forrester had sex before he died, plus there's soap under his fingernails."

Aziz nodded thoughtfully. "That's good, and quick."

"Well," said Oldfield, "We're awaiting tests but they're a good team, know their stuff. There's one thing they're pretty sure of already. He was attacked with a wide, flat double-sided blade."

"And?"

"Looks like the same as the one that killed tramp stamp girl."

## CHAPTER 23

They took turns, Danny and Karol, leading the others in ones and two from the barracks to the barn, according to their age, mobility and their ability to grasp what was going on.

None were unwilling but some needed more help than others to creep softly and quietly along the walls of the buildings beneath the CCTV cameras in the brief gaps between guard patrols.

Danny could feel his nerves stretching with each group that moved. It didn't seem possible that no one would trip, cough or panic. But they had all seen The Axeman in action, knew what the consequences might be.

He thought of old film clips of refugees, shuffling, broken and desperate. Whoever had dreamed up this little scheme needed a good seeing-to.

But Karol's refugees seemed determined, the loss of much-needed wages a price worth paying to escape the nightmare they had innocently walked into.

As Karol led the last one towards the barn Danny squatted in the shadows, Browning pressed against his thigh, trigger finger resting against the side of the weapon.

All this was planning on the hoof. It seemed impossible they could move so many people silently in darkness. If it kicked off and the guards were armed, Danny would lay down covering fire, maybe drop a few to deter the others.

This wasn't the way it was meant to be but it was happening. The situation had to be dealt with, however it developed. Danny looked across at Karol and saw the last man had stopped, gripping the wall for support.

Karol put an arm around the man and gently took his weight, careful to avoid pressure on his damaged ribs, and they shuffled forward. Danny watched, willing them to get a move on. He could hear a slight hissing sound from the injured man's tight lips as his trainers scraped the ground.

Danny pulled up his sleeve and screened the dial of his watch to check the time, then looked up at Karol and the injured man.

"Come on."

They reached the barn, stretched the padlock chain to make a gap, slipped through and pulled it closed. Danny saw Karol's pale hand snake out to adjust the chain just as a guard came round the corner of the farmhouse, heard the crackle of the man's radio earpiece.

He watched the guard. The man was bored, dreaming about his girlfriend or his football team, how he'd spend the money when he won the lottery.

Thank God for sloppy work, thought Danny.

When the guard was gone he checked carefully around and slipped across the yard into the barn. The Axeman's workers stood in a huddle, sleepy and confused, arms wrapped around themselves as if they might offer some protection. Heads came up as Danny entered and concern rippled through the group, like anxious chickens.

Danny slipped the pistol into his pocket and tried to smile some reassurance. Karol turned to him, face worried.

"Stepan is missing."

"Who?"

"Stepan, in the end bunk. I checked the barracks before I brought Olexei. I thought he was the last."

"Has he gone for a walk? To the latrines?"

"I must find him," said Karol.

Danny gripped Karol's thin arm as Karol moved towards the door.

"Hang on, there are too many of us already and we've been here too long. We've got to move."

"All, I insist," said Karol.

"Get real. We've been lucky so far but we've still got to get this lot through the wire and away before daylight."

"All," said Karol.

Danny was groping for a new argument when the chain on the door creaked. Every head turned. The gap widened and the dim light of Danny's shaded torch fell on a thin man with glasses as he edged sideways into the barn.

"Stepan," said Karol.

The man looked across the frightened group and smiled without speaking.

The hair on the back of Danny's neck rose with a prickle. Alarm bells rang in his head as his hand dived into his jacket pocket.

His fingers were closing on the pistol's butt when he heard the chain rattle through its eyes and drop away. He took a step back as he gripped the weapon.

The door swung open. He began to draw the gun from his pocket but he knew he was too late by tiny fractions of a second.

The Browning was halfway out of his jacket when the doors swung wide. A grinning tower of steroid-fed muscle stood in the light from the yard, flanked by two of the guards. Each held a Kalashnikov levelled at the group in the barn.

"Well, well, well, what do we have here? You lot all having a party and me not invited. Now is that polite?"

\*\*\*

She couldn't remember how long it had been since she gave up smoking. It had been tough at the time, really tough, but once she had succeeded Wanda blocked it away in a corner of her mind

Just thinking about it might make it happen again. Like a recovering alcoholic, every day was a challenge. Every day ran the risk of lighting up again.

Wanda tapped the glass of her wristwatch. She felt sure it had stopped but as she held it up to what little natural light filtered down through the canopy of trees she could see the second hand jerking its way around the dial.

It seemed as if they had been gone for ages but it was just under an hour and twenty minutes. If time hadn't stopped it had certainly slowed to a crawl.

Wanda clasped her arms across her chest and paced behind the van, trying to generate enough warmth to keep out the creeping cold.

To the south, sprays of rockets crackled and burst across the icy sky. Patches of throbbing orange from big bonfires pulsed upward into the darkness.

She watched the sparkling arc of a big rocket curve upwards. It burst into an orb of multi-coloured stars. Then another, then another, each orb overlapping the one before, burning bright before fading and falling away.

A silver haze of smoke hung like a false ceiling over Lewes, glowing where it was punctured by rockets or drifted close to the bonfires.

Wanda could picture the packed streets, families fat in heavy winter clothes, red-nosed children, eyes shining with excitement, as they watched the flaming torches of the bonfire societies' parades. It reminded her of when she was a child. Dad's Bonfire Night firework displays in the back garden, roast potatoes, rockets in milk bottles, a guy made from his old gardening clothes that mum said had to go.

The brilliant colours and the stutter and crackle of fireworks bursting over Lewes drew her in, almost masking the reason for her being there. Then her mind snapped back to an image of Bob and his ridiculous boot-polished face, trying to drag that stomach of his through the undergrowth, trying to keep up.

Danny would be in his element, she knew, out there in the dark. He was a big kid at heart but he missed the soldiering, the mates, the adrenalin. She had seen it in his face often enough.

She shook her head as she tried to recall how he had talked them all into this, her standing under a tree freezing in the middle of nowhere, Bob and his high blood pressure crawling about on the damp ground.

She couldn't imagine why he was so keen to go with Danny. It was as if he was trying to prove something. God alone knew what. Just another big kid who didn't want to grow up, thought Wanda.

\*\*\*

A hiss of terror fizzed around the huddled workers. Danny heard one voice gasp the words, "The Axeman."

"Drop the gun, Lancaster," said the big man.

"Hello, Deano. Does Eddie know you're out on your own?"

"Funny man, I said drop the gun."

"You want it, McKeown, come and get it."

"Tough guy, eh? You want to argue with this?" He hefted the Kalashnikov.

They looked at each other. Then Danny pinched the butt of the pistol between his thumb and index finger, drew it slowly the rest of the way from his pocket and dropped it on the ground."

"Kick it away," said McKeown.

Danny gave the gun a tap with his foot and it skidded across the floor.

"That's good," said McKeown, glancing to left and right at the guards beside him. "Right, what do we do now?" He pretended a thoughtful face. "Well, we've still got a bit of work to get done so maybe we'll give these peasants a good kicking and start them on a night shift if they've got so much energy after dark. You, Lancaster, are a problem, but not a very big one."

McKeown sniggered, then paused, waiting for the other two to join in.

"I don't think a washed up ex-squaddie is going to give me much of a workout. I think you'd be more use for target practice."

"What about the axe?" said Danny.

McKeown looked down and, holding the Kalashnikov level by the grip, unclipped the axe from his belt.

"You think we should fight even, both make a grab for it." He laughed. "You must think I'm stupid."

Danny laughed. McKeown's eyes blazed as he flicked the axe. It embedded itself in the floorboards between them with a thud.

"Try for it if you want."

McKeown made a show of switching the fire selector on his weapon, nodding approval as it clicked into place. He raised the assault rifle into his shoulder, nestling it into position with exaggerated care, and took aim at Danny's chest.

The axe was too far away. Danny's eyes were locked on the big man's right hand. He had nowhere to go, chances zero.

Only option to wait till he saw tension in the fingers. Then throw himself sideways. Might avoid a few rounds. Might survive. Not likely.

Everyone held their breath as the big man milked his moment. Then a jagged spear of flame lit the barn, throwing puppet show shadows up the walls and straw bales. The ratchet rip of exploding rounds destroyed the silence.

\*\*\*

Wanda tightened her arms around her body, watching the plumes of silent white breath from her lips, still thinking how right now she could kill for a cigarette.

Another barrage of rockets lit the sky, followed close by a second and a third, each glittering ball of light dancing for attention, competing with its neighbour, like beautiful winged insects with tiny lifespans.

As they faded away it went quiet. Then she heard a rapid popping sound, like Chinese crackers. She cocked her head. It sounded odd.

Wanda stood, listening, trying to understand why that small series of sounds had stood out. She turned and looked into the tangled blackness behind her to the north and knew. The popping had come from the opposite direction.

\*\*\*

The gunfire was deafening. ear-punching cracks that bounced back down from the barn's beamed wooden roof.

Sparks flew from metal brackets stung by high velocity rounds. Spent cases tinkled like tiny bells as they fell. A pile of loose straw took light, then another. The smell of burning fodder mingled with the acid taste of cordite.

When it stopped the silenced roared. No one moved. Then a shape shuffled unsteadily from behind the wall of bales. Bob swayed, stunned, still holding his smoking Kalashnikov.

"Nobody move."

McKeown's bulk turned towards the voice, face puckered in confusion.

Danny pitched forward.

McKeown saw the movement, began to turn back.

Danny hit the wooden floor and snatched up the axe.

McKeown raise his weapon.

Danny rolled across his shoulders and back onto his feet.

McKeown's index finger fattened on the trigger as he applied pressure.

The axe in Danny's hand arced around at arm's length.

The muzzle of McKeown's rifle was an empty black eye staring straight at him.

And in the instant before the axe struck Danny knew he had won the race by tiny fractions of a second.

The butt of the axe slammed into the side of McKeown's head. The big man grunted and staggered sideways, dropping his rifle. The two guards took a step back, getting clear of the falling man.

Danny scooped up the Browning from the barn floor.

McKeown hit the ground and rolled onto his knees, swaying like a stunned bull.

The two guards stood bunched in the doorway, mouths open at the speed of events. One raised his rifle.

Danny shot him in the shoulder and he twisted, pitching backwards.

The second guard met Danny's eye and ran.

McKeown had one foot planted now, one knee still on the floor. Blood ran down his chin as he spat broken teeth.

Danny saw the man pump power to his massive thighs, start to rise. He lifted the axe in his other hand and swung underarm. McKeown suddenly knew what was happening, his eyes stretched wide, just before the axe smacked between his legs. He let out a gargling scream and keeled over.

"Right," said Danny. He turned to the group, still huddled in the middle of the barn. "Let's move. Forget the wire. Out the main gate. Fast as you can."

The workers began shuffling towards the barn door.

***

As the last of the group formed up and made their way cautiously through the wide barn doors Karol ducked behind the piles of crates, pulled out the hessian sack and tucked it under his arm.

Danny checked the barn was empty and turned to follow the others when Karol gripped his arm.

"I insist," said Karol.

"Look, I've had it up to here with your insisting. We've got to get moving."

"Danny, these are evil people. If you call the police, how can you know they will get here in time? If these men move the crates then tonight is for nothing."

"This was supposed to be a rescue mission, not D-Day."

"I still insist."

"We haven't got time to stand here arguing. I say we go."

As Danny stepped forward Karol placed a spread hand against his chest.

"No."

Danny swotted it away and took another step. Karol smacked his hand against Danny's chest again, harder this time.

"Stop pissing about," said Danny. "We don't have time."

Karol took a step back and raised his balled fists. Bob, who had forgotten the empty Kalashnikov in his hands, watched open-mouthed. Danny looked startled for a moment, then started to laugh.

"You're mad."

"This is important," said Karol. "I insist."

"You, all eight stone of gristle, are going to pick a fight with an ex-paratrooper holding a handgun?"

"Cavalry against tanks," said Karol, eyes slitted, face intent.

"You, Karol, are bloody mad."

"This is not some petty criminals, Danny. This is big. Their boss man came here. He was angry."

Maintaining his boxer's stance, Karol tapped the sack with his foot.

"Look inside."

Danny picked up the sack and peered through the open end, saw the Kalashnikov.

"An AK, so what?"

"The boss man held it. It has his finger prints. It could be useful."

"You any idea who the guy was?"

"I saw him only once. He was an old man, wore a suit and an expensive coat. He was bald with white hair, a red face."

Danny looked down into the sack again, then up at the refugees retreating across the yard. When he looked back at Karol, Danny's eyes were stone.

"Did you hear a name?"

"No name, but he spoke to the others about a mission and something about the rule of law. Danny, I have to do this. I know how, I insist."

"No," said Danny, his voice thoughtful. He put down the sack. Karol dropped his fists six inches. Danny held out his hand.

"Give it to me. I'll do it."

Karol put his hand in the pocket of his hoodie.

\*\*\*

Outside in the yard, most of them were still milling around close to the barn, unsure what they should do. Plumes of cold breath rose above their heads.

Danny walked into the middle of the group and waved his arms.

"Come on, run!" he shouted. As he moved towards the gate they began to follow, anxious not to lose contact with him.

He led the charge, dashing across the lit yard. A trail of blood from the wounded guard led to the farmhouse door and raised voices came from inside.

When Danny was near the gate and the others were strung out halfway across the yard, a guard emerged onto the farmhouse step, then another, and a third. They started to fan out.

Danny dropped to one knee, fired twice. The bullets struck sparks from the stone lintel above the door. The men ducked.

Danny fired twice more, the round thudding into the heavy wood of the door. The three men turned and sprinted up the steps into the safety of the farmhouse.

"Come on, come on. Keep moving."

He shot the big padlock from the main gates on the run and threw his shoulder against it. The two heavy wooden panels creaked open. Danny stood in the opening, waving the others on, counting his shots fired, seven left.

Karol and the injured guy were the last out of the yard. Danny watched them limping off down the lane until the night swallowed them.

He turned his attention to the farmhouse. He could still hear voices. As he looked, a small figure detached itself from the shadow of the barn and began a panicked, jerky run across the yard.

The farmhouse door banged open and a weapon flashed. The running man dropped with a sigh.

Danny fired at the door and the gunman ducked back inside. He raised himself up, braced to sprint back into the yard but a hand fell on his shoulder.

"Don't go," said Karol. "It was Stepan."

Another figure appeared in the farmhouse doorway. Danny fired. The ground smacked into the lintel above the man's head. He dived back indoors.

Danny stayed crouching low, weapon held forward. There were still plenty of them in the farmhouse but they didn't seem to want a fight.

He thought they probably weren't being paid enough to face live rounds, or maybe McKeown's leadership skills weren't what they should be.

Either way, Danny was glad. He'd shot enough people.

Then the voices from the farmhouse ramped up to shouting. Two men emerged from the front door and crouched on the top step.

Danny fired twice. The men hesitated. He fired twice again and they ducked back inside.

No one else ventured outside. Danny smiled to himself. At that range he'd be lucky to hit them anyway but they didn't seem to realise. He fired two shots through a lit, curtained window to the left of the farmhouse door to keep them worried.

Time to go. Danny turned and ran.

\*\*\*

They went in darkness, under the lonely night sky, through the shadows. It seemed to take for ever, a crocodile of frightened people picking their way through the winter countryside.

Danny encouraged them on, patting backs and checking the path ahead. They could use his torch now secrecy no longer mattered. Karol supported the injured man as he stumbled along, helping others where he could.

Even Bob managed to ease some of Karol's refugees across ditches and fences as he stumbled along, stunned by what had just happened.

It took a painful hour of bruises and scratches to work their way the 500 yards to where the quad bike was camouflaged under a tarpaulin in a thicket.

They loaded the injured man, Olexei, onto the back. Bob insisted he could drive and Danny let him, if only to save him the walk.

They used the headlamps to light the track downhill which made the journey easier. As the workers tired they took short breaks riding on the rack at the back of the quad. Danny saw some of them flinch at the crackle and boom of fireworks that lit the night sky above.

Using the quad, the journey back to the van was shorter and easier than the first section from the farmhouse. Wanda stood by the driver's door, shaking her head in disbelief as Danny's ragged army straggled out of the trees.

He caught her eye and grinned. "Picked up a few passengers on the way."

Wanda was going to say something when the quad bike swung to a halt beside the van and she saw it was Bob driving. She was beside him in three long strides.

"You shouldn't be driving one of those. They're dangerous."

Bob's face split into a wild grin, half victory, half madness. Wanda threw her arms around him, hugging the wheezing breath from his big body. Then she kissed him hard on the mouth.

They held the kiss until everyone had noticed, stopped to watch. The weary workers were smiling now, some even clapped at their first sight of something warm and human since the nightmare at Payne's Farm had begun.

When Bob and Wanda broke for air her face was black with boot polish.

"Time to get you home." She turned to Danny. "How did he do?"

"Outstanding," said Danny. They laughed.

"Anyway," said Danny. "Stick our new friends in the van. It'll be a squeeze but we'll sort them out when we get back to Brighton, somehow."

"What about you two?" asked Wanda.

"Karol and me have a little business to finish. We'll take the quad down to the edge of Lewes, dump it and grab a train home."

"I'll come," said Bob.

"I think the rest of your night's spoken for," said Danny. He winked at Wanda who pretended outrage before breaking into a smile.

"If you're dashing off to cause more trouble you'll need these," she said, pulling a pack of wet wipes from her bag. Danny's teeth seemed even whiter as he grinned through the boot polish.

They managed to fit the weapons workers into the back of the van in reasonable comfort with Bob and Wanda up front.

Danny and Karol watched them go. An arm waved from the front passenger window. Then they curved away round a tall hedge and were gone.

"Right," said Danny, scrubbing his face with a blackened wipe. "We'd better get this done sharpish. We want to be well away from here."

They mounted the quad bike and headed down the road after the van, towards Lewes.

\*\*\*

Danny couldn't help grinning. A potent mix of noise, colours and adrenalin sizzled through him. He felt electric. He slapped Karol on the back, the Pole wincing before breaking into a smile.

Fireworks burst in a spray of overlapping star patterns, not the family back garden variety but serious explosive cocktails that cracked the air as they detonated.

As the sudden concussions punched the night sky Danny felt a split second of panic when the streaks of colour were tracer rounds. He swallowed hard, shook his head, lit a cigarette and looked around. Karol hadn't noticed.

The glow of a gigantic bonfire silhouetted a row of trees to the east, huge tongues of flame climbing over each other at they stabbed up at the cold night sky. The rippling brilliance of the fire made the trees look like giants dancing.

They had dumped the quad in woodland north of Lewes, hiding in under a tarpaulin and some bracken.

Then the two of them had walked into town, past the prison and the war memorial in the High Street and down to the bridge over the Ouse, near the Harvey's Brewery. Beyond the cover of the buildings the wind was bitter.

The narrow, winding streets of the town were packed with crowds who had come for Bonfire. Music drifted from an open pub door. A crowd of people from one of the town's bonfire societies, dressed in their uniform of hooped sweaters and pointed woollen hats, chanted something mysterious as they strode along.

Danny and Karol jostled their way through the crowd of faces alight with beer and excitement, looking around them in disbelief. Beneath the noise and the fire there was a kind of feral ecstasy in the air.

Danny thought it was like being transported back to some wild tribal festival, then realised that this was exactly what it was.

They stopped on a corner and let the shuffling pack of people flow around them. Karol shivered with cold as icy fingers jabbed through his thin hoodie. Danny took out his mobile phone and handed it over.

"You remember the number?"

Karol nodded, "Of course," and his thumb flew across the small keypad. When he was finished he held it up to show the screen.

"Danny!"

They both turned to scan the wall of people pressing in around them.

"Danny!"

A pale hand waved above the dense crowds. Danny and Karol backed against the wall and waited.

"Danny!"

A small smiling face, pale with cold and rimmed by a tightly drawn scarf, peered through the packed ranks of overcoats and parkas.

"Detective Pauline."

"Danny, fancy seeing you here."

"Fancy."

Detective Sergeant Myers turned to indicate her friend, half hidden behind her. "You remember Liza?"

"With a Zed," said Danny.

"That right," said Myers.

"And this is Karol, friend of mine," said Danny.

Myers ran a professional eye over the small, shivering Pole, noting the stooped posture and the spreading bruise around his eye.

"You look like you lost a fight with a brick wall," she said.

"He's very clumsy," said Danny.

Myers looked at Danny again. He tried his best to relax and not reveal the weight of the warm Browning in his jacket pocket. She cocked her head.

"Are you wearing make-up?"

"No."

"It looks like you've painted your eyebrows."

Danny ran a finger above his nose and they all looked at the black patch on his fingertip.

"Been working on the van," said Danny. "Must be oil."

Myers looked around at the crowds and the fire-splattered sky. "This is fantastic, isn't it? A real piece of living history, such a great atmosphere."

Danny nodded. Liza looked doubtful and muttered something about health and safety.

"Do you know the history?" asked Myers. "It all started when Catholics under Queen Mary burned 17 protestant martyrs outside the town hall in the 1550s."

"I didn't know," said Danny.

"And they celebrate it every year," Myers continued. "Always on November 5. And they're very rude about the Pope."

Karol nudged Danny's arm, "Your phone."

As he turned to take it, Danny saw Karol looking at a scrap of something half hidden in the palm of his hand. A photograph.

"Who's the kid?" he said, quietly.

Karol shook his head. "No one, just an orphan boy whose mother took a job to pay for his piano lessons."

When Danny looked into Karol's eyes he could see they were wet. He didn't think it was the wind.

Danny held out his phone to Karol. "You do it."

Karol took the mobile and pressed to call the number.

## CHAPTER 24

The taller of the two men reeled back with a grunt from the force of the blow. The edge of a packing case caught him behind the knees and he fell, automatic weapon clattering to the ground.

"Un-fucking-believable. Just un-fucking-believable."

The man on the ground gargled blood and phlegm as he tried struggling to his feet. The other man leaned away, trying to put as much discreet distance as possible between himself and the sweating, purple-faced slab of rage that was Dean McKeown.

The big man's groin was on fire. Lucky it had been the butt of the axe head but it still felt like he'd burst a bollock. It hurt like fuck.

McKeown threw back his head and glugged from a whisky bottle, something for the pain, one, two, three, four...

Then he doubled over, spitting hard and keening in agony as the alcohol found the nerves in his broken teeth. The whisky spread across the floor on a tide of dirty water. The walls glistened, the hay bales were dripping. The fire sprinklers had doused the flame, saved the merchandise, but made one hell of a mess.

McKeown staggered upright. "You were supposed to be guarding this place, keeping our people in and everyone else out. And this bunch of tossers just swan in here, shoot the place up and leg it with our workers. Which bit of your guarding job description are you two wankers having trouble with?"

The smaller man turned to walk away.

"Stand still when I'm talking. Where the fuck do you think you're going?"

"Conrad's injured," said the shorter man. "I was going to see if he's okay."

Contempt roared out of Dean McKeown. "I don't care if he's dead. He'd be better off that way. When I get to him he'll wish he WAS dead."

McKeown paused, wheezing, thick fingers massaging his shining forehead as if it hurt him.

"Right, let me think. We need to see if they took anything. Then we need to get everything packed up and out of here within the hour. You hear me?"

The two men nodded.

"Well find the others and get working then."

McKeown shouldered his rifle, gripped a packing case, braced himself and lifted it with a grunt, ignoring the wet fire in his groin. He waddled, thighs planted apart, to the shed door, half-squatted and dropped the crate the rest of the way.

The pain in his head and his crotch was excruciating but he wasn't going to be beaten. He was not going to give up, not Dean McKeown. He'd show them.

When he got his hands on that bastard Lancaster he would wish he had never been born. An axe, that's what he'd use. McKeown remembered from way back the satisfying sound it made when it bit into someone's skull. He'd enjoy doing that, just as soon as he'd finished cutting the bastard's arms and legs off.

He turned back for another crate and saw the cat, that bloody cat. The animal sensed the atmosphere, tensed, crouching, started to run, too late.

McKeown's boot came up under its body as it started to move, straight between its front and back legs. He felt its ribcage bow against his foot as it lifted and smiled as it spun through the air like a ball, turning to face the ground, legs extended, and vanished behind the crates.

He was starting to laugh just as a wave of pain broke from his groin and washed upward through his body, taking his breath away.

With another grunt he picked up a second crate, took it to the door. He saw the cat again, crouched and baring its teeth. He snarled at the animal and it shot through the barn door and away across the farmyard.

Back to work. If they stacked everything by the door it would be easy to pass it outside and load up once those useless tossers had got the lorry backed up.

As he walked back to the main pile of crates he passed the shorter man and jabbed with an elbow. "Get a move on. We don't have all night."

The man swayed under the weight of the blow and the crate, regained his balance and tottered off towards the door.

It was as he was bracing to lift the third crate that McKeown saw something odd. He reached into a gap in the pile and pulled out an old rag. It told him nothing and he tossed it aside.

He leaned into the gap again, pressing his wide forehead against the rough wood of the crates. There was something gleaming, just catching the pale light hanging from the roof above.

McKeown pulled back and pushed a meaty arm into the gap, feeling around with his fingers. They brushed something smooth and cool. He fumbled to get a grip, managed to trap it between the tips of two fingers, but as he tried to bring it towards him it slipped from his grasp.

McKeown pressed his face to the gap again for another look. He could just make out the mobile phone now as the light traced the curve of its casing, the one that skinny tart tried to hide.

"Bitch, fucking bitch."

It was lying in a crevice between two big crates. There was all sorts of crap down there, packs of plastic and a grenade. Sloppy job. This stuff should all be sorted and crated. When they were done he'd give Conrad and those other lazy bastards a right bollocking.

The phone was lying keypad upwards, scraps of clear tape still visible along the side where the picture of that brat had been.

He pressed his sweating forehead to the gap again, trying to work out how he could reach in. There was something funny. Something about the grenade. Something about the pin.

McKeown tried to reach for the phone again but stopped when the screen suddenly lit up. He squinted to read the words "Danny calling …"

Then it started to vibrate.

\*\*\*

Myers's face was bright with excitement and white wine. She bounced on the balls of her feet, looking around.

"…and every year they pick someone unpopular and burn them in effigy," she said. "One time it was a caravan of travellers. That one caused a bit of a row. I think…"

The air around them seemed to dimple and flex, quivering like the pulse of an uncertain heartbeat. People talking, walking, laughing, froze where they stood.

The black, starred sky disappeared in a brilliant magnesium white flash. The crowds winced away from the glare, night vision destroyed, red patches in front of their eyes. The ground shivered. As they blinked to recover they became aware of a deep rumble, like a flash flood over boulders, roaring towards them.

"Wow," said Myers, "amazing."

A dome of fire lit the northern horizon, rising slowly like a giant wave, gathering mass and momentum. As it climbed it dissolved into a column of flame that boiled upwards until its energy began to wane and gravity started to beat it back, blunting its head into a mushroom cloud that churned as it spread outward.

They could hear popping and crackling. Streaks of blade-thin light lashed upward. Dull thumps and flashes stoked the base of the inferno.

Everyone stood still, heads tilted back, mouths open, starry eyes wide. A ripple of clapping spread through the crowd. Then a cheer that grew until everyone was roaring approval, faces to the horizon, plumes of icy breath curving upward.

"Wow," said Myers, again.

"Is that legal?" said the quiet voice of Liza, behind her.

Something warbled through the air nearby. A car's rear window shattered, alarm wailing, lights flashing.

The four of them moved forward, clamped in the press of the crowd around them, for a better look.

"What's that?" asked Myers.

Danny craned forward over the heads of the two women, squinting at the object that had split the rear parcel shelf.

"Looks like some sort of crank shaft to me."

Karol nodded.

Liza muttered something about health and safety.

\*\*\*

It was getting light when they reached the flat. Danny looked in on his mother, listened to the breathing, then put the kettle on.

When the tea was brewed, Danny and Karol, dirty and dog tired, flopped on the sofa in the living room.

"Quite a night," said Danny.

"Cavalry beat tanks," said Karol.

They grinned at each other, grimy faces and puffy eyes.

Karol slipped his hand into his jacket pocket and his expression changed.

"What's up?" asked Danny.

Karol pulled a tiny chip from his pocket and held it up for Danny to see.

"Is SIM card, from Axeman's mobile. I pick it up in farm yard."

"Does it work?"

Karol pulled out his mobile and took off the battery panel.

"We shall see."

The speed Karol's fingers flew always amazed Danny. When the SIM card was fitted he powered up the phone.

"One number only," said Karol.

"Let me see."

Danny took the phone and pressed dial. It rang eight times and he was about to give up when someone answered.

"Rookwood? What the hell..." the voice trailed away. Danny put the phone on speaker.

"Hello? Rookwood?" the voice had changed quickly from anger to uncertainty. The two men looked at each other.

"Rookwood? For God's sake, what are you..."

"Hello, Edmund," said Danny.

There was a pause, the line hissing, then it went dead.

\*\*\*

"Bullshit," said Big Eddie Archer, eyes hard, face dark. "That's just bullshit. I don't know what your game is. I thought you were a straight sort of bloke. But that's just bullshit."

"You've been had, Eddie, set up."

"That boy's been with me since he was a lad. He's been like a son to me. I like you, Danny, but I've only known you ten minutes. And you tell me this? It's bullshit."

"There's no easy way to tell it. Maybe you relied too much on the legend, Big Eddie Archer, and took your eye off the ball."

"I'm not too old to give you a smack, son."

"Go on if it'll make you feel better. It won't change the facts."

"Well there's one easy way to settle this. We'll get Deano in here, see what he has to say."

"No you won't."

"What do you mean by that?"

"You seen Dean lately?"

"Not since the day before yesterday."

"You're not going to, either."

"Stop giving me riddles, Danny. Where is he?"

"A pink mist spread thinly over a square mile of East Sussex."

"What?"

"You seen the news? The farmhouse explosion?"

"On Sky News, some firework factory went up."

"Not a firework factory, a shed-load of Kalashnikovs, handguns, grenades and Deano."

"You … ?"

Danny nodded.

"Kalashnikovs?"

Danny nodded. "About 500 of them."

"I don't believe this," said Archer quietly, shock replacing anger. "It was supposed to be a dozen, maybe twenty, to set up Wolfram."

"Look, Eddie, I want to help you but you've got to be straight with me or you'll finish up sharing a cell with that drunken old bastard."

"Like I told you, Danny, I wanted to crush Wolfram. Not just kill him, crush him. I got that family tree guy, Forrester, to sell a bag of crap to the old fool, puff up his ego. I got him into some dodgy property deals, through middle men, that would have ruined him. I told Deano to get the guns, a dozen or so, to make it look like the old fascist had his own bodyguard going, his own shock troops, maybe planning to start some trouble. I never said anything about five hundred guns."

"Deano sourced them, shipped the parts here through Bowman Enterprises."

"Bowman? It's dormant. I haven't used that in years."

"But it ties you to the guns, Eddie. And Dean had the authority to use Bowman, am I right?"

Archer nodded. "He could copy my signature, knew the passwords."

"That's not the worst of it. He used Bowman Enterprises as a front to lease the farm. It all leads back to you."

"But why?" said Archer. "Deano was a good boy, loyal."

"He got greedy, Eddie. He got ambitious."

"No, he was a good boy but he didn't have the smarts to pull off something like this."

"He didn't need to," said Danny. "He had a partner."

Archer looked up, eyebrows raised. "Partner?"

"Edmund Salter," said Danny. "Wolfram's number two."

Archer shook his head. Danny continued.

"They wanted to take over. Salter planned to discredit Wolfram, take over his little campaign, make it harder, make it earn. And if they set you up with a trail to the guns and the farm through Bowman you'd go down for a long time and Dean would have your operation. They'd have your business network and Wolfram's political machine, one feeding the other. They even used codenames. Dean was Rookwood and Salter was Digby."

"Sounds like an old drag act."

"It threw me as well but I've got a mate who's good with computers. Ambrose Rookwood and Everard Digby were part of Guy Fawkes's gang to blow up Parliament, change the country."

"You're having a laugh?" said Archer.

Danny shook his head.

Archer's big fists mashed together, fingers interlocking, squeezing. The muscles around his mouth squirmed as he tried to digest what he was being told.

"And what about Minty?"

"I'm still working on that one."

"My first regret," said Archer, his voice hard and quiet, "is that you did for Dean because I can't tear that treacherous little shit part. What about Salter?"

Danny shrugged.

"He's mine," said Archer.

***

They stood stiffly in the kitchen. Her movements were tense and tight as she poured the tea, her face set and serious.

Danny knew Margaret was trying to stay calm, keeping it bottled up inside her, and only just succeeding.

She stirred the milk into his tea and handed him the cup and saucer. It looked dainty and faintly ridiculous in his hand.

"You said he was good with lawyers, that they'd got him off the hook before."

A shadow passed across Margaret's face and Danny sensed she was trying not to look at him.

"Is there anything that would help? Anything I could use?"

She stood still, arms folded, staring out of the kitchen window.

"There is something, isn't there?"

She said nothing.

"Margaret, I don't want to upset you but it's important. If there's anything ..."

"Important to you, you mean." Her voice was hard.

"Yes, important to me."

She looked up at him, arms still folded, her face unreadable.

"Come into the lounge."

He followed her. The laptop was on a table in the corner. She sat down, booted it up and began flicking through files. Danny saw the mouse pointer hover over a file called QuickTime Movie MM0001. Then she clicked.

As the film flickered to life she stood up, indicated for Danny to sit in front of the laptop as she pulled over a nearby chair.

Danny looked at the screen, two circles oscillating in the gloom, creaking noises, the hiss of breath.

They watched in silence. The movement, the lean body flexing along the bench, the change of position, the lightning, the girl's smile.

Danny was sharply aware of the steady breathing behind his shoulder. Sixty second in, he pressed 'stop' and turned to Margaret. Her eyes were blank, told him nothing.

"Look..."

"Just watch it," said Margaret as she reached around him and pressed Play again.

He put his hand over hers and pressed Stop.

"Margaret, don't put yourself through this. I've seen it before. I just didn't know what it meant."

Lady Margaret stood up and walked to the window, arms wrapped tightly around herself. He walked back and looked straight at Danny.

"Some silly little tart, some actress, threw herself at him at a house party we attended, tried to blackmail him. It was just after he sold the business. I imagine she was attracted by the money. The figures were bandied about in all the papers.

"It's true what they say, there's no fool like an old fool. She thought a quick fuck would make her rich but Charles's lawyers made it very clear to her what would happen if she went ahead with her scheme. No need for violence or any of that sort of thing. They can be very persuasive. It's why they're so expensive."

"You didn't need to..."

Margaret turned away. Danny followed, put his arms around her. He felt her back straighten, arms rigid, but after a moment she relaxed a little.

"Is it what you needed?" she asked.

"I don't know."

"Just do what you have to, Danny."

He leaned forward, pressing his forehead into her hair. "Thanks for your help."

She didn't reply.

\*\*\*

From a doorway in the outpatients building on the other side of Eastern Road, Danny watched him go.

He came out of the peeling white portico and lumbered off towards the bus stop, shoulders rounded, head down, hands in pockets. Danny finished his cigarette, ground it out under his boot and crossed the road.

The Royal Sussex County Hospital was a rabbit warren of low, dingy corridors and walkways. As you worked your way from the canopied front entrance of the original Charles Barry building through the maze of passages towards the modern Millennium Wing tower block up the hill at the rear you passed through nearly 200 years of medical history, each new improvement bolted on to the previous generation.

Danny didn't like hospitals. He really didn't like the Royal Sussex. Too many nights sat in A&E watching the uncomprehending fear in his mother's eyes as she worked her way up the casualty priority list with another suspected mini-stroke.

Too many hours until some overworked junior doctor had the time to see if she'd had another attack, another section of brain shut down, her life shrinking still further.

Distracted by the smell and the memory, Danny usually got lost. But this time he wove his way straight to the ward. As he walked in a nurse looked up and pursed her lips.

"It's ten minutes to the end of visiting."

"I know," said Danny.

"Who did you want to see?"

"Mrs Driscoll."

"All right, she's in bed 12. You just missed her husband."

Danny nodded his thanks and walked across the ward. One old lady, the right side of her face a dark purple bruise, tube up her nose, stared into space.

A woman in her fifties with hair newly permed by the visiting stylist sang the praises of a lovely young doctor to her family who were gathered around the bed on plastic chairs, picnicking from food boxes.

Danny peered around a curtain. Emma was sitting up in bed, reading an old copy of Hello. He watched her for a moment, drinking in the detail.

There was a bandage around her head. Her pale yellow complexion emphasised the big purple bruises that circled her eyes like comedy sunglasses.

As she moved to turn a page she sensed his scrutiny and looked up.

"Danny."

He moved forward and tugged the curtain closed behind him.

"You're looking good."

"Liar." Her voice was a whisper. She reached up to touch her hair but it landed on bandage.

"I look a fright."

Danny smiled. "No, you look good."

"Sit down," she said, indicating a chair.

Danny sat and opened a plastic carrier bag.

"I brought you these."

He drew out a plastic punnet of white grapes and a bunch of flowers. Emma took the flowers, looked at them, then held them to her nose and sniffed.

"Chrysanthemums," she said.

"If you say so," said Danny. "The woman told me they last longer than most. You'd need that in here. It's like a sauna."

Emma gave a short little laugh. Danny saw the lines around her eyes tighten. "They've still got the sticker on them," she said, indicating grapes and flowers already on the bedside cabinet. "You and Benny must use the same petrol station."

They looked at each other and smiled.

"He was here just now," she said in a whisper.

"I know."

"He said you were here, with him, the night it happened."

Danny nodded.

"Does he … does he know…?"

Danny shook his head.

Emma turned the bunch of flowers between her fingers, studying them under the yellow light. Danny knew she was trying not to look at him.

"They said it was a boy."

Danny couldn't think of anything to say so he said nothing. The flowers turned.

"I don't … I don't know who …"

Danny reached out, put a hand over hers. The flowers stopped turning.

"Don't worry about that. You just get better."

Emma nodded, red-rimmed eyes flickered up towards him, moisture catching the overhead light.

"How's your mum?"

Danny shrugged. "The usual."

"Who's looking after her?"

"Emily down at the pub, she had a friend does a bit of nursing."

"Somehow you always manage to land on your feet."

"Foot," said Danny. "Foot."

Emma tried to smile again

"Is she cleaning as well? I don't want the place in a mess. You know the state that loo gets in."

"Don't worry," said Danny. "I'll pee it clean as usual."

Emma laughed.

"And you're still on wages. Call it sick pay."

"That's kind of you, Danny."

He shrugged again, thought he'd never seen her so frail, saw a tremor run through her. Her mouth quivered as she tried to stop herself crying but a single tear painted a silver line on her cheek.

"I didn't know what to do. I tried to tell you, Danny. I wanted to do what was right. I just didn't know what that was. I ... I ..."

He moved to the side of the bed, put an arm round her shoulder, pulled her gently against his chest. He didn't remember her being this small and delicate. It was like holding a child.

She hissed as her bruises pressed against him. He heard her fingernails scratching for a grip on his jacket, clenching, then holding tight.

Danny felt the tremors rolling back and forth through her body. On the bed, her magazine lay open, glossy colour pictures of smiling celebrities walked the red carpet.

He looked down at the white turban of bandages, holding her and waiting, as her tears spread a hot, damp patch across his shirt.

\*\*\*

It was still there, hidden under a tarpaulin beneath a bush where they had dumped it. Karol walked past, kept going for a quarter of mile, then turned back and checked in the opposite direction. No one about.

You had to be careful, never knew if someone had the place under observation. Everything looked clear.

He circled the bush, then moved in from behind, crouching as he pushed groping branches from his face with a gloved hand.

He pulled the tarpaulin clear. The bike was just as he and Danny had left it, keys in the ignition, a quarter tank of petrol.

He threw a leg over the quad and wriggled to get comfortable, then tried the controls. When he was satisfied Karol took a last look around and started the engine. When it had warmed a little he rode off down the woodland track.

\*\*\*

Danny looked both ways again. It was still quiet. He could hear traffic on the road in front of the building. A shadow crossed and recrossed a lit window, preparing something in their kitchen at the rear of the block of flats.

He could hear faint music. It must have been loud as no one would have their windows open in this bitter cold.

He set the heavy sports bag down on the tarmac, took the key from his pocket and opened the door.

Before he entered Danny glanced back at the figure swamped by a wax jacket many sizes too big. They nodded silently to each other and Danny slipped inside.

The garage was exactly as it had been when he first saw it but the Mini One was missing. The old Jaguar under its layer of dust, the new Jag with the broken headlamp hastily parked, keys still in the ignition.

He pulled his gloves on tighter, took the ignition keys and opened the boot. It looked neat and unstained, spare tyre showroom-fresh, no marks on the jack.

Danny opened the sports bag at his feet. He pulled out a hessian sack, peered in at the Kalashnikov, then laid it in the bed of the Jag's boot.

He delved into the sports bag again and pulled out the polythene package that Archer had provided through "a friend of a friend". Danny pierced the wrapping with the ignition key and sprinkled some of the white powder over the carpet in the boot.

Then he rammed the packet into the corner, tamping it down hard into a crevice, something missed by someone working fast and furtively.

He stepped back to examine the interior of the boot. It didn't have to be perfect, didn't need to be. It was too big to be ignored. Even if he wriggled out from under there would always be the cloud of doubt, suspicion.

Satisfied, Danny slammed the boot, wiped the key and slipped it back into the ignition.

As he stepped out of the garage the figure in the wax jacket crossed her arms tighter against the bitter wind.

"Is it done?" asked Margaret.

"Yes."

"Good, don't tell me any more. I don't want to know."

She turned away and Danny followed her in silence. They entered the apartment block through the rear service door and walked up the stairs to the flat.

Inside, Danny washed his hands and forearms, scrubbing carefully to remove any traces of the gear he had left in the car.

He could hear movement in the bedroom next door. Margaret had been quiet and calm, too calm. Danny knew there was a lot going on behind the mask of a lifetime's loyalty, the stiff upper lip.

When he had dried his hand he found her in the kitchen tidying the draining board. She picked up a plate and looked at him with a reluctant smile.

"Look, I'll try and come over tomorrow, check you're okay."

"I won't be here," said Margaret.

"Oh?"

"I'm visiting my daughter in Perth. I'll see my grandson for the first time and, perhaps, do a little painting."

"Will you be gone long?"

"Yes."

"You treacherous bitch!"

Margaret's eyes widened. The plate smashed on the floor. Danny turned very slowly.

Sir Charles Wolfram stood in the doorway. His clothes were rumpled and his comb-over hung like a door missing a hinge. His eyes were red and watering and the hand that held the pistol was shaking badly.

"I turn my back for two minutes and … and…"

He raised the quivering pistol, screwing his eyes half shut. Danny smelled the sour taint of old booze on his breath and stepped in front of Margaret.

Sir Charles laughed, the sound catching, tripping over itself in his throat.

"Gallant … very gallant. Quite the hero."

"Charles, please…"

Margaret tried to push Danny aside but he held her gently but firmly behind him.

"I only popped back to pick up a few things," said Sir Charles. "Forgot my passport … urgent trip abroad … and I find … I find …"

His arm jerked out towards them. It was a crack rather than a bang but the sound in the confines of the kitchen still punched painfully at their ears.

Strands of blue smoke drifted up from the muzzle. Danny heard a tinkle of glass behind him as he thought about Emma in the hospital and about Eddie Archer and his granddaughter.

Wolfram was six feet away. It would be easy to step forward, take the gun, punch the drunken old fool to the floor. But maybe Archer was right, that crushing the man's soul was the only proper revenge.

Sir Charles looked down at the pistol in his hand, then up over Danny's shoulder at the tiny hole in the kitchen window. His mouth twitched with frustration which made his chins wobble.

He thrust his arm out again. A quiet, dry click silenced even their breathing. Sir Charles held the pistol up to his watery eyes, then held it at arms length again and jerked the trigger a second time. Nothing happened.

He shook the pistol. "Bloody thing … never was any good."

Danny reached forward and pulled it from his unresisting fingers. He looked down at the gun, a .22 Ruger target pistol. Small calibre but deadly in the right hands, or at close range.

"You've got a stoppage," said Danny. He snapped back the slide and the jammed round fell to the floor and rolled away. He looked into the breach.

"This needs a good clean."

He chambered another round, gripped the barrel and held the pistol out to Sir Charles, butt first.

"You want another try? Or maybe you should go into the library and do the decent thing."

The old man almost dropped the Ruger as he snatched it back. He looked down at the weapon in his hand, then up at Danny, his face a dangerous purple.

"You … bastard."

Thick spit began to well up at the corners of his mouth as he tried to pump out words at his wife.

"You … bitch."

He stuffed the pistol into his overcoat pocket and he was gone.

They stood in silence, listening to heavy, uncoordinated footsteps thumping around the apartment, draws opening, wardrobes slamming. Then the front door crashed shut.

Danny turned to face Margaret but she moved away from him, took a dustpan and brush from an alcove, began to sweep up the shards of the broken plate.

Outside, an engine was over-revving, tyres shrieked.

## CHAPTER 25

She winced when her teeth clashed on something hard and unexpected. Detective Sergeant Pauline Myers fished some unidentified piece of gristle from between her back teeth and placed it in the cardboard sandwich box.

There should be laws against things like that, she thought. Liza was right, she should try to improve her diet, eat more fruit and veg, avoid the junk food.

But with the hours she worked it was a case of grabbing whatever came to hand when hunger pangs struck, gristle and all.

A night out in Lewes with Liza had been a luxury. And with their current caseload things were not going to ease up any time soon. Lord alone knew when she would get any more time off.

The phone on her desk rang. Relieved at an excuse to put down the sandwich, she picked up.

"Detective Sergeant Myers."

"Hello, I am a concerned citizen with information about that hit and run."

Her eyebrows curled in puzzlement.

"Is that you, Danny?"

Silence.

"Danny, is that you?"

A pause, then a voice.

"Okay, yes."

"If you're playing silly buggers I'm not in the mood."

"Right."

"You said you had information about the hit and run."

"Yes."

"Well?"

"There's a guy might be able to help you but you've got to be quick off the mark. He's just left Brighton, going abroad, so he said. He's driving a Jaguar."

Danny described the make and model of the car and gave her the registration number. Myers scribbled it down.

"Okay, Danny, and how did you come by this information?"

"Guy in a pub."

"What guy?"

"Never seen him before."

"Oh, really? What did he say?"

"Not much, just that there was this guy in a Jag you might be interested in."

"And you didn't know this man in the pub? What did he look like?"

"Don't remember."

"Look, Danny, if you're pissing me about ..."

"You know how it is, Pauline. He'd had a few drinks. I'd had a few drinks. Suddenly you're the best of friends. Like I said, I'm just a concerned citizen trying to help the forces of law and order. You'd better get a move on."

"So we're not going to find your prints on the car?"

"You have a suspicious nature."

"It comes with the job. Don't leave town, Danny."

Myers put the phone down and looked at the notes on her pad. If Danny was serious, and he had better be, his mystery Jag driver could he heading anywhere but the two likely destinations were a flight from Gatwick or a ferry from Newhaven. She dropped the sandwich in the bin and picked up the phone again.

***

Douglas Gardner picked a piece of fluff from his sleeve and glanced again at the Tag Heuer watch on his wrist. If the client didn't arrive soon it would be too late.

Golf India Papa, the twin-engine Piper Navajo, stood on the apron in front of the art deco terminal building of Shoreham Airport, not far from the black and yellow McDonnell Douglas Explorer helicopter, call sign Hotel 900, used by Sussex Police. The Navajo was ready and the paperwork prepared.

Gardner had hoped for a quick, trouble-free trip. He had promised to take Diana for a late dinner if everything went well.

But someone with the money to pay for a private charter could be late if they chose to be. Gardner was used to it, Thankfully, so was Diana.

He looked at his watch again. They had a little under half an hour. Shoreham Airport closed at 8pm and Carpiquet at 10pm French time which would be 9pm UK time. They could just make it but if they didn't take off soon his client was going nowhere, however much money he had.

Gardner glanced up at the sound of a siren. Looking across the airfield he could see blue flashing lights on the Shoreham bypass.

With nothing better to do to pass the time, he reached into the cockpit and took out his binoculars.

Scanning the road he saw a car slewed at an angle against the crash barrier, one door open, looked like one of those new Minis. There was a van stopped behind it and a group of men, looked like some sort of argument going on.

Vehicles were squeezing past but traffic was building up and the blue lights had slowed as the police car tried to force a path through the jam.

That would explain it, thought Gardner. Someone in too much of a hurry. Mr Digby stuck in the tailback. He looked at the Tag again. He would give it another thirty minutes, just to be sure, then surprise Diana with an early supper at the Regency Restaurant on the front where they had done their courting.

\*\*\*

"Karol?"

"I am busy."

"Karol, I need your help."

"I am at the ninth level. I am busy."

"It won't take a mo'."

Karol's fingers were a blur as they flew across the laptop keyboard. "What part of this English word 'busy' are you not understanding?"

"It's important."

"So is the ninth level."

Danny pulled something small and silver from his pocket.

"It's a JCB."

Karol looked up, brows knitted, and sighed. He looked at the object in Danny's hand, paused his game and slammed the laptop lid shut.

"Is USB. What part of these English words 'universal serial bus' do you not understand?"

"All of them."

Karol made a hissing noise. "You are 19th century man in 21st century world."

Danny shrugged. "I can do email."

Karol shook his head in disgust and took the USB, turning it in his fingers. "Is broken."

"I know. Can you fix it?"

Karol pulled a sour face. "I can try but I tell you now it won't work, probably."

"Give it a go, will you?"

Karol shrugged. "Why not, I am poor immigrant worker from eastern Europe. I have nothing better to do."

"Look, mate," said Danny. "Cut the funny accent and help. It's important."

"Is hopeless," he said.

"Okay," said Danny. "There's something else."

"Always there is something else."

"You're even more cheerful than usual today. Look, I need some background information."

With a theatrical sigh, Karol opened his laptop again.

"You know what is ninth level?"

Danny shook his head.

"You English know nothing. Is miracle you ever have empire."

"Look, I'll buy you a beer."

"This is your answer to all."

"Karol."

"Okay, okay, what is information?"

"I need a bit of family tree stuff."

Karol's fingers started to fly again.

\*\*\*

"Unbelievable," said Detective Inspector Eddie Aziz. "It's just unbelievable." They were gathered around the desk, a dozen of them, reading the incident report.

"This guy," Aziz continued. "Sir Charles Wolfram, businessman, politician, patriot, self-styled saviour of the nation. I mean, you'd have to be mad to vote for him but this? It's unbelievable."

"Just goes to show," said Detective Sergeant Myers. "You can't trust anyone."

"It's always the cunning buggers you've got to watch," said a voice at the back, Oldfield. "Shifty bunch, politicians."

Aziz looked up at the ceiling, face glowing with excitement. "This is why we're in major crimes. This is what it's all about. Three murders plus there's us, counter terrorism, firearms, SoC and Emergency Ops and Planning all peering down a bloody great hole outside Lewes. It's days like this that make careers."

"Or break them," said Myers, quietly.

Aziz looking back at the Wolfram report. "And just look at this. Traffic and Firearms pulled him over on the M23 just south of Gatwick. He had a handgun in his pocket, recently fired, and a loaded Kalashnikov assault rifle with his fingers prints on it. Substantial traces of cocaine. And all in the boot of a car registered to him and used in a hit-and-run that injured a pregnant woman."

"And we've had an anonymous call," said Oldfield. "Linking him to another hit and run in Haywards Health five months back, killed a two-year-old kiddie. Her mother was in treatment for months."

"Wolfram's lawyers will be earning their fees on this one," said Myers. Her mobile rang. She stepped away from the group and answered it. Aziz watched her as she listened intently, nodding, before cutting the call.

"What's up?" he asked.

"Someone claiming to have information of the dogging site murder."

"Any idea who?"

"Says he's a concerned citizen."

"Another one?" said Aziz. "Unbelievable. This Big Society idea is really taking off around here." He turned back to the group around the desk.

\*\*\*

Pub regulars are like a herd. Thinned by death and disease over years and replenished by births, they migrate down the generations to their favourite watering hole.

There is a hierarchy of regulars. The herd will support the weak and gather together against threats and outsiders.

Members of the herd know a warm glow of coming home when they push open the door to see familiar faces inspecting the new arrival.

They may acknowledge each other with only a first name or a nod, guard their own space jealously, but the sharing of alcohol beneath the same sign breeds a powerful, unspoken bond.

Danny was leaning on the bar of the Bellerophon, chatting with Emily, when she walked in. He didn't recognise her until she swept back the hood on her long, dark padded coat and gave him a weary smile.

"Pino Grigio?" asked Danny.

"Please," said Claire.

Emily already had the door of the chiller cabinet open, reaching for the bottle. As she poured she passed a critical eye over the new arrival.

"Shall we sit?" asked Danny, picking up a fresh pint.

"Yes," said Claire. "Somewhere quiet."

He looked around. There was a lone drinker at the bar. Sudoku Wally was in his usual spot, head down, ignoring the world. Two women, foreheads and fingers almost touching, whispered together across a table near the toilets.

Danny led the way to the far end of the bar room and waved at a table with his pint. Claire nodded and they took their seats. She pushed her big shoulder bag under the table.

"Any news?"

Danny shook his head. "Nothing concrete, sorry."

Claire looked down at the worn wooden grain of the table top. "I see."

"I hate to mention this," said Danny. "But could we get the money out of the way first?"

Claire looked confused for a moment, then nodded. "Oh, of course." She dug in the pocket of her coat and pulled out an envelope. "There you are. There's another two hundred plus fifty for the expenses you mentioned."

Danny took the envelope, tested its thickness between his fingers and slipped it into his jacket pocket.

"Sorry about that but a guy's got to live."

"I understand. So what's the situation?"

Danny, elbows on the table, locked his fingers together and studied her. "Well, the situation is that the police have a body, unidentified at the moment."

Claire's Pinot Grigio quivered in the glass as she gripped the stem. "And you think it's Minty?"

Danny nodded. "I'm afraid so."

"Oh my God." Claire's face tilted to the table. A thin strand that had escaped her hair grip drifted across her eyes. They sat in silence. Danny was tempted to sip his pint but resisted.

When she looked up again her eyes were red and there was the faintest quiver in her lips. He picked up his glass and drank. The bang as it went back down on the table sounded loud in the quiet bar.

"So my sister's dead?"

"Looks that way."

Her eyes snapped up to look straight into his.

"But you said the body was unidentified?"

"At the moment, yes."

"So how do you know it's her? How can you be sure?"

"Detection, it's what I do."

Claire shook her head, face creased with conflicting thoughts.

"What do you mean? How can you know?"

Danny picked up his pint and sipped.

"Because I know who killed her."

"How? How can you know if the police don't?"

Danny set down his pint.

"It's all to do with butterflies."

"Butterflies? What are you talking about, butterflies? You sit there and tell me my sister is dead and you talk about butterflies. Is this some kind of sick joke?"

"No joke," said Danny. "I don't think it's funny at all. But it's still about butterflies."

"What do you mean?"

"Something I read in the library, something about butterflies causing hurricanes."

Claire's eyes were wide with disbelief. "Chaos theory? Does the flap of a butterfly's wings in Brazil set off a tornado in Texas?"

Danny nodded. "That's the one."

"My sister's dead on some slab and you're talking about philosophy. You're sick."

"Maybe, but not as sick as you."

"What did you say?"

"I've seen the film."

"What film?"

"Sir Charles and the blackmailing tart."

"Okay, Minty did some stupid thing but she was a good person at heart. She was my sister."

"Whatever Minty did, she didn't bang Sir Charles."

"But you've seen the film."

"I have, and at first I thought the girl putting on the Oscar-winning performance was her. That's what everyone was meant to think. But it wasn't Minty."

"How can you know that?"

"Minty had a tramp stamp, a butterfly tattoo in the small of her back. The girl in the film didn't."

Claire sat back, hands in her lap, watching Danny as he sipped his pint.

"Minty's model card," said Danny. "It says her eyes are blue. The girl in the film has grey eyes. Your eyes are grey."

"You don't imagine…"

"Yes, I do. When you hired me to find her you said you were sisters, as close as it was possible to be, you said. But you two weren't just sisters, you were twins. Not identical, I admit, but very close. Close enough to pass for each other with the right wig, make-up and clothes."

"That just ridiculous."

"Minty said you both did acting as kids, that she carried on with it."

"I suppose she gave you the line about mum and dad saying she had the looks and I had the brains, that I would scrub up well if I only made the effort."

"She did. And you do. There's a website a friend of mine showed me, the Internet Movie Database. Lists loads of TV shows and films with the cast and crew. You took a bit of finding. You used your mother's maiden name and I had to get your birth certificate before I could find that out. You did a few soaps and cops shows, just like Minty, and a bit of theatre, Bristol and here in Brighton. Quite the actress, really."

"I am an archaeologist."

"That too, a woman of many talents, acting, digging and killing people. I'm guessing this bit but I think you tried to blackmail Wolfram to fund your career. Pay for an archaeologist is piss poor and digging is an expensive hobby.

"You copied your little dirty movie onto Minty's laptop to cover yourself. She was so disorganised she'd never notice. But Wolfram's people faced you down. A court case would have ruined your career.

"Then Minty mentioned Wolfram's obsession with his family history, the money she was taking from Eddie Archer to Giles Forrester to doctor his family tree, and you saw another chance.

"If he was caught shagging he could ride it out with a loyal, forgiving wife by his side. But if he was found bigging up his ego, presenting himself as someone he wasn't, that really would cut the legs from under his political campaign. I'm guessing you tried to steal the info from Forrester's computer and he caught you at it."

The Pan-Am smile that spread slowly across her face startled him.

"Forrester caught me downloading his genealogy files so I had to deal with him. When I got home, Minty came in and found me getting out of one of her ridiculous dressing-up costumes. She was right, I am the one in the family with the brains. I had no choice."

"You killed your sister," said Danny.

"The world turns. People fall off. No one cares."

"I do."

Danny was about to speak again when a sharp pain seared up his right thigh. Claire was leaning forward now, still smiling. The pain came again and he winced.

"Still caring, Danny?"

He blocked the pain and smiled back at her.

"Pretty much, yes. I think that's my second proof."

"It's hardened steel but it's amazing what you can do with an ordinary kitchen knife sharpener. Do you care about your testicles, Danny?"

Danny stayed perfectly still as the pain danced along his thigh.

"It took me a while but it was obvious really. Copper I know mentioned a wide, flat double-sided blade. It was on your mantelpiece the whole time, your archaeology award, the trowel."

"You have been busy."

"Busier than you wanted. I couldn't work out why you didn't want to involve Archer or the police if you were so concerned for Minty's safety. Then I twigged. You thought I was just some passing idiot you could use for a little stage setting."

Claire smiled again. It didn't touch her eyes. "If I'd known you'd make this much effort for a few hundred I'd never have hired you. You were only supposed to make it look as if I gave a damn." Her lips tightened as she twisted the point of the trowel in Danny's thigh.

"And the man who attacked us in the street?"

"Just some guy. Amazing what men will do for a smile and a BJ."

"You'll never get away with this."

"Why not. What are you going to do? Arrest me?"

Danny locked his eyes on hers, watching a shadow in his peripheral vision, desperate not to let it show in his face.

"If I stab you now I'd be out of that door before anyone knows what happened. Besides, now that simpering little bitch is dead I don't care any more, I really don't. I hated her from the very start and now I'm free of her."

The shadow was a few feet away now. Claire Marshall suddenly sensed the presence, began to turn.

"You want DVD?" said the short man in a green anorak clutching a Tesco carrier bag.

Danny rammed his leg upward. Claire tried to pull the trowel blade free but it was pinned hard between the underside of the table and his thigh. She pulled again. Danny dropped his leg and the trowel came away so fast Claire's chair toppled backwards, catching the DVD seller's legs and rolling sideways.

Danny started to rise and was surprised at the speed Claire was on her feet. As he moved around the table she swung at him, trowel at arm's length, slashing through a wide arc, so close he saw the fresh metal of the newly sharpened edge. He rocked backwards but the tip of the blade clipped his left nostril. Blood poured.

Danny staggered sideways, pushing the table away. Their drinks slid off and hit the floor with a crackle of breaking glass. The DVD seller was on all fours, scooping wet film packets back into the carrier bag and wailing in a language Danny didn't understand. As he stepped over the man Claire was halfway to the door.

Danny began to power across the bar room. As Claire's hand closed around the handle of the street door something trailing a spiral tail of liquid spun through the air, bounced off the wood and struck her forehead.

Claire screamed and tottered away, one hand clutching her face. Her feet tangled in the old blanket spilling from Slate's wicker basket and she toppled over, the trowel clattering off across the old wooden floor.

Danny was level with the bar now but the two women from the table by the toilets were ahead of him.

Slate was on his feet, prancing and barking. Claire struggled up out of the dog's basket but as she regained her feet the first women cannoned into her, knocking her down.

The second woman grabbed her wrist, jerked her onto her front and pulled her arms behind her.

Detective Constable Liza with a zed stood panting gently, holding Slate's collar as she spoke into her radio. Detective Sergeant Myers sat astride Claire's back.

As she snapped on the handcuffs she began to recite, "Claire Marshall, I am arresting you on suspicion of the murders of Giles Forrester and Minty Marshall. You do not have to say anything. But it may harm your defence if you do not mention when questioned something which you later rely on in ..."

Danny bobbed down, picked up the empty bottle of pinot grigio from the floor and looked at the label. The last of the wine trickled out onto the floor. He placed it carefully on the bar and Emily picked it up and threw it in the empties bin.

"That stuff packs a punch," he said. "Nice throw, Em."

She nodded. "I won't have trouble in here. This is a good pub."

Four uniformed police and a detective in plain clothes came in through the street door. Myers handed over her prisoner and turned to Danny.

"You look a mess."

Emily handed him a bar towel and he dabbed at the blood streaming from his split nostril.

"I'll need statements from both of you." They nodded. Myers turned to Danny.

"Nice job. You do the concerned citizen pretty well."

"I try." He opened his jacket and unbuttoned his shirt. Myers grinned as she ripped away the tape securing the microphone. Compressed breath winced through Danny's teeth.

"There's my big brave soldier. I see you got yourself paid first."

"A guy's got to live."

\*\*\*

He couldn't remember the last time he had felt like this. His thighs ached, his back hurt like hell and the scratches on his hands were stinging.

He was sweating, too. He could feel it trickling behind his ears and through the hair at the back of his head.

And his heart was pounding, really pounding. He could hear it in his ears like a steam hammer.

Bob Lovejoy looked up at the ceiling. The thumping of his racing heart was making his moobs jiggle.

He rolled over and looked up at the ceiling, still breathing heavily. The rivulets of sweat on his head changed direction.

Fingers skittered across his chest. Bob squealed when they pinched a nipple.

"No nodding off!"

He looked up at Wanda, her flushed, smiling face framed by a wild tangle of hair. Her eyes were alight.

"Let me get my breath back." He wheezed.

He patted his cheek. "Oooooh, my poor wounded soldier."

They both laughed. He reached up and ran his fingers through her thick hair.

"Better than Wii exercises then?"

She shook her head and her hair tumbled over her broad shoulders.

"Oh, much, much better."

"Any chance of something to eat?"

Wanda nodded enthusiastically.

"Certainly, we've got to keep your strength up, haven't we?"

"I fancy chops," said Bob. "One of those with a kidney in it. Can you still get them?"

"Do you fancy anything else?"

"I'm not Superman, you know."

She smiled, revealing large white teeth.

"And there was me thinking you were my man of steel."

Bob felt Wanda wriggling down the bed beside him. He tried to shuffle up on his elbows, wincing when stretched muscles protested.

When he looked down the bed Wanda had his sticky semi-erection between her big freckled breasts and a wicked grin on her face.

\*\*\*

The door opened on the second ring. "Well, well, if it isn't Inspector Morse. Come on in."

Big Eddie Archer's weary smile couldn't camouflage the pain and fatigue grooved across his face. Danny followed him into the kitchen where hot oil was starting to sizzle. Archer turned down the gas ring.

"I've just got the bacon on. You want a sarnie?"

"Why not."

"Tea with that?"

Danny nodded. He sat on a stool beside the marble-topped island and watched Archer as he worked.

"You know, son," said Archer, waving his spatula. "You did good. I wasn't too sure about this detecting business at first but you've got a real talent. Cut through all the crap."

Danny shrugged. "It's still a mess, still a lot of dead people."

"Don't put yourself down, Danny. You cracked it when the rest of us were clueless, Plod included."

"Thanks, maybe I can use you as a reference."

"Any time, son. And I've got your money in the other room. Cash, thought you'd prefer that."

"Thanks."

"No, Danny, it's me who should be thanking you. I don't do that often, believe me, but I can't believe how I was being stitched up by those two bastards. I never saw it coming. You could be right, I must be getting old."

Despite the banter, Danny thought Archer looked smaller, shoulders rounded, older. It wasn't the betrayal that had knocked him back, it was his failure to spot it, anticipate. Maybe he really was losing it.

"You're right, Danny. It is messy," said Archer, chasing a rasher of bacon around the frying pan. "But it's sorted now. You got a result. My only regret is that you sorted Deano before I got to him. Being blown to bits was too good for that treacherous little shit, too quick."

"And Wolfram's inside."

Archer nodded just as the toaster pinged.

"Yes, he'll have his work cut out wriggling out from under that lot. And if he does he's going to be a marked man. I don't think even the nutters would vote for him now."

"I'm sorry about Minty. I didn't see that one coming."

Archer flipped three rashers onto a slice of toast and pressed another slice down on top. He handed the plate to Danny.

"No, well, like you said. It's sorted but it's messy. Minty's own bloody sister, eh? And she did for that little shit Forrester as well. Just shows, you can't trust anybody these days."

"Any news on Salter?"

Archer shrugged. "How should I know? Pack a bag, charter a plane at Shoreham, he could be a thousand miles away in a few hours."

As Danny lifted the sandwich to his mouth he smelled the rich aroma and realised just how hungry he was. Archer put his sandwich on the work top opposite Danny and carried over two mugs of steaming tea in the big Seagull mugs.

"It's about loyalty, son. Words are cheap, Moonpig cards are a bit of paper. It's what you say and what you do, that's what counts. There's no side to you, Danny. You do what it says on the tin. That's rare these days. Deano didn't have it. Wolfram and Salter didn't have it. Neither did that bitch sister."

"What about Salter?" asked Danny, blowing the steam off his tea.

"I'm tired. To tell the truth, this whole business had knocked the stuffing out of me. I mean, me and Minty, it was never going to last. But she was a good girl, fun, kept me young. She loved the sea, you know, dragged me down there every chance she got just to walk along the front."

"She mentioned it," said Danny.

Archer looked down at his sandwich. "She didn't deserve that. I think I need to take some time out. Remember I told you I'd got a little farm up near Pyecombe?"

Danny nodded.

"I think I'll go up there for a few days. A bit of time on the land will do me good, commune with nature. Keep my head down while my lawyers sort out the Bowman problem. I've got a guy who keeps an eye on the place but I've neglected it of late. You can't do that with livestock. Starve the pigs for a few days and they'll eat anything."

"You didn't say if you'd heard about Salter," said Danny.

Archer shrugged. "Search me. For all I know he's retired to some gated community in Florida with Sammy Spoon for a neighbour. How's your sarnie?"

Danny looked down at the half-eaten sandwich in his hand. A thick length of bacon curled out between the slices of white bread, rind glistening.

"Very tasty, nice and moist."

## CHAPTER 26

The knock at the door startled her. No one was expected. Perhaps there was a problem. She hoped not.

The boy rose from the table where he had been sitting quietly, reading a book, but she waved him down.

"No, I will answer it."

The woman placed her knitting carefully on the table beside her chair and gripped her walking stick to help her up.

She was half way along the hall when the bell rang again. What could it be that was so urgent? Not a problem, please.

The woman turned the door handle and peered through a three inch gap, annoyed with herself that she had left her distance glasses on the table beside her chair.

The man was tall, his height emphasised by the long dark coat he wore. He raised his hat in greeting and revealed a bald head with tufts of curly white hair sprouting out over his ears.

Without her glasses it was hard to tell but the woman thought the man's expression was uncertain.

"I think you have the wrong address," she said.

The man put his hat back on then, realising the woman was nervous, took it off and pressed it to his chest.

"You are Mrs Pawlowski?"

"Yes," said the woman reluctantly. "Is there a problem?"

The man hesitated. The woman narrowed the door gap by an inch.

"Please," he said. "My name is Mr Dudek. I am a lawyer. I have come here at the request of a client."

"We need no lawyers," said the woman. "Is there a problem?"

"No, no problem. I come with a message."

"A message from who?"

"I cannot tell you. My client requests privacy."

"Please go away. I do not want a lawyer."

The door closed another inch. As the woman braced to close it a white envelope slipped through the gap and fluttered to the floor. As the door banged shut the woman heard a muffled voice. "I apologise for disturbing you, Mrs Pawlowski."

She listened to the fading footsteps as she stood in the hall, waiting for her heart to calm. The envelope lay on the mat, crisp and white.

Mrs Pawlowski didn't want to touch it, didn't want anything to do with it. But if she ignored it the envelope would be there when she came back, there every time she passed. It would not go away by itself.

With a grunt of discomfort she bent, scooped it up and shuffled back into the living room, rested her stick against the armchair and settled down again beside her knitting.

The boy, head in his book, said nothing. The woman looked at the envelope in her lap. Was it a problem?

After ten minutes she picked it up, turned it over, squeezed it. It felt light, just a few leaves of paper inside.

If it was a problem it would not go away. Problems distressed her but they did not go away. If she knew the problem, perhaps she might find a way to solve it and then it would go away.

She took a spare knitting needle, slid it under the flap and tore it along its length. She pulled open the envelope and probed with bent fingers before extracting a single folded sheet with something inside.

Settling her reading glasses on her nose she opened the sheet and began to read.

"Madam,
You do not know me but I like to think I am a friend to your daughter. She went away to help her son and I regret to say she will not be coming home to you."

The letter went out of focus and the woman's head dipped. Her chin quivered for a moment, then she took a handkerchief from her pocket and wiped her reading glasses. She took a deep breath and raised the letter again.

"I managed to trace your address from a telephone number on Katya's mobile phone. There is little I can do for her now but, trust me, what I can do I will.
I have a little money and I have recently sold a four-wheel motorbike so I am enclosing a draft to pay for Peter's piano lessons as his mother wanted.
I am sure he will make her proud."

The woman looked for a signature but there was none. The letter fell into her lap beside the envelope and the international money order. She sat watching the boy sitting at the table, reading his book.

\*\*\*

Danny clamped his hands on the boy's shoulders and jerked him upward. "Stand upright, hold your spine straight. keep your arms straight by your sides."

He glanced sideways at the sounds of chuckling. Joe Walsh sat in a wheelchair, his frail body quivering with mirth.

"You okay, Joe?"

"Me?" said the old man. "I'm fine. Just fine."

"There's people, crowds of them," said Barry, his voice wavering.

"Ignore them," said Danny. "You just listen to me. Grip it firmly by the top with your right hand. Keep in step with me, swing your free arm. When I stop, you stop. We stand still, bolt upright, bow our heads. Then you lay it down on that frame I showed you. We bow our heads, hold it for a couple of seconds, then turn smartly to the right and march back. You got that?"

The boy's eyes were wide as he tried to take it all in. Then he nodded vigorously. "Yes, I think so."

He seemed to relax slightly as the instructions sank in and Danny thought he was about to start enjoying the experience.

Barry looked around at the crowds that lined the road but his eyes kept being drawn upward to the sweeping stone arch high above their heads. He looked at the names engraved on panel after panel, the lettering crisp on the pale stone. Each time he did it his eyes could not help but follow the lines of names upward until they dissolved into a blur of indentations way above his head.

He picked out the names of regiments, Kings Liverpool Regiment, Lancashire Fusiliers, Devons, Somerset Light Infantry, East Yorks, West Yorks, West Kent, Ox and Bucks, 40th Pathans. The last vehicles passed by and the police closed the road. The rumble of conversation from 500 people, many of them schoolchildren, echoed from the vaulted roof until the fire brigade buglers stepped into line and a shuffling silence descended.

Danny looked at his watch, nearly 8pm. As the second hand hit the hour the bugles began The Last Post, the notes trembling in the cold air as they echoed off giant stone panels heavy with the names of the dead.

Barry's eyes stretched wide as if he had been suddenly stabbed. Danny patted the boy's shoulder again, whispered, "You'll be fine."

The last note faded away and the crowd stood still for a minute's silence. Barry glanced sideways to see what Danny was doing. His head was bowed, hands clasped behind his back, and Barry did the same.

They stood shoulder to shoulder with their thoughts. When the silence ended they looked up. Beside them an elderly stooped Canadian with hearing aids in both ears quivered as he tried to hold himself erect.

A man in a beret and immaculate blazer with a long line of medals gestured for the Canadian to go forward and he stepped smartly off across the road and up the steps to the shrine of wreaths.

He bent stiffly, placed his tribute, turned and marched back, his face rigid, eyes far away.

The man in the blazer motioned Danny and Barry to go next. They lined up on the kerb. Danny took a step forward and Barry was a split second behind him.

Joe Walsh watched from his wheelchair as Danny and his grandson marched crisply across the road and mounted the steps. Barry gently laid his poppy wreath among the other tributes and stepped back. Their heads bowed for a moment, then they turned and marched back across the road.

Joe felt his heart palpitate when he saw the tears streaming down Barry's red face.

They resumed their positions beside Joe and watched while the other tributes were laid, some British Legion members from Portsmouth, a secondary school from Yorkshire. Then the buglers played Reveille and the ceremony was over.

The crowds dispersed quickly, the traffic started to roll again, and soon the three of them were alone.

They walked together under the arch, Barry pushing Joe's wheelchair, their heads tilted up, looking at column after column of names, ranks and units.

"There's something like 55,000 names," said Danny, "All killed around here in the battles for Ypres, all with no known grave."

Barry opened his mouth but couldn't bring himself to speak.

"And there's another 35,000 up the road at Tyne Cot. Makes you think, doesn't it?"

Barry nodded.

"That's how you remember them, Billy, your grandad's uncle Cecil, and all the others. You spend a quiet few minutes and think. It's not about things. You don't nick stuff, just think and remember. It keeps them alive, sort of."

Barry nodded again.

They reached the outer arch of the Menin Gate and turned back. Joe reached a bony hand over his shoulder and pressed Barry's fingers, indicating for him to stop.

He looked up at Danny, red eyes shining.

"I don't know how to thank you, I really don't."

"No need, Joe. It was a pleasure."

"Look," said the old man, waving an arthritic hand towards the lights of Ypres. "I raided my savings before we came. How about I treat you two to a dinner of moules frites and a bottle of vino? French grub with German portions, that's what they say, isn't it?"

Barry pulled a face.

"Sounds good to me," said Danny.

Shrugged deep into their coats against the winter wind whistling through the memorial, they started back towards the Grote Markt.

***

You have to keep walking, have to keep mobile. Use it or lose it, that's what the doctor kept telling her.

He was a lovely man, Doctor Singh. Such nice manners. And a lovely family, too, from the look of the pictures in his surgery. Three boys and a girl and all doing well at university.

Sara had no time for those scroungers who kept coming in the country, hiding in lorries, clinging to aeroplane wheels. But Doctor Singh, that was different. He made a contribution, earned his keep.

And he was a wonderful doctor, had worked wonders when she'd had that nasty digestion thing.

If Doctor Singh said keep mobile to stay healthy, Sara would walk every day. And she loved Hove Lawns, with the sea to one side and the big grassed area with the impressive cream facades of the Georgian terraces on the other.

Mind you, it wasn't so easy in the winter. The cold weather sliced right through her, made her numb, slowed her brain.

Still, it wasn't so bad today. The wind was cold but it was dry and the sun was out. Pity more people weren't taking advantage, thought Sara as she looked along the deserted promenade. Perhaps they didn't have Doctor Singh for a GP.

Energised by her mission to follow the good doctor's instructions, Sara lengthened her stride, pulling herself forward with the stick she always carried for her odd wobbly moment.

She could see the café now, steam drifting from the end of the counter where they brewed up and toasted the sandwiches. Sara would have loved a toasted sandwich but she couldn't risk those hard crumbs getting under her plate.

Perhaps that nice young man who always wore the Pride t-shirt would be serving today. He had such a lovely smile for her.

Sara thought again about toasted sandwiches but shook her head. No, she'd settle for a nice cup of tea and, perhaps, a slice of cake, so long as there were no nuts.

The pain in her chest took her breath away. She gasped and leaned down hard on the stick, panting and grasping the promenade rail.

Steady, girl. Exercise is all very good but you can have too much of a good thing. Sara leaned on the railing to give herself a few moments to calm down.

The beach was empty apart from a few squabbling seagulls fighting over something at the water's edge. She could see the tide was coming in.

Feeling better, she walked on another twenty yards then stopped to rest against the rail. As she looked to the sea a figure bobbed up. She hadn't seen him before. He must have been crouching down.

He was a big fellow, broad shoulders and short hair. Sara thought he might have a white beard. She couldn't be sure but she was quite proud her eyesight was so good for someone of her age. As she stood and watched the man swung a bag from his shoulder and took out a small spade.

The blade was flat against the handle but he swivelled it into position and secured it by spinning a nut. Then he began to dig, which puzzled Sara.

He couldn't be looking for bait, not with a big thing like that, not among the shingle. He might be one of those metal detector people digging for coins but she hadn't spotted the telltale pole and disc and her eyesight was good, Doctor Singh had commented on it.

As Sara watched, the man dug a shallow channel maybe six inches wide and three feet long. When he reached the end he started another channel at an angle, then a third parallel to the first.

Fascinated, Sara watched the man until he had completed four linked channels in the gravel that formed something like a zigzag, or perhaps the letter M.

The big man put down the shovel and took a box from the bag. Sara saw him unscrew the lid and pour a cascade of powder evenly along the zigzag.

He shook the box to make sure all the contents had fallen, then secured the lid and put it back in his bag.

Sara had a moment of panic. What if it was gunpowder? Some sort of bomb? He looked like a big, tough sort of man. Perhaps he was a terrorist.

She looked up and down the promenade and knew there was nothing she could do. She chided herself for being silly and settled back against the railing to watch.

The man stood by his zigzag shaped like an M. Sara wondered why nothing was happening and it was minutes before she realised the incoming tide was surging up and down the channels, washing the powder away.

Well, thought Sara, you get a lot of queer folk in Brighton but that was the joy of the place. You never knew what each day might bring. The chap down there on the beach could be anything from a performance artist to one of those poor fellows who keep forgetting their medication. Still, live and let live.

The tide had submerged the zigzag and was splashing over the man's boots before he picked up his bag and turned away.

Sara watched him as he crossed the beach towards her, large feet sinking into the shingle as if it were trying to hold him there.

He plodded up the stone stairs with heavy footsteps and looked up in surprise when he saw Sara for the first time, watching him.

Sara studied faces, old professional habit. She thought the man's face might have been a bit fierce if it wasn't for the red eyes and wet cheeks.

Big Eddie Archer took a last look over his shoulder, back to the spot where the restless waves were carrying Minty Marshall's ashes out into the English Channel, and walked away.

\*\*\*

A shower, breakfast and plenty of strong tea. Those were Danny's priorities as he slipped the key into the lock of his front door and stepped inside.

It had been a good run, stretched the body and cleared the mind. He was sweaty and tired as well but, all together, it was a good feeling.

And he'd cracked two cases, found out who killed Aqualung and murdered Forrester and Minty. Perhaps he was starting to get the hang of this detecting lark.

A thick roll of twenties through Cheryl's letterbox, for the kids, and a shoe box full of cash in his wardrobe said he was. Things were on the up.

As he stepped inside he noticed the postman had been. He felt his muscles aching gently as he stooped to scoop the pile of letters from the mat. In the kitchen, he put the kettle on, then walked into the living room and turned on the television.

He stood for a while, feeling his body calm after its exertions, and channel-hopped through the morning's TV.

He paused on a re-run of The Sweeney. The squad's silver Granada, tyres squealing, heeled into a corner then accelerated hard after a van with its rear doors flapping open.

The van skidded through open gates flanked by tall brick columns and onto a rubbish strewn dockside lined with derelict warehouses. When it reached a dead end it slewed to a halt.

The Granada pulled up hard behind it and all four doors flew open as the cops bailed out, ready for a fight.

Danny hopped through more channels and stopped on Sky News. An immaculate blonde with sexy eyes and pink lips was smiling over the news ticker. "... and the shadow home secretary has today called for a full inquiry into cutbacks in the prison service following the death of Sir Charles Wolfram.

"The controversial right-wing politician and former business leader died of stab wounds, believed to be from a sharpened tooth brush, two days ago while being held on remand in connection with drugs and firearms charges at..."

A library photo of a smiling, suited businessman flashed onto the screen. Danny paused to study it, thinking back to something Bob had said, after the farm raid, about how Wolfram was a complete nutter but he did have a point, talked a little bit of sense at times.

Danny knew what Bob meant but he was wrong. Wolfram wasn't a solution, just another part of the problem. The fact that he attracted any support at all showed the extent of the problem.

Politicians were all the same, just body surfing over the top of ordinary people, confident that there were enough mugs to keep them up there until they'd made their pile. Danny didn't do politics because politics didn't do him.

Wolfram's mugshot was replaced on the TV screen by film footage of the smouldering wreckage of Payne's Farm, police officers guarding a taped area while forensics measured, photographed and took samples.

Then Wolfram's few seconds of fame faded away until his next appearance in the 15-minute news loop, replaced by a story about genetically modified tomatoes.

Danny channel-hopped again. A bunch of surly villains were being led in handcuffs to a van. Jack Regan was probing a bruised jaw when Sergeant Carter walked up to him. "You okay, guv'nor?"

Danny smiled and walked back into the kitchen. The kettle had boiled but he switched it on again. You needed piping hot water for proper tea.

As he waited he began to leaf through the sheaf of letters. More than usual. One from the council. One from the health authority. There was a letter for someone he had never heard of who might have lived in the flat before he and his mum moved in. Someone else was offering a deal on uPVC windows.

At the bottom of the pile was a cardboard-backed brown envelope with stamps he didn't recognise. One had a colourful bird and another had two serious-looking guys with long beards. Danny ran his thumb under the flap and delved inside. His fingers closed on a sheet of card and he drew it out, tilting it to the stubborn winter light from the kitchen window. It was a blank sheet of stiff white card.

He turned it over and stared for a moment before his face cracked into a smile. On the card was a charcoal sketch of a naked man sleeping. He lay on his right side, one arm was folded under the pillow beneath his head. The other arm lay thrown out across the mattress. The man's hair was rumpled.

His penis lay across the thigh of his crooked right leg. His left leg, which rested on top of the right, ended just below the knee with a curved scar almost like a crooked smile where a fold of skin had been sewn across.

Danny plunged his hand into the envelope again and pulled out a small notelet. It was a pale candy yellow with the image of a smiling koala in the top right corner.

In a careful, sweeping blue script it bore the two words "no worries" and a single x.

Danny tapped the sheet of card against his chin and smiled just as the kettle boiled.

**THE END**

## THE AUTHOR

Bill Todd is a journalist and award-winning travel writer who has visited more than 40 countries from the pure white wastes of Arctic Finland to the great deserts of Namibia. He has a keen interest in Greece, maps, genealogy, military history, strong cheese and good beer. Bill is married with a daughter and lives in London and Brighton. The Wreck Of The Margherita and Death Squad are the first two Danny Lancaster stories.

## THANKS

Danny's story is a work of imagination but I have attempted to make it as real and as accurate as the demands of fiction allow.

Any errors or omissions are mine but I could not have written Danny's story without the help of many people who contributed their time and enthusiasm.

I would especially like to thank Kaimes Beasley of HM Coastguard; Keith Ring, former Brighton Borough Commander of East Sussex Fire And Rescue Service; Peter Ritchley of Headley Court; David Shipwright and Debbie Simpson; Phil Stevens of eyetek.co.uk; Malgorzata Kosidowska; Paul Moreton and Stuart Higgins.

I would also like to thank Fran, Zoe, Antony, John Gaule and Paul Thorogood for their help, patience and many suggestions. Additional thanks to Zoe and to Mike Nicholson for the cover artwork.

Also Pete and Steady for the fag darts and the many others who have given their time and expertise, you know who you are.

I also offer my gratitude and respect to John David, Frederick and Neville.

**Bill Todd, London, 2012**

Danny Lancaster returns in Death Squad. Here's a taste of his second investigation

## DEATH SQUAD

### Foreword

**FORT LAUDERDALE, FLORIDA**

EDDIE Shapiro was obsessed with Cindy-Sue. She indulged his fantasies. She took him to the heights. Eddie had been with more women than he could remember. But Cindy-Sue was the real love of his life.

Ahead of them the air shimmered like oil above the baked black tarmac. She exhaled blue smoke. He could tell she was impatient. Cindy-Sue was hot. She was aching to go.

Eddie glanced to his left. Pamela looked tiny amid the great expanse of scorched ground, sheltering under a large straw stetson.

The designer T-shirt and spray-on jeans forced the eye to follow the curves of her body. She had this great liquid way of moving that glued your eyes to her butt.

Little Bobby, all freckles and a shock of blond hair falling across wide blue eyes, looked even smaller than his six years as he reached up to grip his mom's hand.

Eddie often wondered why he had married Pamela. Sure, she was beautiful. Hell, what Playboy centrefold wasn't? She was bright. She gave great head. She had the best breasts money could buy.

Back then, marriage had seemed the perfect thing, a union of her looks and his talent, the raucous mob of photographers jostling for angles as the smiling couple emerged from the white tent beneath the palm trees on the golden beach.

Eddie was convinced it was Pamela who had changed. Kids did strange things to a woman. But there was always Cindy-Sue. Eddie tightened his straps. As he gunned the throttle she strained against her wheel brakes.

The big cat growl of the V12 Packard Merlin engine gave him goose flesh as it powered the Mustang's huge four-blade propeller into a blur.

She was a real beauty, a thoroughbred, 1,649 cubic inches of cylinder giving 1,510 brake horsepower, 437mph at 25,000 feet, six fifty-calibre Browning machineguns.

Cindy-Sue had flown with the 334th Fighter Squadron, 4th Fighter Group, 8th U.S. Army Air Force, from Debden, Essex, England, in 1944. Flown bomber escort over Nazi Germany. Real action. Real bullet holes.

Eddie had documented the aircraft's complete history. He had photographs of her at Debden, even one taken in the air from a B17.

He just could never understand the way Pamela rolled her eyes, pulled that face, whenever he took down the leather-bound volumes of Cindy-Sue's history, the way she bitched at the mention of her name. It wasn't like it was another woman.

He'd only got them to the airfield today by persuading Pamela that Little Bobby needed some fresh air in his asthma-wracked lungs. Don't want the kid living on drugs forever. Women, jeez.

From the corner of his eye Eddie saw Little Bobby give a hesitant wave. Pamela was clutching her hat to her head, a hazy shadow through the veil of dust and vibration thrown up by the P51's prop wash.

The sleek silver fighter trembled as Eddie increased the engine power. He checked the dials one more time, engine temperature and oil pressure. It was like playing keyboards, all about harmony and timing. Then he released the brakes and they were away, surging down the runway.

As her wheels left the ground Eddie retracted Cindy-Sue's landing gear and held her nose down as she picked up speed. Ahead to his left Eddie saw a bunch of turkey vultures circling some fresh roadkill by the I95.

Then he pulled back hard on the stick and sunlight flashed on the fighter's slender silver wings as she soared upward into the blazing blue sky. The ground in his rear view mirror looked like one of Little Bobby's model layouts, growing quickly smaller.

Eddie relished the pressure pushing him back into the bucket seat as Cindy-Sue soared up into the creamy air. The patchwork of greens and browns below him spread wider as they climbed. Away to Eddie's left was the startling blue of the ocean stretching away to a curving horizon.

No more hassle, no more lawyers and contracts, no more unsmiling suits. Now it was just Eddie and Cindy-Sue riding the shimmering sky.

He eased out of the climb and levelled off, sweeping the Mustang into a series of gentle S turns as he scanned the dome of blue above through the big Perspex bubble of the canopy, searching for the Messerschmitts and Focke-Wulfs he knew were waiting to prey on the lumbering Fortress bombers under his protection.

He could see them clearly now, all around him, box formations of B17s stacked up through thousands of feet. Around them prowled knots of Mustang and Thunderbolt fighters, watching and waiting. Nothing would stop Eddie Shapiro getting these guys to Berlin and back.

He scanned the sky until his neck ached, holding a gloved thumb over the searing sun to search its outer glare. Beware of the Hun in the sun, that's what the Brits used to say.

Then Eddie spotted them, tiny shark shapes coming at incredible speed. As they tore past he stood Cindy-Sue on her wingtip, hauled her round in a tight fighter turn and dived after them.

The engine screamed. The whole aircraft trembled as she plunged like a hawk. Sweat prickled down Eddie's spine. This was better than sex.

He picked his opponent and manoeuvred for his shot. The SoB tried to jink away but Eddie was too fast for him. Then the Kraut tried a turn. Big mistake. Eddie pulled the nimble fighter inside his curve, chancing a sideways glance at the ailerons biting the air.

The vast dome of sky was clear and silent apart from Cindy-Sue's screaming. But not for Eddie. He felt the judder of his guns, each of the six Brownings spitting 800 fifty calibre rounds a minute.

He smelled the smoke, saw bits break away from the desperate enemy. He fired again in his imagination and the squat black cross of the Focke-Wulf rolled on its back and spiralled down into its death dive. No 'chute. Another swastika to paint on the fuselage.

Eddie pulled up and graciously acknowledged the grateful wave from the pilot of a passing B17 struggling home with one engine out and chunks chewed from his big tail fin. Cindy-Sue began to climb and again Eddie scanned the hostile curve of the horizon.

Then he saw it and his heart constricted. Racing towards the bombers in a blur of speed 2,000 feet below him. An Me262. The first operational jet. The ultimate prize.

In his excitement Eddie messed up his turn and Cindy-Sue slewed sideways, her screaming engine protesting. Then they were in a howling dive, steeper than ever, exchanging height for speed to counter the jet's superior performance.

When the first vibration came Eddie ran his eye over the instruments. Everything looked normal. Then it came again. Not the straining of speed but an uneven judder. Like something spinning out of balance. As if Cindy-Sue had shivered in pain.

The bang shook the whole airframe and Eddie bit his tongue. The salt taste of blood filled his antique oxygen mask. He throttled back and eased out of the dive. Something was wrong. Eddie turned gently homeward.

He had to get down fast. He was sweating hard under the Perspex canopy. It trickled from under his leather flying helmet and into his eyes.

The runway was ahead now, a long ribbon of spear-straight black tarmac in the heat haze, surrounded by the brown and grey of baked earth and bleached concrete.

He could see his Jeep parked by the old hangar. Pamela and Little Bobby were two specks, just where he had left them.

The vibration was worse now. Eddie clenched his teeth to stop them clashing together. He throttled right back and started to glide her in, prop windmilling, gently turning left and right to get a clear view forward and down beyond the big engine with its matt black anti-glare panel on top of the cowling.

Eddie tried to lower the landing gear. Nothing happened. He tried again. Nothing. He was too low to go around. For the first time real fear knotted his stomach.

He pulled back on the stick and trimmed Cindy-Sue, holding her just above stalling speed as she swept over the runway threshold. It was racing under him now, a blur of black like a fast flowing river. Eddie caught a glimpse of Little Bobby waving.

Pamela Shapiro Kennedy watched the Mustang's descent. Eddie's obsession bored the pants off her and she resented the place that stupid airplane occupied in his life.

She still loved him, sort of. He was Whirlwind, Mr Flying Fingers the keyboard guru. He had been a legend, private jets, limos, best tables in the top restaurants, and she still found that a turn-on.

But just lately she couldn't stop her thoughts straying to the idea that he'd been on top before she was even born. It was more than 30 years ago, for chrissake.

Eddie was still a special person, still had that fire that had first drawn her to him. Only now it took Viagra to light it.

Pamela glanced up at the Mustang growing larger. It was unusual for Eddie to come back so soon.

She looked at her watch again. Marcello, her personal trainer, was due at the ranch in an hour and she didn't want to be late. Eddie would be tinkering with Cindy-Sue's engine for hours.

As the silver fighter swept low over the runway Pamela thought Eddie was taking it very gently. It struck her as strange because he loved to show off. Once he'd taken Little Bobby up in his lap and they'd had a ferocious fight over it.

Then Pamela saw the Mustang's wheels were up and knew Eddie was going to make a low pass before pulling up hard and climbing away. He thought it surprised them but they'd seen it before, too many times.

Cindy-Sue drew level and Pamela could clearly see the leggy Blonde painted on the aircraft's nose and the row of swastika combat victories beneath the cockpit.

Little Bobby pointed a pudgy finger: "Cadillac of the skies, mommy."

She squeezed his hand. "That's right, baby." The bang startled her. She saw smoke spurt from the exhaust stubs and the propeller stopped dead. Cindy-Sue seemed to hesitate for a moment, then the big air scoop under the fuselage kissed the ground. The shrieking of metal on tarmac sounded like death laughing. The silver fighter careered along the runway, trying to dig in its nose, shedding lumps of shredded wreckage.

Sparks sprayed in her wake and then Cindy-Sue was riding a carpet of boiling flame that erupted like a poisonous flower from her underside as the ruptured tanks spewed blazing fuel. Black smoke with its core of orange fire swirled in the vortex of the crippled fighter's wake.

Pamela flinched as the heat wave washed over them but she couldn't tear her eyes away. Then she remembered Little Bobby. His grip on her hand was painful. She tried to turn his head away but he fought her.

Thick oily smoke washed across them, making the pair break into coughing. Cindy-Sue gave up the fight and shuddered to a halt two hundred yards away. It was then that the fire caught up with the petrol haemorrhaging from her broken tanks. With a sudden whoosh Cindy-Sue was swallowed in a writhing ball of hungry flame.

Pamela could see the dark silhouette of her husband in the cockpit through the rippling curtain of fire. His head was tilted down. He wasn't moving. As she watched, the shape seemed to shrink and fade as it was absorbed by the inferno. Somewhere a fire truck siren wailed.

Little Bobby began to cry but his sobs were cut off by a savage bout of coughing as the stinking smoke bit into his tender lungs. His chubby body was wrenched with spasms as he tried to be brave like his dad always told him.

Pamela pressed his reliever into his mouth and put an arm round his shoulder, turning him gently but firmly towards the black RV with the dark windows and fat tyres that was parked by the hangar. This time Little Bobby didn't resist.

As he sucked on his reliever, Pamela looked up and saw a bunch of turkey vultures flapping clumsily towards the rising column of black smoke.

She had a sudden image of the first time she had seen Eddie, dressed like some hero from Lord of the Rings as he exploded out of a cloud of dry ice and pounded his keyboards with the opening chords. Her stomach had trembled with the vibration as the stage burst into light and the guitars and the crowd roared.

Pamela tried to hold the image but it kept fading into one of her husband dissolving into a sheet of flame.

Her mind couldn't grasp what had just happened. Eddie had been such a big part of her life for so long. Now she was alone, a rich rock widow. She wondered if Marcello would be on time.

## CHAPTER 1

It wasn't my fault, it really, really wasn't. I'm the blue sky guy, big canvas, broad brush strokes. It's the minions who fill in the detail, that's not my skill set.

I'm a businessman, the guy in charge, fingers in lots of pies. I can't be expected to micromanage every trivial little detail.

If I was CEO of some major corporation, engineering or media or whatever, would I be expected to know every little dribble and fart of the business? Foresee every possible outcome?

That's the sick thing about this country. Everyone propping up a bar or glued to the soaps on TV wants the jobs, the money, the security, the products and services. Yet those same people are only too happy to rubbish the guys who bring them all of that.

You don't get to be an entrepreneur, build something up, by being touchy-feely. It's a hard world. You can't make an omelette without breaking eggs.

The rewards are high but so are the risks. And it's entrepreneurs like me who take those risks, not the soap fans and the boozers with their comfy lives with their PAYE and package holidays.

Any idiot can have an opinion. But building something from nothing, something profitable, something successful, now that takes talent. You need guts, drive and vision to get off your backside and make it happen. You have to have a clearly defined goal and the ruthlessness to go forward and reach it.

And there will be broken eggshells. So, you see, it really, really wasn't my fault.

***

**BRIGHTON, MONDAY NIGHT**
The creeping damp of the night air didn't bother Danny Lancaster. It probed the folds of his jacket but he had grown hardened to cold over the years to a point where he hardly noticed any more.

It had been a lovely day but in the early evening a squall had blown in from the Channel and with it a cutting wind. It didn't matter. You could get used to anything if you tried hard enough, or you had no other choice.

What Danny wanted was a cigarette but he dare not risk a light. The knowledge that he could not have one heightened the desire to spark up but he knew he could resist.

A stiff breeze, tinged with a tang of salt, muttered through the trees. Danny looked around carefully, eyes straining into the blackness. It was habit more than necessity. He wasn't expecting trouble. Apart from the sounds of the night, everything was quiet.

Danny shifted slightly to ease the aching in his thighs. He had been crouched, motionless, for more than an hour and his body began to protest at the inactivity.

He often thought he was a little mad to get into these situations. But there was no harm in a little madness if it helped you through the day.

The wind whipped up suddenly and Danny scrunched down deeper inside his jacket, keeping a firm grip on the camera. It was a clunky old digital job with a heavy telephoto lens. Fingers crossed it would do the job.

The darkness around him seemed to move like a restless tide on the night wind as he studied the large, wooded garden. Somewhere nearby a car passed. Danny closed his eyes to preserve his night vision and grinned into the blackness.

Something would turn up, and soon. He looked at the luminous dial of the Rolex on his wrist, then pushed the strap back up his forearm, deeper into his sleeve, to avoid it catching the light.

Not long now. As if on cue, a car crept guiltily along the quiet street beyond the garden and edged nervously into a narrow space at the third attempt.

The driver's door clunked shut. Danny heard the bleep of central locking. The car's side lights blinked as if winking at the conspiracy.

Hesitant steps tip-tapped along the pavement, taking on a crunchy tone as the feet moved onto the gravel front path of the large Edwardian villa with its scattering of fallen pebbledash, like dandruff, on the surrounding flower beds.

Small feet, thought Danny. Is that good or bad for a ballroom dancer?

Somewhere a cat yowled. The breeze gusted, wafting the sour aroma of overflowing bins. The reluctant steps halted in the porch. The house was divided into eight small flats. Danny sensed bespectacled eyes peering at the bank of buzzers.

A doorbell bing-bonged. Danny craned to see what was happening. Fingers crossed this plan was going to work. He needed the money.

The old door with its stained glass panels groaned open. Danny heard a woman's voice, husky with gin and Bensons. "Mr Smith, nice to see you again. Come on in."

Follow Danny Lancaster's second investigation in

**DEATH SQUAD**

Available as a paperback and ebook

www.billtodd.co.uk

Printed in Great Britain
by Amazon

81827537R00221